A WINTER OF CHAINS

JASON R. KOIVU

Black Rose Writing | Texas

ISBN: 978-1-68433-955-6

PUBLISHED BY BLACK ROSE WRITING

www.blackrosewriting.com
Printed in the United States of America
Suggested Retail Price (SRP) $22.95

A Winter of Chains is printed in Caslon

*As a planet-friendly publisher, Black Rose Writing does its best to eliminate
unnecessary waste to reduce paper usage and energy costs, while never
compromising the reading experience. As a result, the final word count vs. page
count may not meet common expectations.

This one's for my brother, creator of mysterious monsters.

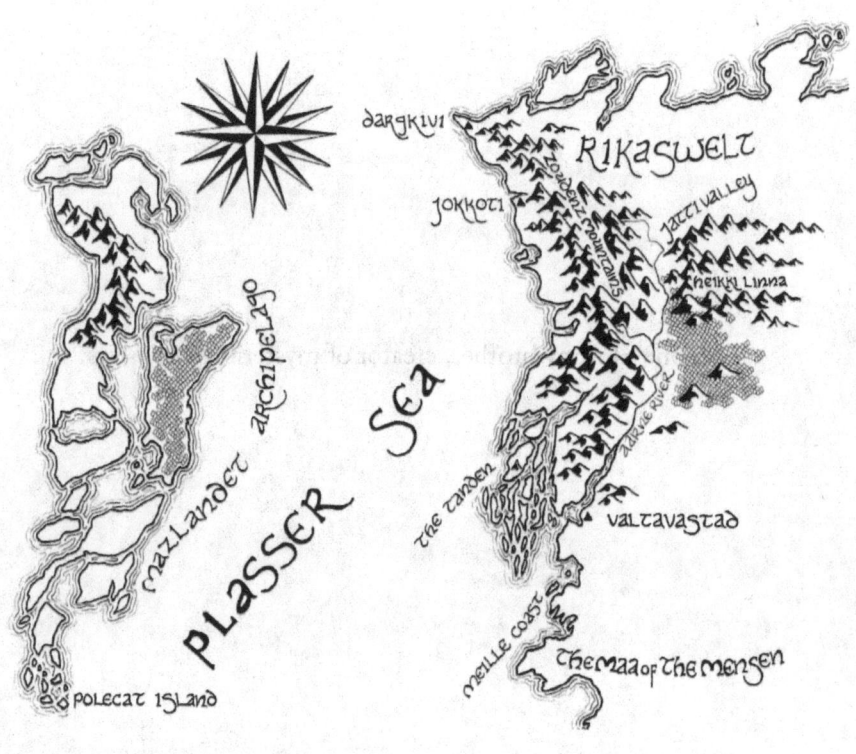

dargkivi

RIKASWELT

JOKKOTI

Jatti Valley

Tonden Mountains

Heikki Linna

Addvie River

The Tanden

Valtavastad

Meille Coast

The Maa of the Mongen

Mazlandet Archipelago

PLASSER SEA

Polecat Island

A WINTER
OF CHAINS

Contents

Chapter 1 - Tiers of Freedom   1

Chapter 2 - The Lyswennod Shallows   8

Chapter 3 - Polecat Island   16

Chapter 4 - Tracking Down Trousers   30

Chapter 5 - The New Morgan Brewer   48

Chapter 6 - Wintering   64

Chapter 7 - The Killers   89

Chapter 8 - Sails Set to the Sky   111

Chapter 9 - Bay of Riches   128

Chapter 10 - The Mines of Dargkivi   150

Chapter 11 - Tat Tarl   169

Chapter 12 - The Kavenauk Deeps   177

Chapter 13 - The Pit   189

Chapter 14 - Games   203

Chapter 15 - Not Too Blind To See   218

Chapter 16 - Happy Together   234

Chapter 17 - The Hunt   252

Chapter 18 - Veks Miris   260

Chapter 19 - The Return   285

Chapter 20 - Under and Over   307

Chapter 21 - The House at Heikki Linna   334

Chapter 22 - The Last Step   351

About the Author

Note from the Author

Chapter 1
Tiers of Freedom

Cutting through the slate-gray water of a wide-open sea. A crisp, salty breeze through the hair. Gulls gliding alongside. Endless expanses. The abounding joy of the sun's light and warmth. It all sang of freedom's glory.

Ford Barlow took in this splendor from the loosened rail of the *Barrow's Oak*, a moribund slug of a three-masted vessel much closer to the breakers yard than to its maiden voyage. Many, including its captain, reckoned the ship was making its last eastward passage along the Aelwydian coast into the Plasser Sea. It would deposit its cargo of prisoners there at the penal colony known as Polecat Island. Ford spread his pillar-sturdy legs for stability against the ship's rhythmic rocking, leaned over the side, and retched with the force and splash of a bull disgorging a chunky mash. His massive back and rounded shoulders heaved with the volcanic eruption. The relief was instantaneous. Now that his stomach was empty and his head clear again, he could focus on other things, like the mystifyingly-curved planks of the bow and how they threw ocean water aside. The water was churned into white foam and the foam was whisked away along the side of the ship to be jettisoned by a steady wake ever aft into the vast sea behind them. Being on a ship under sail at sea was a new experience for him. He could go on watching this entrancing sight all day.

The three men on either side of him turned greener than the pea soup pallor already brought on by the ship's constant lurching. Their horror and queasiness mounted the more Ford leaned over the side, for they were all chained together and would plummet into the sea along with him if his tremendous weight broke the flimsy rail or he lost his balance.

"Holiday's over, maggots!" snarled the quick-to-anger overseer of prisoners, an impatient jailor with a perpetual sneer. Ford thought the sneer might be for show. He doubted anyone could be that angry all of the time. "Get yer stinking arses below!" The overseer's leather cat o' nine tails cracked over their heads. It would come down upon their backs next if any of them showed the slightest hesitation in obeying orders.

The prisoners at the head finished up as quickly as they could, then fell into line with the others. Ford's chained group of four stepped into place and shuffled along with everyone else toward the hatchway to the lower decks. The crew gave them a wide berth and made snide comments about having to clear the air of the prisoners' stench after they were gone. These usually jovial sailors turned on the prisoners whenever they were allowed on deck. The disruption of their routine annoyed the most callous-minded among them, while the more sympathetic found it discomforting to see their countrymen reduced to such a miserable, unwashed state. Many sailors took out their frustrations on the prisoners. The prisoners weren't looking to be a nuisance. They fervently wished to be a hundred or more miles out of the way.

Ford pitied these downtrodden and defeated men and women in chains. None of them would be here but for the caprices of lords and ladies. He pitied his own plight as well, but he had known what he had been getting himself into. Brastersceatt, a minor lord from a wealthy family, poor in power and overburdened with ambition, had combined with a zealous religious movement to foment rebellion. The castle garrison, the heads of the city's only chartered school of magic, and other important bastions of power that could be bought off had been bribed by the rebellious lord to either stand down or assist in the overthrow. Ford had played a small role in the ruling lord's defense. A forlorn defense as it turned out to be. Now he was paying the price.

Ford didn't regret aligning himself with Iarl Middlefield. She was a woman of principle, who would have maintained the laws that, until the overthrow, had allowed Ford's mother to provide for herself. Fortune-telling and prostitution were not his occupations of choice for his mother, but they had kept her clothed and fed. This was as much as could be hoped for after she had been driven from the sheltering arms of family when her affair with Ford's father had gone awry. A woman of little means alone in a city far from home did what she had to do. But now, with the new regime in control and threatening to abolish such vices, Ford worried what would become of her. Thankfully, the Iarl had escaped, due to the efforts of a handful of devotees like himself. Perhaps one day the Iarl would return to reclaim her city and set everything to rights again.

After the Brastersceatt family's victorious uprising, all high officials who had refused the bribe and not sworn fealty had been put to death, if they could not meet the steep ransom. Minor officials and insignificant servants had been spared. Killing commoners seldom made a good impression on the populous. Ford was among those spared. So, he had that to be thankful for as well.

At a word from the captain, orders spread the length of the ship and the helmsman readied to turn the wheel. Only half of the prisoners on deck had made it below. The captain didn't care. He wouldn't let anything disturb the running of his ship. "On the deck!" balled the sailors and the remaining prisoners hunkered down where they stood. Belaying pins jabbed into ribs and threatened to crack the skulls of those who unknowingly squatted where the sailors needed to be. Offenders got the hint and scampered out of the way. They seemed to be a nuisance wherever they crouched. "Move, ya lead-bottomed whore's ass!" Sailors roused some prisoners out from under the larboard fore shrouds and shoved them down in the space occupied by Ford's gang of four. The ship tacked and the bow turned away from the strip of land along the northwestern horizon, a ragged shore that looked much like a worn-down sawblade with broken teeth.

A wind across the beam threw strands of Ford's long dark hair over his square-built face, a face still holding plenty of its youth, while beginning to map out life's terrain: a laugh line, a shiny cheekbone and a knotted nose. His features could have been sculpted from granite, not by a master, but a competent artisan with a wide-bladed chisel and a love of bold edges. He tossed his head to one side, the hair fluttered out of his eyes and he found himself staring at a Haunan curate in the ancient Order of the Sud a Waed. The priest's name was Willem. Ford knew him as Will, but wished he didn't know him at all. The sight of him was like a lemon squeezed over an open wound, embittering a mood already soured by thoughts of returning to the fetid depths of the ship. Ford wasn't high on priests at the moment, since religious zealotry got him into this mess to begin with, but Will held a special place of hatred in his heart.

"I owe you," he said to the priest in a low rumble, menace muddying the words. Will smiled back at him and that nearly broke Ford's remaining restraint.

"I'm sorry?" Will leaned his long and lanky frame forward and slid back the sleeve of his robe to cup an ear. Less than a yard separated them. Not even the ever-present creaks and groans of the ship could have made him miss what had been said. Ford's eyes narrowed and sought the truth in Will's question. He would not be made game of, and the sincerity gazing back at him said that he wasn't.

"I owe you for what you done," he went on, devolving into street brawler lingo. His tone and language would often eschew the little education and refinement he had had when among certain company or in the midst of a conflict. What he felt he owed Will was a beating. He had beaten down many a more substantial man than this in the past. Even won a few purses filled with coin for having done so. He would gladly level this priest for the sheer pleasure of it, and would have done it right then and there, if not for the overseer. Surely, a fight would get him the whipping of a lifetime.

There had been so few chances for retribution since that rather rough night some weeks past when his miserable mood and heavy drinking drove him to nearly kill a man. The following morning, he awoke in the dungeons of Stanrocc Hold. Piecing together his fragmented memory of the night before, he recalled Will walking in on him as he stood over the bloody body of a man he'd just thrashed in a frightening release of rage. Other than the hysterical wife of the beaten man, the only other witness had been Will. So, it had to have been the priest who had turned him in. It didn't make sense to him that the woman would betray him. After all, he had stopped her husband from beating her.

Ford envisioned messing up those lemony light locks and bloodying the priest's boyishly- smooth, white skin. He'd blacken those sleepy eyes staring so innocently back at him and wipe off that irritatingly irrepressible smile. "I promise you, I will repay that debt."

Will raised a hand as if to prepare a defense but said nothing. He was far too contemplative a man to rush into a situation he was unsure of. *A rash word may thrash concord* was a favorite saying of his Shepherd, a mentor of Sud a Waed novices. His Shepherd had been fond of adding poetic flourishes to doctrine. Some of it sounded flighty, but most were well-grounded proverbs. Will curtailed his thoughts before they wandered any farther. Clearly this man Ford was upset with him. He growled like the bear he resembled. If it was directed at him, Will floundered for an answer as to why. Their paths had rarely crossed. He guessed it might have to do with that terrible night when he simply had done what needed to be done, but why it would anger anyone was beyond him.

The whip cracked and the rest of the prisoners were herded below to the rhythmic clanking of chains. Down into the darkness they plunged, to be secured on a lower deck of partitioned, cramped cells crawling with rats and lice, and oppressed by the foul air of bilge water, body odor, and human excretions. Twice a day they were allowed topside to relieve themselves, but for some, it wasn't enough. Many were unaccustomed to the sea and took ill. One man had already succumbed to unrelenting seasickness. Everything he ate or drank came back up and he soon expired. Those affected couldn't wait for their turn on deck. Soon buckets of acidic bile, urine and feces overflowed and spilled their contents. Within the first few days out of harbor, the prison tier reeked beyond endurance.

When not itching or lashing out blindly at squeaking tormentors, Ford spent his waking hours in the dark, windowless cells pondering a bleak future and his hard-luck past, or plotting an escape. Not long after the ship set sail, he and the three men chained to him had brought their heads together to whisper their plans.

"We'll jump over the side, all together, and make for the nearest land," Ford had suggested with eyes so bright with hope that they might have lit up the cell. "I can't swim," admitted one. "Nor I," said another. Undaunted, Ford began counting the crew and concluded that there were more prisoners than sailors. "We could take over the ship!" he just about shouted in his glee to his co-conspirators. "All them sailors got dirty little knives, they do," said Rhod Ellys, a former guardsman of solid, if not overawing build. Though a mop of nut-brown hair and a beard thicker than most bushes framed his face, it was a face that all could see was as scored and open as a butcher's block. If their jailors provided the prisoners with enough water, Rhod would have spat to show what he thought of them and their knives. He could have also added that the crew wasn't hampered by chains. Any break-out or overthrow would be next to impossible and cause much bloodshed. This was proved the very next day when an escape attempt ended before the prisoners made it to the main deck. One had his throat slit and another took a blade to the belly. The other two dropped to their knees and surrendered. That settled it for Ford's comrades in chains. There would be no attempt, not by them.

That hadn't settled it for Ford. He *had* to get back home. There were no two ways about it and plenty of reasons for it. He had made a promise to look after a dying friend's devoted wife and houseful of little girls back in the city. There was also his mother to think of. But perhaps the most important reason for getting back home was himself. He was a free spirit. He grew up in the country with long legs that liked long walks. In the city, he had felt penned in. Here in this cell on this ship, headed to a prison island, claustrophobia of the heart and mind gnawed at the core of his being. He needed to be free.

"They call us traitors. I'm no traitor! Are you?" he urged, making a last-ditch effort at rallying his reluctant cellmates. "Not I!" they replied, but that's as far as it went. They wouldn't be budged. They were decent folk, but he resented them for their timidity. It actually surprised him that he couldn't win over the tough and willing Rhod, a brawler like himself. Rhod didn't have the heaviest of hands, but he was a quick-fisted fighter. Quick to temper, too, though a good friend. He once broke three ribs and knocked the teeth out of a man over a lewd comment made to a friend's sister. Ford would never have pegged someone like that for a coward, and yet Rhod had been just as stubbornly reluctant as the other two: Dior, a slight foreigner with incredibly fuzzy eyebrows as jumpy as his nerves; and Miller Edd, an oft-grumpy Aelwydian.

While chained to them, Ford stood no chance of escaping. When in darker moods, devious means of breaking free from the other three crept up on him and made him ashamed for even imagining such things. No, he didn't blame them. They were right to be frightened. The odds were stacked against a successful escape. But that didn't diminish Ford's urge to give it a go. His whole body twitched just thinking about it. Entire nights of sleep were lost to yearning for it, endless nights in that cramped cell. He couldn't stretch out or even roll over onto his side without the rest of his cellmates doing so as one. His back was sore, his body ached and his every waking thought soured with each new day. How could a person do this to another? What kind of a man would torture another man in this way just for standing up for what he believed in? Every day of his young life spent wasting away in a cell devoured him from the inside out. It was no way to live. At times, when his dreary ruminations sank to their lowest and he was working on his last ounce of sanity, he wondered if he wasn't better off dead.

"I got to get out of here. Get me out!" he blurted during a long night when the ship was becalmed and nothing stirred the silence but the scratching claws of rats deep down in the bowels of the ship. The words spilled from him like a basket of apples overturned, tumbling over one another, bumping into each other, ricocheting at random. A muddle. Before the voyage, Ford and other prisoners like him had spent weeks rotting away upon a prison hulk moored in the bay back at Port Morton awaiting their fate and expecting death as the inevitable end. Back then, it didn't seem as if it could get any worse. For Ford, it had. "Get me out!"

A deep thud in the dark woke the prisoners in and around Ford's cell. It repeated in a regular rhythm.

"What was that?" shouted Miller Edd in a voice unnaturally high for him. All of the prisoners were sensitive to any new, unusual sounds.

"Something's beating on the side of the ship," said Rhod.

Fear-filled questions could be heard coming from the neighboring cells. They worried that the sound might portend some monster of the deep bashing a hole through the hull to get at them. Or perhaps the ship was hitting bottom. One of their biggest fears was having the sides stove in and the lower decks flooding, sending them to a watery grave.

More thudding came faster. The prisoners' shouts doubled in volume and fright. There was no light to see by. Prisoners weren't permitted flame. The captain and his crew ignored them. They were left to tremble in the dark, unaware of Ford leaning his back against the side of the ship throwing his elbows into the planks with powerful backward thrusts. He let loose a groan more of anguish than pain. His cellmates understood. They felt about in the dark and found Ford rocking back and forth. Soothing words had no effect. They tried holding him down, but the chains binding them got in the way. Rhod took Ford's head and knocked it against the side of the ship to drive out the derangement. None of it did any good. Ford was too strong for them. He had worked himself into an inconsolable furor, throwing his body at the heavy oak timbers with the single-minded desire to smash through the side of the ship and swim home. More likely he would break his bones, but he didn't care. The scheme made perfect sense to his addled mind. He would be free or die trying.

Chapter 2
The Lyswennod Shallows

"What are you playing at? I said keep to the sea!"

It was an hour past dawn and the captain of the *Barrow's Oak* had just discovered that his helmsman had altered the charted course. Once past Rockport, the last town of any note along the northeastern Aelwydian coast, the ship was meant to stay to the seaward side of the Crog Islands. These jagged rocks were the stuff of many a captain's nightmare. The shallows between them and the mainland had wrecked countless ships. To seaward, the bottom dropped away precipitously, quite beyond the reach of the ship's lead-line, leaving plenty of water under the hulls of even the most heavily-laden merchant ships. A sensible captain sailed for these deeper seas. However, the common sailor was not so sensible. They inherently believed the terrifying rumors of gigantic sea monsters living in the ocean's depths. Tales abound of slimy tentacles attacking ships and dragging crewmembers into the forbidding waters. If a sailor had his way, the ship would always creep along the shore, especially at night. The helmsman carried all of the baggage of their superstitious beliefs and had been emboldened by a bottle of spirits to navigate to his own liking. He fully expected to have passed the islands in the night before his captain awoke, but the wind died and left them drifting toward the center of the deadly islands.

"Serves him right, the lazy bastard," murmured a foremast hand of his captain to his mates gathered about the bowsprit. If there was one thing to be said against the captain, it was that he liked to sleep in. Most of the hands on duty wore smug grins as they strolled about deck or leaned easily upon a backstay, confident in the ship's progress as the morning winds picked up and sent the Barrow's Oak smoothly through the Lyswennod Shallows. A boy at the mainmast crosstrees called out the most dangerous rocks, some submerged just under the surface, in a fife of a voice that carried all the way down to the prison tier.

"Take her easy and the rocks won't be no problem," said the captain to his new helmsman. Having regained his composure, the captain directed all of his concentration on preserving his ship. The rocks could be avoided. He knew their location. In shallow waters like these, running aground was the real danger for a ship as weighed down with human cargo and provisions as the *Barrow's Oak*, especially since low-tide fast approached. The captain listened intently to the man heaving the line and calling out the depths as the ship crept along under scant sails.

"They're making an awful row up there. What you suppose it's all about?" wondered Ford's cellmate Dior. Though he spoke the language of Ford's people with as thick an accent as any good Aelwydian, Dior's almost dainty physique and amber skin set him apart as a man of the distant lands of Mane. The way all four of the cellmates dropped the growling constants at the ends of words and attached the same intonation upon softly expiring words— perhaps to toughen them up, few knew the true reason for such inexplicable linguistics—without being able to see what they looked like, one might mistake them for brothers. Manerds of Port Morton, like Dior, had suffered from their lord's overthrow by the Brastersceatts. The commonality of their plight had strengthened the bond between Dior's people and Ford's. "Brothers in iron" or "twinned by chains," they would say to one another.

Dior cocked an ear toward the door of the cell and tried to make out the nature of the commotion on the deck above. Their cantankerous cellmate Miller Edd squeezed in beside him to listen.

"They got their own worries," said Ford. It was a new day and he was ready to rejoin the fight in winning over the three men he was bound to. "They won't notice and we can get a head-start! If land's in sight, I say we give it a go! I can carry you on my back. I swim real good," he said to Dior, finding his arm in the dark and giving it a tug for reassurance. The chains that tethered them together, weaving through the hoop in the iron shackle each of them wore on his right wrist, would be a great hindrance, but it could be done, he was sure of it. "We *have* to at least *try!*"

"Maybe if land's in sight and everything else is all right," said Rhod. Ford's revival of the old topic was no surprise, but his heightened fervor and his recent manic episode made them regard him with caution. They had no intention of agreeing, but went along with what he said out of a fear that he might grow violent. "First ten!" called out Rhod as he made room at the door to peer through a split in the wood at head height through which passed their only air. A sliver of light might seep through it as well if a sailor with a lantern passed. Rhod had started the game to distract Ford from thoughts of escape. The frenzy he worked himself into when his mind locked onto the subject unsettled the others.

"Second," said Miller Edd.

"Give me the fourth ten," said Dior.

"What's that leave, third?" grumbled Ford. By now he knew his attention was being intentionally diverted, but he also understood his friends meant well. And when all was said and done, he loved a bit of fun and would rather play a game than stew in his own juices over something he could do nothing about at the moment. So, he lumbered to his feet to join in this game in which each of the four would guess when the next sailor would pass by their door. Rhod was already counting off. "One buggers by…two buggers by…three buggers by…" If the next sailor went by before he finished the tenth line, he would win the game. If not, Miller Edd would take up the chant, followed by Ford and then Dior. If no sailor passed their door after four counts to ten, the rotation began again.

Having nothing to bet with, they wagered promised items left back home, which no one expected to collect on. That wasn't the point. The game passed time and winning was prize enough. By the third rotation, the chant had diminished to a hushed whisper, not only to comply with their annoyed neighbor's entreaties to "Shut your damn hole!" but also because the tension mounted along with the stakes as the game progressed. Miller Edd had just put up a night with his wife's sister against his winning during his tenth of the next round. His wife had no sister, but no one would likely find out. The enticement was to induce one of the others to bet something that perhaps *could* be claimed should he win. "Come on, Dior, what've you got? You win and you can give her a good old…" As he pumped his armed in a suggestive manner, a jolt unlike anything they had felt aboard ship thus far threw all four of them against a wall.

"What was that?" shouted Dior.

"We assuredly struck something this time," said Rhod.

"Or something struck us," mused Ford. Cries of alarm came from the other cells, but Ford's cellmates held their tongues while waiting for the next strike. If one was coming, they wanted to hear it in hopes of discovering what it might be. A soft grinding, almost a hiss, reverberated through the side of the ship.

"What's that?" shouted Dior with a tremor as shaky as the hand with which he gripped Ford's wrist.

"Sounds like something's rubbing alongside the ship," said Rhod. They all backed away from the side of the ship and pressed against the door.

"Let us out!" someone screamed from a neighboring cell. Others echoed the cry.

"Do you feel that?" Ford asked.

"Feel what?" wondered Rhod.

"We're not rocking about no more." The regular rolling of the ship had ceased. As sick as the ship's normal motion had made some of the prisoners, the lack of it made them just as ill, because now they sensed their bodies swaying to the ghostly memory of the roll.

"You sure? I feel like I'm going back and forth," said Miller Edd.

Almost as one, the prisoners went silent as they listened to the distant uproar of the crew and shouted commands of the captain over the thunderous pounding of feet upon the deck. The frenzied activity topside maddened the prisoners with curiosity. They hollered demands for answers. Was the ship under attack? Was it sinking? Eventually the most useless crew members were sent below with pots for the prisoners.

"A pot to piss in!" they called out. "Who needs a pot to piss in?"

"Don't none of you worry!" said Chick, the sailor in charge of the fowl. Crates packed with chicken and geese lined the decks. "Nothing at all to worry about! All's well in hand!" was his constant refrain as he passed from door to door. This merely infuriated the prisoners further. The disgraced helmsman, clapped in irons along with the prisoners for his transgression, finally wheedled a real answer out of a friend.

"Captain drove her straight on to a sandbar," the former helmsman confided to his new cellmates. He seemed to derive great satisfaction in relaying the news. The ship may not have been floating anymore, but this man's attitude sure was buoyant. His cellmates spread the word and soon all of the prisoners had a good laugh at the captain, despite the fact that the ship would not have been in a position to run aground if not for the disgraced helmsman's hubris.

While the prisoners grumbled about the ill luck of having such an incompetent man controlling their destiny, the captain raced fore and aft directing his crew in a desperate attempt to get the ship off before low-tide broke her back or keeled her over completely. Unnecessary and heavy items were tossed overboard, including hundreds of pounds of provisions meant for Polecat Island. The ship's two boats carried out lines and their small crews pulled their hearts out at the oars. When that failed, anchors were run out and attempts to pull the ship free of the sand via the capstan were made, but by then the ship was settling in and taking on a decided list.

Seeing his crew exhausted by the backbreaking labor, the captain risked enlisting the help of the prisoners. Without being unchained, a few prisoners at a time were made to haul on a rope or take a turn at the capstan. The resting sailors leaned against the rail on either side and turned guard by keeping their blades at the ready. When Ford emerged onto the main deck, he found the world tilted on its side at such an angle as to make it seem that the entire ocean might pour over the ship. An occasional wave did wash over the side. Constant bailing had already gotten underway. When it was explained to the uninitiated that the keel of the *Barrow's Oak* rested on the sand and there was reasonable fear that "her back might break" and no amount of bailing would save them then, the phrase quickly made the rounds and terrified all aboard.

Ford had heard about the sailors' heroic efforts to drag the ship clear of the sand and now could see the truth of it in their worn faces and limp bodies, as well as how the blood had drained clear out of the captain's horrified face. He had seen other prisoners pouring with sweat as they heaved sloshing buckets up through the hatch. Infected by the sight of everyone pulling together like this, Ford threw himself into the work. He tossed buckets about and drove all of his weight into the bar at the capstan. He loved pitching in, working together with others, so much so that escape flittered from his mind for the time being. When their shift was finally over, Ford and his cellmates gladly trudged back down to the prison tier. The tilt of the ship was so extreme that they sat with their backs against the side of the ship due to the uncomfortably steep angle of the floor. The awkward arrangement didn't keep them from dropping off to sleep almost immediately.

By the time the sailors came for them again, the tide was on the rise and there was still work to do, but the danger of the ship foundering had passed. Before their next turn got underway, Ford and his weary cellmates waited by the ladder to the main deck for the sailors to rouse another party of prisoners from their cell. Everyone was exhausted and the appeal of going topside was not as great as it had been before. While Ford waited, he stared up into the patch of pale blue sky through the hatchway. Clouds drifted by. No longer caught up in the desperate fight to save the ship, he could think with a clear head of the land he had spied during his last turn. That strip of gray riding atop the sea had a crown of green. He fancied he could even make out individual trees, so he imagined it could not be much more than two miles away. Three or four at most. He had never swum that far before, but he was willing to try.

When the other prisoners joined them at the base of the ladder, a handful of thuds, like a dozen or more dead bodies hitting the deck above, brought everyone to a standstill. Sharp screams from the crew sent a sailor, halfway up the ladder, toppling back down. A turmoil of cries, shouted commands, crisscrossing footfalls, and thumps and stomps from indeterminate struggles all along the main deck created a dizzying confusion. Bodies flashed past the hatchway and a sailor either jumped or was flung down the hatchway.

"What is it? What's happening?" they demanded, but got nothing from the dumbstruck man before he frantically yanked himself free of their clutching hands and fled aft out of sight.

A shadowy oblong shape, like a giant thumb, appeared in the hatchway and blocked out much of the light. Inclining itself to peer below with an eyeless face like smooth black rubber, it reared skyward. A slit of two brilliantly white rows of razor-sharp teeth in a gaping maw opened into a devilish smile. All twelve feet of glistening giant eel body, as thick as the mainmast, dove through hatch and crashed down upon the lower deck at their feet. The prisoners jumped back from the flopping and writhing body. They stumbled across the tilted deck and fell against the wall to avoid the giant eel's snapping jaws and the slap of its powerful tail. The prisoners drove their heels into it to keep it at bay. Ford and Rhod whipped at the eel with the length of chain linking them together. Miller Edd might have done the same, but Dior fought to escape and, as slight as he was, he pulled Miller Edd along with him. The sailors hid behind the prisoners, using them as human shields. The bravest of them made impotent stabs at the air between themselves and the sea creature. A waif and inveterate thief nicknamed Gulp screamed as the eel bit down on his thigh. One of his cellmates, the priest Will, fell onto the creature. This jerked down the other two chained to him, so that all four of them rolled across the slanted deck and crashed into a wall with the eel. The boy Gulp broke free. The chain between him and Will had caught in the creature's mouth. It whipped its head about trying to rid itself of the iron gag. Bodies crawled over one another. The creature's tail swung around in a wide arc, smashing a sailor's head into a beam. Ford and Rhod fell upon the back end of the giant eel and pressed the length of chain between them down on its tail. Will's group fought to hold down its head. The sailors moved in and finished it off with their knives.

"Never seen an eel the size of that in my life," said Rhod for the third time later that evening over a well-earned mug of ale. The ship had been floated off the shoals and was once more underway. They were leaving the Lyswennod Shallows behind them and good riddance said one and all.

"I hope I never do again!" said Miller Edd, while spooning an inordinate amount of thick stew into his round, ruddy face with its long moustache catching much of it. The prisoners were enjoying themselves as they sat companionably in the sun on the main deck wolfing down the heartiest meal they had had so far aboard the *Barrow's Oak*. After the incident at the shoals when unwanted visitors had been attracted to the ship by the jettisoned provisions, meat was found in both of their next two meals, much to the prisoners' delight. Though fishy, it tasted far fresher than anything they had eaten since being imprisoned. No one asked where it had come from.

The captain had indulged the prisoners for their help with the ship. He ordered their chains removed for brief periods to relieve them of their burden. Attention was given to the care of their chaffed wrists and any injuries suffered in the defense of the ship. Extra time was granted while they relieved themselves, and male and female prisoners were permitted to be together on deck during these breaks.

Later the following day, Rhod found himself standing at the rail next to Moll Turner, a female prisoner who had caught his eye back when they were in the prison hulks at Port Morton. Like Ford, Moll had been a watchman and put up a valiant fight at his side during the defense of the Iarl at Middlefield House. The former drover's no-nonsense demeanor, sturdy legs and a torso that put many a tree trunk to shame, secured her a position in the night watch. Her lips, often pulled thin across clenched teeth, presented a jaw ready and even willing to take a shot if needs be. Getting the serious and steady Moll to laugh felt like receiving a gift. Her delightfully wide, toothy grin plumped her lumpy cheeks and pushed smiling wrinkles up under eyes suddenly warm and inviting. Rhod was learning to make her laugh.

Due to the captain's spell of benevolence, the prisoners had had more to drink than normal and Moll urgently needed to relieve herself. Without waiting for a more private moment, she turned about, lifted her leather apron, hiked up her frock and sat upon the rail, pulling her two chain companions along with her. The sailor charged with holding the prisoners by their chains with a boathook when they stood at the rail, had become infected by the lax atmosphere. He stood nearby, but turned his back for privacy's sake. An unexpected lurch of the sea left Moll swaying uneasily on the rail. Seeing her white-knuckled grip and even whiter eyes, Rhod reached past another prisoner and took Moll firmly by the upper arm. She latched onto his arm and finished her business faster than she ever had before. Hopping down, she kept hold of him, a bond that held him more securely than any chains.

The boy at the crosstrees cried something shrill and indecipherable. A call from the bowsprit was relayed fore to aft from sailor to sailor until reaching the ship's second-in-command, who took two steps sternward toward the captain standing by the helm in order to report, "Polecat Island has been spotted, sir!"

Chapter 3
Polecat Island

The *Barrow's Oak* approached Polecat Island at sundown and anchored in its bay after dark. The people aboard her had seen nothing more of the island than a glimpse of the rocky shores of a low, gray land. After passing another anxious and mostly sleepless night in their cells, the confused prisoners emerged from below onto the main deck in the morning and looked about them with wide-eyed dread, like cattle herded toward a slaughterhouse.

Gulls wheeled in and out of the gloomy dawn mist that hung over the rocky shoreline like a dark mourning shroud. Sandpipers nestled in the nooks of the grass-topped cliffs that encircled most of the island. These cliffs spread before the ship like cupped hands to create a small bay no more than a few hundred yards wide. Smooth rock arms reached into the surf from the land at either side of the mouth. This was the only harbor serviceable to ships. A stout pier poked into the relatively calm waters of the bay from a narrow, pebbly beach upon which clustered the dozen damp little houses and shops that comprised New Morgan, the only village on the island. The land behind the beach rose to a garrisoned blockhouse that barricaded a gap in the cliffs and created a gateway to the rest of the island. The wings of a wall topped with spikes spread out on either side of the blockhouse, connecting the building to the cliffs and hemming the village into the beach side of the island. Crossbow-wielding guards intermittently appeared in the upper windows of the blockhouse to stare down at the beach and along the cliffs, with the occasional glance out at the ship. The tallest structures on the island sat at the end of the two promontories which created the bay. On one side stood a watchtower that surveyed the entire bay and much of the southern side of the island, as well as serving as a lighthouse. The grandest edifice of all stood opposite. Three-stories of solid stone crowned at one end by a square tower with a turret, Crowell House was the residence of the island's governing lord and the symbol of power upon the island.

The chains between the shivering prisoners tinkled together as their wait on deck lengthened. The captain had gone ashore to meet with New Morgan's officials, who had to be roused from their beds. Eventually, a crowd of functionaries and important personages gathered on the waterfront. Foremost among them was Pater Atwall, Keeper of the Pen, the overseer of all the prisoners. The colony also had a Master of the Guard, but his presence was not necessary at these occasions. The Island Forester was on hand to select a suitable laborer or two from the newly arrived prisoners for his particular line of work. Also present were the jolly-looking brewer of the island's ale, a baker who did most of the general cookery, and a former inmate of the penal colony who kept the fishermen on task. They called him Fish, because his surname was Baker.

The current Warden of the Island and the lord appointed to govern the penal colony, Barwnig Bryce was not among them. A child pulled back one of the window's curtains in Crowell House, revealing the stiff-backed Bryce languidly gazing down at the ship with only the mildest of interest. A rail-thin and just as rigid woman beside him jerked the child by the arm and the two vanished. The curtain fluttered closed. Soon the child appeared in a higher window with another shorter child by its side. The two waved and then disappeared and reappeared in various windows until reaching the very top window of the tower, where they leapt about and shouted down at the ship. The distance and roll of the surf masked their cries.

In the barwnig's stead, a clerk stepped in as proxy and was one of the first to reach the pier. This young and eager Weaverite priest stood by the ship's clerk and the two chatted amiably as they went over the ship's manifest. The lord's clerk happily showed off his fine quill when his counterpart made an appreciative remark.

"Lovely day we're having," one said to the other. The autumn morning's mist had formed into a chilling drizzle. A crack about the island's notoriously poor weather broke the pack of officials into sour laughter just as the sailors and Polecat's guardsmen began parading the prisoners down the pier.

"That's my man!" shouted Dara Millet the tall and pear-shaped brewer, growing shorter and more pear-like with age. She waved a triumphant hand to indicate Ford and fairly bubbled with glee. "Ha-hah!"

"No," protested the Forester in resigned exasperation.

"Be reasonable, Dara," said the Keeper of the Pen.

"Fair is fair, Pater," said the brewer, as magnanimous as anyone secure in their victory. "You promised me first choice this ship, and that's the one I want." A satisfied grin stretched above her double chin as she leaned back and slapped her belly. "Ho, ho! What luck! Look at the size of him!"

"I'm looking. I'm looking," said the Keeper of the Pen. Such a large and undoubtedly strong specimen as Ford Barlow would be a valuable asset on any of the work parties Atwall was charged with assembling. Certainly, the brewer needed someone to lift the heavy barrels, full buckets and those cumbersome sacks of grain necessary to ale making, but it was never a full day's worth of work. None of the village work was half as strenuous as what was in store for the prisoners out in the fields and in the quarries. Such a figure of a man as Ford would be a worthy addition to the expedition parties to the dangerous outlying islands, where information needed to be gathered and footholds established for the colony to grow. This prison island was but the beginning of a greater plan. But the brewer had been made a promise and the Keeper of the Pen didn't like sour ale, so he nodded to the clerk and the assignment was scratched onto parchment. Ford didn't recognize it for what it was at the time, but he had just had a brilliant stroke of good fortune.

The prisoners were ordered to line up along the beach. Mirthless guards prodded laggards into place with spears and halberds. Atwall stood before them and delivered a bored recital of the island's laws and rules of conduct. He had been at his current position long since the recent upheaval brought on by the Brastersceatt rebellion and their installment of Bryce as Warden. None of this was new to him. The various cruel punishments for breaking the laws and disregarding the rules marched out of him like foot-weary soldiers. To the prisoners, each monotonously delivered line was another disheartening step toward the soul-crushing depression that eventually affected all of the penal colony's inhabitants. Most long-term prisoners lost their will to remain in the present. Their senses shut down and they disappeared into a more pleasant past self or dove headlong into oblivion. The nervous energy of the newly arrived prisoners dissolved into the old familiar lethargy of their weeks upon the prison hulks and aboard the *Barrow's Oak*. Then their interest was revived by a turn in Atwall's speech.

"Sooner or later it will come to your attention that there is land directly north of this island. Ignore it. Drive it from your minds entirely. I say this knowing some of you will still be foolish enough to see it as a means of escape from Polecat. Do not be fooled. It is nothing but another island, one with particularly deadly inhabitants. Escape to that island would bring certain and swift death!"

Excited thoughts of escape sent tiny sparks of life through a few of the prisoners. Ford craned his neck in search of this land to the north to no avail. But most of them only had eyes for their new surroundings as they were led through the hamlet-size village and a pair of gates that took them past the wall and blockhouse into an area known as the Pen.

The Pen was a walled-in square enclosing squat, weather-beaten barracks for the prisoners, men on one side of a tall partition and women on the other. On the men's side, the wooden, nearly windowless barracks were rotting in the mud from the bottom up. What first caught the eye and sent a distressed murmur rippling through the newcomers was a gibbet-like cage and stocks. Neither was being used at the moment, but every prisoner immediately imagined themselves trapped within. A latrine pit had been dug for the prisoners' use behind one of the barracks. Its stench pervaded the entirety of the Pen. Next to the pit stood a four-foot-tall offal pile. As the temperatures rose, so would rise a buzzing cloud of flies above the pit and pile. A small animal carcass and a few scattered bones littered spaces between the barracks, where no living thing grew in the mud, not so much as a blade of grass. All prisoners had to report to the Pen at nightfall. "Be present and accounted for or pay the consequences," Atwall warned. "No exceptions!"

"Welcome home," said Rhod with a rueful sneer while taking in the scene.

"Just look at this miserable ol' place," muttered Ford as he rubbed at his sore wrists. The shackles that bound them for the journey were being removed, so the clunky metal binders could be returned to the ship. A handful of sick and emaciated prisoners emerged from the darkness of the barracks to slouch in the doorways to get a look at the new arrivals. They watched in a stupor through glazed-over, pink-rimmed eyes deeply sunken into their sockets. They dabbed at running noses rubbed raw. Phlegm-filled coughing rattled away inside the barracks.

"And I thought the ship had been a nightmare," said Aeddamon Born, a podgy and round-headed priest in the Order of the Sud a Waed, who wore only a thin moustache rather than the typical full beard. Though merely an acolyte, he often belied his own youth and inexperience with insufferable officiousness and the kind of vocal opinions that had landed him a spot on the next ship to the island with other priests the Weaverites wished to rid themselves of.

"This ol' hole is one step above the grave and that's no lie," said Rhod.

"What kind of dung heap have we landed ourselves in?" Dior wondered amid the prisoners' growing displeasure.

"Clamp it or I'll put a real ache in your belly!" barked Atwall. Such surprising command from such a physically unimposing man brought them all to immediate attention. "Each of you useless vermin will have a job to do here on the island! You'll do it and do it without being told or you will suffer! This is a promise, make no mistake! Understand?" He didn't seek a response, as he didn't much care if they understood. Nearly every prisoner new to the island tested their boundaries and each needed to be dealt with in some way at some point. They would all be made to understand eventually. His eyes fell upon his parchment, which listed all of the new prisoners' names, as well as information about them obtained during their interment back in Port Morton. He read out a handful of names, including Ford's, and segregated them from the main body. The remaining prisoners were separated into work divisions and then led to another gate that opened to the rest of the island, where their overseers would teach them their duties in the quarries and the fields.

The names of those left behind were read out again. Ford answered when his was called and found himself being led back through the gate toward the bay. While passing through the village, he thought about making a run for it. Now would have been a perfect time. There were few people about, none of them paying him the slightest attention, and the patchy-headed older man casually leading the way would be no obstacle. A stiff breeze would knock him down, never mind what Ford could do to him. What stopped him was a realization that he had nowhere to run to. The few boats pulled up along the beach were chained and padlocked to an iron hoop mooring. He could leap into the sea, but where would he swim to? There was no land in sight. And even if he wasn't spotted sneaking onto the ship, they would find him sooner or later. A man his size couldn't stow away for long.

"You'll do your meals and necessities back in the Pen." The sentence slid out sibilant through the missing teeth of the man leading the way.

"Necessities?" wondered Ford. He couldn't remember ever having heard the word.

After meeting Ford's eye and making sure he wasn't been made game of, the man answered, "Necessities! Your water and waste, boy! Water and waste! The privy's hands off." He pointed the stub of his right arm toward a small and rough stone building perched atop a slab of rock at the water's edge at the far end of the beach. Inside was a broad plank with holes cut into it propped up on rocks and laid over a gap in the floor. Anything passing through the holes fell into the gap and dribbled or plopped down between the rocks on the beach below, where it was washed away at high tide.

Ford had seen privies before, but it wasn't every day that you saw someone missing both of their hands. He had a good, long look at the man. Everything about him was scruffy, from his worn clothes to his graying beard. He certainly didn't look like the island's well-dressed and nicely groomed officials, nor even the guards in their clinking ring armor and smart leather. Ford assumed he was an inmate and chanced familiarity when he asked, "What's happening now?"

"Now?"

"I mean, where are we going?" Since leaving the ship, everything was new and confusing. He felt discombobulated and wanted to be on solid ground again in more ways than one.

"Gyl's taking you to your new trade." The old man jerked his other stub at the island's brewery. Smooth-stoned and newly-roofed brewery, it stood a little taller than the other buildings crowded in the bay. They found the place empty and the brewer nowhere in sight. "There's nothing for it, but we wait." Gyl gestured Ford to sit at a long table in the narrow front room of the brewery. The space, tightly-packed with only one table and seating, was meant for the island's officials and off-duty guards to gather and drink. Gyl took up a mug and with admirable dexterity for a man without hands, filled it with a golden ale from a tapped barrel. "We'll have to share this seeing as you're not allowed."

"I'm not?"

"Not from this tap," said Gyl, taking a seat opposite Ford. "Prisoners get their drink in the Pen. Watered down muck. This is the real stuff! Here, get your lips around that." Gyl slid the mug across the table to Ford. "Don't worry, I ain't got the sickness."

"What is it they got?"

"Search me," said Gyl, as if the illness plaguing everyone meant little to him. Though he had his friends on Polecat, like most long-time prisoners on the island, Gyl had developed a careless attitude about life and death. All the same, he willingly provided a wealth of information about the place in a short amount of time. Much of it was pointless gossip, but the one thing that really struck home for Ford was Gyl's insistence that he should take care not to lose his position at the brewery. "Keep it long as you can. Fish ain't bad and the trees is easy, but you'd never get in with either one. Nah, you'd be for the quarries, guessing by the size of you."

"And that's no good?"

"You wanna break rock and carry it all over the island all damn day every day?" Gyl turned his head away, spat, and then gave Ford a sideways look.

"No."

"No, you do not."

"Oh," said Ford. He took a moment to absorb what Gyl had just said and then asked the next thing to pop into his head.

"Women? Sure, there's a few. Double now your ship's come in. They's barracks's over other side of the wall from men's. They got the chickens and sheep in there with them. But just you beware. They's all spoken for, the women I mean. Nose around and you're liable to find trouble, even someone your size. There's plenty of trouble to be had on the island if you stick your nose into another man's affairs."

During a second mug of ale, Gyl moved on from subject to subject in a rapid-fire parlance that flooded Ford's memory beyond capacity. Soon he gave up trying to retain any of it. As much as Gyl had to say, never during the one-sided conversation did he broach the subject of how he lost his hands or why he was on the island. Ford assumed theft. Severing the hand of a persistent thief was used as a deterrent. But to lose both hands, that was a rarity.

"They all want my ale, but never have a free ear when I need the littlest thing!" bellowed the brewer as she bowled through the door and made straight for the tap to pull herself a long draft. Being quite familiar with the brewer's frequent outbursts, Gyl smiled back at her, while sliding the mug away from Ford as they both listened politely. "All I asked for was a bit of black honey, and will they accommodate me, the one who's done so much for them? Not if their lives depended upon it!" Millet had grown quite voluble, but having exorcised her complaints, the redness in her cheeks died away and her shouting immediately dissolved into a grumble. "And it just might one day, if they don't watch themselves."

A sudden smile did yeoman's work in lifting Millet's heavy, drooping jowls that dragged her face into a frown. High-arching eyebrows and laugh-lines helped transform the dour expression into effervescent pleasure, when the brewer beamed upon Ford. "I see you've brought me my new man, Gyl! Millet's my name, brewing's my, well, it's my damn reason for getting up in the morning." A deep chuckle rumbled up from a jumping belly that she restrained with a broad, pink hand. When the fit was finished, she extended the hand to Ford and took his in a rock-solid grasp. "You can call me Dara."

"Ford."

"Ford. Ford," mused the brewer as she scooped up Gyl's mug and topped it off. "Get that down you, Gyl. Then you'd better be off before Rechard finds you here lingering in your drinks again. Ford. There's a name you don't hear every day," she said, dropping down next to Gyl and across from Ford. The little old man bounced in his seat, but managed with intense concentration to keep from spilling a single drop of ale. Ford braced for the inevitable joke about his name. Every other person who heard his name for the first time made a joke about him being born at a river crossing, or even *in* the river if they were feeling particularly witty. "The important thing is, it's short and easy to remember. I once had a man working for me who went by Calbhachnan. Oddest name I ever heard. I just called him Nan. We didn't get on. He had no liking for a good tune. What can you do with a man like that? Do you like a good tune, Ford?" She watched him out of one eye as she took a big swig of ale, some of it spilling from her lips.

"I do, very much." Ford felt an immediate warmth for this tubby, cheerful woman with ale running over her chins. For one, she hadn't made a crack about his name. Also, Millet being such a large woman—over two hundred pounds and nearing six feet—she had had to duck under the doorway just as Ford had. He felt an affinity for those who shared the woes of the overly tall. *Commiseration makes fast comrades*, someone had said to him once.

He sensed he might like working under Millet, but a pair of niggling questions doused this pleasant thought. Millet was a sturdy woman who could no doubt manage barrels and the like on her own. So, how much did she really need him? The other issue was that Ford knew next to nothing about brewing, so he had to wonder what he was doing here. Why had Dara requested him specifically? The whole day was turning a shade surreal. Ford had gone from being a prisoner in the bowels of a ship to landing on an island as a brewer's assistant. He was mired in these thoughts when he realized Millet had carried the conversation on and he had missed much of what was being said.

"After him, I got in a fella who went by Aeron. Not the smartest, nor strongest, but a perfectly fine name. As fortunes go, I lost him to the sickness." Millet sighed and took another gulp. More ale dribbled down her chin. She dabbed at it with her knee-length apron, which had begun life an off-white color and been stained a dozen shades of yellow over the years. "Only three dead from it and one of them has to be one of mine. Can you believe that luck?" The brewer shook her drooping head and sighed again. Suddenly, her face lit up. Her chest swelled, her smile rebounded and she threw her hands up between herself and Ford. "But now, speak of luck! Look at you! You'll do, you will do indeed!" She went on staring at Ford, grinning and admiring him far longer than Ford was comfortable with.

"Begging your pardon, but what is it you want me to do?" Ford finally had to ask.

"That's me off," said Gyl, downing the last of his ale and letting a few drips escape his lips, which brought Millet great pleasure. "Thanks for that," he said tapping the brewer's fleshy shoulder with his stump before heading out the door with a wave of his arm.

"Always a good friend, Gyl!" Millet shouted after him. She waved and turned from the door back to Ford. "Gyl's a good sort. Handy to have around. Let's get to work then!"

Ford followed the brewer into a back room much larger than the front. A central hearth with a leaden vat set atop was surrounded by numerous barrels and buckets in various sizes. Cups, pans, a mortar and pestle, yard-long spoons and ladles sat on shelves, leaned against the walls, or hung from hooks. There was even a boat oar among them. Sacks of grain were neatly stacked in one corner. A ladder led up to a loft.

"That's the biggest barrel I've ever seen!" Ford declared with a look of appreciation that pleased the brewer.

"That's no barrel. That's a tun. It's where the mash goes. Haven't you ever brewed before?"

Ford considered himself fairly well-versed in drink. Much of the money he had made over the previous few years had been spent on ale. He had also visited a brewery or two in his capacity as a porter lugging goods to and from the dockyards. However, he had never so much as made it past the backdoor of a brewery, never mind having worked therein. He worried his lack of experience was about to put him out of work before work had even begun. Gyl had put the scare into him. Ford knew he would much rather work in a brewery than a quarry. Plus, he already felt attached to the place and its slightly eccentric proprietor with her peculiarly proper diction and jovial nature.

Ford gave an ambiguous grunt and that was enough for Millet, who immediately dove headlong into a lengthy discourse on brewing: the various kinds of grains; the baking and roasting of grains; her preferred flavor of water; the heating and cooling of water at different stages; the importance of pouring water from a height; the importance of keeping the room at the right temperature. Everything seemed important. Millet was passionate about her craft. She had formed many of her own ideas on technique, equipment, and ingredients. Ford tried to take in the bewildering amount of information, but was soon lost. Each of the numerous barrels had its own name and he couldn't remember any but the tun. He heard *malt* and *mash* as the same word. Even when described, they sounded the same. Worst of all, he couldn't be sure which were his duties and which were not out of the many procedures explained to him throughout the long lecture. He also didn't wish to interrupt and reveal his ignorance. Lucky for him, when Millet did get down to giving an order, it was direct.

"Carry those sacks over to Alyk, the baker. Then muck out that barrel. I'm going to go talk to the tailor and see if he can't whip you up a set of clothes." The brewer looked Ford up and down with a raised eyebrow. Ford's clothes were uncommonly bright, his friend having sewn them up for him on the spur of the moment from readily available materials. But that wasn't what put the wrinkle in Millet's nose. "You've got a whiff about you like a dog I once had. By the end, he would sit in his own filth, the poor creature. You look half as ragged, too. We'll get you out of them old things before my stomach does a flip out of my throat and drowns itself in the ocean. Boy, the way they treat you people on them ships." She shook her head. Ford didn't know how anyone could smell anything above the yeasty sourness pervading the place. "Better bring along a taste to quicken his needle," the brewer added as she filled a large tankard with ale and then headed for the door. "Do not touch my yeast!"

"Now, *there's* a smell that'll take some getting used to," Ford thought, while gladly drawing in the salty air off the ocean upon leaving the brewery with the grain sacks. Within a few steps, he caught a whiff of freshly baked bread and followed his nose to the thrown-open windows of the round bakery. When he arrived, the baker and two assistants were bustling about flour-strewn tables, waist-high troughs, cooling shelves laden with loaves, and a beehive oven they kept heated almost constantly, making this the warmest place on the island. A short-haired Amitan cat crouched against a wall intently staring at a mouse hole.

"The usual then, eh?" asked the baker when Ford handed over the sacks. To this question Ford gave a small nod. It seemed a safe bet. He hoped he wasn't wrong. He just wanted to get back to the brewery and plunge into some barrel cleaning.

"How do you go about cleaning a barrel?" he muttered upon returning to the brewery's back room.

"How I am to know?" said the most feminine voice Ford had heard in weeks. As soft as the words were spoken, they were quite close to his ear and came at him like a blow to the side of the head. He flinched and threw out a punch at the wholly unexpected sound, then stumbled sideways into the spoons and ladles as he stepped back into a defensive stance. A pile of shiny black hair jiggled as the short, frail-framed young woman attached to it dodged Ford's fist with breezy ease. He caught what utensils he could from falling and then whipped an accusing eye around. What he saw looked very much like an overgrown pixie perched cross-legged upon the huge hogshead standing by the door. At first sight there was a vague familiarity to the lovely face hardened by horrors, but the flesh had dropped away, thus thrusting out cutting cheekbones, cornering the chin, and thinning the neck. The lack of the usual black make-up ringing the round, entrancing eyes coupled with the gay yellows and pinks of the woman's smock and kirtle, conjured an image not readily recognizable to Ford.

"Now I am forgotten to you?"

"Elle!" Ford broke out in a wide, toothy smile and came at her with arms spread. She threw up her hands to ward him off, but had no chance against his overpowering embrace. Truth be told, she was happy to succumb to his touch. She didn't normally permit herself to be emotionally close with anyone, so the press of a warm body against hers was rare. For his part, he feared he might break her bones. She felt positively skeletal. He needn't have worried. His long arms couldn't squeeze together tight enough to crush such a thin frame.

Ford and Elle had been friends since his earliest days in Port Morton. It was she who had stayed up all night tailoring the very clothes he wore. They had worked various street schemes together back when neither had two coins to rub together. This was their first time seeing one another in weeks. Back in Port Morton just before Ford was imprisoned, Elle had been taken up for theft and Ford had agonized over what had become of her. His every ounce of joy at finally seeing her again was genuine. He let it show with another hug.

"All gods, please!" Elle wheezed, while slapping at his sides.

Eventually he let go, but he dropped his paw-like hands upon her shoulders and wore a silly grin while looking her up and down. His eyes misted over with the inexpressible pleasure of reuniting with a friend. However, her ghostly pallor and frailty quickly turned him somber. "Are you ill?"

"No."

"Are you sure? You look pale and tired or something," he said while looking into her eyes and describing vague circles around his own eyes with his finger.

"Now I see," she said, folding her arms together as she caught herself from turning away from his gaze. While she could be vain about her appearance and wished she could make herself up as she preferred, she had a vigorous streak of defiance running through her that overrode nearly everything else in her nature. She lifted her chin and met his eye. "What to do? The food is terrible and nowhere on this island is no paint for the face. And too, of course, I have nothing what is mine."

Tricky as it could be to follow her at times, Ford had grown accustomed to his friend's odd way of speaking. Elle's speech pattern and choice of words were adversely affected by an uprooted childhood. At an early age, she had been taken from her homeland in the Forest of a Thousand Names by a courageous aunt, who had to leave her in Port Morton to be fostered by a mistress who cared only about the little foreign girl's skill as a seamstress, not whether she spoke properly. In fact, speaking during working hours would often get one's back switched, so Elle had little chance to practice her adopted country's language until she ran away and found refuge in the city's thieves' guild. Eloquence and expanded vocabularies were not high on the guild's list of priorities, so she stumbled along picking up new words and piecing them into her patchwork lexicon.

Ford could usually follow along with what she intended to say without getting too lost. When she said she *had nothing*, he knew she meant she had lost all of her own possessions when her room was raided and she was arrested for theft. He knew this because he was the one who had gotten her arrested. She had been transported to Polecat Island because of him. The joy of seeing her again faded at that thought and was replaced by the fear of her discovering this truth.

"A man of the watch, he come to my room with the guard of the town. Maybe you know this man of the watch? Maybe he is here on the island. I find this man, I slit his throat!" Elle's desire sharpened her tone, her eye, her whole demeanor. Ford backed away. The man she spoke of was his former boss, Weylon Whetstone, the city's night watch captain, or at least he had been before joining the losing side in the Battle of Middlefield House and being captured. Prior to that, Ford had spoken to Whetstone about getting Elle transported to Polecat Island, because she had her mind set on stealing a valuable journal and some maps that belonged to Lord Middlefield. Ford knew the security around Middlefield had recently been tightened and he feared Elle would be caught. He wasn't as sure of her abilities as she was. If she had been caught it would mean hanging. Getting her sent to the island for petty theft seemed like the only sensible and non-lethal alternative, and it had worked. But now she was imprisoned upon this remote, desolate island, and for how long? She was still young and might spend the rest of her life here.

After toying with the spoons and ladles again, Ford wandered away behind the giant tun, putting it between himself and Elle while she carried the conversation on to other topics. When Ford's attention returned to the present, she was explaining her role on the island. Apparently, due to her delicate appearance she had been given lighter duties.

"They say I am no good for the wheat or the rock," she said with a happy shrug of her narrow shoulders. She had been made a runner, like Gyl, because of her quick way of walking wherever she went. Island officials trusted her, because of her newly adopted manner of dressing like an innocent peasant girl. Such a pretty and fragile girl as her surely would not overpower the guards or attempt any such nonsense, so they assumed.

She went on speaking of her time on the island thus far. Ford heard little of it, only nodding and grunting when it seemed appropriate. His aloof wanderings took him to the back of the room, where he examined the rungs of the ladder to the loft while battling his worry. If Elle discovered his role in her arrest and transportation, he wasn't sure what she would do, but he knew it wouldn't go over well. If she never knew the truth, it would probably be for the best. Let the past lie, he thought to himself, only an idiot would admit what he had done.

"I'm the one who got you sent here," he blurted out.

Chapter 4
Tracking Down Trousers

"Take off your trousers. Come now, we don't have all day," said Millet, standing in the back room of the brewery with her arms folded waiting for Ford to get undressed. He stripped down to his smallclothes and hoped he need go no farther, at least not while she looked on.

Millet kept her deeper thoughts and feelings to herself about watching Ford undress, but she had been crystal clear in her annoyance at how long it had taken to come by new clothes for her assistant. The recent influx of prisoners created extra work for New Morgan's artisans, pushing back the tailor's promise to have Ford's clothes ready within days to something closer to a week. In the meanwhile, the old clothes had been washed and washed again. That didn't satisfy the brewer. She wanted her assistant out of the ridiculously colorful and irredeemably stained tunic and trousers. "You look like the part of the rainbow where it meets the mud."

At Millet's instance, Ford drew himself a bucket of hot water and washed up with the rag they used to wipe down the table and clean out the mugs. Eventually, she made herself busy in the front room to give him some privacy so that he could go to work on himself. This was the second bath Ford had had in a week. He couldn't remember being this clean since the summers of his childhood when he and the other village children would swim in a nearby brook every chance they got. That brook had been icy cold all the year round. Washing with hot water was a wonderful experience

"I could get used to this," he said letting the steaming rag linger over his skin and spending more time than he ever had trying to reach the small of his back. His mind wandered all the while over the past week's events. On his second day at the penal colony, after the prisoners were assembled to witness a punishment by flogging, Ford found himself walking over Polecat's highest peak on island duties that Millet could not get him out of. Though the hill was little more than a glorified knoll, it still gave him his first real view of the island. Two miles at its widest, but twice as long, the whole of the island could be seen from the hill at its relative center due to a dearth of trees. Only a cultivated grove of oaks and maples masked a small area to the northeast. The rest was unremarkable open downs with the occasional patch of blueberry bushes, crop fields, and boggy wetlands.

What caught Ford's eye was Forbidden Island, the intentionally-named and enticingly mysterious landmass to the north that Atwall had been very specific in warning the prisoners against. It spread out like welcoming arms, giving him hope that maybe, just maybe, it was more than a mere island. Perhaps this was a mainland, he thought, maybe even a portion of Aelwyd he had never known existed. Rocks protruded from the half mile of water between Polecat and Forbidden Island. Seawater passed through the gap in random, irregularly breaking waves. Perhaps the shallows between the islands were wadable. Even if it wasn't, that was a swimmable distance for Ford. More possibilities than problems arose within his willing mind. The danger of the jagged rocks and pounding surf nagged like a fly, but he wouldn't let that spoil his daydreaming.

"Hurry it up in there!" hollered Millet from the front room. "We've got a good deal of work to catch up on!" Production at the brewery had slowed considerably when Ford caught the sickness seemingly having its way with every inhabitant of the island, especially the newly-arrived prisoners, who shook and ached, lost their appetites, vomited, and shed weight at an alarming rate. Ford had been fortunate, escaping with a light bout that lasted only a few days. On the second day, he had been obliged to take to his bed for the afternoon, but by the fourth day he felt something like his old self again.

On the morning of that fourth day, while his sore body still moved with the speed of a sluggish tortoise, Elle had entered the brewery for the first time since Ford confessed his role in her arrest. They had not spoken since then. She had come to deliver a jar of the "black honey" Millet so desperately desired. Where it had come from and how she had obtained it, she didn't offer and the brewer didn't ask. Elle was always doing these kindnesses for the village artisans and in return they often got her out of work. The baker might ask her opinion of the latest batch of loaves—a recipe that never altered—or the brewer would sit her down at the table for a mug of ale and a long pleasant chat. Such delays spared the young woman an extra trip across the island to deliver a message or some other such foot-wearying task.

Millet enjoyed Elle's visits and had been sad when the most recent one ended suddenly and without the usual warmth. When Ford followed Elle out the door, shouting at her retreating back, Millet had been astounded and confused. Nothing good came of that meeting. Ford had been too muddle-headed from the illness to convey his remorse and couldn't begin to clearly explain his intentions in getting her transported to the penal colony. Most of his explaining was done to Millet, who demanded to know why he had scared her off. Upon discovering Ford and Elle were old friends, Millet clapped her hands in delight and declared, "It'll all blow over in time. Friends find a way. You mark my words!"

Ford pulled on his clean, new tunic and got to work. Regardless of her outward show of impatience, today was a better day and Millet whistled contentedly while leisurely scraping away at the tun. That afternoon they were embarking on a special brew, one which Millet made Ford swear to keep secret.

"It's not that I'm afraid of them, but they don't like change, these folk," she said of the island's officials who regulated her production. "Maddeningly stuck in their ways, they are, but I won't let them stop me! Art of the craft flows through me! It makes me feel alive! Take my meaning?" Ford didn't, at least not exactly and not right away. But during his frequent trips back and forth from the well with sloshing buckets of the freshest, purest water the island could offer, he reflected upon how Millet's passion for her trade and his own freedom were a lot alike actually. Without freedom he felt much less alive, even somewhat dead on the inside.

"Wish I could help more with the lifting and whatnot," said Millet for the fifth or sixth time in the past week. It was the sort of thing she said whenever there was a barrel to shift, buckets of water to fetch, or sacks of grain to haul. Ford was more than happy to handle it all. He had finally discovered why he had been chosen to be the brewer's assistant, and the knowledge made him feel more secure in his position.

"The old injury's acting up!" she grimaced, grabbing at her groin while launching into the fifth or sixth retelling of how she had injured herself in a fight. Sometimes the fight seemed similar to a wrestling match or the prize fights Ford had participated in back in the city. Other retellings made it seem as if Millet had once fought in a great battle. Where and when were left vague, but Ford was assured that Millet had fought bravery and come out of the nightmarish fray without a scratch, aside from this unfortunate groin injury. Ford knew the variations on the tale fairly well by now, but he didn't mind the retelling. After all, he liked a good story no matter how many times he heard it, sometimes more so for the repetition.

"There's our man! Thought maybe you'd run away on us," Rhod called out as Ford entered the Pen that evening just before it was too dark to see. His friends greeted him with as much cheer as they could muster after a wearying day of work with little food and drink. Even some of the old timers added to the kind welcome. They had taken to him. Most did. Even if Ford were only half as affable, his obvious strength and size made lesser men wish to befriend him. They figured it was better to be on the big man's side than not, come what may.

"Not yet," said Ford as he pulled off his boots and collapsed onto his pallet bed in the barracks.

"A long day, Master Ford?" asked his overly-respectful friend Dillon Baw in a piping voice. Dillon may have been doleful in appearance, but he was often chipper and ready to please. He and Ford had worked as night watchmen together, even defended Middlefield together. By chance, Dillon had arrived on Polecat earlier than Ford because there was space to fill on a swift ship dispatched by the Brastersceatts to bring the new Warden and his loyal guard to the island in order to make the transition in rule here. Torn away from his family and knowing no one on the island, Dillon had been particularly happy to reunite with Ford. "I saved a tail for you," he said, handing Ford a lobster tail.

Dillon was built like a sapling. He stood two inches over five feet when his back was at its straightest, so island officials decided he was best fitted for the lighter duties of the fishery. Not much actual fishing was done by its half dozen prisoners. They mostly waded about knee-deep in the shallows plucking lobsters and crabs from under the seaweed beds.

"You're a savior, Dillon." Ford chewed and chewed on the rubbery meat. The prisoners nicknamed the lobster "the little devil of the deep." Thinking it intrinsically evil, they would *cook the demon out of it*, making it tough to eat. Lobster being so abundant and easy to catch, for a time it was all the prisoners were fed on. Then one day they revolted against it and demanded anything else to eat. Even now, many of the old timers refused to eat the stuff. Ford could see how one might tire of the taste, but for now he was thankful for anything that would satisfy his near-constant hunger.

Exhausted from the day's work, prisoners mostly fell into bed and dropped off to sleep as soon as they walked through the door. There was hardly any light to see by once inside the barracks, aside from what moonlight came in through the door and holes in the walls. Besides, there was little to do in such austere accommodations with their mud-caked floors, festering mold in the corners, and the ever-present odor of bodies compressed in tight quarters. Pallet beds on the floor, swinging hammocks above those, and a loft over both provided three levels in which to pack in the prisoners. There was nothing else, aside from a small hearth seldom lit due to a scarcity of fuel.

Ford normally fell asleep immediately, but the trouble with Elle lost him a few rounds of guttural snoring. He twisted about on the flattened, dusty rushes covering his hard pallet bed, trying to think of ideas on how to make up with her. As the room quieted, he could hear mutterings coming from the other end of the building. It was the priest Willem, who had inexplicably decided to bunk with Ford and his friends, instead of sticking with the other priests, who had all chosen other barracks.

Discovering Will there on the first night, Ford had gone barreling across the room, ready to exact his revenge, but the other prisoners held him back. Some of them had been communing with the priest since their time on the transportation ship. Many had taken him on as their Layman's Shepherd, confessing their sins to him and seeking advice on living a better life. They liked the priest, because he never played the holier-than-thou card or showed contempt for their failings. Ford had to sit back and watch as even his closest friends took to the priest, who had a knack for providing spiritual guidance that soothed their wretched hearts and heads. Even now Ford listened from across the darkened room as Will spoke to Dillon reassuringly. The words caressed the air and took the edge off the night much as a mother might comfort a child.

"Keep faith and you will come through this," said the young priest. Dillon murmured a reply meant to be indecipherable, but the quaver in his voice could not be hidden. "You must be strong," Will went on. "Every one of us is born as an arrow. We fly fast into the future. Some straight, some waver, but we would not fly at all if not for the bow. When one gives birth and raises a child, they become the bow and all energy must go into firing that new arrow into the future. You are the bow and without you, how far would your little arrows fly? Be strong for them. You will come through this."

Ford wished the priest would shut up, so he could get some sleep. He also admired the simplistic beauty and truth of the words, and wished he had someone to give him advice. For the life of him, he couldn't think of how to resolve his trouble with Elle. He knew he could never speak so eloquently, but if he could at least think up something good to say to her, to get his point across and clear up the mess he had made, that would be enough. If only she would listen.

The whispers of the priest and Dillon continued on as Ford crept closer to sleep. The instant his eyes closed, he shot up in bed and bumped his forehead on the bottom of the man swinging in the hammock above him.

"Not tonight, my dear!" Rhod's quip sent a ripple of drowsy mirth through the men around him that turned into grunts and groans as Ford trampled them on his way to the door. He lunged into the night with hands held before him, stumbling left and right about the towering shadowy shapes of barracks and Pen walls until both hands finally fell upon the tall partition separating the men from the women.

"Elle! Elle! Please, listen to me, Elle!" he shouted upwards. If the priest's whispers could carry through the quiet of night like that, he guessed his shouts would be loud enough to leap the wall and be heard by the women on the other side. "You have to believe I didn't do it to hurt you!"

"What's all this noise? Keep quiet!" demanded one of the guardsmen through an upper window of the blockhouse. The door beneath flew open and armed guards poured out.

"It was the only thing I could think to do to keep you safe!" Ford went on. "If they caught you, they'd hang you! I couldn't let it happen!"

A lantern was trained upon him and the holder shouted, "There he is!"

"No one out after dark! You know the rules," shouted another guard as they surrounded him with leveled halberds.

Ford spent the rest of the night in the Cold House, a frigid hole in the ground too narrow to permit even a single body to lay down. It was dug to a depth of six feet, so he had to stoop and bow his head when the guards shut the hatch over him. It was one of the coldest, most miserable nights he had ever spent, but he hoped it was worth it. For all he knew, Elle might not have even heard him.

Halfway through the following day, an exhaustingly long day, Ford sat before the brewery's hearth beside a giddy Millet watching a small batch of barley roast well beyond the golden brown that Alyk baked for them in the usual large batches. Ford couldn't help but keep wondering whether Elle had heard him begging forgiveness. If she had, was it enough? When he finally spotted her again, coming out of the baker's two days later, she hurried through the wall's gate beyond his reach without acknowledging his waves and shouts. Perhaps it was only confirmation of what his heart was already telling him, but now he knew for certain that he needed to keep thinking of ways to make it up to her. The thought of her hating him was too unbearable.

When it came down to it, Ford was not a great thinker. Brilliant ideas did not come easily. In fact, he was pretty sure he had exhausted them all coming up with his shout-over-the-wall speech. Conjuring something better didn't seem likely. So, it was a complete surprise when he suddenly shouted, "My trousers!" Millet was certainly surprised.

"Eh? What's that?" wondered the brewer, gingerly coming down the ladder from the loft after checking on her sprouting grains. Ford hadn't noticed she had moved from his side.

"I have to get my trousers back!" he insisted.

Tucked away behind the temporarily vacant potter's shed stood the tailor's shop, pressed against an almost perpendicular boulder taller than the building itself. Though, to say it *stood* was a bit of a misnomer. The sparsely timbered building stood only because it was wedged between the potter's fairly sturdy structure and the boulder. Also, calling it a hallway rather than shop would have been more fitting since it was the narrowest building on the island. Half of the interior was taken up by a waist-high shelf, a single ten-foot plank that ran the length of the building to provide the tailor with a workbench. An overhead bar allowed him to hang fabric and garments. When not in use, his shears, needles and thread hung from wall hooks.

Near the end of the work day, Ford begged off early to speak with the tailor. The tailor also being a prisoner, he would be closing up soon in order to get to the Pen on time. Ford strode across the village with purpose, hoping to catch him at his shop and retrieve his old pants right then and there. Poking his head in, he reared back. It seemed he had mistaken a wraith's den for the tailor's. Peering back at him was a cadaverously thin man of indeterminate age with sunken cheeks pockmarked by a childhood illness that not only stole the man's looks but stunted his growth as well.

"What?" snapped the tailor, reaching for the door with the idea of closing it if Ford didn't quickly produce a good enough reason for interrupting his work. Quite simply, he did not enjoy the company of others. As a boy and young man, he hated to distress people, but the horrified looks they gave him became depressing over time. Now he just wanted to be left alone. The island offered him a good deal of the solitude he sought. Everyone on Polecat, who came in regular contact with the tailor, had grown used to him. Few shied away or would not return his gaze and remind him of his disfigurement.

"I come to get my trousers back," replied Ford with less certainty than when he marched up to the shop.

"You want them back?"

"Yes."

"You're from Millet's?" asked the tailor after taking in Ford's length and sizing up this large prisoner's strange request.

"Yes. Do you have them?"

"Sure, I have them, but they're mine now."

"I have to get them back," said Ford, thrilled to find his old pants hadn't been destroyed as he had feared.

"*Have* to, you say?"

"I do. It's important."

"Important, are they?" In the flutter of a bat's wing, the tailor went from uninterested to intrigued. One of the few people on the island whose company the tailor enjoyed was Dara Millet's, mainly because whenever the brewer needed a job done, she would bring along ale as a welcome bribe. Now, this brewer's assistant wanted something from him. Ford worried at seeing the predatory gleam in the tailor's eyes. He could almost see the wheels spinning behind them.

"Yes. Can I have them?"

"Oh, I couldn't part with my wares, not for nothing."

"What do you want with those dirty old things?" asked Ford, noticing for the first time the backdoor beyond the tailor which led to a towering pile of used clothes in a tiny nook outside. The tailor slid down the length of his shop and pulled the backdoor closed.

"I have my uses and never you mind!" he said, playacting at indignity. Ford thought about throttling the little wretch, taking his pants by force, and be damned the consequences. All it took was a twinge of his raw, aching muscles to remind him of his bone-bruising night in the Cold House. The thought of another night wiped away the notion and made his whole body slump. "Well now, let me think," said the tailor, a note of concern that he may have overplayed his hand tempering his attitude. "I suppose if you have something in trade for them?"

"I don't have a thing."

"Nay, don't say that. I'm sure you do," said the tailor, swinging his back door open again and hobbling over to the clothes pile on legs grown stiff over the years. "Just remind me which are yours. No, stay right there! You'd only knock the place down if you came in," he muttered as he picked through the pile. Ford's massive pants were hard to miss, but dragging out the suspense never hurt negotiations. Finally, he held up a filthy pair so large that he could have climbed into one of the legs and worn it as a bodysuit. "This them?"

"Yes! Thank you!"

"You've nothing to thank me for. Not yet!" The tailor's warding hand shot up with the pitch of his voice. It seemed to him that Ford's bulk had instantly grown twice its size, filling the doorframe with a quick-to-anger prisoner, who was on this island for crimes still mysterious to the tailor. He had to assume it was something violent. "You'll get them, but I need something in return, a fair trade."

"What do you want that I have?"

"I'll tell ya. Next I come around the brewery, I'll be thirsty. I expect to have my whistle wetted."

"You want me to steal ale for you?"

"Not steal! Never say steal. It's a simple fair trade, is all."

Ford was dubious about the arrangement, but not entirely unwilling. "But what if Millet's there?"

"I'll make sure I only get thirsty when she's elsewhere. And you make sure it's none of her weird, foul muck, ya hear?" Ford had to stop and think if he had accidentally spilled the beans on Millet's secret special brew to this man. By the time his mind returned to the discussion, the discussion was over.

The following days dragged out to excruciating lengths. Ford's time at the brewery became a misery. He was sure the tailor would show up while

Millet was there and get him fired. Or the tailor might come looking for him when he was called away on some random island duty.

"Torture is what this is," he muttered to himself while sitting by the brewery fire one afternoon. He jabbed with the poker to kick up the lazy heat waves playing over the embers. With the other hand he counted off the days since he'd last seen the tailor. Losing count, he wiped the sweaty palm on his thigh. "The man's a born torturer."

A knock at the back window jerked Ford's heart into his throat. He looked up and there was the tailor placing a cloth-wrapped bundle on the sill. Ford breathed again. Millet was away at the blacksmith's seeing what could be done with a barrel hoop banged out of shape in a fit of frustration.

"Them ain't my trousers," he said looking dismissively down at the tailor's bundle.

"Would I wrap this in your stinking old clothes?" said the tailor, unraveling the cloth to reveal one of the biggest tankards Ford had ever seen. "Fill that up."

"*That?* What you need with that much ale?"

"Would you believe I'm gonna drink it? Now fill it up! Or would you rather have a nice little chat about it? It's your choice." The tailor turned away and leaned his back against the sill.

Ford snatched the tankard and rushed to the front room. Before going to the tapped barrel, he peeked out the door to make sure his master was not on her way back. At the barrel, he pulled the tap as wide open as it would go. The ale could not flow fast enough for him. The pour seemed to last forever and the tankard refused to fill regardless of Ford's urging. He began to wonder if the damn thing wasn't bottomless. A knocking noise made him jerk around. It was only the tailor getting impatient, but when Ford turned to look through the door into the back room, a half pint of ale spilled upon the floor before he realized what was happening. He grabbed a rag and wiped up as best he could, pushing most of the ale down between the cracks in the floorboards. Carefully but quickly, he carried the tankard into the back room and handed it to the tailor, who began sipping at it with a leisured delicacy.

"Can't you do that somewhere else?"

"Wouldn't want to spill a drop, would I?" said the tailor, but after downing an inch-worth of ale, he did finally bundle up the tankard, and with painstaking caution, he began shuffling off.

"Hold up," Ford half-whispered out the window. "What about my trousers?"

"They had two legs. This is for one leg," said the tailor hefting the bundle. "I'll be back for the second soon enough and then you'll have them."

Ford wanted to leap for the man through the window, but instead he sat back down by the fire and heaved a sigh of relief. At least they hadn't been caught.

"Ho! What do we have here?" called out the brewer from the front room. Ford cringed and reconsidered jumping out the window. "Come here, Ford!" Ford knocked the embers about some more, laid down the poker and got to his feet. He put a spoon back in its place and pushed the Forester's dwarfish rundlet a little more out of the way than it already was. He hadn't plucked up much courage, but he still forged on, entering the front room with a hung head. Millet stood in the doorway with her eyes seaward. "Have a look!" Ford cast a glance at the damp spot on the floor and joined her at the door. "We've got visitors!"

They stared out over the southern horizon at a grayish dot. Over the following hour it turned into a shape vaguely more ship-like. The vessel was clearly headed their way. It would be the first visitor to the island since Ford's arrival.

"Shift that barrel," said Millet, pointing a finger in the direction of a half dozen barrels in the back room. "No, the one full of fresh ale! This one. Set it by the front door. I guarantee the captain of that boat'll request one." The task complete, Millet allowed her assistant as many glimpses at the vessel's progress during afternoon as he liked. The brewer couldn't repress her own merry fascination and was happy to speculate at the brewery door with company about the ship's purpose and contents. In fact, Millet was the first to form up the line on the beach of island officials, just as they had when Ford's ship arrived.

By all appearances, the vessel was from Aelwyd, probably Port Morton and likely filled with prisoners. Ford hoped the brewer wouldn't be seeking his replacement among them. He liked working at the brewery and he still needed to get his old pants back. After the ship's captain and her clerk came ashore, the most well-dressed assembly of prisoners the island had ever seen disembarked and proceeded along the pier toward the beach.

Compared to the dirty and depressed prisoners shipped along with Ford, these relatively clean and groomed gentlefolk appeared merely shaken and slightly frightened after a swift, unceremonious abduction from their comfortable lives back home. They were mostly minor lords and ladies and mere distant relations to the Middlefields, holding little power and hardly worth ransoming. However, they were still loyal and any potential danger to the Brastersceatts had to be dealt with one way or another during a tumultuous change in rule.

The relaxed sailors watching over this timid and fragile lot did not hold them at knifepoint or treat them roughly in the least. The threat they posed had been considered so minimal that they had been left unshackled for much of the voyage as well as the transfer from ship to shore. The most rebellious of them, a bold and sometimes brash cousin of the head of the clan Wyn Welland, seized the opportunity of this lax security and leapt from the pier, diving in a graceful arch into the water in an attempted escape. With furious strokes, he made for the rocky shore that Crowell House stood upon, but then turned about and fought back through the surf for the ship, slipping around the stern and out of sight of the frantic sailors racing back and forth along the pier.

"The keys! Where are the damned keys," demanded Atwall until the longboats were unlocked and shoved from the beach by eager parties of guardsmen. Once they were afloat, no amount of shouting from Rechard the Master of the Guard could stop the guardsmen from leaning dangerously from side to side while trying to spot the prisoner or jumping up to point when they did see him. One boat took on too much water and began sinking. Another boat pulled alongside to assist. This left only one boat to chase, and it was making for the Crowell House cliffs, the opposite direction of the prisoner.

Those watching on shore, who didn't know what a proficient swimmer looked like, thought they were witnessing a drowning. With eyes shut to the salty water, a black hole of a mouth gaping between the waves and arms and legs thrashing the water, the escapee's practiced strokes took him speedily toward the smooth rocks which stretched out like an arm on the other side of the bay.

The officials standing on the beach could see the prisoner was getting away and they grew embarrassed, even worried. After all, the ratio of guards to prisoners at the penal colony had been growing decidedly in favor of the prisoners. Sooner or later there would be too many to control, making a revolt more and more likely. An uprising, even as small as this one man's desperate attempt, could be deadly for them all if it encouraged the others. Displaying calm authority had always served the officials in the past, so they stood about looking stern and doing their best to seem unconcerned. The few prisoners allowed in the village, such as Ford, pinned their own hopes and dreams on the escapee.

He emerged from the water and stumbled to his knees onto the rocks. Regaining his feet, he bent over and rested with his hands on his knees. Even from this distance, the people watching from the beach could see his arched back heaving with each deep breath. A work party of prisoners beating down brush along the cliff's edge above him whipped up a hearty cheer, waving their threshers and shouting encouragement. Nearby them, a guard from the watchtower hurried down a steep and slippery stairway cut into the cliff and scurried along the smooth arm of rocks toward the escapee. Without a clear idea of where to go, the prisoner waded back into the water.

The longboat in chase had been directed back on course by the captain's mate gesticulating from the stern of the recently docked ship. The guards in the boat gained perceptibly on their quarry moment by moment. Swimming parallel to the shore, the escapee veered away, heading for some rocks where white water shot into the air like sporadic geysers. The men in the longboat lifted their oars and allowed the boat to glide while they decided what to do. A strong wave carried the escapee through a pair of jagged rocks and dashed him against another. He recovered and tried to cling to it, but the next wave dragged him away and pushed him past the rocks, where he continued along his original course in open water. The longboat got underway again and soon caught up with him. The guardsman leaning far forward in the bow knocked him over the head with an oar and others pulled the unconscious man in. Their champion defeated, the prisoners watching from the cliff slunk back from the edge and returned to work. The officials on the beach heaved a sigh of relief.

The prisoners were still talking about of the escape attempt days later as if it had just happened. Ford was thinking about it while stacking peat bricks by the brewery hearth when Millet came into the back room with a curious look on her face. Being used to her chatty nature, he worried that she hadn't said anything yet. He looked up to see if something was wrong and caught her giving him a rather covert glance before quickly shifting her attention to the small batch vat holding her special concoction.

"I just spoke with the tailor," she said with her back to him.

"Oh?" asked Ford, keeping his eyes upon the bricks he was now stacking with unnecessary precision. So, the game was up, but he thought maybe if he worked hard enough, he might get off with a slap on the wrist.

"For once, he had something interesting to say. Seems he had a theft over there. Someone stole some clothes or cloth or something. I don't know." Millet looked to Ford and tried to smile. "Whatever it was, he asked me, that is, he asked all of us, to uh, to ask our help if they knew anything about it. Do you know anything about it?" She had gone quite red and could no longer look at Ford. "I don't suspect you. No, no! What I mean to say is, maybe you heard something, you know, among the others?"

Ford had taken a few punches in his time. This felt like two to the gut. At first, he assumed someone had stolen his pants. Realizing no one would want his castoffs, his mind leapt to the idea that the tailor was doing him dirty again. Millet stood by waiting for an answer, one she hoped would reassure her that Ford had nothing to do with it. She was beginning to have her doubts. After all, just the other day her assistant had requested time off to speak with the tailor about retrieving his old clothes.

"No," Ford finally replied. "Not I."

"Good. Very good. I didn't think so. I told him, but you know his sort," Millet said with a half-smile. "If you should hear anything, do let me know. One other thing came to me just now. Did you ever get your, whatever it was, back from him?"

Ford shook his head and hoped that would be enough to put an end to the questions. It was. Millet didn't care about the prisoners' little transgressions. As long as everyone was happy, she was happy. Ford was just happy not to be fired. To his even greater relief, on one of the following days when Millet was in the Pen at the request of the Keeper to discuss an issue of extra ale to be purchased by the new prisoners, Ford received his second and final visit from the tailor. The man's tankard was filled and the trousers were handed over.

Autumn truly set in later that week. The air felt crisper and the days grew increasingly gray. On a chilly morning, Ford found himself on the far side of the island hunting bog iron. He and a half dozen others took thin, blunted iron rods about a yard long with them as they fanned out over the choking layer of decomposing plants blanketed over watery mud.

"Step and poke! Step and poke!" commanded Aedgar Swain, the work party leader coordinating their search for the hard, glob-like chunks of ore found a foot or so beneath the surface.

"Brewer's boy!" the field workers upon the slopes above called out to him in passing. "You bring us any drink?" It was the same question every day, every time someone saw him. The baker's assistants were begged for bread and he was hounded for ale. Of course, he had none and they knew he had none, but they would persist. It made him want to avoid them.

Perhaps not all of them. During the midday break, he saw Rhod sitting with Moll in the field nearest the bog. He had an urge to go sit with them, to savor a moment of rest among friends and forget where he was, however brief the moment might be. The notion evaporated when he realized who the third person in their group was. The lanky figure of Will reclined in the grass talking with them. There were smiles all around.

His friends' growing attachment to the priest was annoying, because it prevented him from scratching a very personal itch. One good shot to the nose or chin would be so satisfying. Perhaps an elbow to the priest's stomach. The thought of a well-placed knee to the groin made Ford's day seem all the brighter.

"Get poking!" Swain shouted at him. The sour-tongued old-timer took his responsibilities too seriously, thought Ford as he dug his poker into the ever-softening sod. Water soaked through the bottom of his boots with each spongy step.

He soon forgot about Swain and the time between each of his pokes lengthened as the trouble with Elle began to weigh on him once more. He needed to see her again, yet ever since getting his pants back, he simply could not find her. Occasional sightings of feminine figures approximately Elle's shape and height could be seen in the distance. However, they always turned out to be prepubescent boys or one of the many slender Manerds on Polecat. Ford's right leg sank down to the knee in the cakey sod. He yanked it free and was grateful to find his boot still attached to his foot. Then again, he went on thinking, none of the boys and foreign men wore dresses, and only one had a red tunic faded to pink which might be mistaken for the garb Elle currently wore.

A person paying attention to his job would have tread with more caution after sinking to the knee in a bog, but Ford forged on unwittingly with all that was on his mind that day. The slushy earth gave way and he plunged in waist-deep. The ground churned into humus. It was like trying to stand on porridge. He flailed his arms about, found nothing to grab ahold of, and sank deeper. His fellow prisoners froze in horror and would not come near. A strong and desperate man as big as Ford might take them under with him. Cold water dribbled through his tunic up to his chest. He began to panic. People died in bogs all the time. Back where Ford had grown up there was a swamp famous for the souls lost in it. Since the penal colony began, this bog had claimed three lives.

"What you think you're doing? Get out of there!" chided Swain, while edging forward and leaning out with his poker. Ford reached with scrambling hands. If Swain lost someone under his supervision, it would go badly for him. He stretched as far as he dared. Ford caught the end of the poker, but it slipped through his wet fingers. Struggling quickly brought the sludgy surface of the bog up to his chin. "Come here, you yellow rats!" It took more name calling, but eventually Swain managed to shame the other prisoners into taking hold of his hand, as well as each other's to form a human chain that stretched to more solid ground. Swain could get close enough now to grasp Ford's hand and with much tugging and plenty of grunting, they dragged him out.

After some ribbing, Ford carried on working, much wetter and more carefully. Eventually, Swain took pity on him and tasked him with carrying a load of ore chunks to the village blacksmith where he might dry off by the forge before returning. The loaded rucksacks they draped over his shoulders weighed him down so that he hobbled over the downs like a man four times his age. The village seemed endless miles away. Halfway there he stopped to drop the sacks to rest and lift his head so he could see how much farther he had to go. Up ahead, someone that looked like Elle was crossing the fields on her way back to the Pen. Yes, it was most definitely Elle. Ford made a dash for her. As far as he could tell, and he couldn't tell much with his head bowed under the weight of the ore, her back was to him and she hadn't seen him yet. Even so, whenever he took a glimpse, he could have sworn she was moving faster and increasing the distance between them. If she made it there before he caught her, she would disappear into the women's section and be out of reach to him. Men were not permitted in that area.

Randel Hayward, an unrepentant lecher riddled with venereal disease, had the same idea. Hayward's transgressions were well-known among the prisoners, because he was also a braggart. He would speak with relish of how he had lain with man and beast, and slipped conviction of the allegations brought against him by claiming a lack of evidence. Eventually Hayward was entrapped by a local lord using a prostitute as bait. "I never paid for no whore!" he would claim, but they did convict him of "an unnatural act." However, imprisonment and transportation to the island did nothing to stem his carnal desires. The day after Moll arrived, he dragged her down in the tall grasses of a field. Before Rhod could reach her, she had broken two of Hayward's fingers and sent him howling back to the village.

Ten paces from the gate to the women's barracks, Hayward latched onto Elle by the elbow. She spun around in his arms, as slippery as a fish, and hopped straight up. The top of her head cracked his chin and his teeth clattered together. But Hayward's thick head had taken far worse. He recovered quicker than Elle expected. Grabbing her by the hair, he blocked her knee thrusts and dragged her around the corner of the tall Pen walls to one of the few blind spots on the island, where guards were at a visual disadvantage. Only those looking down from Crowell House could see them, but none of the residents cared to watch the dreary prisoners go about their daily lives.

"You're my sweetie at last! I'll have me some of that sugar now!" He threw her down, flopped onto her, and laughed. His weight sat on her like a dead cow. Her back pressed into the grass, rock, and dirt. She wished it all might give way and absorb her body, letting sink down and escape beneath the earth. But no. He tore at her clothes and fumbled with her breasts. Her fingernails dug red grooves in his hairy forearms to add to the many other hardened scars there. His joyfully mad eyes sought hers while his excited fingers groped under her skirt. A dull thud sounded just before "Guh-erk" bubbled out of Hayward's throat. His body flew off of her and slumped in the grass. A sack of bog iron chunks came to rest beside him. Ford stood over him waiting, but Hayward was out cold.

He knelt beside Elle and helped her up. Her garments were torn in places and dirtier than they had been, but she wasn't hurt, just shaken. He sought to catch her eye, trying to see if she was alright and then to read her mood. She fought to maintain a stony façade, but the emotions roiling around within broke free and she slapped him. He reeled back, not out of pain or even surprise, merely instinct.

"Guess I deserved that," he said. Elle turned her back on him and would have disappeared into the women's side of the Pen, but he called out to her, "Wait! I have something for you. Please wait." The urgency and catch in his voice made her stop. She wouldn't turn to look at him, but she would listen. He frantically drew back the sleeve of his tunic and removed a ribbon tied to his upper arm. This ribbon was the reason he so desperately needed to get his pants back. "Here." Realizing she wouldn't look at him, he held the ribbon over her shoulder so that she could see it. Elle's eyes locked on the thin strand with tiny green and gold embroidered oak leaves on a black background. The design represented the colors and insignia of her people and it was the only remaining keepsake she had to remember her family by. She had made a tremendous sacrifice in using it as a last resort to sew up Ford's pants at a time when he was in desperate need and she had no other materials. She had given it as a friend and given up on ever seeing it again.

Ford continued to hold out the peace offering for her while she stared at it. If she didn't accept it and forgive him after this, he had nothing else to give and no idea how to salvage their friendship. She caught the tremble in his hand. Her hand opened. He placed the ribbon in her palm. Her fingers closed around it and then she walked into the Pen.

Chapter 5
The New Morgan Brewer

"Here's to Gyl," bellowed Dara Millet as she tapped mugs with Gyl and Ford, who flanked her at the table in the front room of the brewery. "Hands down, the best runner this island's ever seen!" The brewer was in a particularly good mood, and had been for the last two days. Her small batch of experimental, dark roasted ale had come out to her liking. She delightedly dubbed it Dara's Pitch. To get the black, thick pungency she desired with the limited ingredients available, it had to be a small batch. There was so little of the stuff that it hardly seemed worth naming, but Millet insisted. She liked to name all of her creations. The standard brew she made for Polecat was called Island Ale.

The "black honey" Elle provided for Dara's Pitch might have been used to make a barrel's worth of a decent, mildly sweet golden ale, but Millet's desire for something with "strength and body," meant a yield of only twenty gallons, slightly less than two of the miniature casks known as firkins. After filling the first firkin, Ford had accidentally poured the remainder into another that still held two gallons of the regular Island Ale at the bottom of it. The flavor of the mixture was a bit muddy, but drinkable and Millet decided to name that one Porter, after Ford for all the lifting and carrying he did, as well as a nod to his previous occupation back in the city. But then she changed her mind, deciding that Barlow's Brew had a nicer ring to it.

"Try a Barlow," she had said just yesterday evening to the blacksmith and then that morning to Mason, the guardsman she had grown fond of because of the man's appreciation for finer ales. "Then I'll give you a taste of my Pitch and you tell me what you think." They were better taste testers than Gyl and Ford. Gyl did not share Mason's enthusiasm for Millet's strange brews. As for Ford, most of the ale he had had in his lifetime had been thin dockyard tavern swill tainted by mucky canal water.

Whether it was their preferred tipple or not, all three gladly carried on toasting to each other's good health and wealth, and a lasting friendship. Then they had another in observance of an upcoming holiday. Or perhaps it had passed. They couldn't recall and it didn't matter. They drank to the good ol' days and better days to come. They drank to the end of the illness, which seemed to be banished for good. That was worth celebrating twice.

"Ya seem to hath a leak in your cup there, Gyl my friend. I'll fiss it," said Millet, standing on wobbly legs to top off his mug. They had come up with another reason for a toast and her guest couldn't be expected to do so with a mug that was as good as empty. Ford was trying to focus on the black ale in the bottom of his mug to make sure he had enough too, when the front door flew open and guardsmen clomped in. "Gens!" Millet hollered, spinning about with spreading arms that flung a half mug of ale across the room. "Eggcellen ta see ya! Come! Come and have a drink with ush!"

The frowning guards weren't in a mood for celebrating holidays or drinking to anyone's good cheer. These well-armed men gripped their weapons tight and trained them upon Ford when he stood to make room at the table. Whenever the guardsmen visited the brewery for a drink, he made himself scarce, because they made it clear they didn't like carousing in the presence of prisoners. Unfortunately, Ford didn't realize how potent the ale was. He swayed toward them dangerously and they mistook it for a hostile act. Sharp points inched closer to his vitals. Rechard stepped forward, took the closest mug and upended its contents on the table. Black ale rushed over the planks and on to the floor.

"Dara Millet," he said in his most officious voice. "You are charged with brewing unauthorized ale after receiving fair warning against such practices. You are also charged with madness for the purposeful and wanton waste of rare goods."

"T'was a wee splash, a firkin's worth and no more," reasoned Millet with upraised palms and a pleading smile.

"Remove him," said the Master of the Guard. Three of the four guards moved in on Ford, pressing their blades to his chest and forcing him back against a wall. Rechard had gone in expecting trouble from the brewery's assistant. If the brewer were alone, Rechard could have handled her on his own.

"He didn't do nothing," said an ale-befuddled Millet. A guardsman took her by the arm and led her gently through the door.

"You'll have your say, Dara," said Rechard following after them. The three guardsmen on Ford backed out of the door. Ford stood with his hands dangling at his sides, staring blankly at the door, unable to believe what he had just witnessed.

"Bound to happen sooner or later," Gyl said from the back-room doorway. "Them lords don't like a waster and, I'm no brewer, but that ale's a waste."

"What'll happen to her?"

"Don't know," said Gyl while running the stump of one arm over the perspiration that had built upon his brow during Millet's arrest. "But they used *madness* against her, so they'll lock her up for that. The rest is just fines. There'll be a trial. Of sorts. But that's her done."

"She won't be coming back?"

"No, she's gone. And I suppose I'd better get gone too before they come for *me!*" Gyl made for the door, but it swung open and knocked him back.

The Keeper of the Pen came in and started back at finding Gyl so close to him. Atwall was getting jumpy as the number of prisoners on the island mounted. "Get to work, you!" The command shot out of him with a nervous intensity. Fear of an ambush by a prisoner was always at the back of his mind. Gyl jumped and scurried off. Atwall regained his composure and turned to Ford. "Barlow. You're the new brewer." He put a hand on the door, but turned back as if he had forgotten something. "For now."

Ford flopped down at the table and stared at the wall. After a while he scratched his head and eventually blinked. Then he got up and went to the back room to look at the brewing equipment. He walked around the tun, peered into the empty barrels, and wondered how he was going to fill them with an even remotely drinkable ale of his own making. Visitors from the village dropped in sporadically over the following hour, full of concern, but bubbling with gossipy interest just below the surface. They wanted to know what happened to Millet, why she had been hauled away. Once word was spread to everyone's satisfaction, they left Ford alone to get to work. He was peeking into a sack of wheat when the watchtower bell rang. The end of the day had come and he had done nothing.

In the barracks that night, it was obvious Gyl had gotten the word around about the happenings at the brewery. Ford's friends still had questions, but most simply congratulated him. "Stroke of luck, that!" said Rhod with a clout to the back.

Their interest wore off quickly. They had their own concerns and plenty of complaints. Backs and shoulders ached. Someone's toe still throbbed from a rock dropped on it that morning. Bog workers complained of swollen and numb feet. "That ain't nothing. Nothing!" bragged a nine-year Polecat veteran. The unremitting thief with a love of sugar and brown teeth to show for it, removed his boot, held his leg up in the last of the evening's light coming through the open doorway, and peeled off cloth from a foot covered in putrefied flesh. The stench instantly infiltrated the room.

"Put it away, ya rottin' ghoul!" cried Miller Edd as he stumbled away.

Ford let his friends' woes wash over him as he laid back upon his pallet and fought down a touch of nausea. They were miserable and he wanted no part of that. He *had* to hold on to the brewery post.

That night sleep came in snatches split between wakeful worry and troubling dreams which made little sense aside from the residue of anxiety he was left with upon awakening. His stomach ached and he thrashed about, ruining his friends' sleep. It was easy to do now that everyone was doubled up in the barracks. Miller Edd had to share Ford's bed and Dillon's hammock was slung over them next to Rhod's. Ford took a few elbows for rolling fitfully into his friend one too many times.

"How hard could it be?" Rhod said to him over their morning's bowl of bland pottage when Ford voiced his concerns. Others wished him the best, figuring it could only benefit them if their friend succeeded as the island's new brewer. By the time Ford left the Pen, they almost had him convinced he could pull it off. After all, had he not watched Millet for weeks, listened to her lectures on malt and mash?

"I can do it. I can do it," he repeatedly chanted all the way through the village. The women at the bakers wagged their heads at seeing him muttering to himself. "I can do it. I *can* do it!" he said as he passed straight into the back room of the brewery, where he drew a complete blank about everything to do with brewing ale.

In his first week on his own, he added yeast to boiling wort, tried to crack unroasted grains, and laid out the roasted grains in the loft to sprout. Some of his mistakes he caught in time, others he did not. There were so many steps to the brewing process from start to finish. Perhaps if he remembered them all and was allowed to complete them in chronological order, he might have succeeded. On rare occasion he did have his little victories, such as completing a pair of steps in the correct order. But whenever he felt on the verge of figuring it all out, something forgotten would crop up or two duties needed doing at the same time. He would freeze in panic and neither would get done right away. Juggling multiple batches, all in their various stages, at the same time was beyond his abilities. By the end of the week, he felt as if a giant had palmed his head and shook all the facts about so that they rattled around in his brain hopelessly muddled.

During midday at the beginning of his second week, he climbed the ladder to check the temperature in the loft. "Keep it warm up here, but never hot," Millet had instructed him. When the hearth had been burning away and building up heat, the small window up in the eves needed to be opened. "Keeps the little sprouting grains happy." Ford crawled on hands and knees past the little sprouting grains to the window. This was one of his least favorite tasks. Though the brewery was sturdy on the whole, Ford still did not like the whining creak of the spindly loft planks. He reached out, slid open the window's shutter, and crawled back with painstaking care.

"And keep the water warm. But not too hot. And stir," Ford muttered to himself on his way down the ladder, taking one rung for each line he spoke, getting into a mesmerizing rhythm. "And stir. Then cool—"

"When..."

Ford missed the last rung and fell with a tremendous *thud* flat-footed onto the floor. Elle crouched like a frog before the hearth warming her hands. She gave him a cursory glance, soured by the suspicion that he'd made the loud commotion just to annoy her. Turning back to the fire, she went on. "When you do the thing that put me here, I hate you for this. Now but I understand your, what you say, your *why*." Her speech was rough, her language awkward, but she maintained control throughout, giving away no sign of the emotion within and never veering her gaze from the fire. "Now you do a thing for me and we are same."

"I do something for you and we're even?" said Ford, taking a hopeful but cautious step forward, as one would when approaching a wild animal.

"Just so."

"Anything! Whatever it is, just tell me." No matter the danger, he would do it, because having her there in front of him, talking and not running away at the sight of him, that was worth anything. She was the closest thing he had to a real friend on this island. Sure, he had new friends and acquaintances, but Elle's friendship went back further, deeper. To him, she was the personification of home. Already his heart felt lighter. He hadn't realized what a heavy anchor of guilt he'd been dragging along with him. The warmth of the world shined again.

"Come." She led him to the front door and gestured to the sea, where a ship sailing for the island already approached the mouth of the bay. They could easily make out its three square-rigged masts, a full bowsprit and a wide beam which indicated the likelihood of a large human cargo stowed below. A few island officials already gathered on the beach jabbered away with one another. Ford had been concentrating on his work to such an extent that he hadn't heard them pass his door. *His door.* Even thinking the words sounded magical to a man who had never owned much of anything, never mind his own shop and trade. It may not have actually belonged to him, but for all intents and purposes, he was a tradesman, and that felt liberating.

"You put me on that ship," said Elle, waking Ford from his pleasant revelry. The statement was like cold water dousing a dream.

"Put you on..." The words flopped out of him purely as placeholders until his mind caught up with his mouth. "You want me to help you escape?" he whispered.

"Yes," she said, leaning in close and dropping her voice. "You help me escape, we are even."

"How?"

Elle led Ford into the back room of the brewery, where she laid a hand on a barrel and said, "This."

So that was that. Having already agreed to do whatever she asked of him, there was no going back on his word. He would help her escape at the risk of losing his job and likely being sent to work in the quarries each and every day, perhaps for the rest of his life. And if they were caught, they would both be punished severely and he would be replaced at the brewery by one of the spent wrecks from the fields. It wouldn't be difficult to find someone as equally unqualified to brew ale.

Their meeting over, Elle made her way through the village. She didn't go so far as to dance or skip, but there was a little hop in her step, as well as a nod and smile for the Keeper of the Pen, who returned it with a suggestive raise of the eyebrows and a devilish grin. She had never learned to enchant with social graces or use her body to entice, but she could be charming enough when it counted, and right now every bit of it counted.

There was no way Ford could concentrate on the finer points of brewing, so he grabbed a pair of buckets and made a few trips to the well. When he could, he kept an eye on the new ship coming in.

Like the last ship, the miserable souls aboard *The Blooming Cherry* were not the usual criminal Polecat Island was designed to house. There were craftsmen of all kinds, which puzzled the island's officials. Seldom did a lord imprison and ship skilled workers out of their domain. However, these guild leaders and masters of their craft had been vocal supporters of Middlefield, and the Brastersceatts wished to cripple their trade so that the families fell out of favor and influence within the city. After the joiners, masons, and smiths came a pack of prostitutes being assisted off of the ship by waggish and overly-accommodating sailors, who even blew them kisses at their departure. There was no trapesing down the pier for these painted ladies as they had done on the streets of Port Morton. There wasn't even paint. They had been made to go bare-faced, thus the telltale lines and shadows of their profession were missing. It didn't matter. Their high-cut skirts and sheer chemise were enough to identify them.

Ford dropped his buckets by the brewery door and watched these women with a keen eye as they came off the boat. He had a hope and horror of seeing his mother among them. It was a double-edged desire cutting up his insides. He didn't want her to end up in the same situation he was in. And yet, he hadn't seen her in fifteen years. Just before his imprisonment, he had tracked her down and knew where to find her, but there hadn't been enough time. It occurred to him that he had no notion what she might look like now, but something within told him he would know her when he saw her. So, he wasn't surprised when the last of the ladies disembarked and he felt sure his mother wasn't among them.

Behind the women shuffled a line of what appeared to be downtrodden boys tethered together with a rope about their slender waists, some wearing nothing more than a light tunic. These were more men from Mane, that land of short and tawny people where the males could and often did pass for female in their dress and manner. In Port Morton they had established a brothel that serviced a clientele with wider ranging tastes. These Manerds had never seen a place like Polecat Island before. Apprehension of the unknown and fear for their uncertain futures set creases about their sad eyes. They shivered in their thin garments from nerves as much as the cold. The transportation of these working men and women fulfilled the Brastersceatt's promise made to the puritanical Weaverites.

Ford went back to work and tried to concentrate on brewing. He had another peek at his first attempt. The murky brew looked much as it had the day before: no foam and no bubbles.

"Fur-manned, damn you. Fur-manned!" he yelled at it. He would go on yelling at it, as well praying for it, until the watchtower bell signaled the end of the day.

He tossed and turned that night, fighting for a few winks of sleep while worrying about Elle and ale. "Get off," grumbled Miller Edd when Ford rolled on top of him. After getting an earful more, he lay awake for a while, with two people pressed on either side of him and the backsides of three men hanging just above his nose. The crowding was getting out of hand. New barracks would get underway soon, and though the unexpected influx of skilled workers was a boon for such an undertaking, it would still take time.

The following morning, Atwall walked into the brewery soon after Ford arrived to inform him that he was exempt from barracks building duties. That provided some relief. The new New Morgan brewer needed all the time available to him. Ford expected to have more time, but the captain of the newly arrived ship had put in a request for as much fresh ale as the island could provide. Atwall read the fright in Ford's face and raised a reassuring hand. "I won't let him deplete the brewery's reserves. Give him a barrel and no more. He'll have to make do with fresh water."

Ford exhaled and said, "One barrel it is." Perhaps he had Atwall all wrong. He might not be so bad after all. Ford thanked him and went to the back room to start work.

"How's it coming along?" asked Atwall, walking in and taking a ladle in hand. He meant to taste test the latest batch. Instantly, Ford disliked the man more than ever. Atwall bellied up to the great tun, slid the top back, dunked the ladle, and slurped up a helping of ale. "Not bad. Not bad at all!" He shoved the ladle into Ford's hands and made for the front door. "Have that barrel ready by noon. He's leaving on the next tide."

Ford smiled Atwall out the door. On the inside he wasn't smiling at all. The ale Atwall had just approved of came from Millet's last batch. Ford's first attempt was in the small batch vat. While that was a lucky break, he still had to consider his remaining supply. The tun held a little less than six barrels in it. One barrel would go aboard *The Blooming Cherry* and the remainder would have to satisfy the needs of the island. It wouldn't last long. Once it was gone, things weren't looking good for the new brewer.

He sighed and went back inside to prepare the captain's barrel. First though, he would have another peek at his first attempt. If it didn't ferment soon, it likely never would, that much he knew. What could be done about it, he hadn't a clue. Millet had mentioned some sort of *ale cure*, she called it. Ford remembered the term because it sounded funny, but for the life of him, he couldn't remember what the cure was for a batch of ale refusing to ferment.

"This barrel," said Elle just as Ford walked into the back room.

"Don't you never say *hello* first?" he said with a hand to his chest to see if his heart was still ticking. "I'm beginning to think you do that deliberate."

"Yes," she said rather more ambiguously than he would have preferred. Truth be told, he was happy to see her, fright and all. She was looking well, much more lively, almost cheerful. Her hair held a healthy shine and she seemed slightly fleshier, less withered. Although, all of this may have been mere impressions, the illusion of a strong constitution conjured by a sunny disposition. "This barrel you give to ship," she said, getting back down to business.

Now he understood her good mood and the vibrancy flowing through her: she was ready to put her plan into motion and the thrill of it enlivened her whole being. Disappointment clouded his horizon. He wanted to help her, of course, but he wasn't prepared for her to leave. Maybe he never would be. Or was it that he didn't want to be left behind? Before selfish reasoning took hold of him, he put it out of his mind and focused on the external. "Are you wearing something new?"

"Your eyes, they are awake," she said without much enthusiasm for discussing her snug breeches and cloth doublet. She had made them from sea-green and bark-brown fabrics, the sort stolen from the tailor not too long ago. In her hurry, the cut was imprecise and she had left distances between the stitches that created gaps in the seams where her thighs showed through. She wasn't proud of the work, nor in the mood to talk about it. "This barrel," she began again. "This one you give to the ship."

"Right. Understood."

"You put it on the ship."

"You want me to carry it onto the ship? Can't be done. They won't allow it. None of us from the island can go aboard a ship. You know the rules."

"Try. You do it and try." She cocked her head and slung him a savage eye that dared him to argue.

He did not. Instead, he turned away, busied himself by scraping out a barrel, and murmured a simple and unadorned, "I'll miss you." Between the grinding scrapes, he thought he heard her feet pad across the floor closer to him, but after a while of hearing nothing from her, he looked around and found her gone. His mixed emotions were weighted by a sadness, though it did not last. With the plan was set in motion and his course of action decided, he reveled in the deception and grinned like a fool.

Trade buzzed back and forth between the village and the soon-to-depart ship throughout the morning. The blacksmith provided the ship's carpenter with some readymade nails. Dillon led a group of fishermen over the downs with a cartload of shellfish. One of the baker's prisoner assistants carried a lumpy sack to the end of the pier and left it for a sailor to carry aboard.

The sack laid there untouched. The sailors had more important work to attend to. Bulkheads needed removing and rearranging now that cells were unnecessary. A large oaken chest of drawers for Lady Bryce had to be hauled up from the hold all the way up to Crowell House. Then there was the stowing of cargo and shifting the ship's ballast, which took ages. When the captain got all he could out of the island, he finally ordered his crew to hand over the sugar, seeds, and other supplies Aelwyd had promised to Polecat. Sailors, island officials, tradesmen, and their assistants swarmed all over the bay like a disturbed nest of ants. It may have appeared chaotic, but enough order reigned so that only occasionally did something go awry.

"Where's the sack?" a harried sailor asked the pier guard. The guard paid him no mind, having too good a time chatting up a female prisoner delivering two laying hens. "Hey, arse for ears! Where's the sack from the baker? Upwater said it was right here!"

"How should I know?" the guard shouted back.

"'Cause you was standing close enough to kick it, ya blind bat!"

"Someone else must've got it, so go climb a mast and leap off!" When the guard turned back to his female friend and found she was slipping away through the village, he took his frustration out on the sailor in a shouting match that got them both told off by their superiors.

The ship's boy, a tormented twig of a child with nine hard years in him, skidded into the brewery's front room while Ford was in the middle of pouring a bucket of new ale into the barrel that had already been tapped. The boy's pink face was as pale as ever his scorched skin would allow. The amount of white showing in his frantic, round eyes was the measure of the urgency of his task and his fear of not finishing it. "Captain wants his ale!" he shouted between panting breaths. The boy had asked for the ale earlier in the day and been put off.

"It's coming."

"Captain won't miss his tide for no ale!"

"It's coming! Go on, boy!" Ford slammed the bucket down onto the table. The boy ducked from a phantom blow out of habit. "If he don't get it, there'll be trouble!" he piped as he shot through the door.

Ford had done his best to hold them off for as long as he could. He needed to deliver the barrel at the last possible moment, but a quarter of an hour more was all the time his delays could buy.

"Brewer! Master brewer!" called the captain's mate well before the tall, thick-thighed woman stomped through the door. *The Blooming Cherry* could not have had a much more efficient second-in-command. She would get the ale from this tardy brewer if she had to wrench it from him, throw the barrel over her broad shoulders and carry it aboard, even if it was filled with two hundred and fifty pounds of awkwardly balancing liquid. "Where is the captain's ale?"

"It's that one there," said Ford, pointing out the barrel by the door just to her left.

"Right," she said and turned about to call out the door for the nearest sailors to give her a hand.

"We have a cart," offered Ford. "It's not here, but it wouldn't take long to fetch it."

"It's already taken too long," she said and filled her lungs for what Ford imagined would be a powerful bellow.

"Wait!" he shouted and took hold of the barrel, tilting it on one end and rolling it out the door. What passed for roads in New Morgan were little more than hard-packed stone pathways between the buildings. The barrel rocked and bumped every inch of the way, jostling the contents terribly. When his lips were quite close to the top lid, Ford whispered, "Hold tight" and smirked, satisfied that there was no way the captain's mate could hear him over the grinding of the barrel rim on the stones. Besides, she led the way by a good ten yards and was busy surveying the village and beach in search of some task that needed hurrying along. Everything was going along fine until the barrel dug itself into a patch of loose pebbles. Ford heaved and grunted, carving a hard-fought furrow for a few feet before he gave out and the captain's mate gave up on him. "Leppi! Kauko!" she called out to two passing sailors. "Ferry this along to the ship for the good brewer!"

Ford would have liked to at least gotten the barrel to the pier, but before he could protest, the sailors wrenched it away from him, and had it hoisted and on its way. Ford tagged along beside them like a worried hen. The sloshing from within the barrel sounded louder to him than the waves crashing upon the shore. He feared it might give the game away, for there was a good deal more of sloshing than there should have been for a supposedly full barrel. Ford prayed that they didn't feel any jarring movement from within. He certainly could when he was rolling it.

"That's far enough, Barlow!" barked the pier guard. Ford stopped halfway along the pier and could only watch as the sailors dropped the barrel at the end. It landed with an unmistakable *thunk-thunk* from within.

"Avast there!" called out the captain's mate to the sailors working the ship's davit, halting them before they could secure the barrel and hoist it aboard. "What's the meaning of this?" She looked to Ford and then to the pier guard, who had heard the noise as well and was signaling to the blockhouse for assistance. A brief exchange passed between the guard and captain's mate, but she wasn't interested in excuses or delays. The request for ale was canceled. What was one barrel to an entire ship's crew anyhow? Orders flew from stem to stern. The crew completed the final tasks necessary before weighing anchor.

"What's the game, Barlow?" asked the pier guard donning a theatrically knowing smirk as he sidled up to Ford. Conlow was amiable enough whenever he visited the brewery for a drink, but right now Ford despised his sly, conspiratorial manner, one that invited the sharing of secrets as if they were old friends.

Gyl was sent by the blockhouse to see what Conlow wanted. The message runner's somewhat breezy pass through the village was punctuated with a brisk hop onto the pier to give his arrival the impression of promptness. Gyl walked a tightrope daily. He always did his best to drag his feet when he thought his errand might go badly for a fellow prisoner, but he also had to keep his jailors happy.

"Fetch Rechard. We got a problem here," Conlow commanded. Gyl cast a worried glance Ford's way. "Don't dally! I'm certain this one's up to no good."

An early winter wind swept up the bay, chilling any idlers not bustling about with work enough to keep them warm, but a chill of Ford's own making was already spreading throughout his every fiber. He stood stock still as commanded while waiting alongside Conlow. Cold sweat dribbled down his back.

"Whatchu got in there?" said Conlow. Ford would say nothing and Conlow didn't expect him to. No matter. They would have this barrel open soon enough and then they would see what was inside. In the meanwhile, Conlow would amuse himself. "Smuggling, is it? What you smuggling? Sounds like rocks. You smuggling them bog rocks? Can't be much coin in that. Takes a cartload of them to make one axe." The guard scratched at his curly beard and then rocked the barrel back and forth in hopes of inducing the thumping noise again. "What could it be?"

The ship had already been hauled about in the middle of the bay by a longboat and was beginning to make sail. Ford watched the billowing white sheets fill, and wished he and Elle were onboard sailing for home. Thinking of how he had failed her turned his stomach.

The Master of the Guard's heavy boots stomped onto the pier. Another guard followed at his heels. "What's going on here?" Conlow briefed him, laying a sneering emphasis on the suspicious noise that had come from within the barrel. As he wound down his account of the situation, Ford stepped forward.

"I must've grabbed the wrong one," he said. Looking down at the barrel with a hand to his furrowed brow. "My mistake. I'll take it back." He nudged between them and laid his hands upon the barrel. Everyone stepped back and drew their weapons. The Master of the Guard brought down a baton upon Ford's fingers. A shock of pain shot through his hand and numbed his arm up to the elbow.

"Hands off and step back," Rechard said, poking Ford's chest until he stood well back clutching his hand. "I don't know what you've done here, but we're going to find out and when we do, I suspect you'll find yourself in worlds more pain than that." Rechard called for a hammer and chisel, sending Gyl and a guard off at a scamper.

While they waited, Rechard interrogated Ford with a more insistent and formal tone than Conlow's casual attempts to pry the story out of the slump-shouldered prisoner going disconsolate before their eyes. Whatever lies Ford concocted would only make things worse when they discovered the truth, so he resolved to remain silent throughout. The Master of the Guard did not take that well. His questions grew louder and his arms flew into the air. Ford began to imagine the weeks he would spend in the Cold House. Worse punishments started springing to mind about the time Atwall came trotting through the village.

"What's amiss? What's wrong," the Keeper of the Pen shouted as he neared the pier.

"One of your scum's causing trouble again!"

This set Atwall on edge and soon he too was raising his voice as questions, answers, and accusations shot back and forth. The rest of the village went completely dead as all eyes and ears fell upon the pier. Once apprised of the situation, Atwall began laying into Ford.

"Whatever it is, Barlow, I'll take the hide off you, of that you can be sure!"

By the time Gyl and the guard returned, each holding one of the tools so they both appeared indispensable, the ship had passed from the mouth of the bay and was under its own power, steadily gaining speed and already beginning to shrink in size as it headed directly away from New Morgan. "Hand over those tools!" Rechard barked at the two couriers. Their task complete, Gyl and the guard joined the crowd around the barrel, itching as everyone was to see what was inside.

Clink! Clink! Clink! The sound of doom. Ford resignedly kept his gaze on the sea, to where he thought Aelwyd was over the horizon, to where many a better place than this lay, and to where a slim dot dressed in wet green and brown clinging cloth climbed out of the water by the rudder of *The Blooming Cherry*. The dot scrambled up, perched there precariously for a breath, and then slowly and carefully stood to reach for one of the stern windows. Stretching out, but still inches too short, the dot made a desperate leap and caught the frame with clinging fingertips. A terrible moment of wild clambering and swinging by one arm, that forced a gasp out of Ford, ended with the dot summoning all it had left to hoist itself up and through the window.

"What reason in the world have you for smiling, Barlow?" Rechard wondered with a piercing glare that would have skewered the truth deep within Ford's bosom had the penetrating look been corporeal. "Wipe off that smile or I'll slap it off."

Ford adopted a somber expression, but Rechard's rebuke did nothing to dampen the joy he felt right then. Nothing much could, not even seeing Elle disappearing with the ship toward the horizon. The knowledge that she had used him to make her escape didn't bother him in the least. It was only fitting. Quite fair to his way of thinking. He drew in a lungful of crisp sea air and felt wonderful in every way.

"Very well, keep mum," said Rechard. "But you're up to no good, that much I know. We'll all know soon enough."

A metal ring rattled on the pier, followed by the hammering of staves, and then the thump of a wooden lid.

"What is it?" said a half dozen different voices as everyone pressed together for a closer look.

"Ale and...rocks?" said Atwall lifting out a stone the size of a human heart.

"Just ale and rocks?" Rechard asked, looking from the barrel to Ford in confusion.

"Like I said, wrong barrel," said Ford.

While they peppered him with another round of interrogation, Ford's smile returned and he had to fight down laughter. Elle could go on duping him until the end of days if it meant keeping her friendship and gaining her freedom.

Chapter 6
Wintering

The Keeper of the Pen lifted the mug to his lips. Ford winced as he watched from the corner of one eye, gripping the tun for support and squeezing the life out of a ladle with his other hand. Testing the ale was one of the perks of Atwell's job and since Ford had taken over, the Keeper had stopped more often than when Millet ran the brewery. This time he was actually tasting Ford's first attempt at an ale. His initial look of astonishment gave Ford hope, but it swiftly dissolved into betrayal. That look marked the end of Ford's brewing career on Polecat Island.

Ford knew it wouldn't go well. Flat, murky barley water did not a good ale make. Not only had he boiled the living yeast to death, but any survivors or airborne cultures making a new home in his cooling wort found the living conditions still too warm for their liking. Remembering Millet telling him to "Keep the temperature up!" in the brewery, Ford always kept the hearth fire high, too high and for too long. His consumption of fuel was questioned, but since neither Atwall nor any other island official knew how to brew, Ford had been left to his own devices for weeks. He spent the time sweating from nerves, heat, and exertion, and all for naught.

Though Atwall couldn't make the stuff either, he was a fairly expert taster of ale. Having discovered the fraud, the Master of the Guard was summoned and Ford was thrown into the Cold House for impersonating a professional tradesman. They hadn't punished him for the rocks-in-the-barrel deception, because they couldn't decide what he'd done wrong, other than being rather stupid. Some wondered about his possible involvement in the unexplained disappearance of a female prisoner, but no questions were asked. Officials preferred to hush up the incident. The reason he hadn't been gibbeted or thrown into the pit back then was because the island couldn't be without a brewer. Now was a different story. Rechard and his men threw Ford into the hole in the ground with no qualms, because there were other prisoners to replace him at the brewery before the day was out. A sister-in-law to another of the Middlefield cousins had offered her services as brewer. She and her maidservant set to running the place with the servant doing the grunt work, while the lady mostly entertained visitors. Over the following weeks and months, the servant would prove to know a good deal about brewing. She even knew enough to use a special bottom-fermenting yeast, which didn't require as much warmth during the cold winter months, thus saving on fuel. This made the officials happy.

After Ford's confinement, they put him to work in the quarries. Instead of having an ale at his pleasure by a warm fire, he faced the empty stomach, cold bones and cracked skin of every other prisoner on Polecat Island in winter. He didn't complain when he bent his sore limbs to pick up a stone so frigid that it might as well have been ice. He kept it to himself when the skin of his knuckles split and bled. Though it didn't make him loath the work any less, Ford knew he'd had it easy so far. Many had been here much longer, most of his friends had been at it since they all arrived on the island together. He kept his mouth shut and learned from them. They knew all the tricks to avoiding work as much as possible.

"Pick it up, Suds!" The name was a taunt, an intentional reminder of what he had been and no longer was. It came from the pinched lips of Lambert, a domineering prisoner promoted to one of the overseers of the quarries. As payment for keeping his fellow prisoners in line, Lambert was allowed time by the fire in the blockhouse and the strong ale from the guards' supply. To keep himself warm while on the job, he barked orders and insults as he pivoted about keeping an eye on his crew and making sure they met their daily quota.

Ford's task was to lug stones to a cart. He stood in the slushy, foot-chilling mud hovering over his next stone waiting for Lambert to look his way. This was known as *the quarryman's reprieve*. Every prisoner did it. Lambert knew they were doing it. If the prisoners didn't try to get away with such tricks and just got on with their work, his position wouldn't be necessary. The usual time elapsed, so Ford began leaning forward for his stone. But Lambert hadn't looked his way or prodded him with a taunt.

"Get up, ya laggard!" Lambert shouted at a figure lying in the mud like a fallen scarecrow missing half its straw. "Get up or it's lashes for you! No lying down on the job!" Lambert was shouting into the ear of Pup Brown, a frail and malnourished man of weak constitution, who never fully recovered from his bout of the illness that ravaged the island at summer's end. Brown had collapsed over a stone and rolled off of it onto his back. Lambert shook him by the shoulders and slapped his cheeks. Nothing would bring Brown about. "You and you," Lambert shouted to Ford and one other. "Hoist him onto the cart! All the rest of you get back to work!"

As Ford bent down to take hold of Pup Brown by the arms, he looked the man over and saw a spent soul of pale lips, yellowed fingernails, and thinning wisps of hair. His gums had pulled back from the few remaining teeth not taken by scurvy.

"I looked into his eyes and I saw nothing left," Ford said to Rhod as they walked back to the Pen when the work day was done. "I'm not ending my days like Pup. Not here, not like that, cartin' stone 'til I die."

"Hmm," said Rhod, not catching his friend's deeper meaning. Thoughts of escape had revived in Ford and he was trying to ignite them within others, but Rhod was more intent on scanning the ground as they walked. "You seen any of them berries by any chance?" He constantly sought out the ankle-high wintergreen plant. Chewing its tiny aromatic ruby-like berries improved the scent of one's breath. Rhod liked to mash a few between his teeth before seeing Moll.

"Not I."

"Probably all snatched up by them greedy bastards," Rhod said, meaning everyone and no one in particular. All prisoners horded whatever they could get their hands on. On a barren island such as Polecat, fish bones, shells, eggs from cliff nests, and even the feathers off of the birds who laid them had value. The island's resident prostitutes did a steady trade for ale rations. They all joked that the one nicknamed Humpback would have been drunk every day if she didn't have the drinking capacity of a whale.

That night the temperature plummeted and the ground froze. The spitting sleet of the last few weeks turned to heavy flakes as the year closed with a blizzard which blanketed the island and brought work to a halt. Most of the prisoners wore nothing heavier than tunics and trousers. Warmer clothes were on the way, or so they were promised. In the meanwhile, they did the best with what they had. Female prisoners huddled among the sheep at night. Male prisoners sprouted bushy beards.

Ford's beard had come in better than it ever had, but he didn't care. He had other things on his mind. The old fire had returned. He wanted off the island. To him, the others didn't seem as ambitious. They lacked his desire, at least that is, until winter and all of its deprivations set in. The prisoners, who celebrated and praised the snow for releasing them from their daily toils, now spent their days stuck in the Pen thinking of food and growing bored of one another's company. Chickens went missing from the coop within the women's side of the Pen. Blankets were often swiped. Even the shoes disappeared off of their owner's feet in the middle of the night. Fights broke out constantly. Gone were the days of relative peace or any semblance of goodwill. Gone was the pride the young wastrel thief Gulp had shown in helping to grow and reap the harvest. The sweet berries, fresh greens and other delights of summer were replaced by stale rations of dried oatcakes. The only thing that stirred their weary, weakened bodies from the sullen malaise infecting them was the desire to spread their anger and bitterness. Once the money the Middlefields managed to smuggle onto the island ran dry, they too were reduced to a pack of sneering backbiters in tattered finery. The situation worsened as more prisoners arrived and the newly built barracks also filled to overflowing.

"Look on the bright side," said Dillon to Ford one morning on their way across the island with a small party of workers sent to smash the ice from the well in the fields and retrieve what drinking water they could. "Least it's warm at night." Ford thought his friend was being a little too cheerful about the overcrowded beds, which packed prisoners together and generated body heat.

"Remember the mutton we had?" asked Bastien the Manerd, taking pleasure in recollecting the last meal they had had which included meat. A snowflake landed on Ford's nose. He brushed it away and nodded. They all remembered that meal fondly and they all asked the same thing: "When will we see more?"

"Have a look at that," said Dillon pointing to the island's tallest hill where a man and a woman stood side by side in front of a lanky, solemn man. Gray, silent and still, they might have been the pillars of some ancient ruins or monoliths atop a burial ground. The falling snow whirled around the figures and covered them like goose down upon their heads and shoulders. To the eyes of the onlookers, they were transformed into ghostly white beings caught up in swirling winter spirits.

"Are they real?" asked Ford and immediately felt foolish. "I mean, who is it?"

"I suppose that'll be Rhod and Moll with Will…" Knowing Ford disliked Will and feeling his familiarity with him might not be appreciated, Dillon sheepishly added, "That priest fellow."

"What are they doing up there?"

"Getting married, if I'm not mistaken." No sooner had Dillon spoken than the couple locked arms and Will clasped their hands together in his. Back at the barracks a small celebration broke out. Their happy friends sacrificed their ale rations in order to get the newlyweds drunk. Everyone treated them with kindness and gladly listened to them sing songs to one another over the wall partitioning the Pen until the sun went down.

The following day was a mishmash of the same old island miseries and remembrances of the previous day's celebration. But after that the good feelings vanished and everyone went back to wiling away the days dreaming of warming stews and other wishful thoughts while they wallowed in the Pen. They loved the idea of not working, but soon came to realize that sitting around doing next to nothing was actually worse than working. Without the distraction, one thought of little else beyond the gnawing hunger and biting cold.

By late winter, life began to lose its appeal. This could not have been more clearly demonstrated than by the case of the quiet chandler who missed his bees. The pudgy little man arrived upon the last transport ship of the year without a single friend on Polecat Island. His extreme sense of loneliness caused him to weep at night from homesickness. Overhearing this, the more hardened prisoners took to ridiculing him. The cruel delight some take in harrying the defenseless and the man's inability to take a joke perpetuated and intensified the torment. No visible end in sight could be seen by the chandler. One day in late winter he went missing. The watchtower bell rang the alarm. All prisoners were rounded up and locked down, and an island-wide search was undertaken. Excitement spread through the Pen that one of their own had escaped, and in the middle of winter no less. When they discovered the daring soul to be *the crying candlemaker*, they couldn't believe it. Some refused to believe it until his blue corpse was fished from the partially frozen seafoam covering the rocks at the base of a cliff. Life had lost its appeal.

On a sunny day that warmed the ground into a slushy mire, Ford was trying to urinate at the latrine while a few of his friends stood nearby watching a fight between an old and a young prisoner. The younger of the two had raised the usual complaints and the older had taken umbrage. "You ain't been here long enough to grouse about nothing," he asserted. The argument was pointless. The fight made even less sense. But such scenes had become commonplace since they had been put on half-rations. Mind and body suffered.

"We got to get off this island," said Ford rejoining his friends.

"Ain't that the truth," said Rhod.

"If you got a plan, count me in," said Miller Edd. A couple of others within earshot concurred and before Ford knew what was happening, people had clustered around him.

"Not here," Rhod suggested from the side of his mouth. "Too open. Too obvious."

A group gathered together for too long would draw attention from the blockhouse. They moved indoors and covered their gathering with a game called Rocks. Thought up by Will, a games enthusiast, Rocks comprised tossing three stones onto a relatively flat surface and guessing which sides would land face up, or in the case of the pyramid-shaped rock, which side would land face down. Game play was usually quick and wagering furious. Today they tossed the rocks at random and pushed an oyster shell back and forth for show. The stones clattered across the floorboards, bumped against the doorframe and came to rest. Instead of commenting on the results, they kept their mouths hidden in shadow and murmured their future plans, faceless voices whispering conspiracy.

"If only we could…"

"We could! We could get our hands on one of them boats."

"They lock 'em. We'd need the key.

"And the guard?"

"One guard's nothing."

"So, we sneak out of the Pen, steal the key, get over the wall, deal with the guard, unlock the noisy chains, and away we go?"

"Don't forget the oars. We'd need oars."

"Demon's balls, the oars!"

"Which they keep hidden somewheres, too."

"In the guardhouse."

"Exactly. In the guardhouse."

After taking his turn, Ford leaned back from the circle of players and listened passively while his thoughts played their own game. Momentum for an escape attempt was snowballing like it never had before, and for that he was grateful. What troubled him was how the other prisoners, mostly his friends at this point, had rallied around him as if he were the chief of a clan. It was one thing to talk up an idea and just do it, but it was another thing entirely to head up the planning for a big undertaking. He had never led men and didn't know if he had it in him. These ideas that were being batted about, few were his own, and he didn't know if they were any good or not. He didn't know how to prepare for a desperate escape over water and land. If they put the brunt of the planning on his shoulders, he would have to admit to them that he didn't know what he was doing. Something Dillon said caught his attention and drew him back into the conversation.

"What did you say?" he asked.

Dillon shifted uncomfortably, cleared his throat, and repeated, "Fish has a boat."

Everyone was caught up in a stunned silence. Few prisoners ever saw the island's little fishing cove or knew about the boat there. Those who did know about it, didn't give it much thought, because it wasn't much of a boat. It was, however, the least well-guarded of any boat on the island, and that gave Dillon's idea possibility. The skinny little man's freckled cheeks rose up with a smile as those gathered about him slapped his back and shoulders. Ford could have hugged him. Giddy imaginings of a happier future started trickling toward the realm of wilder dreams.

A shadow passed over the patch of sunlight upon the floor of the barracks where they played. Normally, prisoners moved about the Pen like slugs. There was no reason to hurry. This unnaturally frenetic, skittering crab walk could only belong to the unpopular Dubell, an inveterate gossip and eavesdropper.

"You think he was listening in on us?" wondered Rhod.

"Of course he was! Snooping's same as breathing with that one," said Miller Edd.

Ford jumped up and out of the barracks. Within a few long strides he had a handful of the gossip's shirt. Yanking him in close, he growled, "Was you listening in on us?" The question wouldn't trip up someone as sly as Dubell, but it was all Ford could come up with in the moment. Dubell's bush of blond hair flopped over his eyes each time his back slammed into the barracks wall. His squidgy body melted under the larger man's sturdy grasp. Ford shook a wet gurgle out of him, but got nothing more before a guardsman in the upper story window of the blockhouse shouted so sharply that Ford released Dubell instantly. The gossip slid away while Ford slumped his shoulder against the barracks wall and leaned there as if that was his intention all along.

"You think he'll give us away?" Ford asked his friends as he sat back down in the doorway a moment later.

"Count on it. His tongue's looser than some whores I've known," said Miller Edd, gathering up the rocks and absentmindedly throwing them down again without a guess or wager.

"But he wouldn't give us up to them, would he?" said Dillon with the slightest flick of a finger toward the blockhouse. The conspirators answered in shrugs and vague nods.

"Word'll get around," said Ford. He knocked his fist against a bent knee. The knee belonged to the man sitting next to him. "Sorry."

"Already has," said Rhod leaning back so Ford could see the two new faces that had joined the circle's periphery. The often-smiling, ever-in-trouble Carter brothers, Layn and Olstan, wagged their eyebrows and beamed their boyish grins back at the everyone. They stayed in a barracks one over with their set of friends. It was rare for them to pal around with Ford's circle.

"We overheard. We want in," said Layn. Olstan bobbed his head and showed a friendly mouthful of teeth.

"Demon's balls, that was fast," said Ford. "I suppose…Is there room enough in the boat?"

"Barely," said Dillon looking around at the growing number of people that would need to be accommodated.

"Damn," said Ford, who didn't need to be good with figures to know that the number of those involved was probably already untenable if they wanted to pull off a secret escape. He would go on saying *damn* over the coming weeks as each new person came up to him asking, sometimes begging to be a part of *the hop*. It had been dubbed thus by one doubter who had scoffed, "What, we just gonna hop over the wall and swim away?" Many a doubtful question was posed.

How would we get off the island?

Where would we go if we did get away?

Ford still didn't always have the answers. The constant asking wore on him. "Dillon thought of the boat. Why don't they go to him?" He put the question to Rhod after a flock of visitors pestered him one day.

"Cause Dillon, and I don't mean no disrespect, he's a good man, but he ain't you. He ain't got your..." said Rhod, looking Ford up and down, taking in the length of him, the width of his shoulders, the bearpaw size of his hands, and then waving his own hands before Ford as if showing him off for display. "He ain't you!"

"You! Just the very one I'm looking for!" In the doorway appeared the apple-red, orange-round and utterly indignant face of Aeddamon Born. Since arriving at the island, Ford had privately turned to Born once when he felt the need for a priest's ministration while in the midst of a losing battle with brewing. Now Born sought out Ford. The fussy little priest marched into the barracks with his shoulders hunched the way one would just before picking up a barrel or a heavy stone. The man had a job to do and had worked himself into somewhat of a fervor in order to get it done. "Give up your absurd notions!" he commanded through a pair of jiggling jelly-like cheeks that seemed to suck up all the blood in his body, leaving even his smooth chin quite pasty and reminiscent of butter. "This fanciful idea that you will rescue all these good people and corrupted souls, it is grievously dangerous to their wellbeing!"

They begged the priest to keep his voice down, but Born threw up his hands into the faces of those closest, as if he would shove the words back down their throats. "You are playing with men's hearts! They believe in you, believe you can save them!" Born found the idea so ridiculous that he couldn't help but let out one of his scornful tinny titters. "And that, my voluminous friend, is a power beyond your station to command! We are all here as a form of punishment seen fit by the gods for our missteps and transgressions. It is our lot to accept their will, not to trifle with the path they have laid for us. Quit this folly or the blood of all these men will be upon your hands! Desist! Your perilous venture is not condoned by the Order of the Sud a Waed!"

After declaring this condemnation, he looked beyond the men standing around the doorway and pointed a rod-straight finger at Will where he lay on his back on the floor in the middle of the dimly lit barracks. "And you there, Willem!" Will, shaken from his meditations, eased himself up onto an elbow and shaded his squinting eyes with a hand to peer at the silhouetted figures framed in the doorway. "You are expected to fall in line with the wishes of the Order! Even if these fools are too thick-headed to see sense, you must, Brother Willem! Talk to them! Show them the way!" Having executed his mission, Born turned his back on them and strode from the barracks in just as officious a manner as he had arrived. The gathered men were left speechless. At least momentarily.

"I thought priests were rich," Rhod eventually said.

"They mostly is," said Miller Edd.

"Then why can't that one afford himself a beard?" A few laughed. A few others brought up other body features that they felt the priest lacked. However, not everyone was in a light mood.

"What do we do now?" asked Dillion. A conspirator's guilt gnawed away at the certainty of his words for his part in simply mentioning the fishing boat. He looked to Ford for reassurance and wasn't the only one. The jesting stopped and everyone gathered in the doorway waited to hear what the man they were entrusting with their future had to say. Ford frowned and ground his fist into his palm.

"We ignore the nosey priest and do it anyway," he declared. The Carters let loose triumphant howls and Ford's back took a cheerful thumping from the gathering.

Their jubilation did not last. A new sense of concern had been fostered among them. The clergy's hold over the people was strong. Regardless of the conspirator's determination, a week passed and no one approached Ford about the escape. It was as if Born's warning had been a gale blowing all away before it and leaving the landscape of their future plans utterly changed in its wake.

"Funny how things go," said Ford to his friends while they sat around wrapped in blankets on a chilly day in the midst of these doldrums. "When they was all buzzing around me like bees, I wanted them to go away. But now, I wish just one'd come by."

"And sting ya?" said Rhod.

"It'd be better than nothing."

Not everyone on the island cared what a Haunan priest had to say. Excited by all the talk of escape and too antsy to wait any longer, a pair of prisoners made a break for it on the warmest night of the new year. The result was not encouraging. One was caught snooping about in the blockhouse in the dark hours before dawn, searching for the key to the patrol boats. Not long after he was apprehended, his desperate partner was found with a bundle of provisions on the beach pulling futilely on the chains that bound the longboats to the shore. Restrictions were put in place. Security tightened. Prisoners were questioned, Ford more than most.

Winter flexed its muscle one last time, blowing a storm in from the north overnight. It blanketed the island and everything on it in a foot of new snow. Atwall sent out work crews to clear paths, sweep steps and catwalks, uncover the longboats, and knock the snow off of the roofs. Ford was set to work within the Pen clearing the thatched roofs of the barracks. After the previous attempt at escape, one of the things the Warden of the Island banned was the prisoners' use of ladders. Since ladders were necessary for certain jobs, the guards kept two in the blockhouse, but the prisoners had to make do with human ladders.

Ford found himself making up the base of one such ladder that morning with Gulp standing on his shoulders, while the boy used an oar to knock off the snow. The well-built Randel Hayward, still oblivious to who had cracked him over the head the previous year, made up the base of another ladder. Through the snow falling in clumps beside him, Ford watched Hayward giggling away like a deranged child as he tickled the feet and ankles of the man standing on his shoulders in an attempt to make him fall. The man, a lightweight Manerd who was even lighter than normal after the harsh winter, threatened Hayward with his paddle. The two did very little work and were getting away with it, because their jests entertained the otherwise bored guards watching from the blockhouse. Ford and Gulp finished their half of one side and moved around the corner.

"My name is Cadogan Wyn Welland," a pleasingly smooth voice murmured into Ford's ear. Ford turned to find standing beside him Cadogan, a handsome lordling from the minor clan loyal to the Middlefields, that daring young man who had made the desperate escape attempt while disembarking from the transport ship. Because the nobles kept their distance from the other prisoners, Ford hadn't seen the man up close, but now he was closer to him than he ever was to any man.

Though not a hulking figure like Ford, Cadogan was hardy for one raised in delicate society. He wore his dirty blond hair at shoulder-length as did many Aelwydians, but with a name like Wyn Welland, Ford guessed his people originally came from Dubhanan. The blood of the Dubhanan flowed through a good many Aelwydians. Names were constantly changing, but the Wyn Wellands had had enough wealth and power to hold on to theirs through the generations.

Cadogan slapped the legs of both his own snow-clearing partner and Gulp, and mouthed "slow" when they both looked down. Each stared at him quizzically for a moment before realizing what he asked of them. From then on they reached for the snow piled on the roof as if it were miles away and needed special care to drag off.

"I want in," Cadogan said to Ford. The statement came from a jaw so sharp it seemed to cut the fat from every utterance. There would be no mincing of words with this one. Ford admired that and quite frankly preferred it, having noticed in himself that the less he said, the less he embarrassed himself. Fewer words held more meaning. "I can help. If you'll have me."

"I..." Ford began, but he trailed off, wondering how it had come about that a lord should turn to him for favor. And perhaps stranger, to wish to be a part of an endeavor that would likely include great hardship, the likes of which he and his kin had surely never endured. His gaze slid down to Cadogan's hands just inches away, where they gripped his snow-clearing partner's ankles. He found callused fingers and skin chapped just as badly as his own.

They had to move on to another of the barracks and slowly went to work there. Cadogan began probing Ford with questions and rapidly offering ideas. Ford was impressed with what he was coming up with, as well as the aura of command he exuded. He absolutely marveled at the man's agile mind. It was like trying to follow an auctioneer in mid sale. Ford explained his own ideas. Cadogan offered counter alternatives, and before long they were making new plans. They even settled on the perfect date to make the attempt, something Ford couldn't decide with his friends. They chose the night of Afonyda's Circle, a holiday two months away which celebrated the first official day of spring. It would be warmer and they both agreed that was essential for success.

"And there's a good chance the guards'll be drunk," said Ford smiling at the thought. "But that's a long ways away."

"It is, but the moon would be close to full then. We will need the light. We can't risk lanterns and torches."

Just like that, they had nearly everything ironed out. The plan hadn't altered the essence of what Ford and his friends had already come up with, but the details made more sense, seemed more sound all around. Plus, the decisive way in which he and Cadogan arrived at their version felt natural and definite. Cadogan's commanding presence was what Ford felt he lacked in himself. Add to it the man's keen wit and a determined spirit, and Ford recognized in him a great asset and someone he might work with as an equal. There was only one objection Ford could think of. There were quite a few Wyn Wellands. "We can't have everyone join in."

"It would only be me," said Cadogan, hardly moving his lips and keeping his pale green eyes skyward, as if minding his work. Small clumps of snow fell from the roof to the left and right of them. "The rest of my people want nothing to do with this." He made a shrugging motion mostly with his head. "But they are soft. I'll not stay here to rot and die."

When their work was finished, Cadogan added as they parted, "Secrecy is key. Tell no one of the date. Not even your closest friends. Tell them to wait. Say it's coming. We don't want anyone jumping ship too soon."

If anyone was ready to jump ship too soon, it was Ford. Back at his own barracks, he had to fold his arms and tuck his hands in at his sides to hide their shaking. The excitement of the plan coming together had his blood pumping. Reining in his impatience and keeping everything under wraps was going to be difficult. However, in the long run, keeping his friends in the dark would indeed prove the hardest part. Every day they badgered him for details, going so far as to offer their meager rations to coax out of him a time and day for the hop. He found their attentions embarrassing and refused, which only embarrassed and frustrated his friends. Luckily, work saved him. As the snow melted and the ground thawed, work parties were organized to clear mud, fix flooded out paths, and patch damaged roofs. There was plenty to do and keeping busy stopped his tongue from wagging.

"Stupid...fussy...build their own damn..." he grumbled, stamping his feet and hopping in place with his fingers tucked under his armpits while waiting in a nippy mist for another stone to carry to the cart. Quarry work had begun again. They were gathering blocks for a temple that the island's priests requested in order to provide for everyone's spiritual needs. It took a good deal of convincing, but officials finally relented. Some of the prisoners who had to sweat over the project weren't so sure it was all that necessary. "Afonyda's Circle can't come soon enough," Ford let loose in his irritation.

Dubell's ears pricked up and his body tensed, but he remained inconspicuous where he stood waiting for a stone behind Ford. For weeks he and others had watched Ford and Cadogan. The two met rarely to keep suspicion to a minimum, but any new ideas that cropped up needed to be ironed out, and when they were spotted together, there was much speculation as to their discussion. Dubell suddenly found himself surrounded by *friends*, or at least inquisitive acquaintances who hovered about him, licking up whatever tidbits he dropped.

Ford also found himself swarmed. "You'll know in time. You have my word," he endlessly repeated.

"Can't a friend do a friend a kindness?" a flush-faced Miller Edd had barked back on one of those occasions as he stalked away with the oatcake he'd offered Ford crumbling in his balled fist.

At the end of this weeks-long ordeal, Ford lay on his side in bed tracing lines with his finger at random on the wall closest to him. He had taken the end spot vacated by Miller Edd, so that now he was pressed up against the wall and had less room, but slightly more privacy. Privacy being relative to the cramped circumstances, at least he could turn away from everyone and not see the eyes staring expectantly back at him. Night had fallen on the first day of spring. In celebration, the guards in the blockhouse carried on carousing well past dark. Ford listened for hours and passed the time distractedly drawing the outlines of animals he knew by sight. He also drew, in their true proportions, the short, large-headed men he had once discovered living in a small cave at the bottom of a ravine. He had seen some bizarre things in his short life and often the memories entailed bitter loss, but this one was mostly pleasant and he liked recalling it. Such a strange encounter, he mused. The small people had possessed valuable jewelry and a kind of ill-defined magic. Then there came a tapping in a rhythmic pattern. The pattern repeated itself twice before Ford realized it was not a part of his recollections or the auditory illusion of a vivid dream.

He shot up in bed, fully awakened from a light slumber. He guessed it to be about midnight. The bustle of the joyful binge going on within the blockhouse had died away entirely. He got out of bed and crept as silently as he could to the door to peer through its cracks at the blockhouse, the wall, the watchtower and Crowell House. All of the usual lights that emanated from the guard posts seemed to have been doused, and everything was lit up perfectly by a full moon shining down from a clear sky.

He turned back to rouse the small, hand-picked group of prisoners from his barracks that he and Cadogan had determined were the most suitable for the escape attempt. More than half of the barracks crouched just behind him staring back in eager anticipation. His concentration on what he saw outside of the barracks was so great that he heard nothing of what had gone on within. The Carter brothers were right there close at hand with so many more just over their shoulders. Far too many. He wanted to tell them to go back to their beds, but he could see, even in the dim light, that they waited for his word with gleeful expectation. There would be no turning them away. It was either call it off or carry on with everyone included, and there was no way he was giving up on this now. Perhaps it would work. After all, many in the barracks still snored away, oblivious to the shuffling feet and muffled whispers around them.

"Not a word, not a sound," he whispered. They all nodded. He turned back to the door and nudged it gently. It gave way. His teeth unclenched and his muscles relaxed ever so slightly. They were past the first hurdle. The slim boy tasked with sneaking out through a loosened floorboard and unlatching the door from the outside had done his job. Ford pushed the door open enough to slip through.

His troop of hopefuls tip-toed after him around to the back of the barracks, where Cadogan awaited them. Behind him stood an eager troop of his own. He and Ford looked at each other and shrugged. More than three times as many men were with them than were supposed to be, and nothing could be done about it. The mass of bodies congregating behind the barracks was now part of the plan. All that could be done was to get them out of there as soon as possible before being discovered.

Cadogan signaled and a man holding a makeshift ladder slipped out from behind the barracks and scampered across the yard toward one of the walls that penned them all in. This was the only wall with a stone base. It stood five feet high and was topped by the wooden palisade which made up the Pen enclosures. Enough of the stone jutted out for a ladder to be propped on top of the base and held in place up against the palisade. Unfortunately, this section of the wall was out in the open and easily spotted from the blockhouse.

There was nothing for it. The stone wall provided the advantage they needed to reach the top of the palisade.

The ladder was simply a pilfered boat oar with nails pounded into it by Ostan of Overbay, a mason who stole a hammer and nails that day at the potential risk of his life. For his courage, he was now carrying the ladder to the wall and would be the first over. The man's nerve was on the verge of failing him. With each of his first three steps across the yard he passed gas. The full moon lighting his way also lit him up almost as if it were day, so Overbay crouched low to the ground in hopes of making himself as invisible as possible. His excruciatingly slow crawl drove the waiting prisoners mad. They were chomping at the bit to rush out there and hurry him up. Ford and Cadogan spread their arms wide and leaned back against the men pressing to get by. The wingspan of gigantic eagles could not have restrained the throng of long-yearning prisoners, who had waited out a bitterly cold winter for this moment. They surged forward and broke in a mass exodus for the wall.

"Wa—" Ford began, but caught himself. There could be no shouting. He and Cadogan kept pace and did what they could to keep everyone quiet.

Overbay was just propping his ladder on top of the stone section of the wall when the mob overtook him. A dozen hands held the ladder in place. Another dozen heaved Overbay halfway up the wall. His feet found the ladder rungs and after two steps, his fingers found the top of the palisade. He threw one leg up and eased himself over, dropping down the other side onto a cart purposefully placed there at the end of the work day.

Ford couldn't believe it had worked. He looked around him at all the excited, upturned faces caught in the moonlight, beaming with hopes realized. He thought his heart might burst for joy.

Someone else tried to force their way up the ladder, but Cadogan jerked him back and dragged Dillon forward to make sure he was next. Dillon had a special job to do and should have been first over the wall, but Overbay had been obstinate. There was some discontented grumbling, but they hoisted Dillon up and shoved him by the feet over the top of the wall. Their impatience showed in the thrust. Dillon flew over the top like a ragdoll. Dozens of soft gasps covered the *thud* of his landing. No cry followed, so they assumed he was either fine or dead.

Regardless of what happened to him, the rest of them were determined to go over next. It should have been Dior. The Manerd had recently been assigned to maintenance of the patrol boats. While scraping barnacles, he had managed to make one of the boat oars disappear. That oar became their ladder. He told the guards a wave must have grabbed it and convinced them that it must have floated away. For his negligence, he had been given a stretch in the Cold House. Now he waited for someone to come let him out, but the person tasked with that job was absentmindedly pressing ever closer to the wall, doing his utmost to be the next over.

Prisoners started pushing, shoving and climbing over one another. Ford and Cadogan dragged bodies back. Ford took the noisiest of them by the neck and silenced him with a threatening fist. While they were distracted, an innovative and bred-in-the-bone housebreaker snuck away to the door leading to the countryside and went to work on it with a lockpick he had made from a nail. The door was the quickest means of escape, but it was dangerously close to the blockhouse and its hinges squealed like a demonic pig, so it had been designated as strictly off-limits. The whole point of the escape was to do it quietly, so they could get a head start before they were found out. The housebreaker was making good progress with his pick when Ford spotted him and tried in vain to wade through the bodies to stop him. There were just too many people in the way. Luckily, Cadogan noticed what he was doing, and from his side of the throng, he was able to dash across the yard to the door.

Old timers like Gyl stood in the doorways of their barracks watching the escape attempt fall apart. Most of them were not participating, because every attempt since they had been on the island had failed, and they expected more of the same now. They had no wish to incur the wrath of their jailors, who had the power to make life even more miserable for the prisoners.

Ford by himself stood no chance of holding in check the anxious prisoners. The mounting chaos at the wall threatened to break into a riot. Randel Hayward latched on to the ladder with an iron grip, demanding he be next. Tiny Brie of Mane leapfrogged his back and jumped for the top of the wall. The tips of the Manerd's stunted fingers fell inches short. One of the nails protruding from the ladder caught his leg as he slid back down, tearing a gapping gash down the side of this thigh. He fell to the ground, where he writhed about and breathing heavily through clenched teeth. The ladder fell over and landed on top of him, puncturing his side. He screamed a scream that would wake the whole island. It broke the prisoners' final ounce of restraint. They began trampling one another to get at the ladder and climbing the mound of bodies piling up at the base of the wall.

Hearing Brie scream, Cadogan cast the plan aside and urged on the housebreaker. Picking the lock and getting the squeaky door open was their only hope now. Ford swam through the flailing bodies to reach Brie. He clasped a hand over the screaming Manerd's mouth and held on while being kneed and kicked. Someone tried to step onto his shoulders. Rhod and Miller Edd flashed by just before lantern light and shouting erupted from the blockhouse. Every prisoner in the yard sensible to the danger froze, seized by the fear of capture and punishment. If they fled back into the barracks now, they might avoid the worst of it. If they kept with Cadogan and Ford, freedom might very well await them. The squeaking of the Pen door shattered their indecision. The housebreaker had succeeded. Prisoners stampeded for the door. Cadogan waved them on. Even some of the old timers bolted from the barracks. The silhouettes of guardsmen appearing in the blockhouse windows made a few flee back to the barracks. Mid-yard collisions and shouting from all corners cracked and spat throughout the night air, creating utter confusion within the Pen.

Cadogan shepherded prisoners out of the Pen and then resigned his post when Ford finally tumbled through the door. The blockhouse gong clanged away as the prisoners lit out in myriad directions. Not everyone knew the true plan. Some who did thought they had a better plan. Ford led his group toward the open country under moonlight that morphed the island into a mysterious land quite foreign to prisoners never allowed out after dark. Boulders and rotting tree stumps protruded from the soil like tombstones. Spindly leafless bushes broke the wavy outline of the downs. A desperate bird fled its nesting hole in an explosion of fluttering wings and squawks. The night air cut through their threadbare clothes and chilled their sweating skin. The dew on the matted dead grass softened their steps into dull thumps and soaked through their shoes after the first hundred yards.

"Which way? I can see nothing," said Ford, who could see plenty, but the distorted midnight landscape made him mistrust his own eyes. He feared leading them in the wrong direction.

"The watchtower stands thus, the hill thus and us between," said Cadogan pointing out the landmarks. "So westward lies thus. Come!" He led them only a few strides more before they all pulled up at the manic striking of the watchtower bell signaling an escaped prisoner. Never had it rung so loudly. The din drowned out the blockhouse gong.

All over the island the escapees ran with little care for where their feet landed, so long as each step took them farther away. Some made for the fishery, where they hoped to find the boat that was supposed to float them away to safety. Others, convinced the patrol boats were going to be used in the escape, took deadly tumbles down the cliffs and dove into the sea in an attempt to get to the pier on the beach. And still others simply ran for the far side of the island and sought any secluded place to hide out, having no other plan in their foolish heads but to elude the guards in hopes that something would crop up eventually to save them from recapture.

When the clanging bell and deeper gong died into complaints crying from afar, the crash of waves came to the ear of Ford and Cadogan's group with blessed clarity. Just over a ridge lay the ocean. They crawled and slid down the backslope over rock and around bush to a narrow, curling inlet, the tiniest of the sea's fingers poking into the island, scratching at the shore, as if testing its mettle for a future onslaught. On the way down, Ford and Cadogan searched the roiling water below and did not see what they hoped would be there. This turbulent bath, open to the ocean, was empty of all but sloshing waves splashing against barnacle-covered rocks.

"Damn," Ford muttered.

"There!" shouted Cadogan. A round object, like a seal's head, bobbed into view over the tall rocks at the mouth of the inlet.

"Blessed boy!" cried Ford.

The head bobbed around the last rock and into the inlet floated Dillon, standing in the center of the smallest boat the island had to offer. Ford's cheer had hardly left his lips when he got a better look at the short skiff with thin, battered sides. A glorified tub. The fragile thing was already taking on water and Dillon had to fend off the rocks with a long pole least the little craft should be destroyed upon them.

"We'd stand a better chance sailin' off in a barrel," said Miller Edd. His deflated utterance matched the spirits of those watching Dillon being tossed about in the undulating water. There was so very little room in the skiff. Less than half a dozen could cram aboard before it would likely sink.

A pair of women arrived at the inlet, breathless and shivering. The female prisoners had gotten wind of the escape and had designed plans of their own.

More than just these two knew of the inlet part of the plan, but only they had made it this far. Rhod squinted from one to the other through the darkness and then scrambled back up the slope.

"Rhod!" Ford called after him.

"I'm going back for Moll!" they heard him shout as he disappeared over the ridge. Unless Moll turned up soon, neither she nor Rhod would reach the inlet before it was too late. Already the escapees were wading into the water or leaping from the rocks for the skiff.

"Wait," called Cadogan, but the people scurried aboard and upset the boat. A wave surged over the gunwale and it took on too much water. Splashing and gurgling bodies floundered away from the sinking craft. Ford waded in and plucked Dillon out of the water. With his and Cadogan's help, they lifted the skiff upside down and freed it of water. Flipping it over again, they floated it on the surface once more.

"Back in," commanded Cadogan, but no one rushed forward this time. The eagerness to climb aboard had all but vanished. Those who had fallen in were crawling out of the sea, soaked to the bone and feeling every bit of the chill wind. "Come! There's no time to lose!" The dozen or so sopping wet souls hesitated on the shore. A pair of them left the rocks they were perched upon by the water's edge and began climbing back up the slope toward the warmth of the Pen. Also, the sinking of the skiff had realized the fears of the non-swimmers. The power of dark ocean waves at night spooked them into backing away from Cadogan when tried to urge them onto the boat.

"No laggards!" bellowed Ford as he bodily lifted someone from the shore into the skiff. New arrivals skittering down the slope toward them were eager to find space left in the boat. As they began to scramble into the water and onboard, their eagerness spurred on the soaked and cold prisoners, who jumped back into the water figuring they couldn't get much wetter or colder at this point. And just like that, the boat took on as many passengers as it could safely manage. Ford held back. He could see what a burden he would be on the little skiff if he climbed in now.

"You go," said Cadogan, shoving Ford toward the boat. "None of this would have happened without you. Lead them to the island, send back the boat. I'll stay here with the rest and make the second trip." They would be lucky to manage two trips that night. In a few short hours dawn would give them away and no nook on Polecat would be deep or remote enough to hide them until they could be taken off the island. Patrols would be out and about snatching them up in no time.

Ford had a flash of inspiration. There was a way he could make the first journey across without getting in the boat. "Stay right here," he shouted to Cadogan over the crash of a wave as he waded deeper into the water. "I'll bring it back! I promise!"

Once in the water, Ford had never gotten out and didn't think the ocean felt half as cold as he expected it to. Submerging up to his chest chilled him just as much as standing wet out in the open. He took hold of the side of the skiff. If he climbed into the boat it would sink. Instead, along with two others, he clung to the side and helped guide it through the inlet toward the sea. Once outside of the inlet, the ocean showed its true strength. Ford held on just to keep the boat from tipping. Though the waves pushed them back and forth, the current enveloping the island swept them long faster than they knew. The sea lifted and tossed the skiff, nearly slamming it against the shoreline rocks, where it would surely smash into pieces. The water grew deeper, coming up to the chest of the others clinging to the gunwale. They often tripped and were dunked under. Ford held on, wedging himself between the boat and a threatening rock.

"Who has the pole? Where's the pole?" he demanded to know. No one answered. They were too preoccupied with their own peril. A woman in the bow clung to the prow. From his side of the boat, Ford could see a row of white knuckles gripping the gunwale. The pole was nowhere in sight. Not only had they lost it, but Dillon wasn't with them either. He had been accidentally left on shore. It was a shame. He had risked much in his midnight flight across the island to steal the skiff for them. A good and honest man at heart, Dillon had done things that night which he never thought possible in himself: breaking out of the Pen; sneaking about the fishery to swiftly and silently unmoored the little craft; navigating it to the inlet through tumultuous breakers in the dark. He loved his work at the fishery and the overseer had been good to him. If this escape didn't pan out, he would never work there again. And that was the least of the punishment he would likely endure.

Right about then the fishery was alive with a buzz of confusion. Dubell had confidently led a group there expecting to find and steal Fish's boat. This much of the plan Dubell had discovered. What he didn't know, was that Dillon had been dispatched before anyone else to retrieve the boat and move it to another cove. Two dozen would-be escapees stood about the fishery wondering where the boat was. Fish emerged from his hut in his small clothes, blinking and rubbing his eyes as he swayed uneasily on half-asleep legs, wondering what all these people were doing gathered around him in the middle of the night.

Island officials allowed Fish the sought-after skiff, because while useful in the shallows for netting fish or collecting the hated lobster, it was intentionally made into a rudderless, flat-bottomed navigational nightmare. It would never survive the open ocean. Dillon poling it along the shore as far as he had was a minor miracle, which the escapees were beginning to appreciate as the boat slid over waves which knocked the bow left and right, their direction constantly shifting. They might have spun all the way around if not for Ford and the others pushing on the sides to guide their way. Those within the skiff could do nothing to change its course. Even if they could, they had to spend most of their time bailing the water pouring in over the sides.

Ford stumbled over the rocky ocean bottom. His feet slipped and his ankles twisted with each step. Sitting so low in the water and with waves splashing about his head, he couldn't make out much. *Keep Polecat on your right*, he remembered Cadogan saying, and so he did. But eventually they would need to leave the shore and strike out for their destination. "There!" shouted the lone woman in the boat. She stood in the bow as erect as she dared, keeping one hand on the prow and pointing with the other. From then on, they steered by her finger.

The bottom dropped away with surprising suddenness. Ford held on to the boat and treaded water with his remaining hands and feet. The woman navigating kept pointing to the right. They were going well off course. The men on the left side of the boat weren't pushing anymore. They were treading water too and must have been pulling the boat toward them. Ford tugged on the side of the skiff and swam harder until the woman pointed straight ahead again. The awkward motion was tiring, so he shifted to the back of the boat where he might kick and push with more effect. There he found the others kicking their feet to propel the skiff, their teeth rattling away as they clung to the transom like a lifeline. No one wanted to be separated from the boat out here in the dark. They envied those in the skiff, but those people were shivering, too.

Ford slammed his foot into something solid just as the man beside him let out a dreadful howl. A wave ebbed and a massive shadowy object like a huge oblong head rose out of the water beside the skiff. Ford instantly thought of the giant eels that had attacked the ship on the way to Polecat Island. The next wave lifted the boat and hurled them all towards the dark specter. Those in the skiff leapt out just as it crashed into the object, a monumental rock that stove in one side of the tiny boat. Bodies flopped about in the water. Cries of terror drowned out shouts for help. Pieces of wood tossed by waves knocked into people. The skiff was no more.

Ford launched himself through the water with desperate and arbitrary strokes, having lost all sense of direction during the crash. In the confusion, objects appeared suddenly out of the night and roiling surf: jagged rocks better off avoided; a sunken vessel's mast which he mistook for a tree trunk; entangling seaweed and the gods only knew what else. His throbbing foot touched something solid, a rock, he hoped. Putting both feet down, he found he could stand. The neck-deep water thrust him back and forth. Another big wave knocked him away from the rock and he swam just to keep his head above the surface. Hindered by kicks and scratches from other escapees, he struggled on in search of something else to stand upon or latch on to, anything to save himself from this amorphous watery leviathan that was the ocean at night surging all about him.

Screams rending the air penetrated even underwater when waves washed over head. Arms flailed. Someone grabbed him, yanked on his arm. The weight of a body on top of Ford dragged him down. He flung them off and struggled to the surface gasping, paddling blindly, the salt water stinging his eyes. Someone shouted, called out to him, perhaps off to the left. He opened his eyes to a gray dome ahead and made for it. A wave buried him. When he surfaced, a figure before him rose up out of the water like a titan or a hero of the old stories, capable of walking on water. It was the sea receding from the man's body as if the ocean itself drained away from his chest down to his knees. That's when it dawned on Ford to put his feet down, and he too rose from the water awash in relief.

Together they clambered up the slime-covered sides of an immense boulder, supporting one another as they crouched upon its relatively dry dome. From there they could make out the others struggling through the sea amid waves crashing against rocks. Ford stood tall and waved them toward him. A Manerd some yards out or perhaps more, it was hard to tell in such conditions, held weakly held on to a wet rock low to the water. They shouted and waved for him to join them, but the Manerd kept his head down and would not budge. Only the irresistible force of a wave could rip him away, and inevitably it did. He disappeared under the surface, emerged, vanished again and reappeared a few feet away. It was clear the Manerd could not swim well enough to counter the unpredictable power of the ocean. His last gasp above the surface was nothing more than gaping lips and wild frightened eyes. Ford dove for him, reached out in all directions and hooked his catch by an arm. The Manerd wrapped himself around Ford's torso and the two floated and kicked back to the dome-shaped rock.

Another survivor of the wreck, Miller Edd, had also crawled onto the rock, which was becoming crowded with drenched, shivering bodies wrapped in each other's arms. They stood ankle-deep in the water, but were glad to be there.

"Do you see anyone?" Ford shouted. Everyone searched the water. None of their comrades could be seen, leaving them to wonder if the others had all perished or were merely hidden by the dark, erratic sea. In places its smooth surface flowed regularly up and down, and at other points it exploded against rocks and sprayed into the sky.

"Look!" shouted the Manerd, tugging at the ends of Ford's sodden tunic. Behind them someone was battling the churning surf with resolute overhand strokes. They watched rapt by the beating arms splashing away ever closer to the wooded shoreline of Forbidden Island. All of their hopes and dreams were now tied to the lone swimmer. When the tall, slender figure dragged himself out of the water and onto land, the people on the domed rock cheered with abandon. They watched him climb onto a large white boulder and wave back at them with both arms. This success made the gap of dangerous water between them and the shore seem fathomable.

"See, it can be done!" Ford shouted over an angry sea determined to drown him any way it could. "We can do this!"

Ford's confident encouragement got them to wade back into the water. Still hesitant and holding onto one another, they shuffled down the rock. A wave swept two of them off their feet. The rest went down with them. Everyone plunged into the depths, where they thrashed about on their own. The Manerd leapt onto Ford's back. The little man's weight hardly mattered at first, but whenever a large wave overtook them, his grip tightened around his savior's neck. Ford feared he might blackout. He tore the Manerd's hands away and secured them to his shoulders.

Forbidden Island grew larger. The points of its evergreen trees, moonlit silver against a black infinity, reached into the sky ever higher, like a mass of conically-roofed towers of some impenetrable fortress. When they set out from Polecat, their aim had been the island's broad expanse. The target was general and could not be missed, even in the dark. But now Ford narrowed his aim to that large, white boulder, an unforeseen symbol of success. He lifted his head to see if it looked any closer. No, he had to admit to himself, he had lifted his head as an excuse to slow down and rest. The little man draped over his back like a cape weighed no more than a hundred pounds, but it was a hundred more pounds than Ford had ever swum with. And the ocean was no calm swimming hole, like the one back home he spent his summers in. The boulder did look closer, but it was to his left now. He put his head down and tried to mimic the overhead strokes of the man on the shore, who still stood on top of the boulder waving them in. *Harder! Try harder!* Ford shouted to himself. Each stroke stoked his burning lungs. Seldom used muscles cramped. The cold water made him want to curl up within himself. Another lift of the head, and yes, the boulder stood clearly away to the left. The current was sweeping him and the Manerd along between the two islands and back out to the open ocean, where they would drown if they couldn't reach the shore. It seemed so close. *Where was the land,* he wanted to scream. He stretched his feet down, but felt no bottom. With almost nothing left to give, he threw his whole body into threshing the water with every limb. Something under the surface stabbed at his leg, jolting him upright. The Manerd dropped off his back. Or was he plucked off by a wave or something more sinister? A thick and long tube-like mass brushed against Ford's thighs. No, he was brushing against it. His whole midsection pushed into a submerged tree trunk. Creeping along its smooth, slimy, bark-less length he dragged himself to a point where he could touch the ground. Summoning the last of his strength, he carried his spent body up and out of the water, where the elated Manerd awaited him on the shores of Forbidden Island.

Chapter 7
The Killers

Forbidden Island welcomed its new visitors with a coastline rimmed by rocks hidden under a blanket of creeping vegetation and a thick wall of evergreens pressing upon the shore. The trees stood at attention like mute sentries hiding an army of secrets within their shadows. The escapees who made it ashore gathered by the boulder that had acted as a beacon. They peered back at the sea in search of the others, but could see nothing more than the white foam of cresting waves and twinkles of moonlight gleaming off of the water.

"They'll turn up," Ford said. "No doubt they made a landing elsewhere." He did doubt it, but saw no sense in distressing the others. "We'll find them in the morning."

They wrung the water from their clothes and huddled together for warmth. Each would have closed their eyes and slept the night away if given the chance, but a short rest was all they were afforded. "The longer we stay out here in the open the more likely a patrol will spot us," said Ford. He did his best to sound like he had everything under control. "When the sun comes up, we've got to be gone." It also made sense that without means of making a fire, they had to keep moving to warm their cold, wet bodies. Ford got to his feet quicker than the rest. He had a burning desire to discover if this so-called island was indeed an island or if that was a lie disseminated by Polecat officials to dissuade prisoners from fleeing the penal colony and having a look at Forbidden for themselves. Ford was banking the entire escape on the hopes of a misnomer.

Cadogan's reluctance to dismiss it as a ruse came through during their discussions in preparing for the escape. Ford had no qualms in dismissing it outright. Regardless, both guessed that from Forbidden they could get to the Aelwyd mainland one way or another. Perhaps they might even reach

Rockport, the easternmost Aelwydian city. A dangerous place by all accounts, it none the less would put them out of the reach of the Brastersceatts. In a lawless frontier town such as that, they could lose themselves among the rabble, taking up new lives, rough lives to be sure, but free. Both Ford and Cadogan disregarded the tales of monsters inhabiting Forbidden. Such blatant tactics were often used as deterrents. Ford wished the sensible man was with him now.

"Follow me," he said to the bodies nestled like baby birds among the rocks. They looked back at him through dull eyes in drawn faces before burying their heads between their shoulders. These were spent husks, mere shells of who they had been before setting out. Ford felt as they did, but he had learned the importance of pressing on when you didn't want to. The lesson had come during his time living with a bunch of boys in the forest as bandits on the fringes of civilization. Their life of ease among the trees came at the price of inevitable hunger, but the deprivations taught them to get off their backsides and do something about it, even when they didn't want to, because no one else would do it for them. Ford looked around at the bedraggled group curled into balls hugging themselves. Getting just one of these people up on their feet was key. An ally was needed to rally the rest.

Passing over the Manerd who spoke little to no Aelwydian, he looked to the man next to him, Dunstan Wallard, a tradesman from Cadogan's barracks. Ford had never so much as spoken to the exiled Middlefield loyalist and didn't know his character. Beside Wallard sat Layn Carter, whose brother was among the missing along with the lone woman on the skiff after the boat had smashed to pieces. Layn shook violently and was by far the least responsive of them all. Then there was the young priest Will. Ford couldn't believe he was here. For one, the other priests had forbidden him from attempting the escape. Certainly, none of them had tried, and yet here was this defiant fellow. The willowy priest seemed too insubstantial for such rigors. If the emaciated Pup Brown had survived the wreck and made the swim, Ford would have been less astounded. Only now did it occur to him that Will had been there throughout the escape: helping people over the wall, swimming alongside the skiff to steer it, and standing on the white boulder on the shore of Forbidden Island providing the welcoming beacon which helped guide the survivors ashore. It was Will who had made the impressive swim over the last gap to the island, which had given the rest of them the hope and courage needed to make their own attempt. Still, Ford's stubborn streak made him pass over Will as a potential rallying ally and choose the person he felt most comfortable with, Miller Edd.

"Up, Edd," he cajoled. With fingers as stiff and painful to flex as anyone's, he took his friend's arm to help lift him and show that he was there to lend a hand. "We got to go. Help me get the rest up."

Miller Edd's head lolled back and he glared at Ford with the petulance of a child, certain he would have been somewhere warm and dry if not for Ford. But the glare softened, perhaps due to the realization that if not for Ford he would never have gotten off of Polecat Island. He unbent his unwilling body and stood on wobbling legs.

When Ford looked to the others again, Will was helping the Manerd stand. Wallard, watching them intently, soon followed. That left only Layn, lying on his side in a tight wrapped ball shaking uncontrollably, muttering a trembling babble. The most coherent thing he managed was a repetitive, "No. No. No." They pled with him, but it didn't seem to get through. Ford lifted him on to his own two feet, but he immediately flopped back down. There was no budging the man. They stood over him contemplating what to do.

"Leave him," said Miller Edd.

"We can't. They'll find him," said Ford.

"Hide him up in there," suggested Wallard through chattering teeth with a slight nod toward the trees.

"If we leave him, there is no doubt but he will freeze to death," said Will kneeling down beside Layn.

"There's nothing to build a fire with and if we did, we'd all be found before the sun came up," said Ford.

"Then he must move," said Will, standing and facing the others who were beginning to walk away. "Without fire and dry clothes, we must all move to keep warm. Otherwise..."

"Otherwise, we die," said Ford. Will nodded.

"You saw, we tried to get him up," said Miller Edd. "If Ford can't get him on his feet, well...well, I say he's a lost cause." He hung his head, tucked his chin to his chest, and awaited their verdict.

"We'll carry him, if we have to," said Ford. "*I'll* carry him, if it comes to it."

Miller Edd's face stretched to farcical proportions of surprise, considering what had just been proposed. But then Ford caught sight of the cause out of the corner of his eye. Layn was standing. He had stopped shivering and stood with his arms dangling at his sides, as if he hadn't a care in the world and merely waited for the others to get underway.

"Are you well, my friend?" asked Will as he reached out a hand to steady Layn should the need arise.

"Fine. Fine. Fine," Layn replied with a far-off look which said nothing was wrong and nothing much mattered.

"Fine then," said Ford quite confused, but pleased all the same. "Follow me."

Getting started proved difficult. Either way, east or west along the shore, meant climbing over rocks and knee-deep foot-snagging brush. No consideration was made to enter the forest. The moonlight did not penetrate the full boughs of the evergreens. Fear of the dark worked like a shield that they were unwilling to breach without necessity. Ford led the way, crashing through a bayberry bush and stumbling to his hands and knees. Wisps of cordgrass brushed his cheeks and he was none the wiser. His skin might have been lashed by brambles and he wouldn't have noticed for the little feeling he had left in his face.

After climbing over some bare rocks, he halted with one foot trampling a yearling staghorn sumac. Someone behind him had shouted something lost to the waves and the Manerd tugged on the back of his tunic. Ford reluctantly hobbled back around to see what was the matter. Back by the white boulder, Layn was stripping off his shirt and wading into the water. The brush caught their feet every step of the way as they ran back to him. By the time they reached the spot where Layn had entered the water, he was already up to his neck in the sea. No amount of shouting attracted his attention. A wave washed over his head. When it past, his head popped back up, but only briefly. The next wave covered him. They scanned the surface and called out, but he did not reappear.

"He kept saying something about a baby," said Miller Edd shaking his head. "*We gotta get the baby.*"

Ford mounted the boulder to shout and see what he might. Partially submerged rocks kicked up the sea. Floating logs and pieces of the skiff masqueraded as heads and arms. The cry of Layn's name died in the crashing waves.

"Nothing," Ford said to the questioning faces greeting him when he finally climbed down again.

Utterly defeated, stunned by the disturbing loss, and standing almost exactly where they had been when they started off, the dejected group slumped on the ground to pray for Layn's soul. They wrapped their arms about themselves and took to violently shivering once again. Layn was well liked, and they would have grieved with all their hearts, but their own precarious situation turned thoughts inward for most.

Ford's will to go on was slipping from him. He didn't have it in him to rally them again. Exhaustion, the cold, and now this sadness was too much. The worst of it was knowing he had let these people down. He couldn't even raise his eyes to meet theirs. His bowed head flopped from one side to the other with nothing but knees and feet visible. Something was amiss. One of them was standing. Ford lifted his head and saw that it was Will. The priest looked down on them all. Ford couldn't tell the man's thoughts by his face, which displayed no outward emotion. At least, not at first. But then the slimmest of smiles slowly lifted his lips. He knelt with them and grabbed up the hands of his neighbors.

"Take one another by the hand. Palms to palms," he instructed. The others came out of their lethargy and despair as if waking from a deep sleep. They didn't understand what was going on. They simply obeyed. Ford tried in vain to pry open Wallard's clenched fist. The man couldn't move of his own free will. "No matter. Pull back your sleeve and his. Now lock arms and take him by the wrist. That is well."

For what seemed a lifetime, they remained seated holding hands and saying nothing. Little else was heard besides the chattering of teeth. Ford felt his body seizing up just as Wallard collapsed onto one side.

"Do not let go of him!" The priest's fervent tone threw a jolt into Ford's arm, making it lock with his neighbor's. The bond held even as Ford fell to one side, his head coming to rest on Wallard's back. The shaking that had overcome them both receded. A strange tingling spread over Ford's skin and a relaxing calm radiated from his mind to his body and out to his farthest extremities. He could not have put it into words if he tried, but he felt with an inexplicable certainty that he was being enveloped by a reawakening of the spirit.

Ford sat up and Wallard soon followed. Miller Edd and the Manerd were already sitting upright and looking far more alert. Everyone felt refreshed. Only Will's head remained down and his eyes closed.

"Is all well, Father Willem?" asked Wallard.

"I think he's praying," said Miller Edd.

Will's eyes flickered open and his head lifted. "Yes, I was bidding our brother Layn farewell."

"We should be off," said Ford.

"I am ready."

The rocks and knee-high brush proved just as much of an obstacle as it had before, but their new vigor saw them through. They put the worst of the tangling undergrowth behind them and dipped down to a length of sand exposed by the low tide. Ford did not feel warmed throughout his entire body. The tips of his ears and fingers felt like they'd never be warm again. But whatever the priest had done had greatly reduced his shivering. As he walked with the others along the beach, he wondered about the power of "prayer magic," as he called it. Not many possessed it. He doubted any of the other holy men imprisoned on the island had the gift. Then again, he had never suspected Will of having it. The man kept his secrets, that was certain. Ford caught glimpses of him now and then while they walked, and the thought occurred to him that any horse would be proud to own such a long face and prominent snout. Ah, but perhaps he was being too harsh. Maybe he'd been too harsh all around when it came to the priest. Harboring ill will against others for any length of time didn't set well with him.

As they trekked along, the curve of the land put Polecat Island out of sight behind them. None of them noticed the shadowy landmass disappear. All of them had an eye for the future and their eagerness quickened their pace. When the beach ended, they crawled up through the steep, flora-cloaked rocky bank and skirted the trees until a new beach reappeared. Occasionally the keener eyes among them spotted what they took for another island across the water. They would all stop and stare at it trying to determine how far away it might be and how large. Whether island or mainland, whether near or far, none could tell. Moonlight made it difficult to gauge distance without decent perspective.

"Stop! Stop," shouted Miller Edd from well behind the group. After trailing for some time, he finally felt he could go no farther. The others walked back to where he stood bent over with his hands on his knees. "I need a drink or I'm gonna die."

"No water. No food. Let's go," said Ford. It came out too brusque and he knew it, but he was annoyed with his friend. Miller Edd knew that those tasked with providing the provisions hadn't made it to the boat. Perhaps the escape should have been called off then and there, but they'd made the attempt and had to live with the consequences. Repeatedly bringing it up only made everyone feel more miserable. They were all hungry and thirsty, and there was little to be done about it. "Maybe we'll find something," Ford said to soften his gruff reply.

"There ain't nothing," griped Miller Edd. It was true, not even a rivulet whispering through the undergrowth had been found.

"When the sun comes up, we'll find something," said Ford, trying to ignore his friend's unhelpful pessimism.

"We may not have long to wait," said Will. The moonlight had gradually faded, leaving behind a dull, gloomy sky. "I believe dawn is upon us."

The tide moved in and covered the sandy beaches. Picking their way through the brushy high bank in the muddled light slowed them to a snail's pace. Ford led them and was the first to spot a long stretch of land ahead like a peninsula or perhaps the arm of a bay.

"Here's something more like it!" he said. The find excited him, because such a land formation held possibility. It might be the sign of a fresh water estuary from which they could quench their thirst. Throwing caution to the wind, he plunged into the forest to cut across a long thin strip of land which would have taken them the better part of an hour to skirt, rather than bypassing it through the trees. Coming out the other side with daylight rapidly brightening their world, they found a thin cove, no fresh water, and another long peninsula ahead. Ford emerged first from the trees on the other side of the second arm, took in the panoply of the land and water before him, and fell heavily against an enormous red cedar.

"That ain't what I think it is, is it?" asked Miller Edd, the last to join the group, who gathered about Ford holding their heads in their hands or staring dumbstruck across the water. From the sea before them poked the treacherous rocks which had destroyed the skiff and beyond that watery battlefield sat the gray and ill-defined, though dishearteningly familiar outline of Polecat Island. Forbidden Island was indeed an island. Ford dropped to his knees. The incredibly thick vegetation that had tripped them up all through the night padded his fall, but he could have split open both knees and not have noticed, such was the disbelief that numbed him to the core.

"There's the rock I stood upon last night," said Will looking at a huge boulder away down the shore. In the light of day, it was more of a gray hue than the brilliant white it appeared the previous night in the moonlight, but clearly this was the same rock. With all doubt removed, a weighty anchor of despair began dragging down Ford's heart.

"I'm sorry. I led you on a fool's errand," he said over his shoulder to the others standing behind him. He wished one of them had an ax with which to behead him. Certainly, they must want to, he assumed. If they stoned him to death or tied him hand to foot and threw him into the sea, he wouldn't have blamed them, and probably wouldn't have struggled. But they said nothing in reply, only stared over the water, shoulders sagging and heads drooping.

Ford had nothing left to give, no way of making things better, and no grand idea to continue the escape. Someone laid a hand on his shoulder from behind. From his periphery he saw Will's long, white fingers. Of course, it had to be the priest. He almost shook it off. He wasn't in the mood for his pity.

"Look," said Will. "See, there upon the rock?" A kind of hope buoyed his words and made Ford follow his finger to the tall, skiff-wrecking rock. Perched atop the rock like a giant seagull was a distinctly human form.

"The woman!" shouted Wallard. "She lives!"

The woman who had accompanied them in the skiff had survived the entire night upon the rock. When the tiny boat neared its doom, she was in the bow and saw what was coming. At impact, she leapt upon the rock and scrambled on top of it, avoiding the cold water and hypothermia others had succumbed to. Ford and his companions leapt up and down with the pleasure of finding one of their own still alive. They set about scheming ways of retrieving her. Though nothing sprang to mind immediately, it did not dampen their revived spirits.

"We'll find a way!" Ford shouted in his excitement as he began looking around at the ground, as if he might find something lying about which would help get the woman off the rock. It warmed Will to see Ford's big grin as he bound this way and that. He marveled at the elevating effects of good tidings.

"What's that?" asked Wallard looking out to sea. Something low in the water over a mile away emerged from the side of Polecat Island and slid out to sea.

"One of them boats," muttered Miller Edd. He would have spit if he had it in him. A longboat filled with a patrol of guardsmen rowed swiftly over the waves. The dangerous shoals, which seemed to take Ford and the others a daring age to overcome, were spanned by the longboat in a few blinks of the eye. They watched, dazed and despondent, as it swooped up to the tall rock and plucked the woman from it as easily as picking an autumn apple.

"We should conceal ourselves," said Will in the same untroubled tone he seemed to possess no matter the occasion. The patrol boat's oars plunged into the water and its prow turned toward them.

"Into the woods!" Ford commanded, pushing and pulling his companions away from the shore. In their haste, they stumbled through bushes and tripped over rocks. Ford was sure they must have been spotted by the patrol, but he kept everyone's heads down as much as possible and got them into the trees as quickly as he could. This was a reality he understood, a mode of survival he had experience in, and he led with confidence.

Once beyond the shoreline, the underbrush died away and the forest of tall evergreens took over, creating a canopy which darkened almost the entire interior of the island. Here the land plateaued, occasionally dipping into hollows in some places. The crashing waves receded, leaving a sinister tranquility among the shadows. Squelching and slurping sounds, like those from the salivating mouth of some muck-dwelling monster, brought them to an immediate standstill. They waited without a move, aside from their thumping chests, all of them held by a fear-bred stasis evoked by legends and fairytales. Some fully believed the tales, believed them to be absolutely true. Time seemed to stop. No more wet gulping and sucking sounds were heard. Ford could take no more of this standing around, frozen by terror of the unknown. He stepped forward, a squelching step into a pool of standing water. Numerous pools of melted snow from the winter thaw, difficult to see in the dim light, had collected upon the ground before them. How long the pools had stood there and how dirty the water might be, none of them knew, but all of them instantly dropped down on their hands and knees to lap and suck up what they could.

"Ah, that's a mercy," said Miller Edd after drinking his fill and sitting with his back against the nearest tree. The water did them all a world of good. After a short rest they felt more alive and alert, and were even willing to follow Ford deeper into the forest. None knew how aggressive the patrol would be in tracking prisoners. This was all new territory. So, they zig-zagged between the trees, while hiking mostly parallel to the shoreline, never actually piercing the heart of the island. The sun rose through the hours, blossoming into a clear day everywhere else but Forbidden's inky interior.

By noon, three patrols had been spotted circumnavigating the island just offshore. They never left the safety of their boats. Sitting at the edge of the trees on the north side of the island, Ford and his companions caught the tail end of the third patrol as it slipped out of sight on a heading for Polecat.

"They'll keep after us," said Wallard, voicing the consensus.

"Maybe we could make one of them islands," said Ford, pointing across the water from where they sat together on a lofty promontory that gave them a wide panoramic of the sea to the north, a waving landscape dotted by small islands. None seemed particularly promising. A large mass stretched upon the far horizon, but without a boat or the means to make one, it might as well have been on the far side of the world for all the good it did them.

"We got to find something to eat," said Miller Edd. For another hour and more, they continued to stare out at the horizon with growling complaints rising in their stomachs and distant land denying their dreams. They had all searched, but foraging for food proved fruitless. The year was still young, far too early for wild berries and the like. A few edible roots were dug up, but little else. While walking just within the trees on the south side of the island with their heads down in hopes of spotting a mushroom or early-sprouting wild greens, Ford felt a tug on his sleeve. It was the Manerd and he was pointing to a ship passing swiftly over the sea toward Polecat Island. Full sails billowed from a slim, two masted vessel riding high in the water. They wondered, entirely among themselves, how many new prisoners it held. The thought was depressing and most soon returned to foraging rather than staring out to sea.

Very little exploration of the interior had actually taken place. Aside from the thick forest, this island seemed much like the one they'd left: a few sloping hills; the occasional outcropping; a glen which quickly turned boggy, then swampy on its far side before the ground rose up and the evergreens took over once more. When the sun went down, they found a dry hollow and built a shelter of spruce, fir and larch limbs stacked and layered under a cedar. This kept the wind at bay, but not the cold. They lay snuggly side by side for warmth as they did in the barracks. Miller Edd shivered regardless. His nose had been blocked when he awoke that morning. Now he had the sniffles and they were increasing to an annoying rate. Ford's hunger cut his patience to the quick.

"Why don't you use some of your prayer magic and warm us up again?" he said to Will, who sat two bodies away clutching his own knees gathered in close to his chest. Will looked surprised and took his time in answering, Ford assumed because he was insulted. After all, the insinuation was that the priest was holding back. Why, Ford had no idea, so he wanted the question to sting. At least a little. He didn't want to push the man too far, not when they needed his help. However, a little prodding seemed in order.

"I'm not the master of my abilities," Will finally said. A touch of humiliation deadened his voice a trifle. Only those intimate with him would have caught it.

"What you mean, you can't do it whenever?"

"Precisely. Some can, but not I. Not yet. Perhaps one day. Maybe never."

"You did it like nothing last night," said Wallard in a coaxing manner. Like Ford, he too thought a little persuading might induce the priest to act on their behalf.

"I felt the presence within me," Will said with a shrug. "The need was dire. Perhaps that's to do with it." He shrugged again. "It hasn't happened often. For some it never happens, no matter the extent of their devotions. For some it comes about but once." Ford wasn't convinced, but he was still listening. "When I was a boy, my mother was struck down. A malady." The heads of all were now turned Will's way. "She suffered greatly and it seemed no one could save her. On her deathbed something came over me. I reached out, touched her here." He placed a palm tenderly over the heart of the man next to him. A tingling sensation spread throughout Wallard's body and sent blood rushing to his cheeks. "And within the hour she rose of her own accord." The listeners smiled at this story. A happy ending pleased them. "The next morning, my father's father took me to Cupladrach, two oaks upon a precipice, a place of great significance where I come from. Between the trees he laid me down upon a broad rock placed there for rituals. Quite flat. He meant to strike off my head with an ax."

"To know if you had the gift or not," said Miller Edd.

"Precisely. If I had the true gift of the gods, they would surely save me. If I did not, I was demon spawn or a changeling and good riddance to me. This was his reasoning."

"Did he?" asked Ford and then shook his head violently to erase the question. "I mean, what happened?"

"My father stopped him and sent me away, where I was to live amongst others who might help my gift flourish. I suppose he hoped I might make my fortune as some lord's healer. I believe he envisioned our family rising in the world through me, but it was not to be. I was admitted into the Order of the Sud a Waed and languished with the brotherhood for years without fruition, never acquiring control over the power to heal." Will felt he had gone on too long. He didn't like talking about himself.

The others now understood that keeping warm was entirely up to them. They wrapped their arms around themselves tighter. Miller Edd went back to his distracted snuffling. Ford remained silent, lying on his side thinking things over until he eventually said, "But you *did* do it last night."

"Yes. And it was the second time in the past year."

"I don't understand. You said—" began Wallard.

"Don't you recall, Ford Barlow?" said Will. The interruption and cagey edge to his voice was something none of them had seen or heard in the priest before. The group sat up a little straighter and paid more attention.

"I? No," said Ford, confusedly casting his mind over a vast blank slate.

"The man you nearly beat to death?" Will said with an incredulous smile. Even then Ford couldn't be sure who he meant. He'd been in countless fights, some of which ended in near death. "The neighbor of our friend Elle, who would often, I'm sad to say, beat his wife."

"Ah," said Ford when that night of hazy memory flashed back to him. He had been drunk and enraged by the world's inequities. Elle was allowing him to use her room when she wasn't there. Will lived across the hall. Next door was a pair of quarrelsome foreigners. Ford had no idea what they fought over, but something in him snapped when he heard the loud slap of skin upon skin and the woman's cry. He took out his frustrations upon the vile Dadha wifebeater. That bloodied head and limp body lying at his feet took on a more vivid clarity in Ford's memory.

"It was long overdue," said Will. "I am ashamed I hadn't done the same and sooner."

"His wife screamed at me something awful."

"She might have feared your intent."

"I only meant to help."

Will shrugged and said, "Good intentions are sometimes misunderstood."

Ford thought about the incident a while longer, sorting the vague recollections in his mind before saying, "But what has that to do with now?"

"I saved his life," said Will, never taking his eyes from Ford. The flare of anger was not what he expected to see. Hurrying on he said, "You had done the right thing and if that man had died, they would have tried and hanged you for it. It all played out in my mind instantly right then. I saw no justice in such an outcome and a great sorrow swept over me. I felt…" He stopped short of describing the exhilarating, otherworldliness which overcame him in these moments. It seemed too personal to put into words. "I felt the magic, as you say. I felt it return to me and I healed his wounds. It is a shame."

"A shame?" asked Miller Edd through a congested nose.

"Yes. Likely that monster is still tormenting his wife to this day." His listeners nodded. A bad apple never regains its sweetness.

Ford went quiet and his agitation subsided. Something in what Will had said gnawed at him and he was trying to work out just what it was. Nuanced interactions were devilish riddles to him, but he finally latched on to what he thought might be an answer and said, "You did it for me? You saved that man, 'cause you didn't wanna see me hung and so it wasn't you who turned me in and got me locked up in the Hold," said Ford, referring to Stanrocc Hold, the keep turned prison in Port Morton.

"No. Not I," said Will shaking his head.

Ford knew he could be wrong at times, but he had been as wrong as could be about this man's motives and actions. All this time he had assumed the worst about him and even sought revenge for a perceived wrong. He was glad he hadn't acted upon his misperceptions.

Will kept his head bowed and his eyes closed. What he had to say next was highly personal. He did his best to maintain his composure, but he couldn't help his face from flushing and was glad for the covering darkness.

"I believe *you*, Ford Barlow, may be the key to my gift. Or I should say, *a* key to understanding my gift. I can't explain it any better. I don't fully understand it myself, but something about your noble actions brought it out in me." Now Ford was the one reddening.

"Is that why you're always about? Why you joined our barracks instead of the priests'?" asked Miller Edd. He snorted at a thought that struck him funny and wiped away mucus dripping from his nose. "Is that why you come on this little holiday of ours, to be with our Ford?"

"Shut your hole, Edd," said Ford. His friend's prodding jest annoyed him, but more to the point, the truth spoken so plainly put an awkward taint upon a matter of serious import. Ford had a hundred and one questions, but before he could ask one of them, Will answered Miller Edd.

"The simple things in life are what matter. Laughter. Happiness. Without freedom there is no true laughter, no true happiness." His measured speech grew in confidence and conviction. "Imprisonment represses the soul. Manifesting one's power over another is repugnant. Freedom is the natural state of being. That is why I am here."

No one else spoke. They sat pondering what had been said. Ford had never heard his own ideals expressed so well. Life and the desire to live it freely surged through him like little lightning strikes that made his body twitch with pleasure. An urge welled within him to leap into the water and swim for home.

"What's that sound?" said Wallard.

"What sound?" said Miller Edd, blowing his nose into his sleeve. "I can't hear nothing."

"Shhh!"

They sat quietly listening and expecting something awful. Dread of the night, bred into them since childhood, conjured nascent fears. The tales of Forbidden Island's horrors, fed to them by Polecat officials, stoked their anxiety. Expectation of being set upon by a patrol amplified every little crack of a twig or rustle of leaves. But the footsteps and shouts of command from Polecat guards did not come. Instead, they heard a strange call through the trees.

Hoo! Hoo!

"That's an owl," said Ford.

"Ain't you never heard an owl before?" said Miller Edd digging his elbow into Wallard's side as if ribbing an old friend. They could not be said to be friends in any respect, but Miller Edd's relief needed the outlet and Wallard was too ashamed to complain.

"No, sorry. I never have. Sorry all."

Much relieved, they nodded off to the sounds of hooting from what they dubbed "Wallard's Owl." Ford awoke an hour later, fairly sure he hadn't actually been asleep, to the others talking and Miller Edd shaking him.

"What's it..." Ford began in a slur, then stopped to gather his wits. "What's going on?"

"The owl's back," said Miller Edd.

"So?"

"It's very close," said Wallard.

"So?"

"Priest says they's two of 'em," said Miller Edd.

"So?"

"Listen," said Wallard. They waited and listened. Nothing happened. Ford laid back down to sleep.

Hoo! Hoo!

Hoo! Hoo!

The calls were quite close and there were two of them. Ford sat up, put a hand to one ear and waited. He had to do his due diligence by these men who he was responsible for, though what good eavesdropping on a pair of birds would do he hadn't the foggiest notion.

Hoo! Hoo!

Hoo! Hoo!

The calls were more distinct now and variations became clear. There was the usual intonation of most birds, such as the rise in pitch to warn of some perceived threat, but the calls also had the cadence of human speech. Clearly whatever creatures were making these noises were not human, but what they could be was beyond the guess of any of the listeners. The eerie trill that accompanied every other call was not like any owl call Ford had ever heard. Where each *hoo* at a distance seemed to die away and end as naturally as any owl's *hoot*, now at this closer range it was apparent that they actually dragged on in a prolonged, throaty kind of speech almost too low to hear. The response came with its own variations, creating a lyrical discourse disconcerting to listeners sitting in the dark undefended. Any lingering bravado fled the escapees when the two callers moved through the forest to points on either side of them.

"They're surrounding us." Wallard's whisper died off in a tremulous laugh.

Ford tried to convince himself that they were only birds, and had nearly succeeded by the time the calls had stopped. Moment after moment passed in taut silence aside from a wisp of wind. An hour went by with barely a word passing between them before Miller Edd said, "It weren't nothing." Tension eased. Relieved sighs mixed with the wind blowing through their circle. Eventually they all dropped into a restless slumber for the remainder of the night. Ford woke late with the reminder of failure at the forefront of his thoughts. Except for Miller Edd, the others were up and about. Ford closed his eyes and tried to fall back asleep.

"The Manerd's gone missing," said Miller Edd, still wrapping his arms about himself in the same spot as where he'd spent the night. "Nobody's seen him."

This got Ford to his feet before his legs were fully awake. He began searching the area with the others. They didn't stray far from the spot where they had bedded down. When they called out it wasn't with much gusto for fear of patrols lurking nearby. Suspicions arose within each of them separately that the Manerd had been taken in the night, and each discretely searched for blood or any trace of a struggle. Neither was found.

"We should set out on an island-wide search," suggested Will.

"No need," said Ford as the little man appeared through the trees in the direction of the closest shore. He carried handfuls of snails and mussels scavenged from the shallows.

The Manerd's early morning search for food set the tone for the day. The escapees all but gave up on the idea of building a raft. No vines, grasses or bark on the island was suitable for binding together the few dry logs they did manage to find. Most of the fallen trees were either rotted or so soaked as not to float more than their own weight. Even if they had had more luck, their hunger was becoming too much of a distraction.

"What do you suppose that was last night?" Wallard asked Ford as they crouched behind a patch of laurel just within the tree line along the western end of the island later in the morning while waiting for a patrol boat to row out of sight.

"Don't know for certain, but if I had to guess, I'd say a couple of odd birds I never seen before."

"I suppose it was."

"There's strange things in this world, believe me. We should've come armed, but there was nothing for it." Ford stood up. "The coast is clear. Follow me." The pair slipped down to the water's edge and waded in knee-deep to pick through a patch of seaweed in hopes of finding shellfish. The western tip of Polecat was visible from where they stood. They might have been spotted, but it was quite a distance and besides, hunger overruled the risk. Even raw lobster was sounding good to their empty stomachs. Will's strong advisement against eating the crawling creatures of the sea raw had dampened their spirits. However, Ford's pronouncement that a small fire might be built inland as long as it was shielded from sight and put out long before dawn kept them from sinking into despair and put some bounce in their step. After creating a mound of tiny crabs, clams and more at their camp, Wallard and the Manerd went off in search of flint, Miller Edd stayed behind to collect the driest kindling, while the two strongest swimmers made their way to the south side of the island.

At low tide just before dark, Ford and Will crouched at the edge of the trees while they cautiously scanned the shore of Polecat and the water between the two islands. As anticipated, all work parties and their overseers had headed back to the Pen. And as hoped, the sea was clear of patrols. Ford and Will crept out of hiding and climbed atop the enormous gray boulder to look for wrecks. Specifically, they sought the mast which breeched the surface, which Ford had grabbed ahold of momentarily during their escape. He couldn't recall exactly where it lay, but if it wasn't too far out, they might see about recovering pieces of it. What they needed were its metal fittings. Without metal to beat the flint against, they would have no spark and no fire. Of course, it would be rusted, but Wallard thought they might knock off the rust and find enough useful metal underneath. The possibility of getting a fire started with what they could get their hands on had been his originally.

"There! See," Ford shouted and then remembering where they were, he lowered his voice, though not his enthusiasm. "That's not so far!"

"The water will be very cold," said Will, feeling his body balking at the idea of crawling into the sea for another desperate swim. "If we don't succeed, there will be no fire to warm us."

"If there's no fire, we don't eat." Will bowed to his wisdom and they both began removing clothing. "Good gods, that's colder than a witch's tit," said Ford as they waded out in their smallclothes. It being low tide, they were able to walk far from the shore before the water rose up even to their thighs.

"Hullo!" The hail came from behind them. The Manerd and Wallard were wading through a sea of their own, happily hurdling the bushes and rocks along the high-banked shore and waving their hands over their heads. Their recent contributions to the expedition had infused each with a feeling of self-worth and enlivened their outlook on the whole endeavor.

"Lumpheaded fools," Ford said as he turned about and began waving them down, trying to get them to be less conspicuous. "No sense in them two."

Will refrained from answering and contented himself with watching amusedly as the two men capered along a bank above a short scrap of beach like a couple of halfwits proudly holding aloft pieces of flint they had found. A figure emerged in a crouch from the forest behind them, appearing to be an old man in furs with a bent back, stepping gingerly down the slope sideways. "That's never Edd, is it?" Ford squinted. The light was dimming fast and the brown figure, seen against a backdrop of tree trunks and leafless brush, could have been anyone or anything. Another figure, similar to the first, slipped from behind a large cluster of bushes not far from Wallard. As it did, the first figure began hopping quickly down the slope toward the Manerd, who spun about, let loose a scream and stumbled backwards, tumbling over stones, falling over the edge of the bank, and landing in a heap on the wet sand of the exposed beach. The tapered heads of the two mysterious figures turned toward Wallard, who was staring down at where his companion had fallen. Within feet of him, they lashed out their long, whip-like tails and wrapped the ends about his legs. Wallard cried out as they leapt upon his back and drove fangs into his neck and shoulder. In an instant, he was down on the ground and being dragged by the head back up the slope toward the forest.

Ford and Will leapt waves on their run from the water, past the recovering Manerd, on their way to save Wallard. Ford clambered up the bank and a rock came free in his hand. He clutched it firmly, even as he stumbled to his knees among the boulders and tripped over a thin, fallen tree. Wallard's attackers gripped his body in their jaws, rather than using their almost uselessly small arms, and yanked him up the slope with impressive, backward thrusts of their muscular hindlegs. As they slipped away into the trees, Ford hurled his rock at them. It landed harmlessly in the undergrowth.

"Ford!" It was Miller Edd, weaving through the trees and brush toward them. "What is it? What happened? I heard someone holler!"

"Something got Wallard! Two of them!"

"The guard?"

"No, something! I don't know!"

Will had half his clothes on when he caught up with them and thrust Ford's clothes into his arms. All three looked and listened, but the forest gave up nothing.

"We have to go after them before it's too late," said the priest.

"No, we don't," replied Miller Edd, stepping back from the trees, from them, from the whole idea.

"We're going in," said Ford, pulling his tunic over his head.

"I ain't!"

"Then stay and look after him," Ford said, popping his head through his tunic and jerking it in the direction of the beach, where the Manerd was staggering to his feet and dropping back down onto his knees.

"Wait!" shouted Miller Edd, but Ford and Will had already disappeared into the forest.

Cloud cover and nightfall made it difficult to see much of anything under the trees. And aside from a bird twittering, little could be heard above the crash of waves and Miller Edd calling after them. Ford caught a rustling of leaves, but chalked it up to wind threading through the trees. He and Will fumbled about blindly, clumsily crashing through the undergrowth and creating a din over which it would be impossible to hear Wallard or the creatures who took him. Still, they tromped haphazardly on, heedless of tripping root and lashing branch. Miller Edd and the Manerd ran to keep up.

With no trail to follow, no clues as to which way to go, and no weapons to assist them, the utter impotence of their position struck home. They would stare wide-eyed at the slightest forms taking shape out of the shadows and comprehend nothing. Anything vaguely humanoid threw a scare into them.

When a lumpy, mounded amalgamation of what appeared to be heads and bodies clumped together on the ground coalesced before them, they were afraid they had found what they had come for. Hearing faint snorts and slurps, they froze or ducked behind trees. Ford was the first to overcome the shock. He crept forward with the others following just behind. Together they snuck up on what turned out to be a huge rotted stump of a large fallen tree. Half of its roots had come loose and were splayed in the air, creating the corporeal illusion.

"It ain't nothing but an old tree!" Miller Edd blurted out in his relief.

A wild bustle of abrupt grunts and a flurry of thumping footsteps burst from behind the clump of earth and root. Ford rounded on the stump mound in time to see the dark forms of two humped figures hopping into the trees beyond. He leapt over the horizontal trunk and fell to his knees. A patch of moonlight before him outlined in gory detail the body of Wallard.

"Is he alive?" asked Miller Edd, bringing up the rear of the group rounding the massive stump. Will dropped down beside Ford and laid his hands upon Wallard's body.

"Heal him," Ford commanded.

Will's hands moved from Wallard's bowels to his neck. He shook his head. "It's beyond me."

"Do *something!*"

"There's nothing I can do. He's dead."

They gathered about the body, hands to their heads or stomachs, feeling useless. Ford began a prayer. As if in answer, a wailing cry emanated from within the trees ahead, followed soon after by the horrible calls of the night before. *Hoo! Hoo!* One voice sang in tones of woeful misery. The other added to it an aggrieved frustration, a growling call that seemed to beg, "*How? How?*" Soon they were both echoing one another in an agitated frenzy.

"We gotta get outta here," said Miller Edd backing away.

"We're not leaving him here to be a meal for those things," Ford shouted at him, but his friend had already fled back the way they had come with the Manerd on his heels. Will remained behind to help Ford drag Wallard away. Smears of blood and gore made the body slippery. They found their own hands had grown clammy and could not hold his wrists and ankles long without slipping. They wrapped what was left of his torn clothes about his torso and shoulders and pulled him backwards out of the forest.

All the while, the calls of the creatures echoed between the trees. Tonight's catch could easily sustain this mated pair through the summer and they weren't about to let it be snatched away. They stalked through the forest side by side, murmuring reassurance and threat to keep one another in line. As they gradually separated to take in more ground, they began calling out information about themselves and their prey. *No sightings, only smell. Straight ahead to the salty water.* Each step of their wide padded feet pressed with care upon the pine needle-blanketed forest floor, so that their ears did not miss any of the noisy beings' barking talk. The male spotted their quarry first and warned his mate by a *hoo* filled with a quivering excitement. One of the hairless beings, a tall one hovered by their stolen catch. The others fled in the female creature's direction. *Let them go. Surround the tall one. Attack as before.* The male stalked the tall hairless being out in the open. The female slipped from bush to bush from behind. It didn't work. The tall being heard the female and turned toward her. The male rushed forward to leap upon its back and strike the base of the neck. Before the final bounding hop, another of the hairless ones sprung out from behind a boulder just to the left with something raised above its head.

The male creature cried out in surprise and warning when Ford jumped from behind the boulder swinging a thick branch. The improvised club crashed against the side of the creature's head, knocking it to the ground. But the branch broke in half, leaving Ford holding a splintered end. The creature writhed on the ground, never losing consciousness. While it flailed wildly to regain its footing, Ford leapt upon it, driving the jagged end of the branch into its neck. The thick fur covering its body kept the splinters from puncturing deep enough to deliver a death blow. The creature whipped its strong tail around and caught Ford about the neck, pulling him away to free up one of its hindlegs to gut him with clawed toes. That was the moment Will rose up from behind and brought a rock down upon its head, ending its life.

Not sure what to do, the female turned her snout from Ford to Will. The scent of fresh blood filled the air and emboldened her, but she never attacked alone and never against more than one prey capable of fighting back. She let out a hiss seldom heard, which spoke of hatred, regret, loss, and longing. Then she fled into the forest.

At dawn the following morning, a longboat pulled out from the beach at New Morgan, rounded the island, and cut through the choppy waters between Polecat and Forbidden Islands. The guard keeping an eye on their heading from the stern shouted a command and pointed straight ahead. On the shore of Forbidden Island, four ragged figures sat shivering upon the rocks next to the enormous gray boulder. The rowers pulled harder.

"Sit down!" commanded the guard in the bow, but Rhod could not be restrained by mere words at a time like this.

"Hullo! Hullo!" he cried as he leapt about in the boat with joy at seeing friends whom he thought were lost to him forever. "There! Run it ashore there!" His eyes had not deceived him. As rough as they looked, it was indeed Ford, Miller Edd, and the priest who had married him to Moll, not to mention one of those Manerds.

The four fugitives barely moved but for the shaking of their bodies in the cold morning air. They didn't want to be captured, but then again, they didn't want to be on this island any longer with no fire, no food, and the gods only knew how many more of those hopping, fanged beasts out there. So, they sat on the shore and waited for the inevitable to come for them. None waved, none smiled. Ford squinted in confusion at seeing his friend jumping in the boat. This was not what he had expected.

"It's over," shouted Rhod, slapping at the hands of the rowers attempting to settle him before the boat overturned. Finally, they got hold of his wrists and yanked him down. From the bottom of the boat, Rhod sang out his glee at the top of his lungs. "Middlefield has returned! We are free!"

Chapter 8
Sails Set to the Sky

The *Fida Mal*, the sluggish merchant ship taking Ford and the rest of the political prisoners from Polecat Island back to Aelwyd, settled into a regular rhythm as it sailed into the vast Plasser Sea. Once Ford stopped vomiting, he began enjoying the voyage, especially the fresh salty air, the gulls soaring serenely overhead, and the feeling of being truly alive evoked by the ever-undulating ocean.

"Having a piss whenever you please is awful nice," he said to Rhod and Moll upon his return from the ship's head. They both gave pleasant murmurs of assent and went back to nuzzling one another's necks.

The three of them, along with Cadogan, Will, some of the artisans, the remaining priests, and a few of the Manerds had caught this second ship back home. The first ship to arrive with news of the Middlefield victory, *Awyr's Blessing* was a speedy, square-rigged, knarr-like vessel that beat the *Fida Mal* to the island by days even though they set sail from Port Morton within twenty-four hours of one another. Space in the *Awyr's Blessing* being limited, only the minor lords and the most important of the priests and artisans could return upon it. Cadogan declined, deciding to stay behind and assist the transition of the new Warden of the Island appointee. Iarl Middlefield greatly appreciated those who had defended her retreat when she was deposed and marked their return in her orders as a high priority, so the freed-up berth in the *Awyr's Blessing* was given to Dillon Baw, he being on hand at the time of the ship's departure.

Ford was immensely happy for his friend and not at all sad to leave behind the likes of Hayward, Dubell and a few others who had made life on Polecat miserable. Sadness he reserved for his goodbyes with Miller Edd, who would be staying on the island to serve out his sentence for continually breaking weights and measures laws.

Of course, Ford would have preferred returning on a swift Aelwydian ship heading directly home, rather than this foreigner's vessel setting out on a trading voyage that would take them eastwards, somewhat to the south and then back west, hitting numerous ports before returning to the Aelwyd mainland. Ironically, their last port-of-call was set for Morgan, the town west of Port Morton that founded New Morgan on Polecat Island as a place to exile their undesirables. It was the previous Iarls of Port Morton who bought the island after realizing its potential as a stopover along overseas trade routes. The village and harbor were being expanded to be more serviceable for larger merchant vessels. As important as it was to the Iarl to have her loyal subjects returned to her, after a long drought and a revolt, Port Morton needed to replenish the city coffers with trade.

"Bevan Underwall, if you don't keep your hands to yourself, I'll hammer one of these into your skull," said a sailor with flaming red hair playing a game with carpenter's nails on the deck with his companions. "After I shove it up your arse!"

Despite such outbursts, the crew of the *Fida Mal* were a happy lot. They hailed from various and sundry ports across the known world. Languages and customs differed vastly, but somehow, they all combined into a single floating nation populated by bodies white, brown and black. And with no mandated standard but to keep pants short or hemmed at the ankles to prevent tripping, their broadly varied clothing made the *Fida Mal* look like a gathering of flags and banners on a battlefield. Tattoos, piercings, gold teeth, no teeth, and a tendency to go shoeless provided some similarity among them. Also, most carried a prized feather from the whero bird, which was woven into braids and belts or tucked into sashes. Red as fresh blood and soft as a kitten's fur, it was said to prevent falling or at least slow a fall enough to survive the impact. Since no one on this voyage had yet died from a fall on the *Fida Mal*, the feather's magical properties were as good as proven.

"See there! That's why I was a nudgin' it back," exclaimed Bevan Underwall with an imploring look to all in the tight circle of sailors. "Because Prota there, that cheatin' shit-swillin' swine, knocks 'em intentional like!"

Prota Corekci, a bronze Bzinsani man with a melon-round skull shaved all but for a topknot, smiled back at Underwall as if he had just received a compliment. He stuttered out a confused laugh to disguise the fact that he understood well enough the words spat at him. With muscles hardened by years of pulling on ropes and oars, he could have pummeled the smaller Underwall into a fine powder, but preferred to keep the peace. A slur such as that could be overlooked since Underwall lost so frequently. On the whole, they got on with one another. Their jovial nature was helped along by a captain, who allowed them generous leeway when it came to discipline. As long as they did their work promptly and kept their voices down when he was about, Captain Abel Najeem happily let them play.

Najeem was of the Amita people, a southern race occasionally found in Aelwydian trading ports. Stooped and brooding, he had the dark, angular features of his people. In the mornings and late evenings, when sleep clung to him and dragged down his body as he leaned over a rail or clung to a backstay, the man looked not unlike a bronze gargoyle. Like many an Amita before him, he sought to make his fortune in foreign ports. Much scrimping and saving, as well as an old debt handsomely repaid, set him up in his captaincy. However, after suffering lean years under Middlefield rule, Najeem had been enticed and rejuvenated by the Brastersceatt promises of wealth to come. None would know if there was any basis of truth to those promises, for Pennaeth Brastersceatt's reign had come to an end before a year had elapsed. Likely, Najeem would be hauling cargo for a pittance no matter who ruled, but to be doing it again for the Middlefields was nettling.

The captain kept to himself, leaving his passengers in the dark as to how he felt about them.

It didn't matter. Nothing could dampen their festive mood.

Ford rejoiced at being homeward bound on a ship with a crew he deemed good-natured, even if they did keep to their own kind. He watched them play their game with a longing eye, wishing to join in, but receiving no invitation. Even a welcoming smile cast in his direction would have been invitation enough for him to insert himself into their circle. It was not to be. He sighed and turned away, leaning against the ship's side with his elbows propped upon the rail and his broad buttocks jutting into the main deck. Once he tired of the horizon, he let his head droop and watched the sun-sparkling surface of the water flash like diamonds. Soon a cloud swallowed the sun and turned the water gray.

"I…" he began to say to Rhod just as a deep purple shadow emerged from the depths to coast alongside the *Fida Mal*. A body half as wide as the ship loomed near the surface, turning a single, enormous eye directly up at Ford. Before the horrifying image fully registered in his mind, it dove in a smooth arc back down beneath the ship, a bundle of ribbon-like, inky green legs trailed behind like strands of seaweed. Doubting what he had seen, Ford looked to his neighbors to the left and right along the rail, but none had been looking over the side. Rhod and Moll were taken up with gazing into each other's eyes. Ford filled his lungs to bellow an alarm, but a cry from a boy at the mainmast crosstrees cut him short.

"Monster! Larboard! Monster on the larboard side!" came his shrill, semi-hysterical warning. Instant panic. Brynmor the first mate shouted orders that brought about the serving out of pikes, cutlasses, hooks, and belaying pins to all hands and any passengers on deck. The most daring and curious among them ran to the larboard side to see what they were up against. All eyes were riveted there, especially the more cautious and outright frightened souls. They edged away or pretended occupation on the far side, but would not take their eyes from the larboard side. However, it was on starboard side where tentacles crept aboard and felt about, wrapping around rails and lines, yanking any loose items overboard. One such loose item was Awoodi Kara Weynhoolka, a young Dadhan sailor without the strength to stop the tentacle wrapped about his ankle from jerking him off his feet and into the water before he could shout for help. The rest of the tentacles slipped back into the sea without being spotted. Eventually, when no horde of sea creatures crawled up the larboard side to attack, everyone relaxed somewhat and the boy was questioned. The captain scoffed at his answer.

"Twas not but a fish! A beastly great fish, maybe, but just a fish," Najeem said loud enough for all to hear. When Ford corroborated the boy's story, being the only other person to have laid eyes on the monster, the captain questioned his eyesight and knowledge of the sea, crushing his creditability and thus his evidence. Ford and the boy felt unjustly dismissed, but calm returned to the ship, which was all Najeem cared for.

"Some you see skimming just above the surface, just for a while like," an older sailor said later in the day to a gathering of his mates. Ford sat on the periphery, having been accepted on the fringe of their close-knit fraternity for having backed up the story of one of their own. These were men who believed wholeheartedly in monsters, even though the settled lands of humans seldom encountered them these days. The ocean was a different beast all its own. They had spent enough time upon it to see some of the weird things of the world with their own eyes.

"And some I seen spit in the air!" said a tired and leathery rigger with tormented eyes and more hair growing from his ears and nose than atop his head.

"They hide in coves and sneak out to snatch you up. Pulling boats under like they was nothing," put in Ward Bywell the long in the tooth boatswain with bags upon bags under his eyes and a mouth which usually hung open in a dark, oval hole. Though a busy man, he adored the supernatural, the stranger the better, and would always make time for a tale.

The eventual discovery that seaman Weynhoolka was no longer onboard reignited alarm and anxiety. To staunch the fear infesting his ship once more, the captain latched onto a rumor that the sailor had gotten drunk and fallen overboard. Few bought the cover story and this further annoyed the captain.

"Below! All below," he suddenly shouted, having decided to punish the stubbornly scared, while giving the Bryces extra time topside. Three times daily the former Polecat warden and his family were allowed out of confinement to relieve themselves and enjoy some fresh air, unfettered and free to roam the deck as they pleased. The passengers grumbled. They remembered all too well the tighter restrictions and confinement they had undergone during their transportation voyage, not to mention the deprivations they suffered under Bryce at the penal colony.

"Come along, mate," Bywell muttered by Ford's shoulder as he came up beside him to cajole the big man below. "It won't be long and you'll be back up here with us. I'll get you in on the next game, eh?" He hoped to coax Ford along in the same way a drover would persuade the dominant bull into going where he wished, so that the herd would follow without fuss.

The Bryces were nobility and they were rich. In Najeem's eyes, this made them the right kind of nobility, so, naturally he sympathized with their plight and did them all the kindnesses he could. This extended to topside excursions, where they had the main deck to themselves without fear of reprisal from the former prisoners. The Bryces used every last minute of this time to their advantage. While the sailors showed the children around the ship, carrying them into the rigging and telling them stories of far-off lands, Bryce and his wife worked on the captain subtly, but relentlessly. First, they took the measure of the man. Then they plied his more susceptible side with temptations of all the riches he could acquire if he took their counsel and made certain life-altering decisions which would benefit them both.

The weighty pros and cons of these decisions teetertottered wildly in Najeem's agitated mind in the days in which the *Fida Mal* left the Mazlandet Archipelago behind and sailed across the cobalt blue Plasser Sea. A prolonged southerly storm pushed the ship north and a good deal off course, even though nearly every sail was taken in. Brynmor steered clear of his captain. This was just the kind of trouble which would put the man in a foul mood. But surprisingly, Najeem hardly seemed to notice. He was too busy contemplating his options and playing out the probable resolutions of the gamble the Bryces proposed, a gamble that didn't seem so chancy the closer they came to the Meille Coast and the Maa of the Mensen. This land's capitol city, Valtavastad, contained a fluid port that made moving illicit cargo a fluid enterprise. The gods had thrown a detour into Najeem's path in the form of the storm, but he only read this as a sign that he was being given more time to make his decision.

The storm tossed the ship about and kicked off another wave of seasickness among the passengers. They had grown used to the ship's natural roll, as reliable as the rising and setting of the sun, but the wild pitching and strange lurches brought on by a choppy sea sent them all below into the increasingly fetid atmosphere of the lower decks. By the fourth day at sea, the storm and the turmoil it created had passed them by and life aboard ship regained a sense of normalcy. Ford emerged from his swinging hammock feeling recovered after a long, satisfying night's sleep. At the forehatch, his growling yawn and suddenly outstretched limbs surprised and spooked the Bryces as they came down the ladder. They looked him up and down with wide-eyed suspicion and hurried aft with Najeem leading the way.

"Under no guard?" asked the priest Aeddamon Born after Ford related what he'd seen to his companions when he met them on deck.

"They might as well been arm in arm, the way they all went right into the captain's cabin together, nattering away like old friends," Ford said.

"I don't like it," said Cadogan. After seeing that Polecat Island was back to running the way it was originally intended, Cadogan felt his next duty was to ensure delivery of the Brastersceatt's people to the Iarl for trial or whatever awaited them back home.

"I thought little of it when first I saw them conversing lightly on deck together with the captain, but now…" put in Will.

"I shall complain to the captain," said Born.

"Shout it any louder and you won't have to," said Rhod, inserting himself into a conversation with his friends after a long absence. Kissing and caressing Moll in secret corners of the ship seemed to him a better way to spend that time. Moll was a perfectly fine person in Ford's opinion, but he missed Rhod, his one true friend on the ship. While he had warmed to Will, they could not be called friends exactly. And though he considered Cadogan a friend of sorts by now, he could not feel entirely comfortable around the man, whose station in life put him in a different world than what Ford was accustomed to. They didn't share the same experiences or interests, and thus had little to talk about. While Ford had not known Rhod for long, the two came from a similar background and had bonded quickly.

"Land!" came a call from above a little before noon.

Vessels approaching the northern Meille Coast had to contend with a stretch of long thin mountainous islands called The Tanden. These tightly packed peaks rose out of the water like immense, jagged plates, a shield-wall for the mainland with no visible end. Never a tree sprouted from their gray, stony cliffs. The *Fida Mal* headed on a long southward passage until the islands grew less vertical, though no more hospitable. An eastward course was set and would be maintained for a score of miles before they began the laborious process of beating back northward to reach the port at Valtavastad.

The arrangement of cabins was different that night. Instead of smaller compartments just below the main deck, the passengers found themselves another deck down in two larger spaces, one fore and the other aft. Here, the air was even more stagnant and unpleasant, but they were assured the accommodations were temporary, and so with little complaint they slung their hammocks side by side and spent an uncomfortable night amid a rising humidity generated by too many bodies jumbled together in tight quarters.

"What is this?"

The question penetrated canvas and drifted into Ford's waking ears. The answer seemed obvious: a cocoon. His entire body was wound up in his hammock. He imagined its all-encompassing embrace must be what the caterpillars experienced before turning into butterflies. Normally, he wouldn't have enjoyed such confinement, but this felt more like a comfortable hug. He began nodding off again, but voices in the dark kept sleep at bay.

"What are they playing at," someone asked, no, demanded.

"Who in all of Dan O'dan is making all that noise?" Ford wanted to know. His fingers pulled down the edge of the hammock and he forced one of his eyes open. Enough light from a hatch above filtered down to illuminate a group amassed by the door. They were beating on it, shouting at it. Ford's unraveled mind reeled itself in as he came to. The door was locked. He sprang from his hammock, strode across the room with quickening steps, threw bodies out of his way, and attacked the door. The wood creaked and bowed, but it wouldn't budge. When Ford gave out, the others went back to beating on it and shouting at the grated hatch in the deck above the door, their only source of light. An echoing howl came from the passengers trapped aft. The stem-to-stern din finally drew stamping feet to the hatch.

"Shut your holes!" shouted a sailor through the grate above their heads. Cold water splashed down upon them, bucket after bucket. Ford and his companions jumped out of the way and cursed them. The sailors laughed. "Keep quiet or you'll get worse!"

Eventually they did quiet down, at least until footsteps neared the hatch or shadows passed over head again. Then they demanded answers. All questions were ignored throughout a day of anger and confusion fueled by thirst and hunger. The overnight relief buckets in the room filled fast with sloshing excrement. As time wore on, they began begging for relief.

The fate of their future sank in as evening set in. Footsteps approached, but few bothered to look up. They had exhausted themselves leaping for the hatch and hoisting one another up to yank in vain at the grate's sturdy oak timbers. Those that did lift their hung heads saw Brynmor the first mate staring down at them, his face a passionless mask. A signal from him and within moments the grate was lifted away. Sailors leaned over the opening to deliver food and water. The open hatchway looked like an opportunity too inviting to pass up. The prisoners leapt at it. Bastien the Manerd scaled Ford like a ladder, stood on his shoulders and took hold of the hatchway frame, only to lose the fingers on his left hand to a cutlass. Half a dozen other blades whipped about and stabbed at the opening.

"Get back," hollered Bywell the boatswain. "Get back or lose your life!"

After that, their rations were thrown down the hatch. Ship's biscuit broke into pieces or rolled into dark corners. Half of the waterskins burst. The prisoners scrambled about on their hands and knees, snatching up whatever they could get their hands on. The sailors laughed and watched until the frenzy died down. Then they dragged the grate back into place.

"If you want those piss pots emptied, next time be a little more courteous," Bywell advised as the cover was drawn over the grate.

That night in his cabin, Captain Najeem and the Bryces made their way through one of the ship's wine casks, though no social lubricant was needed to bolster the celebratory mood. All three were in high spirits. Lady Bryce's eyes sparkled in the hanging lantern light and her delightful, tinkling laughter infused the spaces between their already jubilant conversation. The party atmosphere and rapid talk bordered upon the giddy at times. And why wouldn't it? The Bryces had struck the deal which saved their future, while the captain was happy to have finally made his decision and acted upon it. The previous few days had been surprisingly trying, considering he had been expecting the boredom of a mundane voyage. Now, all of his appetites had come galloping back to him. The vivacious feminine company at his table certainly helped to whet that particular appetite. He might have had her if fates twisted the other way and she was his prisoner for the taking, but she belonged to another. He would have to satiate his hunger elsewhere, and he would. This floating world was his. He would take what he wanted.

In the wee hours of the morning within the cell holding Ford, the prisoners were awoken by the quick sliding of metal and the door bursting open. Lantern light flooded in along with a dozen sailors with blades drawn. They invaded the room like hungry rats let loose in a pantry, slashing their cutlasses and knives at the nearest thing that moved. One of the priests took a fist to the jaw and dropped. Prisoners were prodded into the farthest corners at sword point.

"Back down or I'll run you through!" a sailor shouted at Ford. Ford did not. More blades were trained on him and just when it appeared they would skewer him, the gang of sailors retreated through the door as suddenly as they had entered, and the thick metal bolt on the outside was slammed home. The priest's jaw might have been broken and a number of people had minor cuts, but no one was seriously injured. The incident left everyone wondering what had just happened and why.

"Moll!" Rhod cried in the darkened cell. "They took Moll!" It was true, Moll was no longer among them. The only female had been taken.

"Why? Why?" Rhod shouted at the top of his lungs. By the time the sailors threw another tarp over the hatch to dampen his wailing, his voice had just about given out. But he kept on croaking his questions to the dark, a whisper coursing over the room's eerie silence. "What do they want with her?"

No one had the heart to answer him. No one wanted to think why they had taken the only woman aboard the ship available to them. None of the female prostitutes had been taken off of Polecat. Najeem would have picked any one of them over Moll, whose brawny physique did not particularly recommend her to a man seeking something soft and pliable to make his own for the remainder of the voyage. Eventually the reality of the situation struck Rhod like a hammer to the heart. His soul found new torment and his voice new life. "I'll kill them! I'll kill every last one of them!"

Screams from his failing voice no longer reached much farther than the cabin he was trapped in, however potent the pain. Certainly, they could not be heard in the captain's cabin, where Moll stood before Najeem among finery from around the world. Fearing what this unpleasant looking man wanted from her, she leaned from one foot to the next and vigorously itched at the back of her right thigh. That spot, just below the buttocks, always became enflamed when she was nervous. The motion accidently lifted the hem of her frock to the knee. This flash of skin encouraged the captain, though the calf was more akin to a sow's ham hock than some of the more delicate legs Najeem had seen in his day.

The gripes and groans of age accompanied him out of his padded chair as he stepped from behind a desk covered in navigational tools, maps, and books. Suddenly the room felt much smaller and more stifling to Moll. It wasn't the heavy draperies about the stern windows or the many garish furnishings killing the flow of air which caused the suffocating sense of foreboding to descend upon the atmosphere, but rather the captain's leer which carried with it the looming threat. The man was drunk and aroused. It was now obvious to her: she had been dragged here to satisfy his carnal desire. Najeem shuffled from behind the desk to the bed pressed against one wall. The thick and lumpy mattress was covered in plump pillows with tassels. The bed looked barely large enough for one. Moll was in no mood to see if it could fit two. Rhod was the only man she had known and she wanted to keep it that way.

Najeem brushed a hand across the satin sheet laid over the bed specifically for this encounter. Moll stepped back.

"There is nothing to fear. Come away from the door," he said, trying to smooth out his usual skittering speech, like a rat masquerading as a snake. "Do as I wish and this will be yours." He waved an arm at the cabin. "Be mine and you can stay here in the light and air with good food and wine to drink. I said come away from there! Now!"

Moll threw herself at the door, yanking at the handle and ramming one of her sturdy shoulders into the wood. All in vain. There was no way out. She turned toward him with the dread of the hunted. Her jittery eyes leapt from a pair of chests against a wall to a cabinet holding a stack of glazed plates and a tray of tarnished silverware. Aside from a small dining table that might fit four in a pinch, there was just the desk to put between herself and this lascivious man. He motioned her to him. She stepped around to the far side of the table, ducking a hanging gilded lantern and catching her foot on one of his plush rugs. It would be impossible to avoid him for long in this tightly packed cabin.

"Very well," he said, undoing his belt. "We'll make this quick."

A little after noon that day, the tarp was pulled off of the hatchway over Ford and his trapped companions. They raised their heads and shaded their eyes from the dim light. Sailors lifted the grate and buckets of food and water were exchanged for buckets of excrement. Through a wheezing, painful throat, Rhod asked, "What've you done with my wife?" This made the sailors laugh. They didn't realize he was married to the woman they had abducted for their captain.

"Captain's making her his whore!" said one.

"Been riding her for all she's worth, from what I hear, eh Holloway?" said another with a nudge to his mate. Common sailors, often treated as little better than slave labor, seldom had the opportunity to take out their frustrations on someone stuck on a decidedly lower rung of the social ladder than themselves, so they delighted in the rage they created in this pitiful wretch below them.

Rhod pounded upon the deck and drove his body into the door and walls. The other prisoners feared he might be going mad. They let him release the anger, hoping he would exhaust himself before they attempted to calm him down. But then one of the timbers cracked and the sound excited Ford, who joined his friend in attacking the ship with his feet and fists. It wasn't long before a large party of armed sailors entered and forced the prisoners into chains. This did little to subdue Rhod, who pulled as hard as he could at his fetters and then slammed his chains on the deck repeatedly. His friends held him down, afraid he would hurt himself or draw worse punishment from their jailors. He thrashed about to break free, but was soon spent and could do nothing more than lay curled up, softly sobbing and repeating his wife's name.

A white sun slid toward the western horizon. The day was nearly done and so was the captain of the *Fida Mal*. Najeem stood in the center of the main deck as straight as a rod, wearing a defiant sneer with his chin held high. The comforting hand he held over his left abdomen, a black eye, a split lip and a particularly red nose all told the reason for his petulantly curt mood. "Get in line! Get in line, damn you! Take that man and tie him to the capstan. I'll have the hide off him before the sun sets!"

His snickering crew sobered instantly and formed a line along the rail facing toward the deck. Before them, directly in front of Najeem, Moll stood strapped to the mainmast with her hands bound. She'd been there for hours, wearing nothing but her torn frock. Her body ached all over, but she held her chin up. A few superficial fingernail scratches crisscrossed her cheeks and set jaw. A small amount of blood stained her hands and her hair was as wild as the look in her eye.

"This is your last chance," Najeem muttered to her. He would have preferred to do this privately. The whole affair had been embarrassing. The thrashing this woman had given him would be detrimental to his control of the ship's company. He had to display command. "Will you sub—"

"No!" she screamed. "Rhod! Rhod!"

Najeem gritted his teeth and motioned his boatswain forward with an impatient flick of his finger. The first mate leaned in and spoke in Najeem's ear. No one but they heard what he said, but Brynmor waved a hand in Moll's direction.

"No!" shouted Najeem as he shoved Brynmor away from him. "My mind's made up! You and you," he shouted at the sailors standing guard by Moll. "Throw her over!"

It took three men to get ahold of the struggling Moll and lift her over the larboard rail. The sailors leaned against the side to watch, ostensibly to make sure she didn't cling onto any part of the ship, but mostly for their own amusement. Moll plunged into the cold water, the shock of it shooting through her as if she had been electrocuted. She broke the surface flailing about, with as much desire to fling her body from the frigid sea as to keep from drowning. Some of the sailors gave a wry cheer, and cheered again when a wave dunked her under a second time. None in the crew expected a woman bound at the wrists to last very long, but Moll came back up sputtering with her neck stretched its length. She took in rapid, gasping breaths that might be snatched away at any moment by another wave. Mouths along the ship's rail dropped open when she started paddling away. It was a panicked dog's stroke, but fierce and determined to keep her from being dragged under by waterlogged clothes.

"Back to work," ordered the boatswain as Moll and the ship parted. Some of the sailors had to be pulled away from the side. Such entertainment was hard to come by on a long voyage. Even Bywell lingered at the rail to take one last look at Moll as she headed for the nearest island, a small and mostly barren rock. It would be a long, hard swim in the best of times, never mind being hampered as she was.

Najeem buried his subordinates in unnecessary orders and busy work for the crew, then went to his cabin and brooded over the course of a bottle of wine. Halfway through, he whipped the satin sheet off the bed, sat down on it and immediately got up to look out of one of the stern windows. The woman, still paddling away, was nothing to him. *Nothing.* But this deal he had made with the Bryces absolutely had to pan out for him or he was sunk. The *distant relations* they spoke of, who he had been promised would pay him dearly if the Bryces were delivered safely to them, had to be genuine. If it were a ruse, it wouldn't get them far. No, Bryce was not that stupid. It had to be true. If it wasn't? Well, he smiled to himself, the prisoners would fetch a good price, if not from some slaver, then from the charitable Haunan organization within the city which bought Aelwydians out of slavery, but a lord's ransom was where the fortune lay. Thoughts of the wealth he sailed toward warmed his heart. After Valtavastad he could make for far harbors and ply his trade there.

Not much remained of the bottle by the time his order to wear ship was finally completed. He hadn't moved from the window and was now staring at two craggy islands of The Tanden. The sharp angle of the sun caught a thin, black line barely rising above the surface of the water between them, as if something skimmed over the ocean in a way that would intersect with the ship. Immediately, one of those monsters from the sailors' legends came to mind. Of course, they weren't all fairytale. Whales, for one, were real. The green ridgeback was known to migrate through these waters. That was probably what it was, mused the captain as he lifted the bottle to his lips and cursed when his mouth filled with bitter dregs.

"Ship!" cried the lookout. "Ship to larboard!"

"Where away?" demanded Brynmor.

"West by north!"

"Brynmor's an honest, hard worker," Najeem slurred and mumbled as he half-heard the questions, answers and orders swept down to him upon the wind. He had treated his subordinate shabbily of recent. "I'll make it up to him. Maybe, hmm…a case of those Valtavastad cakes he loves so dear. No, that's Moorby. Perhaps some little trinket then. Or a new cup." He peered with some suspicion at a crack in the bottle that he only just now noticed. With an underhand flip, he tossed it out of a window. "I'll buy a pair or a set even. It's always cheaper than—"

"Captain!" Brynmor shouted as he burst through the cabin door.

"You intrude on my, uh, on my sanctuary without being bitter…bidden?" said Najeem, all goodwill vanishing in an instant. "What is it?"

"The Severn!"

In these waters, the Severn were synonymous with piracy. The Tanden made the practice possible. Perhaps probable. The innumerable islands abounded with excellent nooks where pirates could lay in wait. Valtavastad might have been one of the world's leading ports for trade if not for the uncertainty created by this persistent pestilence. Patrols were made, but these seas were too vast for them to make much difference. Among the pirates, the Severn were considered some of the most feared. As a race, they subsisted on what they could thieve from others. Their ships were few, but they made up for it with an aura of ferocity by packing those ships with their more hideous and war-like cousins the Skala. Rumors spread through vessels like the *Fida Mal* that the Skala fought for the pleasure of killing, carried and spread disease, and sucked the blood out of their victims. Together the Severn and Skala piloted swift ships and used slave-manned galleys to dart out of coves and pounce upon fat and slow merchant ships. Falling prey to them meant slavery on one of their galleys or being sold in some distant port.

Once on the main deck of the *Fida Mal*, Captain Najeem took one look at the ship speeding straight for them and knew its intentions. "To arms!" he cried, setting off a flurry of action. The frenetic shouting and stamping of feet above their heads had the prisoners up on their feet and asking questions in the cells below. They were left in the dark as to the cause of the disturbance until the captain himself came barreling into the cell holding Ford and his companions.

"The ship is beset by the Severn! If they take her, they take you, too! Who will defend her with me?" His plea was edged in panic and desperation. The quivering boy holding up the lantern behind him danced on the brink of flight. Only shock rooted him to his duty. Catching up to his captain at last, Brynmor appeared in the doorway in time to catch these last words. A handful of sailors tumbled into the doorway after him.

"Captain! You cannot think to release—"

"We need every man!"

"But…" Brynmor doubted the logic of releasing and arming a score of embittered men who they had just recently imprisoned for no just cause. To Najeem it made all the sense in the world that the prisoners would want to fight against a common enemy. And if self-preservation wasn't enough, he had another incentive.

"Any man who fights gains his freedom," he said, clenching his fists held out before him, as if to wrench their acquiescence from them. "This I promise!" There was no rallying cheer for the captain's fiery speech, but the prisoners did nod their agreement to the deal or muttered an "aye," and held up their hands when the captain ordered his boatswain to remove their fetters and chains.

"Faster Bywell! And weapons! They cannot fight without weapons!" Najeem wore a nervous smile while complimenting a few of them, such as Ford's obvious strength and the fierce gleam in Rhod's eye. Anything to rally the troops in his time of need. "Brynmor! To the other cabin! Release the others! And serve out the blades, man! Bywell, you slug, give me that key and go help him!" Najeem himself began freeing the remaining shackled prisoners. "Go now, find yourselves a sword! All of you, go!"

Sailors and prisoners alike flooded from the room. Najeem waved them out, then spun about seeking anyone he might have missed in the dark corners. The heavy iron bands of fetters cracked into the crown of his head.

The unexpected blow dropped him to one knee. Rhod gathered up the chain and swung it around again, this time striking the back of the captain's head. Down went Najeem. A third and fourth blow sent blood spurting from his skull.

"Dear gods of death and mercy," Aeddamon Born uttered by the door among the few remaining prisoners.

"Stop! Rhod, stop! He's dead! He's dead," Ford shouted as he ran to Rhod and took the chains away from him.

"I said I'd kill him. I said I'd kill him," Rhod muttered as he fell into Ford's arms and the two slumped to the floor. The light faded away. Someone had made off with the lantern, taken from the boy lying prostrate and insensible by the door.

"What do we do?" Born wondered. Ford looked up at him to answer. Before he knew what was happening, Rhod shot from his arms and flew through the door. Ford began getting up to follow, but fell down again when the ship was rocked by a shattering collision.

"Mother of all that is good!" someone shouted by his ear as Ford stumbled through the door.

"Follow me," the first mate commanded from somewhere aft. Ford found him leading a group of freed prisoners and sailors toward the ladder to the upper decks. There they met Bywell and a party of sailors with their arms full of pikes and cutlasses. Ford joined them and tried to reach through the throng to grab a weapon, any weapon. Clashing metal, stamping feet, random shouts and screams of agony told of the battle raging above their heads. Panicky priests and Manerds fled in search of holes to hide in.

"Sir, I—" started Bywell, but he was cut short by a body flying down the companionway and slamming him into the deck. A Skala warrior, as large as Ford, sprung to his feet with a sabre in one hand and a boarding ax in the other. He pushed back a sallet-styled helmet from his hyper-alert and hungry raider's eyes. The helmet had no visor, but a scarf still kept much of his face hidden. A long tunic of lacquered, overlapping leather rectangles worn on top of layers of padding covered his broad chest. A sleeve pushed back revealed grayish skin, rough and bumpy with moles sprouting coarse, black hairs. Close at hand, a sailor carrying weapons dropped them, save a cutlass, which he drew back. The Skala plunged his ax into the sailor's chest and rammed his sharp, right-angle shoulder into another sailor coming at him from the other side. With legs as sinewy as a stallion's spread for balance, the Skala whipped his sabre from side to side while pivoting upon his paddle-wide feet. The whirling blade kept at bay those around him who hadn't yet fled. But the odds were still a dozen to one and would only get worse, as some of the newly freed prisoners were reaching for the weapons spread across the deck. Seeing he would soon be faced by a troop of armed fighters, the Skala resorted to an old trick, yanking his scarf away from his mouth to reveal his jawless maw. Like all Skala, he lacked a jawbone. In place of it, a flap of skin hung over a small plate-shaped piece of cartilage held by ligament, creating something of a prehensile bottom lip. The top of the mouth was filled with grinding molars, like a cave entrance crowded by rocks. The warrior flashed the whites of his eyes and a ghastly, half-faced grin to create an image so grotesque and terrifying to those opposing him—men who had been frightened from birth by thoughts of this very nightmarish horror—that they fell over backwards trying to get away.

Two more Skala plunged down the companionway and together they chased their fleeing prey along the passage through the middle of the ship. Ford's fingertips brushed a hilt just as the tide of bodies thrust him aft and into the cabin which had been the prisoners' cell. The ways of a fearful man were intimately known to the Skala. They knew just what to do. Following close behind, they shoved the closest and slowest, and slashed at any who turned to face them, but always allowed their prey to funnel themselves into the confined cabin. The cell seemed prepared for their arrival. They slammed shut the door, slid home the bolt, and then howled in celebration at one of the easiest captures they had ever attempted.

Chapter 9
Bay of Riches

The *Fida Mal* looked like a slaughter house. Its usually clean-swept main deck was awash in blood, severed limbs and slashed corpses. Where the concentration of bodies was thickest, Skala warriors oversaw chained work parties of captured *Fida Mal* sailors lifting their fallen comrades and unceremoniously dropping them over the side into the sea. Other captive sailors carried the ship's choicest stores up from the hold, while some busily knotted and spliced the few lines that had been cut in the attack. Everywhere the rattling of chain-linked prisoners filled the air.

A weak-chinned man with the same rough and lumpy gray skin as the Skala, but of a less robust physique, hurried fore and aft and back again, briskly directing the preparation of the ship for sailing. He was the Severn who would be taking over as shipmaster of the captured vessel. Like the Skala, he wore a scarf, but it hung loose and did not cover his tiny bump of a jaw, a bone jaw but quite minimal. His bearskin hat and sealskin jerkin had been stripped off and sat upon the capstan. Sweat stained his tunic. The cool, late evening breeze of this northern climate was still too warm for him and his kind. Handling the prisoners was left to the armored Skala, so Severn such as he were able to work in their shirtsleeves.

Ford damned his luck. Two sea voyages amounted to two unjust imprisonments and two encounters with deadly sea creatures. He was beginning to develop a prejudice against sea travel. When he and those imprisoned with him were led up from below in chains, he searched for any sign of Rhod or Moll, but found none, not even corpses. Eventually he learned what had happened with Moll, and whenever he thought about the two of them, it set well with him to imagine that Rhod had escaped in the confusion and swam to an island with her.

As luck would have it, Cadogan and Will had also survived the attack. Just as Ford reached the main deck, he saw them being transferred over to the Severn ship. The long, narrow-beamed galley appeared as sleek and dangerous as a dagger alongside the rotund *Fida Mal*. The galley's sides were pitted with hook and blade gouges, but otherwise the nameless ship was in good shape. Not being shipbuilders themselves, the Severn and Skala relied on theft to obtain such a fine galley, one which perfectly suited their purpose, unlike the slow merchant ships that were their prey. Once emptied of half the prisoners and Captain Najeem's personal effects, now being divided among the Severn and Skala leaders on the galley, the *Fida Mal* and a small single-mast Severn consort vessel recently joining them set sail for the southern trade routes and ports.

The former crew of the *Fida Mal* watched their ship sailing away with a deep sense of loss. The dejected prisoners being herded onto the galley didn't care for the ship, but did feel a deeper sense of defeat at having sunk even further into captivity. The Skala pushed and shoved them below the main deck to the rowing tier, where haggard slaves, thinly clad or stripped to the waist, sat upon two rows of benches to either side of the ship leaning over their long oars. Skala with whips or a length of chain stood at either end of the ship and commenced walking up and down between the benches to keep an eye on the rowers. Ford and a few other hardy prisoners were pulled out of line and chained to an oar alongside wiry-armed and vacant-eyed galley slaves that looked like they had been born to this backbreaking life. Each newcomer was attached to a partner already familiar with the motions of the oar, so that there was little disturbance in the ship's progress once it got underway.

At first, Ford took the regular rhythm of rowing in stride. It bothered him less than the boredom of being confined and idle. But it wasn't long before the novelty of the repetitive motion wore off, and there appeared to be no end in sight to the monotonous labor. The overseers—still afire from the heat of battle—demanded they row faster until reaching maximum speed. Whips cracked and lengths of chain whirled overhead. Laggards took a lashing. One overseer wore leather gloves knobbed with metal studs which he used to strike slaves he caught resting on their oars. One particular repeat offender was hauled down onto the deck and held there while a serrated blade was dragged over his skin. Such savage theater proved entirely effective in keeping the ship's pace brisk.

The Skala's brutal encouragement carried on in absolute earnest, urging the rowers to give everything they had. If this was how it always was, Ford doubted he would last out the day. He wondered how these ragged bags of bones to the left and right of him had lasted as long as they had. Then, an enlightening rumor whispered through the ranks at a time when the Skala were preoccupied, bent over peering through the port holes. Apparently, a ship called *Jo Laiva Jager* had swooped down upon them, threatening to capture the galley. This rabid hunter was well known in the region for ending many a pirate's plundering. *Jo Laiva Jager* was packed with experienced and well-armored men and women, who made it their life's duty to clear their waters of such scourge. If there was a pitched battle upon decks, win or lose, the cost would be too high for the Severn and Skala, whose numbers had been reduced to make up a skeleton crew for their recently captured prize.

The wind favored *Jo Laiva Jager*, allowing its captain to make the most of her vessel's multitude of broad sails. The hunter gained perceptibly on the galley. The annoyed Severn and Skala watched the captain standing brazenly upon her bow staring back them with eagle-eyed intensity, a helm tucked under one arm and hair flowing freely.

However, the Severn were careful and precise sailors with a complete understanding of their vessel's capabilities. Their vigilant look-outs had spied the danger soon after it emerged from behind an island, flying a false pennant and doing its best to look like a fat merchant ship. The Severn weren't fooled. The galley fled like a gazelle. Eventually, when the hunter did manage to come to within missile range, the idle Skala—who were only good for hauling on a rope when it came to sailing—dared to stand upon the stern rail, while they exposed themselves and hurled curses at the chasing ship. *Jo Laiva Jager* catapulted weighted chain meant to tear up sails. These were less effective against a ship relying more on its rowers than its sails, unless oars could be fouled. Nonetheless, one shot did fly over the water and caught a cavorting Skala about the neck with the heavy ball and chain, flinging him lifeless across the deck. This cheered the crew of *Jo Laiva Jager* immensely, and a happy, hopeful crew worked all the harder. But more importantly, a harpoon shot through one of the galley's stern windows, hooking the two ship's together and pulling them ever closer until the cable was cut by the frantic Severn.

The chase wound westward around the southern end of The Tanden and proceeded on a northerly heading. The wind favored the Severn galley now and any Valtavastad-based ship would soon be out of its home waters and floating farther from safety. *Jo Laiva Jager* slowly gave ground, but it did not give up. An earnest chase continued up The Tanden's western veneer. Eventually, the galley was driven from the Meille Coast and well away from The Maa of the Mensen. Only then did the ship based in Valtavastad haul its wind and sit watching the galley until it was out of sight.

The prisoners heard and understood little of what was going on above them. If only they had known how close they had all come to being saved, they might have sat upon their oars and refused to row, be damned the punishment. Midway through the chase, Ford collapsed upon his oar and took a lashing. The searing pain of the leather stripping the skin off his back shot him upright and kept him moving through the motions until he could no longer even fake it. Slumping forward with his head down, he couldn't see the overseers but expected a flogging at any moment. It didn't come. Instead, relief came. He had no idea, but his rowing partner had also given out. In fact, he had given out before Ford and for a while Ford had been carrying on alone. The overseers shifted some of the rowers, brought in replacements, and sent the spent rowers below.

Ford dragged his body along with the others, a line of walking dead delving into the bowels of the ship. Skala hands shoved them down the passage to the ladder, toward what would have been called the orlop deck on any other ship, but what had been transformed into a half-deck slave tier. When the short door to this half-deck was slid back, the Skala holding a lantern near the entrance pulled his scarf up over his nose and held it there with his free hand, a hand that Ford noticed held only three fingers and a thumb almost as long as the other digits. The opening looked like a mine shaft: dark, cramped and utterly unappealing to a large man who didn't like confined spaces. From within, chain links clinked as cadaverous forms sat up and peered at them with sunken eyes, dead eyes within pale, skeletal faces. Appearing like the ghosts of their former selves, these were the prisoners captured earlier in the galley's voyage, plucked from farms and undefended villages in lands to the south. Bodies caked in filth and packed together cheek by jowl, along with the decaying flesh of the dead yet to be removed, gave off a stench unlike anything Ford had ever smelled, and far worse than what he suffered on the transport ship to Polecat Island or within the Pen. He backed away, but a blade point poked into his back and forced him forward into the nightmare of emaciated bodies and doleful moaning.

Ford, Will and anyone nearing six feet tall already had to duck everywhere they went within a regular ship, but here the three and a half feet of head room had everyone on their hands and knees as they pressed upon one another to squeeze in the newcomers. Once the last of them were in, the door slid shut, trapping them in darkness, from which their only reprieve would be another long stint at the oars.

Ford crawled across the deck, pushed from behind and pushing his oar-mate ahead of him until they could go no further. His hand landed in something mushy and slid out from under him, sending his face flying into the boney flanks of a wraith-like form from which he recoiled. His oar-mate hit the deck with a muffled thud, other bodies dulling the impact. He didn't move and Ford feared he had died, but a moan did finally sigh out of him. Ford lay down beside him. Others slid in and stretched out beside him. Immediately, the person laying at Ford's feet butted his soles with the top of his head. Ford pulled up his knees and had to lay with his legs bent.

Only once before, when crawling through a chimney, had he felt so cramped and claustrophobic. The stiflingly humid and foul air being absorbed and expelled by more than a hundred unfortunate souls was nothing he wanted to breathe, yet he breathed in deeper and faster by the second. His fists clenched as he fought to hold back his rising nerves, and still the shaking came on. Just when he thought he would either vomit or scream, a hand took him by the wrist. This was not one of the ghoulish grasping hands that pawed at him when he had pushed his way deeper into the slave tier, and so he stayed the urge to jerk away. Some vague intuition told him the hand belonged to Will, and then he knew for certain when the pleasant murmurs of prayer caught his ear and drove back his dread. Ford began praying with the priest and found solace in his companionship, even as the insect vermin began crawling over them and the rats came out to bite the perfectly still bodies to see if they were dead and ready.

"Water," begged a prisoner from some dark corner, carrying on a constant refrain heard throughout the voyage. There was no end to the pathetic pleas, because there was no remedy. Soon after being captured, the prisoners' water rations were cut in half. When the Severn and Skala themselves had to go to half rations, the prisoners received none but what came in the increasingly cakey, gray pottage they were given once a day. What it consisted of exactly they couldn't be sure. If they found a piece of scaly flesh in their portion, they considered themselves lucky, for it was the only thing approaching meat they would get. The disgustingly sour mash kept them alive and that's all that could be said in its favor. Even so, some desperate souls took to stealing the portions from those too weak to defend themselves.

The transient unpredictability of luck was all the prisoners had to lean upon for hope and mercy. Certainly, they would get no mercy from the Severn and Skala, who took little notice of the prisoners' living conditions, never giving them the opportunity to bath and not even bothering to have the overflowing tubs of excrement upon the slave tier emptied. The prisoners lived and worked under these conditions for more than a week's worth of sailing into the frigid north. In that relatively short span, some of those who came from the *Fida Mal* died, such as Bastien the Manerd, who succumbed to a fever after his wounded hand became infected. Then one day luck did strike in a most literal way. The galley struck ice. The damage was not fatal to the ship. The crack was soon patched, but enough fresh sea water seeped into the ship to partially flood the slave tier. All the prisoners were removed, even the dead. The water was bailed, which cleared much of the filth. All labor was performed by the prisoners, but at least they were allowed to empty the excrement from the tubs.

"Where's the sun?" Cadogan muttered in Ford's direction while they were topside emptying buckets into the ocean and no guards were within earshot. Streaky sheets of gray clouds blotted out the sun and cast the land and sea in a dreary gloom.

"Don't think they have the sun around here. Wherever here is," Ford replied.

"We're north I'd say. Very far north," said Cadogan nodding at the icebergs floating in the surrounding waters, as well as the snowcapped mountains lining the eastern horizon. "Farther north than Polecat, I'd say."

The gaze of the Severn and Skala also turned to the east, where lay their homelands. Even when the galley drifted miles closer to the shore, no greenery could be made out upon the nearly vertical, unforgivingly harsh slopes, just the rocky cliff faces and peaks capped in white. Only briefly in summer did the steep banks of the rivers yield a meager harvest of wild cabbages and root vegetables after the floods crashed through the precipitous ravines and the sun warmed the soaked earth.

"Jokkoti," said one of the Severn sailors to a young Skala warrior new to the ship. The sailor longingly pointed to where the mouth of the largest river cleft the tall rock. He tried to get his poor-sighted companion to pick out some of the hidden dugouts and cave dwellings of the isolated settlement along the cliffsides where a great portion of the Severn population scratched out a cheerless existence in these grim lands by fishing, seal hunting and carrying out sea raids.

The settlement was so well disguised among the boulders that even the perfect-sighted might walk right up to a Jokkoti dwelling before realizing they were trespassing.

The unworldly Skala warrior boasted to the Severn sailor of how his semi-nomadic brethren moved with the seasons, but could also avoid accidental intrusion by other clans when they did settle for brief periods. Each clan's high chief, the Tarken Hoof, he explained, had his insignia inscribed in red dye upon a boulder within a mile of the first dwelling on the landward approach. The Severn sailor's rejoinder was to point out the insignia of a crescent moon surrounding a clawed paw painted upon his own long fur-lined coat. The same insignia adorned the ship's seldom flown pennant. These young Skala knew nothing, the sailor lamented.

Jokkoti passed by as the galley continued north up the rugged coast. There was no point in returning home with a ship laden with slaves they had no need for. They would be ridiculed if they had. Instead, the galley headed even farther north, where the snow and ice never fully abated.

In the guttural language they shared, the Severn sailor told the young Skala warrior that they were making for Dargkivi in Rikaswelt, the land of the Kamen. The Skala knew of the Kamen. His people were their next closest neighbors, but he knew almost nothing about them because Skala did not mix with Kamen. The Severn held back a laugh. He knew the truth of the matter: Skala were seldom invited into Kamen society. The Kamen spurned most other races. The Severn had a purely trade-based relationship with them. Long had their people sold slaves to the Kamen, that wealthy and willfully idle race, who used the slaves for work, pleasure, pure entertainment, and to bestow upon themselves a sense of superiority. The Kamen possessed one of the strongest and most destructive inferiority complexes of all races the Severn sailor had ever encountered, and it was not uncommon in them to make life miserable for the more physically gifted when it was within their means. Since they possessed the means, the Severn and Skala happily provided them with what they desired for a price.

The mountains to the east plunging directly into the sea became more jagged the farther north they traveled. Chunks of floating ice filled the water around them. The last Severn and Skala settlement had been left behind and there was nothing ahead for the galley but the port at Dargkivi. To the rowers' great surprise, they were suddenly commanded to stop and draw in their oars. The galley rode on light sails aloft, and their speed did not diminish. Such was the strength of the reliable wind in this region. The reason for the cessation of rowing was that the ice flows had become too numerous to risk snapping oars. The rowers remained at their stations and awaited word from the sentries upon the bow or masthead, who called out iceberg sightings. Then the Skala made the rowers backpaddle like mad.

"Have you ever felt cold such as this," Cadogan muttered over his shoulder to the bench behind him where Ford sat. The easing of their toil had resulted in a mass of shivering, underdressed bodies. It was their eighth day on the galley and each day had been colder than the last. Ford had survived winters with little to wear and wasn't suffering half as much as most. Still, he had to admit, this bone-chilling air was unlike anything he had ever experienced.

Cadogan was shaking almost uncontrollably by the time their turn at the oars was over. As they made their slow, shambling way toward the slave tier, an exhausted Gel na Nadi woman collapsed in front of them. Her naturally brown skin had gone dusty gray and the dark circles about her sunken eyes rendered in high relief the starvation her body had endured. The nearest Skala booted her twice in the abdomen, then grabbed her by the neck and hoisted her to her feet. She swayed a moment before dropping to her knees. The Skala stood before her and cupped a hand under her chin to raise her head so that she might see his fist poised to strike her. The woman's dead-eyes stared into his with infinite apathy. The Skala backhanded her to the deck, then stripped her and thrust the clothes into the arms of the closest prisoners.

"Uztragen," the Skala shouted at them.

"No," said Cadogan shaking his head. "I can't—"

"Uztragen! Daritagad!" The Skala's metal-knobbed glove swung back and would have struck the side of Cadogan's head if he hadn't immediately pulled on the Gel na Nadi woman's cloak and cowl. The woman's body was dragged to the main deck and tossed overboard. Her skirt ended up in Ford's hands. He put it on over the other he already wore over his trousers. Both skirts came well short of covering his legs, but they were better than nothing. None of the prisoners who had passed away had worn pants long enough to fit him. However, by the end of the day, he would add a mantle to wear over the cloak he had obtained the day before and together his motley ensemble made life more bearable.

Seeing the wealth in their human cargo slipping away, the Severn and Skala began eliminating the weakest to preserve their more valuable slaves. Just about every one of the remaining prisoners now owned layers of clothing taken off of their dead comrades. Ice was brought aboard to be melted, so that water was no longer rationed, and many who were on the brink of death rebounded. Still, Ford worried about Will. The lean priest grew thinner and more lethargic by the day. It wouldn't be much longer before he was deemed expendable.

"He's not eating," Cadogan told Ford while they were standing in line to receive their daily ration of water. "The mess they give us doesn't set well with him." After the first few days aboard the galley, eating the slop everyone was served, Will had become ill and unable to keep anything down. His health had deteriorated rapidly. "If this goes on much longer…"

As Cadogan trailed off, Ford shuffled along behind, his mouth opening and closing soundlessly. The suggestions that leapt immediately to mind weren't worth uttering. A cracking sound came from the water barrel. The Skala controlling the water rations was smashing the ice which had formed on the surface.

"What about water," said Ford.

"What about it?"

"He can keep it down, so why don't we make sure he gets plenty of that?"

"Man can't live on water alone," said Cadogan shaking his head, but then turned it into a nod. "Even so, you're right, we can do that much for him."

"You're going to give that bag of bones your portions?" asked an incredulous Bevan Underwall, the former sailor from the *Fida Mal*. "It'll be wasted on him. Even if your friend survives the voyage, where we're going, he won't likely survive much longer."

"What do you mean by that?" demanded Ford, but their turn had come at the water barrel and they had to hold their tongues.

Afterwards Underwall wouldn't elaborate much further, mostly because his knowledge was based in rumor and hearsay, and he possessed scant of either. "All I'll say is, it's a bad place, where nothing good comes of a bag of bones like your friend."

Ford might have thrashed the man for that if not for the distraction of a sonorous peel, like harmonic thunder. When it struck the galley, it shook their very chests with a racking vibrato. The blare recalled to Ford tales of the Bellowing Beast of Twll Uchel, and he wondered what manner of monster existed in this harsh and remote land capable of roaring with such booming ferocity.

"It sounds like the pipes of the gods," said Cadogan.

Others wondered if perhaps thunder took on a deep and strangely sustained tone in this part of the world. "Do they deliver us up to a race of giants?" Aeddamon Born asked among the other murmured questions deep within the slave tier as the prisoners sat up to listen to the ascending notes blasted across the bay. "To be sold into slavery as some play thing? A pet?"

Under a single scrap of canvas made taut by the region's steady winds, the galley had sailed around a spire-like rock at the end of a peninsula into Licilass no Rikkust, the Bay of Riches. The ship had been spotted by the harbor watch at Dargkivi, who immediately sounded the alarm, an organ larger than most temples. The Severn and Skala knew of the organ, but had never seen it. Those who doubted it existed built up a mythical explanation, deciding that living rock of the cliffs spoke the mountainous bellowing. As a theory, it wasn't all that far off. The organ's song escaped through holes drilled in the rock facing the bay as a warning when a ship was sighted. Once the vessel was determined to be the Severn galley, the organ's tone soared. Yards-long icicles snapped and fell. Sheets of ice slid from the cliff tops and crashed into the rocks and the frozen sea below all the while the notes carried the information to those within the city. Parts of the song were repeated and then the tremendous melody finally died away. The relative quiet which followed sounded like pure and absolute silence after such a din.

The arms of the bay becalmed the wind, allowing the galley to glide smoothly into the still bay. Naming the slender arrowhead-shaped strip of water an inlet would have been more precise. Its mouth opened a quarter of a mile at the widest. The high cliffs pressing in on either side narrowed quickly, giving the impression that a ship would be crushed before it made the docks. Sailors with a fanciful turn of mind imagined they were being swallowed. Such worries were washed away by the entrancing sight of the cliffs themselves, where a heady multitude of balconies, terraces, stairways, windows, and doorways had been carved into the blue-gray rock. Square and rounded towers stood like sentries embedded within the cliffs, while others seemed to fly out over the bay. One flying tower continued on in an arched bridge spanning the water and connected with a twin on the other side. Over time, the orderliness of the old design had been augmented and intentionally masked by ornate facades with diamond, shell, wave, wishbone and weave patterns. It was pure decoration done to break with the rigid past. Some called it outlandish, others saw it as a wondrous marvel to behold.

The port at Dargkivi was seldom visited. During the galley's northward passage, they had met with only one other vessel, a small Kamen merchant ship heading south. The stability of Dargkivi's economy depended upon trade to a certain degree, but it was the value the rich ruling classes placed upon the exotic products of distant lands which kept their icebreaking, steel-nosed barge continually cracking and smashing the constantly freezing bay's surface with its massive hammer.

The galley slid up to the stone wharf where all ships docked while offloading their wares. Straight ahead, lodged between the cliffs, sat a ponderous gatehouse, the main entryway into the center of Dargkivi. Above the gatehouse, where the cliffs narrowed to a twenty-five-foot gap, giant steps of a width, depth and rise of precisely ten feet each rose almost to the top of the cliff more than a hundred feet above. During the minimal summer thaw, water from the hinterlands flowed toward the bay and over these steps, draining into the numerous holes which had been dug at regular intervals into the base of each step. The holes led to a vast warren of tubes and pipes that conveyed water to reservoirs and sewer drainage, as well as directly to some of the individual great houses. It was an engineering feat that the early Kamen settlers had been immensely proud of and the modern Kamen took for granted.

From the perspective of the galley when it sailed into the bay, there appeared to be small balls of black and brown fur rolling about along the wharf and upon the lower terrace just above. Some Skala visiting the city for the first time thought that bear cubs had wandered into the city docks, but up close the furballs proved to be barrel-chested Kamen dockworkers and their masters decked out in heavy furs. The giants among them stood five feet tall, while the average was more than a foot shorter. In their furs with padded inner lining, they appeared to be nearly as wide as they were tall. *Fat-headed wall-eyed runts* was a common slur used by Aelwydian sailors on the rare occasions when their paths crossed on the trade routes. Some called them *the unfinished men*, others simply saw them as marred. Indeed, their oversized heads, bulbous features and superfluous eyebrows would have rested more naturally upon larger bodies. The part the Kamen had once taken in raids upon the eastern Aelwydian coast, albeit minor, created a prejudice against the diminutive race. Their bushy eyebrows, which sometimes hid the eyes and gave them a devious appearance, didn't help improve others' opinions. Modern upper class Kamen women teased, curled and colored their eyebrows enough to make peacocks blush for the garishness.

Ford and the other prisoners thought they knew what bitter cold was until the intense, stabbing air pierced their meager clothing and attacked their faces when they were led in chains onto the main deck. On the slave tier, body heat had generated survivable conditions, but out in the open it hurt to breathe. Even the tough-skinned Severn and Skala were now wearing heavy clothing. They were welcomed ashore by stubby Kamen men-at-arms armored in metal breast plates over buffalo fur jerkins and carrying javelin-sized, needle-tipped spears. However, their beard-hidden smirks and the curling and unfurling fingers of their upraised palms, a sign of welcome, had a decidedly sinister air about it.

"The Sever Man," Aeddamon Born let slip when he caught sight of them. A backhand from a Skala caught him on the temple for his utterance.

The legendary Sever Man of Aelwydian myth was a misnomer and a case of mistaken identity. By association, the Kamen had been turned into a nightmarish bogeyman after accompanying a raiding party of Severn and Skala, who were the real culprits of the rape and pillage that once took place upon the eastern shores of Aelwyd. The band of adventuresome Kamen who had joined them were merely seeking greener pastures in warmer climes, but when some of them stayed behind to create a new life on Aelwyd shores their unusual appearance had captivated the minds of Aelwydians. Misleading secondhand accounts filled with faulty information spread the story and mutated the truth. Ford was one of the few non-sailors not taken aback by the stunted men who greeted them. He had seen a Kamen before. An amiable descendent of the Kamen raiders named Viktor had set himself up as an innkeeper in a small seaside town Ford had once passed through.

Ford stepped onto the galley's main deck during the transfer to shore and his eyes passed over the little people to a giant ape-like creature sitting on its haunches in the middle of the wharf. It leaned forward to sniff through slits for nostrils at the newly arrived humans as if letting its nose pick out the tastiest among them.

"Avar," murmured the animal's handler to calm the beast. The handler was somewhat new to the care of karvane slevkavve such as Avar, but he was getting the hang of it. The woolly, dull gray-haired beast blending in with the cliffside rock despite its stout chest and muscular limbs had been with the Kamen for years now and that helped. Avar had grown used to taking direction from them, knowing that compliance with the wishes of these little beings led to a full belly. The handler kept a loose hold on Avar's leash and leaned back against the wall beside the beast, while they both watched the proceedings with mild interest. The way Avar leaned forward every now and then convinced the prisoners that he was ready to attack. The chained men and women shortened their steps as they drew closer and eventually had to be shoved along. Avar's black, beady eyes peered at them through upward slanting lids that narrowed, as if to better scrutinize the cuts of meat parading before him. Whenever he ground the teeth of his wide jaw or grunted as he shifted his ponderous weight, the prisoners would jump back and nearly fall from the wharf.

While Avar adored man flesh—his last taste was that of a forgetful handler who'd missed one of Avar's feedings—he mostly fed on Juminevesikoer or simply koer as the Kamen called them. These tuber-shaped mammals were clumsy on land but swift swimmers with blunt horns upon their forehead with which to break open ice. The Kamen once hunted them, but now a domesticated breed, kept in a sea cave under the city, provided ready meat for the people as well as Avar. For the sake of his innate desire to hunt, his handler would lop off the koer's flippers or tail and leave it on the ice of the bay for Avar to chase down and eat. Without hampering the koer, the seal-like animal would likely elude him and slip back into the sea.

The last of the prisoners stepped off the ship and joined the line, which stretched along the wharf, through the gatehouse door, up a flight of steps and reappeared on a terrace some forty feet above the wharf. Ford stood toward the end of the line waiting for it to move. Beside him, built into the base of the cliff, were long and low stone buildings used as temporary storage houses for trade. A few large ceramic pots, vases, and jars sat by the doors, but little else. The prisoners crept forward in fits and starts, and Ford found himself standing in front of Avar. Even in a sitting position, the massive karvane slevkavve hardly had to raise its head to meet Ford's eye. Avar leaned forward to sniff the air between them. Ford leaned away. The line shuffled forward a few paces. Ford scooted ahead and breathed a little easier.

"Soliz korval! Mark raum! Rumi!" shouted a truculent Kamen guard as he shoved his way out of the gatehouse door through the line of prisoners. Anyone not stepping aside quickly enough for him were threatened with his searing hot poker: a rod with a diamond-shaped, red glowing rock fastened to the end.

"One of them *warm rocks*," whispered a sailor near Ford. "Careful. Word is, they never lose their heat and they're hot enough to burn you."

The guard's shouting carried on down the wharf toward the galley, full of harsh consonants and never a soft *pah* or *bah* sound. Behind him trotted a line of men and women from Fodag, Hadas, Junipung, Grakt, Dadha, Nagapor, and Hikari, representing a veritable rainbow of skin tones compared with the pale gray and white of the Severn, Skala, and Kamen. Though thin from malnutrition, most were of hardy stock. Every one of them had been shaved bald and wore little more than a dark-colored robe draped over their shoulders. Their bare arms revealed branded skin about the wrists.

"Slaves," muttered Underwall from behind Ford. The slaves passed by, boarded the galley and went below. Under the supervision of the Severn and with assistance from the Skala, the slaves began unloading some of the cargo pilfered from the *Fida Mal*. They carried the goods up from the hold and onto the wharf. Seeing this disturbed Ford. People didn't own other people in Aelwyd. Servants were paid to serve. Debtors worked off their debt.

A commotion broke out at the far end of the wharf, where a Kamen harbormaster dressed from neck to ankle in a golden panther doublet was arguing over goods with one of the Severn. Next to them, a thick and filthy smoke from a furnace rose through a small round hole in the roof of the last building on the wharf. Ford followed the newly rising plume up the cliff and caught sight of what he thought was a ribcage stuck to the rock about ten feet from the ground. Kamen faces began appearing in the windows along the cliffs high above on either side. The short and round people pulled on wraps or cloaks and stepped out onto their balconies to observe the goings on below them. Some pointed out Avar to their companions, while others watched the prisoners with mild interest.

Kamen heads topped by fur-trimmed chaperons and roundlets peered down over the edge from the end of the terrace above, where it stretched past the wharf. They seemed to be disputing something among themselves. Small gems passed from hand to hand. Then Fleury of Mane appeared at the edge. Ford couldn't believe the tiny man had survived the galley voyage, never mind imprisonment on the *Fida Mal*, considering how thin he had grown during their time on Polecat Island. Having been stripped to the waist, the definition of his ribs stood out quite plainly. He was the picture of frailty and one of the most desperate of cases among the prisoners. His eyes, having remained half-lidded for months, widened in alarm as someone grabbed him from behind and hurled him over the edge. His body cartwheeled through the air once before being impaled upon a hook embedded in the cliffside about ten feet above the jagged rocks and ice of the bay. Some of the people watching on from the windows and balconies cheered. The Kamen gentlemen on the terrace laughed and paid off the man who had thrown the prisoner over the side. Avar lumbered down the wharf and clambered over the rocks and ice to stand under the dangling body with his great maw open wide to catch the rivulet of blood draining down. The blood ran over his chin and stained the white fur of his chest.

"Bastards! Bastards!" someone shouted amid an outcry from the prisoners on the wharf.

"I knew it! I knew it was true!" shouted Underwall. A pair of Skala warriors rushed up and down the line of prisoners striking those who had spoken. Ford's entire body clenched and he was hit with an instant headache as he tried to come to grips with this bizarre and hateful reality he found himself trapped in. Had he and the others been led here simply to be thrown off of a cliff and skewered for the entertainment of these cruel people? Despite the beatings, the provoked prisoners on the wharf and the terrace would not be suppressed. They raised their fists, shouted, and rattled their chains. Damn the punishment, if they were going to be killed either way, they would not go quietly.

Avar was brought back among the prisoners with his appetites aroused. Each deep, musky breath flared his nostrils. His massive limbs flexed and his blood-matted chest heaved with the desire for flesh. His presence immediately subdued those nearest him. The guards reasserted control and began pushing the prisoners inside the gatehouse back onto the wharf. The prisoners on the terrace above were pushed to the edge. The line of them overlooking the wharf had a troop of men-at-arms pointing needle-spears at their backs. Avar was led up and down the line of shivering men and women still standing on the wharf until silence and submission spread over the prisoners there.

A Kamen official with an expansive chest marched an Amita woman briskly down from the terrace to the middle of the wharf where all of the prisoners could see her. Although a woman of some fortitude, she had already been on the Severn galley for a week by the time Ford was captured. Her concave cheeks and skeletal frame displayed a body on the verge of collapse. A Skala pinned her spindly arms behind her back and swept the legs out from under her, so that she dropped to her knees. This put her on a level with the Kamen official, who tore away at her clothes, exposing the trembling goose flesh of her dusky body.

"Verot!" he shouted through a thick, woolly muffler. The muffler covered the bottom half of his face, while a fur-lined helm hid the top half. His eyes alone expressed the importance of his speech and its purpose with a sober glare. A nearby guard handed him a spear. The official pulled down the muffler to be heard more clearly, even though none of the prisoners knew how to speak Kamen. "Verot!" In the blink of an eye, he leveled the spear and jabbed the Amita woman in the stomach. She let out a cry. A trickle of blood dribbled from the wound. She tried to cradle her belly, but the Skala held her upright by the shoulders.

"What's this game," said Ford with a low growl through his teeth.

"Wart unt verot!" the Kamen official shouted to the left, and then turning his body, to the right.

Above, a few figures shaved bald and lightly attired in russet robes, stepped forward to stand by the Kamen and prisoners upon the terrace's edge. The robes were sleeveless, which revealed the shaved men had been branded about the wrists like other slaves. Each of them began translating the Kamen official's words into a variety of foreign languages. They were none too pleased to have been dragged from their masters' cozy quarters, where they mostly kept the accounts of wealthy merchants and tradesmen, to be used by the guardsmen of the bay out here in the harsh elements.

"Noverot tas voimakt unt oht! Uzvestez vy to verd notikt uz ju!" the official shouted, again to the left and right. The translators rattled off words and clipped phrases, none of which Ford understood until his ear caught "watch" and "behave." His gaze darted about trying to find the speaker. As he did, he missed the beginnings of small bubbles of saliva forming in the corner of the Amita woman's lips. The bubbles turned to froth and her eyes dancing about. She slumped forward, spit on the ground, and began gasping. Everyone watched, almost as if entranced by the rapid and ever-increasing heaving of her chest. Even the Kamen official stood back a pace, still erect in his stance and patient. He tilted his head to one side, casually admiring his handiwork. A shudder convulsed through his victim and the Skala let her drop to the ground, where she curled up and clutched her belly. Sweat beading on her upper lip began to cover her body. The onset of twitching and dry heaving swiftly developed into wild floundering convulsions. With a sudden jerk, she seized up and moved no more.

The Kamen official shouted, gesturing from the spear tip to the dead woman and then from the spear tip to the line of living prisoners before him, as well as those upon the terrace above. The translator who possessed some Aelwydian eventually said, "Look see? If trouble...you die...of poison spear."

The display had the desired effect of cowing the prisoners, who now formed a line and peacefully proceeded along the wharf, up through the gatehouse, and onto the terrace. Ford found himself bending at the knee and waist halfway up a spiral stairway of one of the gatehouse towers. The short, slanted ceiling forced anyone more than five feet tall to hunch over. Auction calls and bidding could be heard, but there was little to see. The only window in the tower faced the bay and let in a slit of dull light. With no guards about, Ford dared to whisper to Cadogan standing ahead of him in the line close to the doorway leading out onto the terrace. "What do you see?"

"I..." began Cadogan, turning around to face him. His mouth fell open and one of his hands reached for Will, who stood between them in the light of the window. "Ford!" Ford watched as the priest slowly tipped over backwards like a tree being felled. The back of his head dragged against the ceiling and slowed him just long enough for Ford to shove aside the man in front of him and catch Will before he fell.

"Oh," Will exclaimed in a voice so flat that Ford wondered if he hadn't fallen asleep. One of his hands reached out for the wall to steady himself, while the other went to his head. "I'm all right. A little dizzy, nothing more. Thank you." Ford set him upright again and kept a hand on his back. His eyes wouldn't focus and another fainting spell seemed a certainty. To Ford, he sounded weak and his body felt incredibly light, insignificant almost. Ford watched over him from then on, assisting him up the stairway as best he could until they reached the terrace.

Emerging from the cave-like stairwell, the prisoners unbent their aching bodies and looked about them with trepidation. To their left, the rock surface of the sheer cliff continued to rise above them. The carved decoration about the windows and balconies made it seemed as if they stood at the base of a palace. A steady stream of Kamen and chained prisoners passed through one of the doorways built into the wall. On the other side of the terrace there was nothing stopping a person from falling over or being thrown over the edge, as they had already witnessed. In the center of the terrace stood a row of square stone blocks about three feet high with a short flight of tiny steps leading up to it. This was the auction block. In other countries that practiced the trade, it was customary for slaves to mount the block in order to be displayed to prospective buyers. In Dargkivi the buyers stood upon the block as to be tall enough to examine the prisoners. Eyes, ears and mouths were poked and prodded. There weren't many buyers left. Most had already filled their needs. Yet the remaining few still jabbed the abdomens and kneaded the limbs of prisoners, carrying out their usual soundness tests with an invasive thoroughness.

While the rest of the prisoners awaited their time at the block, another of their number was tossed over the side of the terrace. With the rest having already been bought, by now there were more Skala and Kamen guards than there were prisoners remaining. No one at the end of the line with Ford made a peep of protest. If they had, it would have had to be more than a peep to be heard over the auctioneer and buyers.

As Ford's turn neared, he began to worry. If he wasn't bought, would they throw him over the edge? If they tried. He would fight back, so his life would definitely be forfeit either way, ended by a poke of their deadly spears. Beyond all belief, he found himself hoping, even praying, to be bought by one of these runty men. So caught up was he in his own concerns that he didn't notice how some of the prisoners, a very few, were being returned to the galley. The Severn needed someone to man the oars and occasionally balked at a low offer for a perfectly serviceable slave. If Ford had known of this alternative, he would have preferred to take his chances back on the galley, perhaps to be sold elsewhere in the world. Anywhere else seemed better than this inhospitably cold land with its horrid little people.

Cadogan became one of these exceptions. He was dragged in front of the auction block and led away soon after without having been bought. There was nothing particularly wrong with him. The market had merely dried up. A pair of Skala took him and a few others back to the galley. The moment Cadogan disappeared into the gatehouse, Ford's attention returned to Will, who was wobbling toward the auction block. Instead of standing before it, the priest veered away slightly, swayed a bit, and made for the steps, as if he would mount the block itself. The Kamen slave buyer nearest to him threw up his hands to fend off a perceived attack. A Kamen man-at-arms scurried forward with his spear tip aimed at Will's vitals and would have ended his life if a Skala had not jerked Will back in line. For his wayward step, Will was knocked to his knees by a light slap. The blow should have only turned his cheek. Instead, he flopped to the ground with all the backbone of a ragdoll. Ford had seen this happen during his prize fighting days. When a fighter had taken more punishment than he could handle, a tap could tip him over. Will was spent. The toll their ordeal had taken on him was writ large in his vacant eyes, his drooping head, and the limp limbs hanging from his cadaverous body.

Will's auction began without an ounce of interest from the buyers. They clucked their tongues dismissively and raised their arms to flip their hands to the heavens, waving away the worthless thing before them. Will was clearly too weak to work. The supervising Severn in charge of this end of the auction spoke with a small circle of Kamen, gentlemen in fur-trimmed hats standing off to one side of the block. These were gambling men who had been buying up unwanted slaves to make a game of tossing them over the side. The Severn didn't have any use for Will and hoped he might squeeze the odd coin or two out of these men for the spent priest. They talked animatedly among themselves, came to a quick decision, and put in a low bid for Will that was accepted.

Will was marched by a Kamen guard over to the gentlemen and held there while they wagered. By now, much of the gold and gems they had all arrived with belonged to one man among them. The gentleman with the lightest pockets eyed Will's length and licked his lips, salivating over what he felt was a real prospect of getting his wealth back. This Kamen believed he had the arm and aim to make the toss, and he wanted a go at this lanky Aelwydian, for it stood to reason that a long body, rather than a short one, had a better chance of catching upon one of the cliffside hooks. Saying he would risk everything he had left in the attempted throw was all it took for the heavy-pocketed one to agree to the bet. Like a lamb to the slaughter, Will was led to the edge of the terrace with the Kamen gentlemen following giddily behind. They laughed as the one who would do the throwing began limbering up. Meanwhile, the auction continued on as if nothing out of the ordinary was going on.

"Don't!" Ford cried. His chains rattled as he lunged with manacled hands for Will. A Skala trying to silence the unruly prisoner threw a leather-gloved fist at Ford's mouth and split open his lower lip. "Wait!" Ford shouted. A punch to the gut dropped him. The fall yanked the prisoner in front of him away from the auction block. The line of translators called out from the background all of the buyers' vehement complaints and threats not to buy another slave from the Severn for the indignations that had gone on that day. While the supervising Severn hollered at the Skala to keep the prisoners in line, Ford crawled toward the ledge with his hands outstretched toward Will, dragging along the remaining prisoners with him. "You can't do this!" A boot knocked the wind out of him and he fell on his face just behind the Kamen gentlemen. The Kamen guarding Will wheeled about and pointed his spear at Ford. Ford gathered his breath and wailed, "He's a healer! That man has the ear of the gods! He has the gift! He can heal!"

The bored translator who could speak a little Aelwydian perked up and repeated the gist of what Ford had said. The remaining buyers fell upon the betting gentlemen, showering Will's new owner with offers that doubled, tripled and quadrupled what he had paid, and that was just for starters. By the time a deal was struck and Will had been handed over to a new owner, the gambling gentleman, who had been down on his luck, was now twice as rich as when he'd arrived at the auction. To Ford's great relief, a Kamen guard led Will, without the need of chains, away from the terrace and through the door in the cliff wall where other purchased slaves had disappeared previously.

The Skala didn't like a challenge to their authority. The one who had doled out Ford's punishment was annoyed that this prisoner would not obey. He drew his sabre and pressed the blade against the side of Ford's neck. A downward thrust would be enough to severe the artery and spill blood. Ford closed his eyes and felt the sudden thrust of a boot on his shoulder. Skala hands yanked him to his feet and the rest of the prisoners were dragged back to the auction block.

Few buyers at Dargkivi saw value in buying the biggest and strongest specimens brought before them. Besides the logistical problems presented in having a tall slave in a town built for small people, there was little sense in laying out the coin for slaves obviously stronger than themselves. The Kamen were not weak, but they had their limits and knew them well. The danger of having a giant such as Ford living among them wasn't worth the risk for most slave masters.

Yet, two of the few remaining buyers had passed on many another prisoner the moment they laid eyes on Ford. They had a particular use for someone of his size. One was the purchasing agent for the mines. Ford could be used to break rock until his body gave out. But also, the agent knew that Tat Tarl, the shrine to accumulated wealth and prosperity, would need repair soon, and he foresaw the potential of renting out a slave who would need no scaffolding to work on the dome, the pillars, and the like. The other man, a buyer for the Master of Games, wanted Ford for Mullauk, Dargkivi's entertainment arena. Whether or not Ford was a good fighter, he couldn't be sure, but he was willing to bet that the big Aelwydian could at least hold his own. The Dargkivi people loved their entertainments. It was a challenge keeping up with their ravenous appetite for diversion. The buyer considered Ford's attributes and thought he might make the perfect villain in the arena shows. Given the chance, the Master of Games could morph this huge Aelwydian into a monster.

Surrounded by guards, gabbling town officials, and equally incomprehensible and utterly bored translators, Ford did nothing to protest the rather intimate examination he was subjected to. After the beating he had taken, he could do nothing but go along with this madness and hope that better days lie ahead. If there was one thing his time on Polecat Island had taught him it was that opportunities arose for those who were patient. So, he would bide his time and snatch his opportunity when it came.

A small bidding war had broken out over him while Ford was lost in contemplation. When it was over, the Kamen were done buying for the day. The remaining prisoners went back to the Severn galley, to a fate no one could predict, though backbreaking labor at the oars and slavery in some far-flung land seemed the likeliest end. Three Kamen guards led Ford to the cliffside doorway and into the city of the Kamen, propelling him toward his future as a slave in the Dargkivi mines.

Chapter 10
The Mines of Dargkivi

"Faster! In here, you gold-less worms!" the translators repeated in a variety of languages for the sake of a gruff Kamen guard. They were hurling a lot of information at the new slaves. For one, this guard was known as a valvar, specifically an alamvalvar, and should be accorded the respect of a guard of the lower city. The valvar hollered, stamped, and genuinely had himself an enjoyable time insulting and ordering about the line of prisoners he was leading from the bayside terrace into the cavernous city of Dargkivi. Another valvar with him joined in with gusto and made a game of one-upping each other's insults.

Ford had no idea what they were saying or what they wanted. The Aelwydian translator was not diligent in the least. So, Ford followed the herd and hoped for the best. They passed into a rectangular, smooth-walled room carved out of the rock. A pair of stout pillars supported the center of the ceiling of this long and wide vault. Ford had to duck deeply to pass through the doorway and then remain stooped once inside the room, as he would have to do just about everywhere he went in the Kamen-built town.

Most of the prisoners from the slave galley were here, in what was used as a holding cell where they would begin the true transition from prisoners to slaves. Floor-to-ceiling bars divided the room in half. Prisoners on Ford's side were encouraged by Kamen spears to strip until a strap of leather tied about their wrists was all they wore. This tag was wide enough at one end to bear a pyrographic symbol indicating the person's owner. Their old clothes ended up in a pile next to a lit hearth. Periodically, a slave would add a shirt or cloak to the fire, kicking up a good deal of smoke and killing countless vermin. They were made to wait, feeling cold and degraded in their nakedness, until prodded through a gate in the bars to the other side of the room. There were no translators here, which left the prisoners in a state of wary confusion, not knowing why any of this was happening or what would come next until they saw it for themselves.

On the other side of the bars, new slaves were shaved and scrubbed one or two at a time while Kamen guards looked on. The idea was to destroy all the fleas and lice that could be burned, crushed or drowned before allowing the newcomers into the city. A long-serving slave acting as barber sweat away as he busily sawed and scraped with a rapidly dulling blade at the longhaired men from Polecat Island. Aelwydians like Ford had grown winter beards, which were filled with pests after their confinement aboard the Severn galley. When the barber was through with them, they were made to stand in a tub of water to be scrubbed down. They came out of the ordeal looking like shiny new babies, some tanned or wrinkled, but shorn of hair and stripped of much of their accumulated filth. The scrubbers were not gentle and the barber had to work quickly, so skin was rubbed raw and nicked scalps dripped with blood. One woman lost half an eyebrow.

"No! No!" began the chanted complaints of a pack of *Fida Mal* sailors yet to be shaved. These men had developed a superstitious attachment to their hair. The guards approached a step or two closer with their needle-spears and that quieted the sailors for the time being, reducing them to standing at the bars grinding their teeth, tearful at the sight of hair hitting the ground. Their silence lasted until the first among their number was grabbed and shoved into the stocks used to hold the prisoners relatively still for the barber. The sailor bucked and kicked at the barber's hand so that the blade flew across the room. When not manhandling prisoners, the Kamen guards of Lower Dargkivi took their ease by the fire and passed around a bottle. But now, one of them lost his patience over these bothersome sailors. Taking a last pull on the bottle, he stomped over to the hearth and pulled out a flaming tunic with a pair of tongs. Holding the flame close to his lips, he blew a fireball of spirits into the sailor's face. Hair, eyebrows and beard vanished, leaving the screaming and trembling man with a patchy, splotchy head resembling a roasted pig. After that, the shaving went on without delay.

Once the barber and washers were finished, they prodded each prisoner out of the room through a door and down some stairs to a downward-sloping tunnel terminating at another door. The valvar escorting the prisoner would knock on the door and only open it when another Kamen from within signaled to enter. A gush of wonderful warmth swept into the tunnel from the room when the door was pulled back. When it was his turn, Ford gladly stepped in. He thought he heard pained moans coming from beyond a door on the other side of the small square room of gray stone, but was distracted by the peculiar décor in this close and comfortably warm space. Hundreds of long-handled iron tools hung upon the walls. The heat came from a massive brazier standing upon a thick-legged tripod in the middle of the room. It was filled with bright orange coals with dozens of iron rods protruding from it, identical to the ones lining the walls. Next to the brazier sat a stone block with straps wrapped around it. A half dozen bored valvar and slaves stood about these two items awaiting his arrival. Ford was ordered to kneel before the block. While a needle-spear was pointed at his throat, slaves strapped down his arms. Suddenly the room felt too warm. His tag was removed from his wrist and the emblazoned symbol read out to another slave wearing leather gloves, who selected from the brazier a pair of iron rods. These turned out to be one long pincer tool. The claw at the end of the tool had been buried for so long in the coals that it burned a deep red. When the slave pulled the handles apart, the same symbol from the tag could be seen engraved in iron and welded onto the claw. Ford began pulling at the straps holding him down, dreading what he sensed was to come. In the not-so-distant past, he had been threatened with a hot poker. Memories of that horrid incident flashed before his eyes as the glowing pincers neared. His protests mounted to screams. Every word fell on deaf ears. To the other burn and cut marks over his body, they added a scorched brand around his right wrist.

The smell of his own cooked flesh turned his stomach. The burn would not be soothed. He stumbled from the room clutching his arm, wanting to, but not daring to touch the seared skin of his wrist. They had bundled him into a dark hallway, where he found himself wet, cold, in pain and alone. The temperature here plummeted precipitously. The cool air felt good on his wrist, but the frigid floor seared the soles of his feet with an unbearable burn of its own. He stopped once to press his throbbing wrist against the cold floor. It gave him some relief, but for the sake of his bare feet he hurried down the passage, window and door-less, to a distant light.

At the far end of the tunnel was a small room being used as a temporary clothier's. A pair of valvar oversaw trained slaves outfitting new arrivals in clean and mostly new robes, tunics, trousers, and shoes. Piles of clothes and bolts of cloth stacked against the walls were being picked through by a few outfitters and tailors, who created new clothes to the size of the few slaves who absolutely could not fit into the premade outfits. All fabrics were of dark colors. Light colors were reserved for the well to do. Slaves wore dark colors because their work made them dirty and also there was a better chance of spotting them should any one of them attempt to escape into the white world of ice and snow all around them.

When Ford barreled into the room, all needle-spears turned toward the huge Aelwydian. The valvar had a kneejerk reaction to anyone of his size. They grumbled to one another about the foolishness of allowing such a large monstrosity as he into Dargkivi. Submissive and manageable were preferable. Ford fell in with a line of naked and often whimpering men and women favoring their wrists. He stood at the back, hiding his body behind another. Without a stitch of clothes, he didn't think he could feel any more naked, but then he ran a hand over his stubbly chin and the top of his head. Surely, this was how newborns felt upon first entering the world - miserably cold, battered, and utterly unsure of everything about them. All of these shivering men and women, nude and newly shaven, looked disturbingly alien to him. There was something unnatural about the look. People ought to wear clothes and have hair on their heads. It was an opinion he never knew he held until just then.

The outfitters read each new slave's brand and picked from the piles either a robe, tunic or frock to match the industry or kind of household he or she would be working in. The largest clothes available fit Ford like a glove made for a child. He split the seams of everything they thrust at him. Standing by a tailor waiting for new clothes, he covered himself with his hands. The tailor worked like his life depended upon speed, and perhaps it did. The distance between stitches was larger than Ford had ever seen. When finished, the tailormade outfit, sacks with holes for extremities, gripped him like a second skin and threatened to burst at every bend and stretch. The slave acting as tailor could not and would not expend more fabric than he had been allotted per slave. All requests for changes met with silence and downcast eyes until finally a valvar took notice and moved the troublemaker along to the shoer. The shoer stood glumly by the only other door in the room and doled out padded socks with leather bottoms. None fit Ford, so by order of the valvar, he was issued the leather sacks the sock-shoes had been stored in. The sacks had to be tied around his ankles to keep them from falling off. Worse than making him feel rather foolish, the sacks provided him the barest warmth.

The time it took to fashion new clothes made Ford the last to shuffle into the next room at the urging of the valvar. He found a gathering of the guards huddled around a group of translators carrying lamps. It was the only warmth to be had in this sparse room and it wasn't much. Strangely, all of Ford's fellow prisoners encircled the group, mostly with their backs up against the wall or at least at a respectful distance on the perimeter. What was unusual was that none of the valvar paid them any mind. Those who should have been guarding them were too intent on the tiny flames warming the tips of their fingers. Now was the time for an uprising if there ever was one. The prisoners outnumbered the guards five to one. It was just a matter of getting ahold of their little spears. But like them all, Ford was miserably tired, hungry, and recovering from being branded. Most appeared on the verge of passing out from sleep deprivation or starvation. They simply hadn't the strength left to put up a fight.

Alerted by the valvar that all slaves were present, the translators positioned themselves in front of everyone and began reeling off snatches of all the languages they possessed in an effort to gather the new slaves into groups who understood them. "To me come. To me come," one of the them finally said. Ford and those who knew Aelwydian shuffled over to him. Bald and robed like all of the other translators, this squat Fodagan man possessed a grating voice which probably served him well in his former employment as a sailor. He had absorbed bits and pieces of the language from fellow crew members during his many long voyages to and from Aelwydian ports. Though illiterate, he knew enough of a variety of spoken languages to distinguish himself in these remote lands as a decent candidate for verbal translation.

The individual groups were taken through a series of twisting and turning passages, past locked doors, and ever up and up stairways with steep, tiny steps that everyone but the Kamen guards climbed with their hands and feet. After conquering the longest set of stairs and breaching the stoutest door, they finally arrived at the roof of the city. As they stepped outside, a tearing wind ripped at their new clothes and threatened to carry away the lightest bodies. Never had any of them felt a wind as stiff and cold as this. It cut to the bone and hurled stinging ice particles at their exposed arms. They kept their heads bowed and tucked between their shoulders. Those who snuck a peek about them saw a dreary and sunless landscape of ice and rock. Even on the brightest days there wasn't much to see. Dargkivi had no mighty fortresses upon the surface and was surrounded by no walls. Here and there could be seen a handful of dovecot-styled entryways, like the one they'd used. Streaks of soot trailed away from a few stumpy smokestacks which pimpled the land and belched a smoke that the wind instantly dragged away. At some distance, a large dome stuck out of the ground a few feet, looking like a buried egg. Otherwise, there were few structures to be seen, leaving very little evidence of the civilization below.

Ford noticed Barwnig Bryce among another group huddling nearby. The former warden of the penal colony had absentmindedly wandered into this other group by mistake. He had not been himself since the attack on the *Fida Mal*, which left him bereft of his family. No one knew nor asked what had become of his wife and children. The worst was assumed, and so he received pity and forgiveness from the former penal colony prisoners whom he had lorded over back on Polecat Island. The way they looked at it, they had all ended up in the same miserable situation and saw no need for retribution against a defeated man.

"No chains you have!" the translator shouted over the constant howling of the wind. "No use! You run? Want you run? Go! Now go!" The valvar lowered their spears and waved hands to the barren expanse and even smiled to the new slaves, as if welcoming them to leave if they so wished. No one moved, except to shiver and stamp their feet. Ahead of them stretched endless miles of ice-covered rock and behind lay the cliffs overlooking the ocean. They might flee into the wasteland, but they wouldn't make it a mile before succumbing to the cold. In fact, they worried that they might not survive even this much exposure in their flimsy clothes. With teeth chattering away, they wrapped their arms about themselves, as if fearing their innards would freeze. The translator's interminable speech finally concluded with a warning. "Away of Dargkivi you run? No! No, you can not!"

Returning to the relatively warm back tunnels of the city, the valvar herded the new slaves into a vast kitchen. Here Ford and the others waited in a line to be fed on boiled fat from a steaming cauldron. As the line crept forward, they scarfed down the greasy chunks, not caring about scalded fingers and throats. They had to get as much into their mouths as they could before the line moved on and reached the cook's assistant, who then took away the bowl, whether it was empty or not. Feet dragged and the line backed up until a guard waved his spear at them and forced a more regular step. After their bowls were taken from them, they were made to wait at the far end of the room for the others to finish. It made the rush through the food line seem pointless, but this was the way of their captors and no one dared complain.

While being fed, they were made to listen to the translators babbling away, like a tuneless choir singing different songs at the same time, as they recited the long list of rules and infractions set down by their new masters. Ford eyed the cook, who scraped the bottom of the cauldron with his iron spoon, and thought how another bowl's worth would have been a better thing than listening to gibberish. Not everyone wanted more. Those who had suffered extreme malnutrition couldn't keep down what little they did have.

The Fodagan translator stumbled into his broken Aelwydian and fumbled through the topic of punishment. By parsing together a few of the more comprehendible words, Ford understood that so much as a hint of a threat by a slave toward his master would result in various punishments just a hair's breadth less severe than death. Any blatant attack, successful or not, would bring a swift, trial-less execution. The translator reeled off a mind-numbing litany of other crimes and infractions. The list was daunting, and yet, there was hope. "Work you seven years…you go free." Everyone's spirits lifted somewhat at hearing that. The thought that they could work for their freedom was more than they expected. Hearing of a possible end to this madness was a cheering thought. Seven years was a long time, but it was not a lifetime.

"Atsevisk tatz vergz!" snapped an officer of the alamvalvar as he entered the room with more Kamen guards. Aside from a tiny silver insignia pin denoting his rank, all that distinguished him as an officer of the lower guard from the rest of the alamvalvar was a shinier helmet, cleaner clothes and boots without holes. His command set all of the valvar in motion. They checked each prisoner's brand, then regrouped them by owner and industry. More than half of the new slaves would be handed off to the ulemvalvar, the upper guard, who were tasked with serving and protecting the upper echelons of Kamen society.

A pair of Kamen led Ford and three others from the kitchen through doors and corridors which emptied into the main entry hall just behind the gatehouse. Iron-gridded windows facing the bay had been inlaid with colored glass. They let in enough light that no lanterns were necessary to see the statues of famous Kamen sitting atop protruding door lintels, as well as the many etchings in the gatehouse's stone walls. These were depictions of the prominent Kamen who helped found and build Dargkivi into what it had become. This was one of the few places in the city where Ford could stand up straight. He stretched out his back for the few paces it took to pass through the hall and out a far door.

The group plunged deeper into Dargkivi's less desirable districts, traversing tunnels, stairways, and neighborhoods defended by iron gratings. They were specifically making for the town of Drek, home to miners, koer herders, and other laboring Kamen. Few Kamen worked for a living in Dargkivi, but every Kamen living in Drek worked.

The approach tunnel opened to a roughly-excavated cavern filled with echoes of coughing, the tapping of a hammer upon metal, a dull drum beat, a woman singing tunelessly, and children at play. Drek was only lit sporadically by pungent tallow candles flickering in round, knee-high windows, aside from the one oil lantern hanging just under a hole in the ceiling at the center of town. These windows, as well as doors that were almost as wide as they were tall, belonged to snug houses built into the rock walls on either side of the road through town. The cavern's ceiling had been dug out a few extra feet higher to permit stacked housing. The second stories were reached by short stairways built on the outside of each house. Ford could have ascended them in a single step.

A chubby toddler not much larger than a housecat, tottering after a koerskin ball near the edge of a thin second story terrace, stopped its play to watch the new slaves pass. Without exception, this was the roundest boy Ford had ever seen. Conversely, Ford was the tallest man the boy had ever seen. Even as elevated as the child was, Ford still had to look down to meet the child's eye. The boy beamed back a delighted and ludicrously wide smile. His mother stuck her head out of a window to see what the noise was about and started at the sight of Ford. Like a harassed penguin, she waddled out to drag her child back inside by its head.

Most of the people out and about in Drek at that time of day could be found congregating at Revek's, a public house which made up one of the corners of the town square. Revek's wide, shutter-less windows and brick veranda created the best possible approximation of an open-air establishment one could find underground. The drowsy, pink-eyed patrons lifted their heads from the short tables to leer at Ford, the tallest slave to pass through town. They pointed and muttered to one another, took a sip of the blandest fermented koer's milk in all of Dargkivi, and resumed their napping.

The valvar escorts led Ford's group through the center of Drek, passing narrow side streets that disappeared into the darkness where the town extended into more housing and shops. A gang of children rolled out of one street on their stumpy legs and chased after the group, hooting in ways that best bounced their voices off the walls. Just outside of Drek, the valvar stopped at another iron gate.

The gatekeeper brightened at seeing the new slaves approach. Beyond him lay the mines where the recent wealth of the Kamen had been dug from the rock deep beneath Dargkivi. Such riches came at a considerable loss of life, so there was always a need for more slave labor to smash and haul stone in the suffocating and dank labyrinthine tunnels. But that wasn't why the gatekeeper smiled. His natural sanguinity smushed his eyes into crescents and inevitably blossomed that smile into a bubbly laugh. He couldn't help himself. He yanked open the gate to welcome them with upraised palms and fingers curling eagerly inward. His vest, shirt and trousers looked to be made of a black fabric, but that was actually years' worth of mine dust settling upon his clothing, clothing that would never be clean again despite the best efforts of a devoted daughter on behalf of her beloved father. The only thing truly dirt-free upon his person was a polished bronze mining insignia in the shape of a hammer pinned over his heart.

The mining guard and the bay guards dropping off the new slaves growled back and forth. Ford expected a fight to break out, but no, this was their way. The often-curt bearing, blunt speech, and edged consonants of the harsh Kamen tongue made everything seem surly and insolent. Much to the new slaves' surprise, the valvar slapped each other on the head companionably before parting company.

Once left alone, the jovial mining guard beamed benevolence toward his new charges. "Mulle olen Aato. Aato!" said Aato Valodiz, a mining guard known in Drek for telling the children stories he made up during his solitary hours on the job. He patted his own chest and repeated his name until he felt satisfied that they all understood. "Slaves need repetition before they learn anything," he would say to his daughter. "It is a shame they are not as smart as us Kamen, but what is to be done?" All he could do was pity them and treat them with all the kindness he possessed.

Aato gave a beckoning gesture to follow and strolled ahead with his back to the new slaves. He struck up a continuous, rambling monologue about various aspects of the mines, conjuring all the animation of a five-year-old describing a birthday party. From the Kamen's gestures, Ford guessed he was talking about death, something that stank, and tools. He said it all in Kamen, so none of the slaves knew what he was saying. Aato didn't let their lack of understanding slow him down. Guard duty was lonely and now he had people to talk to. His needle-spear hung at his side and was only raised when he wanted to make a point or felt his narration needed a flourish of the hands. The distance they had to walk wasn't far, but he stuffed their short time together like it was a holiday turkey. More than once he stopped to face them, figuring that if they saw his lips moving they might better understand him. They couldn't see much of anything. Aato carried no light, but there was a dull red glow coming through the bars of a gate ahead.

Once they reached this second gate, the mine's inner gate, Aato banged on the bars and continued chatting away about the various kinds of gates in Dargkivi. He banged on the iron frame and poked at the canvas covering as he spoke. One of the Kamen mining operators showed up and interrupted him. This broad-faced Kamen without an ounce of Aato's charisma, but plenty of beard and nose hair, tromped up to the gate, ignored Aato's salutation, and let them through. Aato resumed speaking to the slaves, even after the gate was slammed in his face.

After another, shorter tunnel, the new slaves emerged into an octagonal room lit by the weak, beet-red light of a warm rock held in an amulet-like clasp that dangled from the end of a chain hanging from the ceiling. A half dozen passages intersected at this room, none of which were as refined as the tunnel they arrived in. Though not a pleasant place, the floor in this room was level and clear of debris. A water tap jutted from a wall. Koerskin bedding cluttered the floor of an alcove just off the main room. The mining operator barked a few orders and left them. Not knowing what else to do, the exhausted slaves collapsed upon the koerskins and fell asleep.

"Wake up!"

The shout evoked the threat of thunder before the storm to Ford's ears. He shot up, throwing elbows in the midst of a waking nightmare in which the Skala were whipping him at the oars.

"Easy, lad! Easy," said a softer version of the disembodied voice. Ford squinted at a shadow hovering over the sleeping newcomers. "Mush's here. And yer shift's up."

While the others crawled out of bed, Ford stretched out the kinks in his aching body and peered around wondering where he was. As the true nightmarish reality set in he groaned as much from physical pain as despair. It had been all too real.

The smell of boiled fat propelled him to his feet and toward the dull red light. Under the hanging warm rock, he found a cheerless group of miners sitting randomly about the room slurping up a fatty stew from ceramic bowls and gulping vast quantities of water straight from a communal pitcher. Ford couldn't help but stare at these wasted, discarded souls like so many empty shells. Once free men, now they were nothing more than hammers being made to beat themselves blunt against an unending labor until their handles snapped. The only reason they were alive was that they were as thick of finger as skull and built to work all day and night. The filth layered upon the miners almost blotted them out. Dust covered them head to toe, even the insides of their noses and ears. As regular as clockwork, one of them would snort out or cough up a black glob which he would jettison to the left or right. They didn't care that they were being stared at. Their only interest was food and drink.

The most rugged of the miners, a hardhearted Nagaporian by the name of Prakash, who had calloused, ochre skin and strands of gray in his stubble, kicked up a cloud of complaints. No one fully understood him, for he shouted and cursed in his mother tongue, but his gestures toward the new arrivals made it obvious who bothered him. The newcomers went on eating, though not nearly as ravenously. Cautious eyes kept the apparently volatile Prakash within their periphery. At least now they knew who they needed to tread lightly around. Ford wasn't nearly as concerned as the others. He didn't pay heed to a bully.

While chewing on a rubbery piece of fat, his slumbering mind awoke to the fact that he had been roused by someone speaking Aelwydian. Ford had no friends with him, no one who might help make a bad situation bearable, nor anyone to even speak to. But now, someone here had spoken his language.

The realization sent a shivering thrill through him. He looked at each tired, dusty face and couldn't pick out an Aelwydian among them. Every one of the veteran miners wore a mask of gray dust.

"Any of you understand a word I'm saying?" he asked. No one replied.

"The water," said a drowsy, slump-shouldered slave sitting beside him. His cheeks were as pockmarked as a slice of leavened bread. His concave chest and cagey manner made him appear to be constantly receding. The man jerked his chin toward the pitcher of water. Ford slid it over to him and watched as he drank deeply. "Name's Rynne. I come from Rockport," he finally said.

When Rynne said no more but went on drinking, Ford offered up, "I'm Ford. From Port Morton, but born in, well, elsewhere." He didn't have the patience just then for idle trivialities. This was just as well for Rynne, who was too tired to even listen. Ford read the exhaustion in the man's dead eyes and slouched posture, so he kept his many questions bottled up for now. At least he knew he had someone he could talk to, and that was a mercy to be thankful for.

Prakash threw his dirty bowl into the basin and let loose another angry string of oaths. Ford couldn't help but ask, "What's eating him?"

"Prakash? Everything and nothing." Whenever forced into conversation, Rynne breathed heavily between labored phrases and avoided long sentences when he could. "The meal wasn't here when we got back. The off-duty's supposed to get it and have it ready. But don't mind him. Everything prickles his pear."

The Drek gate clanged shut in the distance. A belch rippled from the tunnel. Rynne and all of the miners who had not yet turned in grunted and groaned to their feet and shuffled off to the alcove. A group of Kamen mining operators let themselves in through the gate into this slaves' common room. Among them were two alamvalvar, whose names Ford would learn later from Rynne were Dustav and Jukk. Proud brutes they were, who thought themselves better than the likes of Aato and other mere gate guards. Having come from their midday meal in Drek, Dustav and Jukk were here to watch over the next shift, ensuring that the slaves got to work promptly, kept at it and caused no trouble. These two were particularly free with their punishment. Ford didn't need Rynne's word for that. The two guards were poking and prodding slaves with the butt ends of their spears almost the moment they entered the common room.

Well-rested and full-bellied, the Kamen sauntered into the common room ready to whip the slaves into a frenzy of activity. Ford and the new miners, as well as a few veterans, were bustled down a much rougher tunnel. Unrefined stone left the active mines with uneven floors, irregular ceilings and tight passages strewn with rubble. Loose rocks twisted ankles, jutting stone bruised heads and pits opened under one's feet. Tunnels forked left and right, cut sharply back and forth, dove down steep slopes and occasionally crawled back up toward the surface. Offshoots would circle back around to the main tunnel or dead-end where disused mines had been walled off. Before long, Ford found himself growing dizzy and disoriented. The confusion only deepened as they traveled farther into Kavenauk, the name Ford learned was given to the mines by the Kamen. The chance of becoming forever lost seemed sickeningly probable.

Less than a hundred paces in, lightheadedness swept over him from the close atmosphere and stifling air. He leaned against a wall to catch himself from falling. Much of his youth had been spent out in the open among the trees or hauling cargo by the seaside, where one bathed in fresh air. Now he found himself crawling into dark holes, choked by smokey oil lanterns and lamps, where air seemed rarer than the precious minerals they mined. He coughed and tried to bury his nose in his tight tunic to avoid the dust kicked up by the men trudging ahead. The early architects of the city had been ingenious when building flues for their living quarters, but that ingenuity had not been brought to bear in such remote locations as these.

Once they reached the end of the newest tunnel, the Kamen official in the group acting as excavator brought his expertise to bear against the ignorance of the new slaves. Through exasperated gestures he showed them how to dig and pry with a pick, as well as where to place wedges and how to drive them in. Before long, hammers clinked, rocks cracked and rumbled over the floor, and the scraping of sleds deafened the ears. Ford's first few swings of a hammer displayed how useless he would be as a rock breaker. His long body had to contort itself just to get into position to swing. And for all his strength, his hammer missed the wedge placed for him, bounced back toward his face, and hit the ceiling. A sliver of a rock chipped off and shot past the head of Jukk, the guard keeping an eye on him. Envious of the long-legged and irritated by his superiors for having foisted a useless slave upon him, the valvar gave Ford's legs a few cracks with his spear, as if to make more room by beating them out of the way.

Before he did someone a mischief, Ford was put on hauling duty in the relatively larger, more finished tunnels, where he could move about easier and be of some use pulling or pushing one of the rock-filled sleds. He and another man would haul their load to a cavern near the common room, where they would dump it in a finishing room. When construction within the city called for blocks, a mason would come down and pick through the rubble for the necessary pieces. The haulers had to carry whatever wasn't wanted to a dumping room.

By the end of the first day, Ford and the new slaves assigned to the mines knew their duties inside and out. Before three days had passed, their duties became a drudgery of hard, monotonous labor augmented only in the slightest by rushed meals and harassment from the guards. By the end of the first week, Ford had carried a dead body out of the mines and into what was known as the Room of Bones, a mass grave of slave remains. In a short span, it was all too apparent to the newcomers, that miners beneath Dargkivi lived a hard existence and died miserably.

There were reprieves. Like all Kamen, those guards and engineers associated with the mine enjoyed their holidays. On days when they did not work, the miners were allowed the time off as well, since there was no one to watch over them. One of these holidays occurred toward the end of Ford's first week in Kavenauk. The slaves spent the entire day on their backs in the alcove. Most slept the day away, waking only to eat. Ford had not been paired with Rynne long enough yet to get many answers to his questions, so he took the opportunity to ask during a meal on their day off.

"One day I was chasing after this son of a whore…" said Rynne through labored breaths. "Who I found with my wife, if you follow." Ford did follow, but it wasn't the answer he expected, at least not to the question he had asked. Ford could guess how Rynne had been captured. What he wanted to know was how he had come to be in the mines. Why had they all ended up here? Why was one person chosen for one task and not another? What were the others doing, and where were they? Rynne was tired and his faculties muddled. Like those before him who endured the dank mines for any length of time, he was at the start of a decline that would end his Kavenauk days in a jangle of nerves. The only way he had found to cope was to live each moment of his remaining life within his own mind as he wished it would be. Instead of answering Ford's question, he answered the question he wanted to be asked, a question that plagued him since his capture. Why had he been so foolish over a woman? "I was hot-headed. I tore after him along the docks, not thinking nor seeing straight." A bout of coughing broke up his story, leaving it in a hacking limbo until he mastered the fit. "I fell off the dock into the bottom of a boat. Knocked my fool self out, woke up on a ship headed for Valtavastad, pulling on ropes, tending the goat, doing whatever I was told. Then we were captured."

Frustrated in his first attempt, Ford moved on to the next question begging an answer. "Is it true, they'll let us go after seven years?"

"Let us go?" Rynne repeated as if he couldn't believe what he'd heard. His eyes roamed over the top of Ford's head to determine the thickness of this young giant's skull. "No. Abandon that hope. Some've been here seven years and more, so I hear. Not many, mind you, and none here in the mines. No one lasts that long down here."

"But they said—"

"They say a lot. Don't believe it. They make excuses and lay blame and…" He held up a hand, cleared his throat, and continued. "And come up with reasons to add years. A man can't seem to stay out of trouble. Every little thing they find fault with and add another year or more. But mostly it's not a problem."

"Why is that?"

"Like I said, nobody lives long. If the work don't kill a man, them bastards will." Rynne nodded to the tunnel leading to Drek. "This one slave lost an eye for staring too long at one of them. Another fellow got above himself and threatened his master with a knife. They broke his arms and legs with a hammer for that. You raise a finger to one of them and they'll chop it clean off, if the stories are to be believed. If ever you see a man wearing a hand around his neck on a string like a necklace, it'll be his own. They got sick heads, they do." The long speech took it out of Rynne. He laid back on his skins and let his lungs catch up. His words had weighed upon Ford heavier than the loads of rocks he was tasked with carting around all day. His mood plummeted. From all he'd seen and heard, this place was worse than Polecat Island by far. Nothing new he heard improved this opinion.

"And there's no way of getting away?"

"No one here gets out of alive, lad. There's no way out but dying." The weary words dropped from Rynne's lips as if bringing them to life had cost him some of his own.

On the morning of a day that would change the day-to-day lives of the miners, Ford woke to a world of metal crashing all about him. Two chipper valvar marched into the common room after waking up to the reheated remnants of their holiday meal. They were bursting with a gurgling mirth over a game savagely won at Revek's the day before. This pair didn't have quite the violent streak in them as Dustav and Jukk, but they made up for it by being annoying in their own way. Each and every time they came to rouse the miners for their shift, they stomped into the common room banging the shaft of their spears on their helmets, helmets which they were wearing. To Ford's waking mind it sounded like a pile of tin pans thrown down an endless slope. The two guards hooted merrily as they used the butt end of their spears to rouse the slaves from their beds earlier than normal or necessary. One of the pleasures of their drearily lives was showing up a hair early to have their fun with the sleeping slaves.

It being Ford's morning to retrieve their breakfast, he followed one of the valvar back to Drek. A large communal kitchen there served out meals for the slaves and workers. On the way back, the guard made him carry the hot pot for as long as he could before it scalded his hands and arms to the point that he had to put it down. With Ford running in a hustling half-sprint and the guard at his heels urging him on, they made it as far as the tunnel leading to the common room. The pleased guard cheered the feat, but smacked Ford's ankles and wrists until he hefted the pot once more and finished the run.

"Ohtiz! Runnak! Koletiz runnak!" The panicky scream came ricocheting through the tunnels from some distance away. The guards waiting to make the shift switch rushed to the tunnel mouth from whence it came. The slaves in the common room, having barely begun eating, sat up and looked to one another.

"Was that from down the mine?" Ford wondered aloud. He looked from tunnel to tunnel expecting something awful to emerge at any moment.

"That'll be Dustav," said Rynne without the least concern. "Sounds like there's been an attack." Ford had become used to Rynne's listless lack of interest in life, but this was beyond even his barren apathy. The man kept on eating without lifting his eyes from his bowl.

The scream repeated and the guards could take no more. They gathered up the slaves and herded them into the tunnel. On his hands and knees, Ford followed after a man with a lantern ahead of him, keeping as close to him as possible the farther they delved into the mines. Without that light, one was liable to fall into a hole. How far he would plunge and what was down there were things Ford didn't want to find out for himself. Dustav's incessant shouting guided them through the passages until they met up with the miners dragging Jukk's body back out of Kavenauk. Blood oozed from where his forehead had been split open. One eye remained shut, while the other protruded from its crushed socket. There were no puncture wounds, just blunt force trauma.

Through a cascade of words and gestures, the slaves claimed that some kind of creature had invaded the mines and attacked him. They beat back the attack, driving the creature through a gap in a previously blocked up tunnel from which it must have infiltrated the mines. This was the worst attack in recent memory. Dustav's hands shook and his voice quavered. He and Jukk had been friends since childhood. The guards gathered up the body and took it back to Drek, leaving the slaves with their picks and hammers to secure the mines and hunt down any other such menace that might still be lurking about.

"What do you think it was," Ford asked Rynne. The guards had taken the hammer from the weakest miner and given it to Ford. The man was then dispatched to retrieve more oil, while Ford followed the band of slaves-turned-monster-hunters deeper into the tunnels. They were squeezing through a passage too tight for comfort. All Ford could hear was the scraping of their tunics and trousers against the stone walls. He doubted Rynne had heard him. If he did, he didn't answer and that left Ford with his eyes peeled, seeking the sinister in every dark crevice which the wavering lights of the lamps would not illuminate. "Whatever beat him to death must've been ox-strong or maybe used a rock." This remote ice land might harbor all kinds of strange creatures he had never heard told in Aelwydian tales. That hulking beast they called Avar, for one. He wouldn't have believed a muscle-bound creature like that had existed if he hadn't seen it for himself. Worse possibilities began infesting his wonderings. What was waiting for them in the dark? And what if they were overwhelmed by more than they could manage? Where would they flee to? They would have to flee to Drek and hope the Kamen let them through the gates. The slaves' common room wasn't safe. There was no protection for the slaves from a full-blown invasion of the mines.

His mind had plenty of time to wander. The veteran miners weren't in any rush. Ford chalked it up to hesitation from fear, but after they left the Kamen well behind and found a small cavern that everyone could fit into, Prakash called a halt and they all made themselves as comfortable as they could among the rubble. Ford was confused. They had found nothing, and yet they'd stopped long before investigating the farthest reaches of the mines or coming to any blocked-up tunnel that had been breached.

The answer came in the tight jawline and pulsing vein above Prakash's clouded brow, two outward marks of the mind-warping, humanity-crushing brutality he had endured while enslaved in Dargkivi. Those markings disappeared when the Nagaporian sat down on a rock, leaned his back against a wall, and began shaking with laughter. The other veterans joined in, stifling almost giddy outbursts as they fell about themselves. The newcomers watched on in wonderment and confusion, concerned that their comrades were going mad. Ford wiped his sweaty palms on his thighs and clutched the hammer firmly. Vexed by the lax attitude of the veterans and refusing to be caught unprepared, he remained coiled and ready for anything, whatever might be lurking around the corner, or even if it came bursting through a wall.

"Calm yourself, lad," Rynne said, wiping away a mirthful tear and noticing Ford on his toes, his body ready to spring upon an imaginary foe.

"But what if it's still out there?"

"What, the thing that did in our friend Jukk? What you think did it? You saw his head. What you think did that?"

"I don't know, maybe something big…with a rock maybe," said Ford. He reached down and snatched one up to make his point. They were all around, a ready weapon.

"Try your other hand," said Rynne nodding to the hammer. Ford looked down at it and back at Rynne with a dawning in his eyes. "That's right. We got rid of the monster. That Jukk was the blight of this miserable, godforsaken place. Dustav's no better, but one at a time. If it has to be done, Prakash won't mind finishing the job." Ford sat back and took it all in. Prakash gave nothing away, at least not to one who had no understanding of the man's odd rambling utterances.

Dustav did not show up for duty the following day. The break didn't help. He came back on edge and easily set off, threatening the slaves with his spear and beating them over the slightest infractions. He was often absent from work. On his next trip to the kitchen to fetch their meal, Ford saw him lingering over a drink at Revek's and looking pale. When on duty, the miners would find him staying behind at the common room on some pretext or other, or offering to take a shift at the gates.

He and the mining operators had their suspicions that a slave had a hand in Jukk's slaying, but they also believed in their own ability to maintain control over their slaves. More acceptable to their way of thinking was the idea that an incredibly strong beast of some kind had broken into the mines. To make themselves feel that they had handled the problem properly, they made the miners double buttress the point where the wall had been supposedly breached.

Dustav was ordered to head up the job, since he had been on duty when the incident occurred, but of course he did no such thing. He waited in the finishing room while the miners spent half their work day walling off an already walled-off tunnel. The patchwork job satisfied the Kamen, who were eager for work as usual to get underway again.

As a result of Jukk's death, Aato was promoted as his replacement. This made the miners happy. And the affable Kamen proved to be a good influence on Dustav as well, entertaining the shattered and irritable guard with games and stories, soothing his troubled mind and distracting him from his more destructive pursuits. Aato being no taskmaster meant that there were longer breaks and fewer beatings. Work in the mines became much more bearable.

Chapter 11
Tat Tarl

Ford lost count of the days since his capture by the end of his second week in the mines. Each day melded into one long monotonous grind in some of the worst conditions imaginable. He had no desire to know how long it had been, because as Rynne suggested, "It's best not to think about it. It'll make ya miserable." It had. And the one day when something different did happen, Ford wished it hadn't.

On a morning when it was Ford's turn to retrieve breakfast, Aato took him to the kitchen at Drek, where a team of Grakts, known for working magic with food, stirred vats over a central hearth or butchered racks of rib and slabs of fat carried in from the cooling vault by blue-lipped porters.

"Vrod!" a voice called out to Ford from across the kitchen. It was Kavenauk's head mining operator, a man the slaves knew as the Big Beard of the Mines. He stood with his hairy arm around a cook's assistant, a witless and silly Manerd of indeterminant sex and age trying to stir a cauldron. The flush of the Manerd's face was dangerously red from the heat and unwanted attention. "Vrod! Good day to you," the operator sang out in Kamen. "Vrod, Vrod, Vrod! Just the man I want to see!"

All of the Kamen in Drek had come to know Ford's name and liked to say it aloud, though none pronounced it correctly. Most of them liked him for being an overly large man. While many Kamen held a prejudice against those taller than themselves, they made an exception for this ludicrously tall man. The way he crouched and crawled everywhere he went made them laugh, and they were always happy to have something to laugh at.

The Big Beard addressed Aato. Aato's expression became even more excited and pleased than usual. He took Ford by the arm and together they left the kitchen, and the breakfast pot, behind as they headed out of Drek by a back route.

Ford fretted. His comrades in the mines would likely go without their morning meal and have to work on empty stomachs. It may not have been his fault, but he would take the brunt of the miners' ire. He thought of Prakash's reaction. The crazy bastard might murder him in his sleep over such an offense. If only the day had been like any other day.

They traveled deeper into Dargkivi than Ford had ever been. Aato talked over his protests. The ebullient Kamen was too excited about the day's excursion to think about the mines or any one slave's concerns. Along the way they stopped off in Alamdorv, a lower town of tailors and tanners. They ditched Ford's filthy, split-seamed sack clothing and outfitted him in something new and clean. His shoe-substitute sacking would have to go, too. Even slaves needed to be presentable where they were headed. Aato was in tears over the size of Ford's gigantic new leather shoes.

"Boats! He walks upon boats!" he kept on saying while he and a tanner fell about themselves.

Once Aato caught his breath and put on a new coat loaned to him for the occasion, they set off for the upper districts. Along the way, he launched into a soliloquy on the wonders of the Shrine of Tat Tarl. Ford caught the name and assumed its significance by Aato's grand gestures. The Kamen's talk lasted the entirety of the half mile journey up countless steps and through winding corridors. Popping out of a side passage, they entered a broad square off of which branched a wide corridor lit with warm rock lanterns that led to Tat Tarl's large doors.

"Are these not the grandest doors in all the land and beyond?" Aato said. The lightness of his voice and the sweeping flourish of his hands drew attention to the door's size as well as its meticulous and intricate repeating line and knob pattern. Clearly Ford was meant to be impressed, but he had walked through larger doors than these, and still he had to stoop to pass through Tat Tarl's entryway. Even so, he tried to appear in awe.

Upon entering the antechamber, one was bludgeoned by reminders of the generosity of the wealthy citizens who paid for the shrine's construction, rather than by memorials for whom the shrine had been made, Tar Suur Adelar Olev, whose foresight and ingenuity had brought previously unimagined prosperity to the Kamen people. Roughly carved busts of the contributors sat on footstool-sized pedestals crowding the highly-decorated chamber. The largest busts portrayed the highest contributors.

When Aato entered, a pair of slaves cleaning the chamber began vigorously scrubbing the stone heads they had been leaning against. They used rags to trace the bulbous eyes and noses, dig into the accidentally bell-shaped ears, and wipe across the tops of the wide heads with broad strokes. Ford was gaining the impression that Kamen artists weren't half bad when it came to wall decoration, but damned awful at most else. The antechamber's intentionally low lighting actually improved upon the childish design of the busts.

Entering the shrine itself, Ford and Aato's unaccustomed eyes squinted and watered from the brilliant light shining down from the magnificent central white dome. It took some explaining on Aato's part, but eventually Ford understood that Tat Tarl meant "The Pearl" in Kamen and referred to this dome. Ford guessed it was the one he'd seen on the surface soon after he arrived. Like an inverted colander with its holes inlaid with reflective stones and thick glass, it caught any and all light whether the sky was sunny or overcast. A brilliant spectrum of color sprayed over the arched aisles and dual transepts.

Though it was not the usual day of worship at the shrine for the lower ranks of Dargkivi society, Kamen tradesmen and their families had been allowed entrance to see the repairs being made, so that they might better appreciate the sacrifices of the ruling rich in paying for these repairs. Their simply garbed backsides filled the marble seats placed at various angles in the aisles. Clusters of their newly-scrubbed faces marveled at the many urns, arks, painted vases, silver coffers, and glass jewelry cases displayed upon squat stone pedestals against the walls. More than a house of holy reverence, Tat Tarl resembled a museum or treasury. These commoners were duly impressed by the collection of wealth. One could easily read in their faces their pride by association in the accumulation.

Aato had only ever visited once before. The occasion remained a strong, favored memory. He took Ford by the wrist, his unbranded left wrist, and led him eagerly to a row of stone plinths. Atop the first was a stocky alabaster figurine depicting a jolly, big-bellied man holding forth a pile of coins in one hand and a golden heart the size of a melon in the other. Ford was wondering if the heart was solid gold all the way through when Aato reached out and rapped it with a knuckle. They were both disappointed to hear the hollow echo. But just five feet away was an intricately designed torque with frolicking figurines all around. Aato gave another tap, and yes indeed, they were solid gold dancers. Next to the friendly fat man was displayed a small crystalline statuette, the representation of Jaa Zadievs, Lord of the Endless Winter, said a small plaque beneath it. This bizarre, almost translucent creature looked like a conglomeration of ice shards, a mound of frozen spikes and little else.

Aato's tour took them past many a silver plate, bowl and chalice. They brimmed with resplendent honorifics engraved around their rims to glorify prominent citizens. The names of the wealthiest families could be read going around and around the circular frame of a wooden plaque representing a sun with flares bursting from its edges. Trees didn't grow in Rikaswelt, making wood a rarity to be esteemed. Reckless amounts of gold and silver had been handed over to foreign merchants for the oak chests, pine stools, walnut spoons, and hickory tool handles that were presented at the shrine as if they were precious relics. Even something as mundane as a long piece of driftwood had its own granite display block. It stood on end with two huge round knots making up a stable base which held the long shaft erect.

The ulemvalvar began hustling the commoners out of the shrine. A small group of important Kamen had arrived. While Aato rattled on about the dancing ladies on the torque, pointing out their nakedness to Ford, the newly arrived group moved like a herd of well-groomed sheep up the aisle in their direction. Jewelry hung abundantly from the necks, ears and fingers of both the men and women. The moment Aato became aware of them, he pulled Ford back so that they both stood out of the way between a plain wooden box and a rostrum.

"The Master of Games and his wife," Aato whispered as much for his own benefit as Ford's. "The Minister of Water and his son. I'm not sure of the family who follows. Verz perhaps. Merchants though, to be sure."

Once past Ford and Aato, Verz stepped ahead and led the rest straight to a thick-legged table that came up to their noses. Nothing sat upon the table's rough, fissured planks. The table itself was the exhibit. The new acquisition had only recently been added to the collection and its novelty hadn't worn off yet. The table looked ordinary to Ford. Every tavern in Aelwyd had one. However, these people admired the ponderous and blocky piece of utilitarian furniture as if it were a work of art and happily indulged Verz as he extolled its virtues. They may not have understood the difference between pine and oak, but the table's sheer size and the quantity of wood before them enthralled all but Kunar Kalev, the Master of Games.

His attention had been drawn away by the sight of Ford standing in the shadows. Kalev's buying agent had informed him of a giant man he had lost to the miners at the auction. It stood to reason that this was that man. Losing out on anything rankled the pride of a man accustomed to getting what he wanted. The big slave would make an excellent addition to the games. One could almost see the machinations of his mind beginning to work behind his eyes. Somehow, he would get this giant and make the most of him. The group finally moved on and Kalev reluctantly followed after them.

One of the Kamen supervising the work site barked an order at Aato from across the shrine and put an end to the guided tour. As they crossed the nave, Aato pointed up at the great dome to show Ford the work he had to do that day. Every few feet an iron truss supported the shrine's ceiling, and even more iron held up the dome, just in case something large roaming about on the surface stepped upon it. These supports were rusting and needed replacing.

The city's tallest slaves had been enlisted for the job since they didn't need ladders to hold up the trusses or to bang them out of their seats with a hammer. Most of these lanky individuals were already at work. Like the rest of the slaves, Ford stood where they told him to, lifted what was shoved into his hands and toted what they ordered him to without lifting his bowed head or making eye contact with the Kamen in charge of the worksite. He was at it for an hour when the elbow of the man with the thin, trembling arms next to him buckled and the truss they were hoisting unbalanced. Ford had to take on most its weight to avoid the beam crashing down upon either their heads or the oak cabinet displayed upon a pedestal between them.

"I'm terribly sorry. Please forgive my clumsiness," said the other man in a hoarse whisper full of apology, but also strangely calm. And more importantly, in Aelwydian. Their eyes met as Ford steadied the beam and the other man adjusted his grip. Smiles broke out between them. "Oh. Hello, Ford Barlow."

"Will!" Ford's exclamation at finding the priest standing beside him brought a swift crack of a spear shaft across his knee from a valvar drawn to them by the near accident. Ford hardly noticed the pain, such was his joy at seeing his fellow former prisoner from Polecat Island. Though they had been working side by side for some time, neither had noticed and recognized the other because of their shaved heads, change of clothes, and averted gaze. Will's eyes welled up at the sight of Ford. Though they longed to speak to one another, they didn't dare. The Kamen of Upper Dargkivi were even more draconian about slaves speaking out of turn in their presence. The rest of the morning passed before they could talk together without reprisal. The Kamen took their midday meal and left the slaves to feed upon a greasy parcel of dried koer strips.

"You look well," Will said as he nibbled at a tough piece of meat.

"You as well," Ford lied. In truth, Will looked bone-thin and his pallid complexion hadn't improved.

Beyond the physical, he thought Will might be even more remote of mind than usual. During the exchange, the priest seemed to float in a haze, like a marionette lost in a dream. "Some days are better than…" he began at one point, but never seemed to finish his thought. "When they are, well, I think of walks in sunny glens, mother's warming pies…" The disconcerting way in which he spoke left Ford speechless. Will didn't seem to notice. "Birdsong in spring." He appeared to be disconnecting himself from the present in order to send the tender portions of his psyche on a leisurely jaunt back to more pleasant times and places.

"My…my…" The words crept out of him slowly and confusedly, like a pair of senile tortoises. He cleared this throat and waved a hand before his face as if to brush the utterance aside and begin again. "My, but your eyes are awfully red."

Ford rubbed a finger and thumb over his eyeballs, which had become somewhat habitual for him since being assigned to the dusty mines. But there was emotion mixed in with the irritation as well. Seeing a friendly face meant the world to him these days, but seeing him so reduced made the meeting bitter sweet. The gap in the conversation lasted uncomfortably long. Ford cleared his throat and said, "By the gods, it's good to see you." He almost said *to see you alive*, but caught himself. "How are they treating you?"

"I don't suppose I have much to complain about," Will said after a moment's contemplation. Ford shoveled in more food to satisfy his hunger. The cuts of meat were superior to what he was given in Kavenauk. His preoccupation with food was intentional. It gave Will the opportunity to speak about himself, even complain, if he so wished. Likely he wouldn't. To

Ford's knowledge, after all they had been through, he couldn't remember Will ever complaining. "I'm fine. Truly."

Ford doubted he was fine. While they were holding up the dome supports, he had noticed deliberate and measured cut marks along the insides of Will's arms from wrist to armpit. "What happened there?" he asked with a slight nod to the cuts.

"Ah. Yes," said Will as he covered his arms as best he could. Sensing the conversation moving from mere interest into the realm of concern, he did his best to focus his thoughts and answers. "Well, you see, the people here are engrossed in the healing arts. Though highly suspicious of magic, the Kamen do like their remedies and cures, those who can afford them. Have you not seen this for yourself?"

"All I've seen is the inside of some caves," said Ford and left it at that. He didn't think the people of Drek dabbled much in medicine or magic.

"Ah. I see. Well, it would seem the Kamen indulge themselves and suffer for it. Common ailments, which might be easily avoided if they only abstained from certain foods and what have you. For all of these problems of the body they seek a *dievs zauver*, a divine magic, as an instant cure-all. They make deep studies into the subject and grasp greedily upon any and all who might illuminate and elucidate upon some dark corner of their learning." Seeing creases of confusion darken the corners of Ford's face, Will clarified. "They want to know how to heal their ills."

"Ah," said Ford bobbing his head.

"They collect specimens, such as myself, and value them for their practical uses. If a healer proves useful, they are satisfied."

"And you were useful to them, were you?"

The surprisingly insightful question took Will aback and made him somewhat uncomfortable, because he knew the truth would worry Ford. He mulled his words and then mulled some more. His long mediations threw off the natural to-and-fro of their conversation, made him forget to answer the actual question asked, and instead provide an answer which sounded cagier than intended. "They thought I was withholding, keeping secrets. They wanted to see miracles, otherwise they considered me worthless." Will hesitated again and chose his words carefully. "They used various methods of inducement."

The complicated words Will used often confused Ford. Regardless of what was said, he was fairly certain he didn't like the sound of it. "Do you mean torture?" he asked.

Will shrugged. "It's not the word I would choose to use. Perhaps call them experiments."

"Expert mens?"

"Experiments. Trials used to discover the source of my *magic*." Ford's red eyes narrowed. His interest penetrated the priest's evasion. Will was never one for guile. "The truth is, they gave me an ultimatum. Either I show proofs of my abilities, they wanted me to heal an ailing elder of my master's household, or their so-called doctors would open me in order to seek out the source of my *dievs zauver*. They believed I was intentionally hiding it from them." Will caught Ford's clouding brow and wished he hadn't been quite so forthcoming. "It's nothing. They're mystified and wish to understand. That is all. I don't blame them. I find it mystifying myself." Ford didn't look mollified by this, so Will took on as placid a manner as he could muster. "But I am well, quite well. I do some transcribing and figuring for the master of the house, as well as his son's. I dare say it's a good deal easier than what they have you doing. So, as I say, I can't complain."

Ford fought down the urge to take up one of the iron beams and bash open the skull of the nearest Kamen.

Chapter 12
The Kavenauk Deeps

The ear-piercing *pings* of hammers hitting trusses still bounced between Ford's ears when he found himself back in the mines the following morning. It didn't help that his job on this day included hammering away at rock. The mining of a recently discovered vein of ore had created a cavern large enough for Ford to stand in and swing a hammer, so the Kamen put his strong arms to work.

"Amazing how warm it gets down here," he said as he stretched his back and wiped the sweat from his brow.

The Gel na Nadi man working with Ford that day nodded back and patted at his forehead with a calloused and gnarled hand to show he understood and agreed. His name was Ajasti Makhamudi. Aside from his habit of chewing his food, spitting it into a bowl of water, and then drinking it down like soup, Ajasti was memorable for having a neck so long that he had been nicknamed Horse.

Ajasti stuck his pick into a crevice and pried until a small avalanche tumbled to the floor. Some of the rock dropped from the ceiling onto their miners' metal caps. Folding up one's tunic, placing it on top of the head, and then setting the cap on top of that provided a decent amount of comfort and protection. Without the headwear, their skulls would be as battered and bruised as their knuckles and knees. If the rock falling from above didn't get them, what was strewn across the ground would. Tripping became a part of walking. The morning before, a miner leapt out of the way of a cave-in only to have a slide bury him to the waist later in the day.

Ajasti dug away at another crack. Another avalanche cascaded down around their feet. Ford stepped back over the uneven, rubble-covered floor and stumbled over shards of the reddish rock. Once the dust settled, a hole large enough to crawl through appeared in the wall about waist high at the spot where Ajasti had pried away the rock. The hole opened like an anguished, wailing mouth or a patch of starless night sky seen through treetops. Ford retrieved their oil lamp and shoved it into the hole. The light didn't illuminate much, but there was a cavern or possibly a tunnel on the other side.

"Can't tell how deep it is, but it goes on for a fair bit. Should we block it up?" said Ford. Ajasti replied. Neither understood the other, but that didn't stop them from having a conversation.

"Did we break into another part of the mines, do you think, my large friend?"

"Wonder where it leads to."

"Mother of all gods knows what could be in there."

"Anyway, it ain't natural, I'll tell you that much."

"We should alert the little men."

"Suppose we ought to let the half-men know."

Their back-and-forth may have led nowhere and answered no questions, but it made them feel better for having spoken. These dark caves could be terribly lonely places. They stood side by side for a while, shrugging their shoulders and scratching their heads while staring at the hole. Another pair of miners found them thus and joined in. Before long, half of the miners were formed about the hole shrugging their shoulders, scratching their heads, and wondering if there were valuable mineral deposits within or something not nearly as pleasant. Ford hoped for something valuable. The slave who had found the last strain of ore had been taken to Revek's and come back drunk hours later.

A lantern light and a merry song from Aato's lips came bouncing along the tunnel toward them. The sub-operator sent him to investigate why the hammering had ceased. They showed Aato the hole and instead of listening to the warnings of his bosses after the incident surrounding Jukk's death—*Take precautions around the slaves* and *Don't leave yourself exposed*—he turned his back to them and poked his head in for a look about, as inquisitive as a cat. Prakash had an unusually firm grip upon his pick and hovered a little too close, but otherwise the slaves showed no signs of malicious intent.

The valvar spun about, rapped the side of his skull with a knuckle, and shined his signature smile upon them. "You fret like soft mothers," he said to the assembled slaves in his own language. In mid-laugh, his lightweight bowl-shaped helmet shot forward from his head. While it clattered upon the ground, he let loose an involuntarily loud shout of surprise. The miners held their lamps and lanterns out toward him and recoiled. Dozens of toe-like appendages were wrapped about Aato's head like stumpy fingers clutching a large ball. From the miners' perspective, it looked as if something had reached out of the hole and had the Kamen by the back of the head. It gripped the skull and palpated the scalp. A weak squeal escaped from Aato and died away, yet his mouth worked on, speaking silent terror. The blood drained from him like water poured from a glass. His eyes rolled back and he pitched forward onto the floor facedown. Staring up from the back of his head was a huge lidless eye of fading, liverish red and white concentric circles. The miners fell back. One of them fled.

"What's that!" shouted Ford, cocking his hammer high over his head, ready to strike at the very center of the eye. If he struck it, he would crush Aato's skull. If it had been any other Kamen, Ford doubted he would have hesitated.

"It's a biter!" Rynne shouted back. They were known as blue ironbiters or biters for short. Over a foot in diameter when mature, these disk-shaped scavengers could scuttle like a crab across walls and ceilings as easily as floors. Mostly they sat motionless or slowly slid about scraping minerals from cave surfaces. Over time they reduced rock and created their own caverns. The miners had broken into just such a lair. Rynne would fill him in on all this later, but for now Ford thought he was looking down at the unblinking eye of some kind of demonic abomination.

Sensing the object within its grasp no longer posed a threat, the biter used its many short and powerful legs to flip from the back of Aato's head onto the wall next to the hole, where it clamped onto the rock to create a seal upon the surface with its carapace. When the biter jumped, so did the miners, and they kept on stepping back from the eerie eye. Though it appeared to be staring back at them, the eye was but mere deception for the sake of defense, a bit of camouflage mimicry of a more dangerous creature's petrifying gaze. The veteran miners knew this, and after the initial shock, Prakash darted forward and swung his hammer, crushing the biter's shell. A blue viscous liquid squirted from its sides. A moment later, the biter fell from the wall and moved no more.

The miners gathered about the prostrate Aato. The radula within the biter's spade-shaped mouth had scraped the back of the Kamen's head, peeling away a layer of skin where no hair would ever grow again. Ironbiters were not flesh eaters by nature, but like so many wild creatures, they used biting as defense and a way to discover if something new to them was edible.

After the miners shook him and shouted into his ears, Aato came to with plenty of questions. The miners pointed from the dead biter to the hole it had come from. The Kamen understood and hurriedly led them away from the spot to the gate at the common room. Erko, the valvar on guard there, let him through, but the moment Aato blurted out that there had been an attack, Erko slammed the gate on the slaves and locked them in. Now Ford understood why this particular gate had been reinforced with plates and covered in tough leather. One of those disk-shaped biters could easily slide through the bars of a regular gate. The slaves pounded upon the bars. There might be biters at their back, they implored, but Erko wouldn't let them through no matter how much they begged. Not even Aato could convince him to break safety protocol. Seeing the wound on the back of his fellow guard's head shocked Erko, who ignored the clamorous pleas, threw an arm around Aato, and ushered him back to Drek.

The slaves would have shouted themselves hoarse if not for Rynne. His calming manner settled them down. "They won't leave us here forever," he reassured Ford. "This happened months back. One of them biters—" He stopped and gave Ford the full explanation, as far as he understood what a biter was. "One of them got into the mines awhile back. I think only Prakash and I were around as far back as that to remember it. They made some of us go in there and kill it and block up the hole it come from. That'll be what they want from us this time too, I'd imagine."

Sure enough, before long a troop of nervous valvar showed up and jabbed through the bars viciously with their needle-spears at the riotous miners until the slaves retreated from the gate. Once clear, the valvar unlocked the gate, shoved provisions through, and slammed it shut again.

"You see?" said Rynne as the Kamen barked orders at them through the gate. "They mean for us to go in there and finish off any other biters that might've got through."

The pile of provisions unceremoniously dumped on the floor contained a four-foot-long metal fork, lamps, extra oil, water and a small sack of smoked meat. The miners set upon the food like wolves and had half of it down before coming to their senses and realizing they might want it for later, should the clearing of the mines take time. The shortest of them took up the fork, everyone lit an oil lamp and they all proceeded as one back into the mines heading straight for the hole. If they were to get this job over and done with, it would need to be blocked up straight away. Any more of the biters that had snuck in could then be dealt with afterwards, preferably one at a time. These creatures may not have been deadly, but all the same, no one wanted to take a bite from one of them. The long fork was specifically designed for prying biters off of ceilings. The short Kamen found the tool indispensable. There was no ceiling in the mines too high for the slaves to reach, yet to a man they preferred the idea of using the fork rather than their hands.

Blocking up the hole took no time at all. Searching the mines took longer, but even that job was executed quickly. Biters did not move fast or far unless surprised or attacked, aside from the occasional aggressive leap of an adult. As far as could be told, no others had wandered into the mining area. Once satisfied, the miners relaxed in one of the more spacious caverns and dug into the remaining provisions. Everyone but Prakash seemed content to spend the rest of the work day down here eating and drinking. Ford couldn't tell what had upset the Nagaporian, but the man kept ranting as he stalked around them waving his hands in their faces.

"What's gotten into him?" The words were barely out of Ford's mouth when Prakash jumped up and started snatching the strips and chunks of dried meat out of the hands of the others. When he came around to take Ford's portion, Ford gave him a cold glare and took a firm grip of his hammer. "You try and take it and you'll get this hammer instead." Prakash's hardened features went sour, but he backed down and then flew into a rage, shouting and gesticulating. "What's he saying?"

Only Rynne spoke enough Nagaporian to understand. "He wants to go into the biter hole," he said while he and the other miners edged away from Prakash. The irate miner had taken to kicking them about the legs and backsides, not hard, but in the way an impatient farmer might coax cattle.

"Go into the hole? Where the biter came from? Is he mad? What for?"

"He figures if those things found a way in, there must be a way out. He wants to save the meat and water and whatnot and go see if we can't escape." Rynne shook his drooping head. He tried to be discreet, not wanting to anger his friend further, but Prakash didn't care. His attention was fixed on Ford's softening demeanor and the eyes that sought sincerity in his own. "Of course, as you say, he's mad—"

"I'm with you," Ford cut in with a nod and shove of his provisions toward Prakash.

"Oh, Mother of Luck and Misfortune," said Rynne dropping his head into his heads. "Now there's two of them! You're making a mistake, my lad. There's likely no way out. And if you do get out, out there in the freezing cold, what'll you do then?"

"I don't know, but it's better than being here."

Ford and Prakash made impassioned pleas to the others, but none would go along with the plan. As a consolation, they did obtain the rest of what little remained of the food and water, all of the oil, and the long fork. Just as valuable was the promise they received upon their departure.

"We'll tell them you didn't make it," said Rynne when they were back at the biter hole pulling away the stacked rocks. "You chased the biters into the hole and we never saw you again."

Prakash climbed through the hole first and disappeared deeper into the cavern, eager to see what lay beyond. The meager light cast by his oil lamp diminished rapidly, even by the distance of a few feet. Ford squeezed through the hole into semi-darkness. Once inside, Rynne handed him his dish-like lamp and the rest of his equipment.

"Good fortune to you," said Rynne as his face disappeared behind the last of the stones he placed over his end of the hole.

Prakash had gone ahead, but now turned back and held out his light, which made it easier for Ford to gather his things. The Nagaporian gave an involuntary gasp. Ford looked up to see Prakash staring at the wall above the hole just behind Ford's head, where some two dozen sickly eyes glared unblinkingly back. These young biters had a watery sheen over the violet and ivory-white circles upon their shells, which gave their "eyes" an ill-defined, angry or even crazed appearance that often caused observers to flee in terror. Ford whipped his hammer at the wall, knocking one off. The tiny biter tottered upon its back on the floor, its many writhing legs on the underside of the carapace looking like a jostled bowl of nuts. A heavy weight dropped on Ford's head. A large, adult biter had dropped from a hole in the ceiling. Its mouth could be heard scraping on the metal of Ford's cap and its toes grasped at the back of his neck and ears. A jolt to the side of Ford's head from the shaft of the fork sent the biter and cap flying across the floor. Prakash dashed forward and brought his hammer down. The biter's innards oozed from under a shell nearly two-feet in diameter.

The two men crouched in silence with their weapons at the ready, watching the eyes on the wall and waiting for a reaction. None of the biters moved or made a sound. Those covering the wall were young, with bodies no more than a few inches across and without the range of movement adults possessed, not having fully developed their many legs yet. At this stage, they mostly attached themselves to a rock, and sucked and scraped away at it as they grew. The ones here had been eating at the ore from the opposite side of the vein the miners had been working on.

Using the tines of the long fork, Prakash gingerly flipped over the large adult biter and found Ford's cap underneath covered in the insect's sticky blue ichor. Ford took one look at it and gave it up as lost. The two men then set to work on the wall with their hammers. By the time they finished, blue gore coated the room and gave off an unpleasant, metallic odor that turned their stomachs.

Once the bloody task was completed, they lifted their lamps from the floor and made a hurried check of the many exit tunnels leading off of this main cavern. The smooth surfaces of these tunnels were clear of debris, but they twisted and turned at odd angles, occasionally shooting off in random directions. As rough as the mines were, they seemed a model of orderly design compared with these absurdly meandering and utterly nonsensical passages, like some kind of bizarre floor plan drawn up by a deranged architect. Most of the tunnels were too narrow, ended after a few feet, or were located in the ceiling and unscalable. The one in the floor disappeared into darkness.

In the end there was only one feasible choice, a hole across the cavern from the one they entered. After a few yards of pushing and pulling themselves on their bellies through the tight gap, they were on their feet again, crouched and shuffling through a curving tube-like tunnel which randomly expanded and contracted. Occasionally, a navigable passage would branch off, perhaps at an odd angle or presenting a tighter squeeze. Whatever the case, they stuck with the passage that felt most promising. More than one tunnel wound back around upon itself and deposited them in a spot they'd already passed. Then there were eerily deep holes to leap and near-vertical rises to climb. One was so steep it almost put an end to the endeavor. The going wasn't easy, but as long as they were moving forward, they were happy, even optimistic. Every foot and yard that carried them farther away from the mines and the Kamen sent a surge of elation flowing through them, lifting their spirits regardless of how strenuous the climbing and crawling. Ford began daydreaming about regaining his freedom and returning home. Prakash hummed a quiet tune.

Their pleasure was cut short by a sound neither of them had made: a scraping of rock somewhere off in the warren of tunnels, like a pickax tip dragged over stone or hard nails across slate. The thought that maybe they were hearing the work of the miners was dashed by the length of the scrapping, unlike any motion a miner would make. It also wasn't the sort of noise a biter would make. It was too loud, too abrasive.

"Maybe it's something like a biter, only bigger," Ford muttered, and wished he hadn't. It only egged on his fears and made his mind jump to a story Rynne had told. A miner's folktale really, about how when Dargkivi was first being excavated, miners opened up a cavern in which they discovered a hollow-eyed troll who'd been chained there for hundreds of years, surviving on whatever blundered within its reach in the dark. How it came to be there, whether or not the story was true, none of this mattered. Anything could be down here. Anything might leap from the shadows. The only thing more frightening was the thought of being recaptured by the Kamen, who would likely kill them for trying to escape. Neither of them could think of a better solution than to put as much distance between themselves and these evils as they could, as soon as possible. They pushed themselves to the point of exhaustion, traveling the oxygen-thin tunnels for hours, until finally the strange scraping died away.

How far they'd gone was a mystery. A half hour might mean no more than a few feet, especially when they had to span a wide hole, but they guessed they were far enough away to risk a short rest, and by now they had mastered their nerves enough to do so. Ford leaned his back against the rock and slid down onto his haunches. Prakash stretched himself over somewhat level ground. Sleep came easily and for longer than either intended.

When they awoke, they weren't positive that they were awake. Impenetrable darkness enveloped them. Both oil lamps had gone out and they had no way of relighting them. Their curses gave off dampened echoes. Each wanted to blame the other, but knew they themselves were just as much to blame. Prakash surprised Ford by quieting down almost immediately. He wondered if the Nagaporian was thinking over their dire situation and coming to the same conclusion that he had. They had to go back. Maybe excuses for their absence would save their necks. It was worth a try. Out of the darkness came a grunted word from Prakash. A tug on Ford's arm turned him around. Just like that, they were off again, ever slower, but moving. However short and shuffling, each step was better than simply standing still. In the dark, the tunnels took on a mindboggling elusiveness. Everything seemed topsy turvy. The first fork in the tunnel confounded him, but Prakash led on.

"Least someone knows where we're going."

Prakash had been in the mines for the better part of a year and grown accustomed to underground terrain. On the other hand, it was a lucky break for Ford if he didn't trip or twist an ankle for a span of ten feet. Prakash's annoyance sighed through the tunnels louder than anything else. His dexterous steps soon put distance between himself and his floundering follower.

"Hold up," Ford said reaching his hands out in front of him and picking up his pace. White light burst across his vision and a shock of pain exploded upon his forehead where he connected with a low-hanging rock. A blind fall dropped him hard on his backside. The next thing he knew he was on one knee steadying himself, unsure if he had been knocked out or not. "Can't tell if my eyes are open or shut," he muttered. Just as his wits were gathering about him, they were mowed down by a rush of dread.

"Prakash? Prakash!" The only reply was his own words bouncing back to him. Either Prakash had left him behind or something had happened to the man. Perhaps he too hit his head. Ford waved his arms about and felt the ground all around him. All the while, he called out the man's name. There was nothing. He felt utterly alone, and as far as he knew, he was. Abandonment and hopelessness began wedging their way in and pushing aside concern for his companion.

He scrambled to his feet and frantically groped about for something tangible, something to make sense out of the nothingness. A wave of dizziness snatched away his balance and toppled him onto his back, where he stayed for a while to rest and regain his composure. His mind wandered. How long had they been down here? Half a day? Or had he been knocked out and it was now another day altogether? He didn't know and he supposed it didn't matter. Time was becoming meaningless.

"If he'd only come back," he said aloud just to hear a voice. "What good would it do? Prakash!" He felt a fool for letting the Nagaporian hold all of the food and water. His tongue felt like a dry lump in his mouth. "It's no good." He couldn't lay on his back and wait to be rescued down here in the dark, where there might be things worse than biters lurking about. There was no other choice but to try to find his way back alone. The decision had been made and yet he didn't move. "A nice little sleep." It seemed like a good idea at the moment. "No." He slapped his own cheek, and again, but harder. "Get up! Now!"

Forcing himself to his hands and knees, he ran his fingers over the smooth tunnel floor until it sloped up into a wall. Crawling in the opposite direction, he quickly found the other wall. Sliding against it, he crept along the way he thought he had been heading when they had turned back. When his knees could take no more, he got to his feet and slid one foot before the other without lifting them. Now and then his toes would trace a divot too deep and he would shuffle around it if possible, or get down on his belly and crawl over it. Once he even lowered himself down into a hole, and though his feet touched the bottom after a few short feet, exposing his legs to a sightless void where anything or absolutely nothing might reside, was an experience he would not soon forget.

"This is going to take a lifetime."

Painfully slow hours passed with his head bowed, a forearm protecting his crown, and his toes tapping the ground ahead. Inches passed with excruciating care. Branches of tunnels were chosen by an imaginary flip of a coin. Fingernails were ground down by hard climbing over rough rock. But it was all worthwhile when he came to an incline almost too steep to scale. It reminded him of a patch of trouble they'd passed already, and he was sure if he could just get over it, he would be home free.

"What a horrible place to call home."

With a resigned sigh, he leaned against the steep incline and reached for the top. A hop brought the tips of his fingers to the top, but there wasn't enough of a purchase to hold on to. That didn't stop him from jumping for the top again and again until he winded himself and slid to the bottom in a heap. There he remained, catching his breath and thinking. A few more inches, maybe another foot, was what he needed to get there. A search for stones to pile at the base of the incline took ages. Loose stones were hard to come by in these smooth-bore tunnels. After gathering up a small pile, he made another attempt at the climb. Now he could reach the top without problem, but he lacked the strength to lift the rest of his weight over without a firm grasp on the smooth rock.

"Useless," he said of his arms, weakened as they were from the work. He sat down in a huff and thought it over. It didn't take long before he was back on his feet, carefully feeling for rock above his head. There was none. It seemed to be quite a tall ceiling. Taking three well-measured steps back from the pile of rock, he lunged forward, leapt onto the pile and vaulted off of it. A mad grasp at the void and his hands latched onto the top of the incline with his forearms draped well over the crest. Wedging his legs against the walls to either side to keep from slipping back, he dragged himself up to the top, where he stopped to give his burning muscles a rest. "Many a blessing to and from the good gods!" he gasped and blew out an expiring laugh of triumph.

If this was the same wave-like lump of smooth rock he and Prakash had passed on the way out, and he was certain it was, the backside would be a gradual slope down to a level and safe floor. His certainty was enough to overcome his doubts and take the plunge. His aching muscles and exhausted body would take any bit of easy momentum wherever it could be found. The trip was exhilarating, scary and short. He slid down the short slope on his belly as planned and shot like a bolt straight into a hole in a wall.

The biters had eaten away at the rock and created a circular hole just wide enough to get his shoulders stuck in. He was laid out with his arms pinned at his sides, his head lower than his feet, and his own weight holding him in place. The hole didn't seal him in completely. There was room above his back, but he couldn't twist his body about or inchworm his way back out. Wriggling his legs and feet did nothing. There was no purchase to be had where he might scoot backwards out of the hole. If he'd gone into the hole with one arm first alongside his head, the other shoulder could have slipped through at an angle. But both shoulders had gone in at the same time and together they were a square peg too large for the round hole. The blood began rushing to his head and he worried he might pass out. Then there was the possibility that anything might come along and have at him, and there would be nothing he could do about it.

"Prakash!" His usually steady voice cracked as panic shuddered through his every limb. Squirming did no good, perhaps made matters worse, but he couldn't stop while he had strength left in him. Only fatigue would calm him down. Eventually his taut muscles collapsed and he went still. Time slowed along with his heartbeat. He relaxed. He breathed. His nose picked up the faint hint of that bitter, metallic scent of ironbiter blood. What it meant, he couldn't fathom. His wits were as thin as the air. Reason failed him. After a laugh burbled out of him, he thought his sanity was failing as well. The strange thought had occurred to him that he didn't know where to find Will. When they had seen one another, he'd neglected to ask where they were keeping him. It meant he couldn't find Will and take him with them when he and Prakash escaped. What a silly thing to worry about now, he thought to himself. He was going to die alone down here and they would never see one another again.

Soon after, he drifted in and out of consciousness. Once he was roused by a muffled thudding which could have been a headache rolling between his ears or thumping coming from somewhere deep within the tunnels. Later, he heard the *click-clack* of rock hitting rock. It might have been the beginnings of a cave-in, another danger he hadn't even considered yet. Now all he could imagine was being buried by rocks, rocks he heard rolling over a cavern floor some distance away, but growing closer. Someone or something was coming. He twisted and writhed, and called out for Prakash, all in vain. Whatever was coming would come. There would be no stopping it.

"What are you? Go away!" Ford barked out, hoping to scare off whatever awful, scurrying underground oddity was nearly upon him. Maybe it was nothing so bad, he hoped and then prayed. As if a golden dawn had come to Kavenauk, the walls in the tunnel ahead of him began to glow. One last growl snarled out of him as the light floated around a bend in the tunnel before him and then hovered above his head. It was no blazing star, just a soft flicker, and yet it was nearly blinding to eyes deprived of light for so long. When he peered up and could see through streaming tears the warm light, it was marred by the lip-curling sneer of Dustav the valvar. The newly sharpened tip of his needle-spear flashed in the light and plunged into Ford.

Chapter 13
The Pit

Dargkivi's wealthiest citizens, draped in gobs of jewelry and wearing the finest apparel gold and silver could buy, cheered with anticipation from the balconies overlooking Mullauk, the city's premier entertainment arena. They came early, not wanting to miss a moment. Before the show began, drink and meat mongers at the entryways did brisk trade selling frothy beverages and roasted koer on skewers. Everyone, even children, hoisted a mug of some kind of intoxicating libation to their lips. The most avid fans liked to watch the action up close. One overexcited man in a ludicrously tall sugarloaf style hat leaned over the edge of a balcony to get the best view of what was below and knocked his mug off the ledge into the pit. When he reached for it, his hat toppled along with it.

While men's fashions tended to be impractical and flashy, such as tall hats and red-winged eyebrows, they were a model of discretion compared with the women, who used hot presses, oils and wax to pile mounds of hair into playgrounds for the latest gravity-defying trends. They rolled their green and blue dyed monobrows into waves over their foreheads and strapped themselves into form-fitting dresses made of dangerously delicate materials. The number one sign of prosperity was excess weight. Weight equaled wealth. If your skin stretched so far as to shine like a diamond, well then, you likely possessed at least a few of those precious stones in your purse. Pure white, fluffy furs were another indicator of riches. So, when Kamen women were all dressed up for a big event like this, they stood out like buffalo in a beanfield, bejeweled albino buffalo.

Balconies overflowed with these cawing and guffawing, bleating and braying peacocks and buffalo. The eldest and most decorated of them looked on from the highest balconies and sat back in padded chairs, napping before the event began. Below them, eager audiences stood in friendly groups all giddy with anticipation. Wives linked their arms with their husbands and readied the plump fingers of their free hands to shield their sight from the gore. Mail and plate-clad house guards hovered behind their masters. These private valvar were often better equipped than the city guard. Gleaming swords and axes hung at their belts. Great helms were tucked under their arms. Each maintained a stony façade of professionalism, but spent most of these evenings at Mullauk on the tips of their toes trying to see the action over the heads of their masters.

This much-loved fighting arena located in the eastern reaches of Dargkivi contained a past that all Kamen knew about, but mostly overlooked. At one time, Mullauk was simply known as the giant hole into which trash was dumped. For ages, Kamen who lived inland couldn't be bothered toting their refuse to the ravines or ocean, so their chipped masonry, discarded bones, rotting food, rusted metal, shards of broken pottery, matted fur, and worn-out clothing littered a mostly round hole approximately fifty feet across and a depth long forgotten. When the smell of the rotting organic matter became a problem and needed cleaning, they imported carrion feeders such as rock urchins, slurpworms, and avaksakluda, giant blind bugs capable of scooping up mouthfuls of bones and mashing them to a pulp with their powerful mandibles. Seeing these carnivorous creatures madly crawling over one another as they fought for scraps gave an enterprising Kamen the idea to turn the pit into an arena. The dumping of trash ceased, except as it suited the games. Balconies were cut into the rock all around the rim about thirty feet above the irregular arena floor. Ventilation holes were bored out and lanterns hung. More access tunnels were installed for the audience above and the combatants below. When Mullauk first opened, brave Kamen warriors enjoyed displaying their fighting prowess and receiving the accolades of an adoring public. Disputes were settled in the pit, honor regained, and even military rank was handed out to winners from time to time. However, all that came to an end when hurricanes of wealth rained upon the Kamen and their culture trended away from manual labor. Not only did they refuse to dirty their hands, but bloodied hands were frowned upon as well. A few of the poorer Kamen were permitted to continue fighting at Mullauk, but it only took the rise of one folk hero, a commoner the people worshipped for his skill in arms, to threaten the established military hierarchy. The pride-pricked Vaslavak Kirivirz, the league of Kamen elite defense, forced a ban on all Kamen combatants from entering the arena.

After the ban, slaves were made to fight one another in order to keep the games going. But the Kamen soon grew bored of watching tired and less-than-enthusiastic slaves sparring, so they turned to the community's hunters and fur merchants to capture suitable creatures upon the icy tundra for use within the arena. The blood-thirstier and more vicious the better. As long as it couldn't fly or crawl up the sides of the arena and attack the audience, anything with a mean streak was desirable. "When I was a boy, there was one in particular that everyone loved best," a Kamen father regaled his son before the show began that night. "An enormous hairy boar with long tusks and leathery skin as impenetrable as iron plate. We called him Doom. His tusks gored more slaves than I can remember." Slaves were tossed into the arena with little more than a spear or shield to defend themselves, just as trash had once been dumped into the pit. Demand for cheap replacements increased.

Tonight's entertainment was going to be special. Instead of the combatants entering at the pit level, winches were lowering the slaves down from the bottom balcony. The audience loved this new innovation and slapped their heads and bellowed to show their appreciation. Men tapped their rings and pounded their fists upon the wide band of thin, oiled sheet metal wrapped over the rim of the lowest balcony that created a slippery surface to prevent creatures and combatants from scaling the walls and attacking the audience. Before the slaves touched down, wagers were made with flying hands and fingers. They even bet on what creatures would come out of which gates near the floor of the pit.

Chain links of the three winches clinked and rattled as teams cranked the gear handles and worked the brakes. Each chain was attached to a harness strapped around each of the three slaves. Two of the slaves wiggled in midair like fish, twisting about and grabbing hold of the chains. But one slave hung loose and limp, yielding to his mortality, to the inevitable.

By chance and misfortune, Ford Barlow was one of these three. Death in the arena was to be his fate. A discarded undesirable. He had survived being stabbed by the valvar's needle-spear, because it hadn't been poisoned. Those in charge of the mining operations' expenses didn't feel the need to pay for poison. It was costly and there were gates to keep their slaves penned in. There were guards to keep them in line as well. In theory, this worked. However, when a valvar slipped up and used his spear, as the rash Dustav had done with Ford, the lack of deadly poison became apparent when the slave survived the stab. That was a knowledge they couldn't afford to have disseminated. So, they hustled Ford from the mines without any contact with the other slaves. They sought to get anything back for the troublesome slave suspected of an escape attempt along with the slave Parkash, who hadn't been found yet. When Kunar Kalev the Master of Games stepped forward as a buyer, they sold Ford off without haggling. Kalev was thrilled to obtain Ford for less than a quarter of the price he would have paid at the auction.

As Ford held onto the winch chain like a lifeline and stared down at the ground beneath him, the distracting spectacle and roar of the crowd receded into the background, like the buzz of a distant swarm of flies. He had no idea why he was here or what was in store for him, but it looked like nothing good could come of this. He had detected among the detritus below a section of the floor shifting. A dark patch slid from the middle of the pit closer to where his feet would touch down. The dangling slave closest to him saw it too and let loose a shriek as he tried to climb back up the chain. Ford returned his gaze from the distracting slave back to the floor beneath him, but he had lost track of the shambling pile of moving earth. Whatever was below had blended back into the muddled, filthy panoply of dirt, bones and waste.

The chains cranked out of the winches at a glacial pace, leaving the slaves dangling above their fate for what seemed like an eternity. The Kamen liked the thrill of the kill, but loved the suspense of a slaying yet to come, and those working the cranks had been instructed to go slow. When the audience could stand it no more, a sudden lurch sent Ford and the other two plunging toward the bottom. Just before their feet touched down, one of the three gates near the floor of the pit creaked open and a flash of fur shot from the tunnel.

A thumping great blurry ball of woolly wolverine bounded into the arena on wide paws full of gut-tearing claws. It skittered to a halt in the center of the pit and whipped its head back and forth, taking the measure of its surroundings. It sniffed the air and peered about with black eyes narrowly set in a dark face which blended into the browns and grays of its bear-like body. At a quick glance, it could have been mistaken for a bush because of its masses of fur, if only the creature could stay still. However, its eagerness as a hunter made it leap and pounce with ungovernable energy. In an enclosed space such as a fighting pit, the creature could maximize its talent for ferocity.

The most agitated of the three slaves spun in uncontrollable circles. All his writhing sent his pants slipping from his hips, revealing a pair of white legs that wiggled like tormented albino worms. The audience erupted in gut-busting belly laughs. The scrawny fellow's frantic motion drew the wolverine's dark eyes to him. Fur flew as it dashed and leapt. Its vice-like jaws latched onto the slave's ankle. A crunch, a lightning-fast yank, and the foot snapped free with a rending of flesh. The man screamed. The wolverine whipped the foot from its mouth and then backed away just enough to gather itself for another leap. Its sharp canines flashed before plunging into skin once more, this time the throat. The man's life ended in screams and a spray of blood. A final spasm brought the body to rest. The wolverine lost interest and moved on.

While the cheering and gasps exploded above him, Ford finally understood that he and the other two slaves were meant to be nothing more than bait for this savage beast. He started reaching his legs and toes for the ground in absolute earnest. The other remaining slave had already touched down and was kneeling with his face to the wall, a strange picture of serenity. The wolverine turned its beady black gaze upon Ford, the more exciting challenge of the two. It charged over the uneven ground, a huge flopping mop stained with blood.

The moment Ford's feet hit the ground, a shambling lump of matted fur, the camouflaged shifting earth he thought he'd seen before, scuttled through the space between him and the wolverine. The unexpected movement spooked them both and made man and beast shy away in opposite directions from the unknown danger in their midst. The wolverine's skirting detour diverted its attention back to the slave kneeling at the wall. Ford backed away and kept looking from the wolverine to this strange dome of fur, like a hairy tortoise without head or appendages. It stopped shuffling about, but the wolverine had not.

While Ford did his best to keep everything in the arena within his sight, the kneeling man remained oblivious to all that was going on around him. Only a portion of his profile was visible to Ford, and with his shaved head making him look much any other slave, Ford didn't recognize him immediately. The man's chin rested on his chest, his eyes were closed, and he held his hands in repose upon his lap. Nothing mattered anymore. He had given up on life. The wolverine would have him without a fight. Ford snatched up a rock and threw it across the arena to distract the beast, but it landed harmlessly and without a sound that could be heard above the Kamen audience's excited din. From a partial skeleton at his feet, Ford grabbed a long leg bone and sprinted across the pit.

The wolverine stalked ever closer to the kneeling slave, showing uncharacteristic caution by attacking much slower than it normally would. Something about the man's repose and lack of fear did not sit well with the animal's instincts. Ford's loping and stumbling strides carried him swiftly over the mounded debris, right up behind the wolverine. He swung the bone, but his body left the ground and he was jerked backward. The bone whistled behind the beast's head. His makeshift club was shorter than he realized. The knee joint of the yard-long femur had snapped off in a previous fight, shortening it and leaving a thin jagged end. Ford found himself swinging through the air. The length of chain attached to his harness had run out and he was being reeled back in for sport and the entertainment of the people. They were in hysterics at seeing him plucked from the stage, his legs churning and kicking like a maniacal dancer.

As Ford swung backward, he could only watch on helplessly as predator approached prey. Hearing the wolverine's snorting breath behind him, the kneeling slave sat up straight and lifted his head. The high chin, the long neck and that perfect posture all pointed to Barwnig Bryce, the lord who had lost his family and had little to live for. The wolverine lunged, bit, and shook. In a reversal akin to the windblown whims of the gods, the winch team hurriedly cranked out more chain for Ford, so that he landed on his back in the middle of the pit. He scrambled to his feet and charged. The wolverine released its prey in hopes of making sport of it, biting again and sinking its teeth in even deeper. It finished off Bryce with a flurry of gnashing jaws shaken back and forth at the very moment Ford stabbed the sharp end of the femur into the crook of its neck. The bone's jagged point pierced skin and muscle, and came out the other side, where it smashed to pieces against the arena wall. Bryce's limp body fell away. The wolverine threshed earth and flesh with its legs, shredding Ford's tunic, arms and torso with long bloody gouges. He held on, even when the animal's jaws snapped just inches from his face, pressing bone against neck, pinning the wolverine to the wall. There was nothing else he could do. Releasing it would bring him a swift death. The wolverine's growls drowned out the audience's wild applause, at least in Ford's ears. Time seemed to drag on. His wounded shoulder ached where the needle-spear had pierced him that morning. The arm felt weak. His sweating hands began to slip down the bone while the wolverine's thrashing widened its own shoulder wound, gashing itself deep in the neck. Tides of blood flowed over Ford's hands and hastening the animal's demise.

"I knew it to be true! The giant is a mad fighter!" shouted Kunar Kalev the Master of Games to the friends gathered around him, laughing so long and loud that he intertwined the fingers of both hands and pressed them against his round stomach for fear it might burst. "Did I not tell you? I knew there was a devil's heart in that one!"

"A good show, Kalev! A great show!" cried his friends. They all congratulated him on consistently providing the best entertainment Dargkivi had ever seen. And yet, the show was not over. Lifting Ford out of the pit required extra hands at the winch and a whole lot of sweat. The straining of the winch team delighted the audience. They begged Kalev to feature the giant at his next event.

Jolly chatter of satisfied Kamen happily recounting the evening's entertainment echoed through the Dargkivi tunnels as the audience made their way home. A squad of valvar volunteered to parade Ford from the arena through a few neighborhoods on the way to his new living quarters. The Master of Games wanted to show off his new find and build excitement for the next show. Any Kamen who hadn't attended tonight's performance would be clamoring to pay the entrance fee for future shows, and that would drive up prices.

Unlike the valvar of the mines, the tips of these guards' needle-spears dripped with poison. Also, more than one wore an unusual contraption welded onto the top of their helmets: an oil lamp shaped like an onion which left both hands free to wield weapons, manhandle slaves, or whatever the need may be. They were being careful with the big Aelwydian who had just taken the life of a most violent and savage beast. However, a child could have led Ford without trouble that night. There was no fight left in him.

His arrival at the cramped and spartan slaves' quarters was met by the vacant gaze of a few emaciated souls from the southern lands. Ford stood by the door that had just slammed shut and shook gently from the remnants of adrenaline still coursing through him. One look at this blood-splattered giant's face and the other slaves hastily offered up furs to wrap himself in and made room for him to lie down. Not even Joord, the tough veteran of the lot gave him trouble. Ford collapsed on the floor. The reek of sweat and other human excretions embedded in the fur wrapped around him barely registered. The pain in his shoulder and the gouges along his body lost him a few winks, but after shifting on to his other side, he was out for hours.

While Ford slept, plans were made for him and his future as a pit fighter. The Master of Games placed an order with the Dargkivi armory. Blacksmiths and tanners busily crafted and tailored armor and weapons to specifications they had never worked with before. Ford was now a Mullauk warrior, one whom his new owner planned to exploit to the fullest.

The following morning, Ford's work for Kalev really began. Besides defying death whenever thrust into the pit, arena slaves were tasked with removing garbage, emptying pots of urine and feces, disposing of vermin, helping collect dead bodies and transporting them up to the Uuz Miris catacombs, the compact and orderly Kamen burial grounds near the cold surface at the end of a long tunnel outside of the city. Part of the deal the initial owner made when purchasing and converting Mullauk from a garbage pit to an entertainment arena was that all future Master of Games would be obliged to provide sanitation service to those who no longer had access to a convenient dumping ground. So, when they weren't fighting, arena slaves collected the refuse of the middle and upper classes. They walked long distances to the outskirts of town toting heavy jars and full sacks to chutes which jettisoned the waste into the sea or a ravine, anywhere away from Kamen living quarters.

"Attakal uz toole! Kiiresti tagad! Sie votid ei hakk rienegen selvst!" shouted the arena slaves' overseer and trainer in a marching cadence that matched the precision of his lock-step stride, each foot dropping like clockwork. Only the renowned drummers of Wrenfeld kept better time. The slaves addressed him using the honorific *kungs*, but Roniik was his given name. Roniik being a female name, no one who knew what was good for them called him by it. Somewhat tall and athletic for a Kamen, he packed his slender frame with muscle and worked hard to become the strongest Kamen in all of Rikaswelt. Some found it a trial not to laugh at him, because his head appeared to be square. The illusion occurred because he cut his full beard straight across at six inches and the low ceilings pressed flat his bushy hair. Unless it was a helmet, he never bothered with a hat. To his mind, the things Kamen put on their heads were odd and ridiculous. As a rule, he had no use for the nonsense of Kamen fashions.

No matter how orderly or crisp his speech, none of the slaves understood the words Roniik bawled at them. They didn't need to. The specific and intuitive gestures he provided defined his intentions perfectly. An arm swung wide to a cardinal point clarified direction. Fingers slapped onto palms made the counting out of figures obvious to the dimmest. Hands clapped together to punctuate an important point, such as when he spoke a location name.

Each arena slave under Roniik's training regime was well-fed with plain but filling meals accompanied by hours upon hours of lifting and carrying heavy objects. In the days that followed, Ford put on weight, gained strength and healed his wounds. These seemed like blessings, but Ford couldn't see that his lot in life had improved that much. Yes, the mines had been dangerous and the living conditions inhumane, but the madness of Mullauk set one's nerves on edge and waste removal was a thankless task. The families they serviced treated them like personal servants, delaying and burdening them with petty demands, and worse, adding time to one's enslavement. On his second day on the job, a year was added to Ford's time for the accidental breaking of a urinal pot. Also, Ford found some of the trainer's methods cruel and unnecessary. For instance, Roniik would stop them in the middle of work and force them to pick up and lay down a full pot they were carrying over and over again. The soup of urine and floating feces would slosh about and make Ford gag during the first week. Eventually, he grew used to the stench, as he had grown used to the coughing fits in the mines. The weight of the pots, too, became easier to bear over time. Other routines of Roniik's that would annoy them included: sneaking up behind them and shouting in their ears; waking them in the middle of the night by clanging his prized mace against a pan; sometimes the room would be cast into darkness or a bag would be thrown over their heads and they would be pummeled from various angles. All of this was done to keep them alert and ready for anything. Ford did learn to be more observant and prepared, but at a great cost to his peace of mind. If he could be said to enjoy any of it, it would be the weapons training. They learned to hack and slash with dull-bladed swords, to pierce and parry with blunt-tipped spears, and to repeatedly pummel with cudgels of all shapes and sizes. Ford appreciated the education and enjoyed daydreaming about the day he would use these skills to slay Kamen without mercy.

Ford wiled away part of a day's work thinking such thoughts in luxuriant detail. It was morning and he was pushing a cart through the tunnels of southern Dargkivi with a dark-skinned and flat-nosed slave from Dadha named Jengo. Jengo's friend had died in the arena the night Ford killed the wolverine. Since then he had gravitated toward Ford and the two got along from the start. The bug-eyed man's looks bordered upon the repellent, but he did possess a pleasing manner and was not one to quarrel. Whenever they were on their rounds together and Jengo lightly hummed a snatch of some tune from his homeland, Ford would attempt to join in, occasionally hitting a correct note on the refrains. The first time he did it, Jengo turned a quick corner to dry his tears. After that, they got on like brothers.

On this day, they were on their way to one of the disposal chutes, navigating narrow tunnels full of tight corners, when a rat shot between their legs. It was quite puny. Probably a stowaway from the most recent Severn galley visit. The rat skittered by without comment from the two apathetic humans, who watched it pass along the floor pressed against the wall. The creature sensed their lack of interest and continued on its way unimpeded. As it neared the next turn, a light flashed in its eyes and another two-legged being emerged from around the corner. The surprised rat hopped into the air, did a flip, and made an end-around run past this new being's stamping feet. Growls and grumbles quickly faded away behind the rat as it rounded the corner and sped away down a blissfully empty tunnel.

Roniik's startled leap away from a rat in front of slaves would diminish his authority in the eyes of all the arena slaves once the story spread. He knew this while still in the air, and it was why he came back down to earth with the intent of stomping on the vermin to cover his surprised reaction. Slamming his foot down on the ground at an angle, he turned his ankle in an exquisitely painful way. He meant to stalk up on the pair of slaves to simulate a sneak attack, but that would have to wait. Most people would have had a seat, massaged the ankle, and given it time to heal. That was not Roniik's way. A firm believer in working through pain, he marched down the tunnel toward Ford and Jengo as if nothing were amiss. Only the slightest hitch in his gait told the lie. If he grimaced, it was hidden within his beard.

Ford and Jengo had gone rigid at the sudden appearance of their overseer. His presence made them tense at any time, but now they feared he was about to tell them off, perhaps worse, for having done nothing about the rat. As it turned out, apparently, he had only come to retrieve Jengo for another job. Few words were wasted in explanation. "Uuzdorv," he said with a gesture intimating that Ford was to go to that part of town and start work there after finishing his current job. Then he bundled Jengo off in the direction of the arena quarters. Ford figured he was on his own now and would have to finish the day's work alone. It would be a long, dull day, but if Roniik were busy with other matters, at least Ford could rest easy in the knowledge that he wouldn't be set upon by another one of his surprise visits.

The tunnel grew steadily colder as he neared the liquid waste chute. Halfway along the last straightaway, he halted to align the cart's front wheels, which tended to veer to the left and drive the nose of the cart into walls every twenty or thirty feet if there was no one at the front to guide it. Arriving at the final intersection in the far outskirts of this part of town, he banged on the bars of the gate to the chute. There wasn't enough foot traffic to warrant posting a guard out here. A semi-retired ulemvalvar living in a stuffy hole down one of the side passages kept an eye on things around this dead-end part of town. Eventually he showed up and unlocked the gate. Ford shoved the cart ahead with a little more urgency. He had to hurry so as not to hold up the aging Kamen, whose duty it was to wait until Ford finished so that the gate could be locked again.

Ford hesitated for a moment with his hand hovering over the bar which held shut the leather-covered grate to the outside world. This was always an unpleasant part of the job, letting in a gust of frigid air. The hole in the rock wall was not quite a yard wide, which made it just possible to lean out with the pots and dump them safely, but kneeling by that gaping hole for even a short while made one feel as if they were going to freeze to death. He almost had to laugh at the ridiculousness of his escape attempt with Prakash. Dressed in rags and with little to eat, how far would they get if they had escaped the city?

The old valvar tapped on the gate. Ford snapped to, sliding the bar back and jerking the grate open. More sunshine than he had felt upon his skin in months struck him in the face. At this time of year, the sun shone almost constantly upon Rikaswelt, but it was a remote glimmer, never a scorcher and often diminished by at least a thin sheet of cloud cover. Now, to Ford's light-deprived eyes, it seemed to glare at him like a flaming eye. He left the pots sitting on the cart and leaned out of the hole, as if he might get a tiny bit closer to the fiery orb in the sky and perhaps slightly warmer. There wasn't the kind of warmth he was used to during those sweltering Aelwydian summers, but at least it wasn't quite as cold as it had been on the day he arrived in Dargkivi.

Then the wind picked up and the pleasure disappeared. He hurried to empty the pots of waste. The semi-solid liquid sloshed down a wide groove cut into an icy cliff. The ice had built up over time, especially during the winter months when the waste would only travel so far before freezing and the near vertical drop became a gradual yellow slide that sloped down to a stunted, round-domed structure made of stone blocks. It was essentially an outhouse in that the worker stationed there was meant to clear any blockages and make sure the bulk of the waste continued on into a gully that ostensibly carried the mess even farther away. The system didn't work quite the way it was meant to, which left the poor individual stuck doing this job—usually someone from Drek, since a slave couldn't be trusted out there alone—shoveling and sweeping feces to keep the waste from backing up.

From the southern waste chute, it was a fair trek back to town and Ford took his time in reaching the fancifully-designed Uuzdorv neighborhood, where new abodes housed young merchants and daring entrepreneurs who cherished architectural embellishment that matched their penchant for dabbling in the mystic arts. Instead of the straight and square structures and orderly layouts of other communities, Uuzdorv had cul-de-sacs and central, circular layouts with streets that wound around the houses. The area came alive with colorful inlays, abstract mosaics, spiral stairways, iron lantern holders with twisting designs, and a variety of odd-shaped doors and windows. Because the tunnels weren't straight, it took a great deal of time to collect the neighborhood's pots, but at least there was something interesting for a slave to look at.

To get from Uuzdorv to the dumping grounds in a gorge on the north side of Dargkivi, Ford had to take a circuitous route around Tat Tarl, the upper treasury vault, and an expansive warren of homes owned by the Komersantz family. He then had to walk out onto a bridge in the cold blasting wind under the supervision of a valvar, who was never happy when a refuse slave showed up to dump the contents of the pots over the side of the bridge into a gorge with a frozen river a hundred feet below. As an expedient to get to this bridge, slaves were permitted the shortcut of walking through the Revane Steps, an outdoor amphitheater located along the gorge.

The Steps were carved into the southern cliffside. Their outmoded block style architecture could be seen in the many right angles and octagonal pillars of the amphitheater. Each cold, gray step was ten feet deep and five feet tall. At fifteen feet wide, the top step was the narrowest. The width doubled with each lower step, the lowest being one hundred and twenty feet long. Kamen-sized stairways connected the lower tiers. The top step could only be accessed by a private door at the back. In the early days of Dargkivi, Kamen elite stood upon the top step making decrees, casting judgements, and handing down punishments to the populous crowds standing on the lower steps. If the people disagreed with a ruling and rose up in revolt, they would find it difficult to mount the steps and rush the ruling class. The bottom step had neither lip nor railing to stop a person from falling into the precipice. More than one troublemaker had been forced over the side by valvar under orders. This went a long way in keeping the lowest rung of society well-behaved during such meetings.

When Ford pushed open the door to that lowest step of the amphitheater, the chill wind that almost constantly blew up from the ocean through the gorge plowed into him and ripped at his clothing. Wanting to be done with this job as soon as possible, he thought about dumping the waste over the ledge at the base of the Steps. However, this was forbidden. On the other side of the gorge was Ulemine Alu, and the wealthy and influential families living there, with their south-facing windows overlooking the chasm, didn't want spillage dripping down the cliffside to ruin their view or for the gorge to be turned into a stinking cesspit. The Ulemine Alu windows which could be seen from the Steps were all shuttered now and there was no valvar here. He waited at the entrance to the bridge. If Ford dumped the pots from the Steps quickly, he might get away with it. Then again, a slave could never be too careful. Instead, he got a running start in the hallway and shoved the cart ahead of him in a dash for the far side of the lowest step. The wind shoved him and threw off his stride a third of the way across. The auditorium hadn't been used in years, so the entire place was coated in ice. Icicles hung from the ceiling and snow piled high in the corners. The cart veered to the left toward the gorge. It looked doubtful that it would make it the entire one hundred and twenty feet of the step. He pulled back and tried to dig his heels in to slow the cart so that he could realign the front wheels, but his feet simply slid over the ice. The weight on the cart was too great. There was nothing he could do to check its momentum.

Halfway across the step, it was obvious the cart was going to go over the edge into the gorge. If he held on, he would be pulled over with it. If he let it go, untold years would be added to his enslavement for the loss of all these pots. He dropped onto his backside and jerked on the cart one last time, slowing it down, but not enough to stop it. The left front wheel went over first. The underside of the cart caught on the edge and held the whole thing in place, but only for a wavering instant. Momentum toppled the cart over into the gorge. Ford's attempts to stop the catastrophe pulled him inevitably toward the ledge. He slid across the perfectly smooth ice surface of the bottom step with no way of stopping himself from going over. Scrambling for his life, he flipped onto his belly to dig his fingernails into the ice. One leg slid over the side. The toes of his other foot gripped the edge. If they gave, he would go over and end up a mangled mess along with the pots and the plummeting cart now crashing against the rocks and ice below. Putting his all into it, Ford pressed his forehead into the icy floor, dragging every part of him that could be dragged over the surface in hopes of halting the unavoidable. A hand wrapped around his wrist. A second hand clapped onto his forearm. Ford looked up into Roniik's straining grimace. The trainer had been following him and waiting for an opportunity to rattle the new arena slave with a surprise attack designed to teach him another lesson, as he had intended to do near the southern waste chute. Instead, Roniik happened upon Ford at the nick of time. His fingers dug into Ford's skin, the veins in his arms bulged, and he let out an almost imperceptible grunt as he pulled with all he had in him. Ford's legs still inched over the side. His hips slid to the edge. He was going to go over. Roniik let him go, and in one swift move, flopped to the ground, gave Ford his legs to hold, drew his mace from his belt and drove it into the ice. The spikes took hold and with an immense effort, he was able to pull them both to safety.

Roniik had seen the cart plunge over the ledge. Ford would pay for the loss in added years, but the cart and the pots themselves meant little to Roniik and his master. What couldn't be afforded was the loss of this particular slave, not tonight, when he would provide the evening's main entertainment.

Chapter 14
Games

Eat, eat! There's plenty for all!"

"Shove it down your gullet!"

"Stop your nibbling! Gulp! Gulp!"

"Yes, yes! Bravo! Get it all in! Well done!"

The raucous exclamations bubbled out of a jocose crowd of well-to-do Kamen on the lowest balcony of the Mullauk arena mobbing a small group of slaves being force fed. The Kamen encouraging this orgy of food laughed hard enough to shed tears. Those few who hadn't given themselves over to unbridled merriment were busily studying the eaters with earnest intent and placing wagers with one another, betting against the slaves who were already sweating, belching and looking distinctly uncomfortable. Those putting away the fatty meat and koer's milk cheese without a sign of distress were backed with vigor.

This strange feast was part of the opening entertainment for the evening's show. It had been dubbed the Erupting Slave Race, and it was usually run by those slaves who acted as clerks and bookkeepers, or any slave who was considered to have it easy in Dargkivi. House slaves considered complacent or even haughty were entered into the race by their masters as a way to demean them. Once stuffed, the slaves were stripped naked and lashed upon the rump with leather straps to get them started around the lowest balcony, which made a complete circuit around the entire arena. Overzealous and inebriated Kamen lining the balustrade lashed their backsides to keep them running. This wasn't a traditional race wherein the winner was the first to finish. The idea was to overfeed them, work them into a lather, and bet upon which of them could keep their stomachs steady the longest. One runner didn't finish the first loop before vomiting, but most went around and around many times, becoming redder in the face and sweating from all pores. Some Kamen considered themselves too refined for such behavior and showed their disdain by remaining in the upper balconies and turning their backs on the spectacle or showing up late to avoid this part of the show all together. On the whole though, the race appealed to anyone who suffered from the malaise brought on by the dreary, long, and dark winters, which riddled the hearts and minds of most Kamen.

After a short intermission while the balcony was cleaned, the next portion of the evening's entertainment began with just as much enthusiasm from the crowd. The Kamen called this game Zielkikraksket, for which there was no translation. Slaves harnessed to the winches on the lowest balcony were tossed over the side, to swing at great speed wildly over the pit, the object being to knock one slave into another. Kamen paid well for the chance to aim and fire a living projectile at an opponent's slave. The Kamen considered it a great victory if their slave bumped into another and knocked the other unconscious. Screaming slaves flew dangerously at one another over the pit. Thus far, none had died. However, one of the slaves had been given more chain than the others, so that his feet clipped the tallest mound of detritus. The shriek that shot from him shocked the audience into a moment's silence before they realized what had happened and broke into laughter once more. The mound turned out to be more than just trash. It was actually a rock urchin blanketed by a bearskin, and the slave had impaled his foot upon one of the many long spikes covering its dome-shaped body.

The rock urchin spent its days shuffling about the pit upon the dozen stocky foot pads that protruded from beneath its shell, using antennae and a retractable proboscis on its underside to feel its way in the world. Its world may have only encompassed an enclosed pit, but as long as it had enough food to scavenge, the rock urchin was a content long-term Mullauk resident. Indeed, the creature had taken up such a lengthy residence within the pit that the Kamen were beginning to think up names for it. Ford had mistaken the urchin for a patch of moving earth in this previous visit to Mullauk. The dirty brown bearskin, which a desperate combatant had thrown over the rock urchin some months back, was finally beginning to come off in bits and pieces, and now its spikes were deadly dangerous once more.

On the backswing, the slave held up its feet and sailed over it safely. On the next few passes, the winch operators lowered the slave slightly. He held up his legs to avoid the multitude of sharp points, which came desperately close to puncturing his posterior. The audience gasped in glee with every near miss. Eventually the slave was drawn back up with no more harm done. This could not be said for all three slaves, one of which had been swung with too much vigor and cracked his head open against a wall.

These games were a warm-up, a bit of fun for the audience before the real action. They were also vital filler. The wild game hunters who provided Mullauk with beasts still hadn't returned. Perhaps they were late due to a lack of luck thus far and had been searching farther afield than usual. Maybe they had been distracted by a long chase. Delays happened and Kalev had to come up with alternative entertainments. Once in the past when they ran short of animal fodder for the arena, the Master of Games used a mercenary Skala to fight in the pit for a decent fee. The Skala had unwittingly entered the arena through one of the iron gates at ground level, not knowing those entrances were only used by slaves and animals. Such was the Kamen opinion of the Skala.

The audience's cheers and laughter echoed through the tunnel that Ford tread on his long walk toward Mullauk. This was a tunnel used by the Kamen, not one usually permitted to a slave combatant. Such was the pedestal upon which Kalev attempted to place his newest protégé. Ford had no idea of the plans being made for him. He only wondered what was waiting for him in the pit. Would it be another wolverine or worse? At least he would be able to defend himself this time. The Kamen had fashioned for him a shirt of metal rings sewn into a padded vest, hard-wearing calf-high boots, and a tall cylindrical helmet. From the waist down all he wore was a skimpy leather skirt meant to show off the length of his legs and accentuate his height. It barely covered his buttocks, and since he hadn't even been allowed undergarments, his manhood dangled out in the open every time he bent down or took a long stride. Besides not giving him a lick of protection, the article seemed ridiculous and Ford couldn't guess for the life of him why they made him wear it. The idea came from the Master of Games, who was not above titillation of any kind. If it got the people talking, all the better for trade. Ford had also been provided a weapon this time: a six-foot long rod with a heavy ball at one end and a foot-long blade on the other. Roniik considered the blade unnecessary. A good solid mace was all anyone ever needed in his opinion. Kalev added the blade as a way to heighten the danger. "Always make it big.

The bigger the better. Create the spectacle," his predecessor had advised him. Roniik was no expert with the odd contraption, however, he did show Ford how to hold and swing the thing without stabbing himself. Also, while training with his new gear, Roniik had warned him against being stabbed in the chest by a piercing weapon, because the individual links of the mail were large enough to poke a finger through. After a few jabs to the kidneys, Ford got the point.

Roniik led the way up to the entrance where Kalev met them and then the Master of Games escorted Ford the last few steps into the arena. The eruption of joy that greeted Ford's arrival surprised all three. The Kamen remembered him from his first fight by his height. Those that had been there spread stories of the giant to their friends. Someone in the crowd with a powerful baritone began a chant of "Vrod! Vrod! Vrod," which spread throughout the arena. Their cheers filled with anticipation at seeing him in warrior's gear. Something special was afoot.

While a pair of slaves hurriedly strapped the harness to Ford's groin, waist and shoulders, he stared down into the pit and saw the rock urchin. The bear fur that once camouflaged it now hung on by a single spike and the creature lay on its back. It had got caught up with an iron rod sticking out of the debris, flipped itself over and was in the process of inflating to increase its roundness, so it could rock back and forth on its spikes and right itself. While its dusty gray underside was visible, its wriggling legs, tube mouth, and creeping antennae unsettled the viewers.

Aside from the urchin, the pit was empty when they slowly lowered Ford by the creaking winch.

He kept his eyes peeled, searching every unusual mound of debris and watching the gates. The lanterns which hung over the side of the lowest balcony only dimly lit the floor, but he sensed no danger, spotted no threat. The audience's initial enthusiasm dissolved into questioning murmurs. After one Kamen started rhythmically banging on the balcony's metal sheet to show his displeasure, others took up the beat. Ford understood the meaning. He had fought in front of unruly mobs before and knew that if they didn't get what they had come for, the place could turn ugly. Maybe something had gone wrong and he wouldn't have to fight. The possibility made him hope all the harder that they might lift him out of the pit and send him back to the slaves' quarters. The thought had barely formed before one of the gates rattled open and a hush fell over the arena. All eyes were trained upon the mouth of the tunnel. They expected and even hoped something horribly vicious would hurl itself from the darkness and cause mayhem in the pit. However, nothing happened and confusion hummed throughout the room.

"Come, Kalev," shouted a Kamen across a middle balcony to the Master of Games. "What is this? You give us nothing?" While the last word still drifted across the arena, out of the pit tunnel burst the embodiment of Kamen angst and ire: a warrior from the Khoratan Plains. The crowd gasped and fell back from the balustrades, pressing their backs against the walls. All of their intense fear and hatred for the Khoratan people, and the death and deprivation they had once wrought upon them during the Kamen continental migration to Rikaswelt, flared up and broke forth in angry howls.

The warrior's shock of flaming-red hair and his face awash in blue with blackened eyes and a deep red about the lips down over the chin, evoked the horrific imagery so vividly recounted in Kamen oral history. All Kamen, young and old, instantly recognized from the stories his small helm with its visor that only covered eyes and nose, boarhide jerkin and leggings, the round shield strapped to the back, and his pair of scimitars. A chubby merchant's daughter fainted away at the sight of her nightmares embodied. Few noticed her being carried from the arena, so caught up were they in hurling curses and spewing venom at the fiend in the arena.

Ford didn't know why the Kamen jeered the man behind the warpaint. He might have been a saint or any benign being, but even Ford had been here long enough to fear and despise whatever came out of those pit-level gates. This warrior did not disappoint. He ran out swinging the two swords over his head and mugging up at the people with a face distorted into an insane grimace. The sight of Ford wrenched from him a demonic scream that drove the audience and Ford back a step. Such an unnaturally crazed state of mind had to have been altered in some way. Ford wondered if there was truth behind the rumors spreading through the servants' quarters regarding a devious alchemist working deep in the heart of Dargkivi. Secret doors and back passages were believed to hide a laboratory where the most brilliant Kamen created alchemical concoctions that altered the mind and body. There was no doubting this man was bent to violence.

The Khoratan warrior came at Ford with a berserk fury. The curved blades caught the light upon their sharpened edges, so that each wild swing flashed through the air like a shower of shooting stars. He leapt over the debris with an unbridled exertion which squeezed inhuman grunts and cries out of him as he swung those swords with a relentless determination meant to cleave Ford in half. Ford hauled back on his long, two-handed weapon and caught it in the chain attaching him to the winch above. The Khoratan's scimitars slashed his chest and slid away harmlessly. The warrior tried to stab Ford, but the curved blades were not designed for piercing. Ford stumbled back from the blows. They swung at one another and neither landed. The Khoratan came on, ever on, hacking and slashing. Glancing blows all, but frenetic and unremitting. Ford parried and swung back when he could. What the fight lacked in skill, it more than made up for in hectic action. The audience showered them with applause. The iron rod, which had fouled the urchin, tripped up the warrior and gave Ford time to whirl around the heavy ball at the end of his weapon, but it moved too slowly and sailed too high. This opened him up to slashes over his ribs that the ring armor held off. Ford's backswing also flew over his opponent's head. He took another painful jolt to the chest, cutting short his wind. And then it was all over. The death blow seemed to come out of nowhere. When the ball end missed, the blade end of Ford's weapon swished through the air and caught his opponent across the neck, opening the artery and spilling the life's blood from the man.

That ungainly swing of his oversized weapon toppled Ford and dropped him to one knee beside his vanquished foe. Much of the warrior's war paint had been sweated away and patches of brown skin shown through. A glimpse of brown stubble peeked from the edges of the fiery red hair, which sat askew on the man's head. "A wig?" thought Ford, who had seen actors wear such at shows in the city back home. He tentatively removed the helmet. Away came the wig, revealing a slave's shorn scalp beneath. In repose, the man's mad grimace had disappeared, leaving behind a natural, almost serene countenance. Ford knew him. The helmet's visor no longer hid the bulging eyes and the paint could not disguise Jengo's long face. The applause ringing in Ford's ears woke him like a lighthouse bell in a fog, revealing the truth. He had just killed a fellow slave and a friend for their pleasure.

Unadulterated anguish roared up from the pit. The startled Kamen mistook it for Ford's war cry and began cheering him all the louder. He threw down his weapon and helm, meaning to break them. They clattered to rest among the trash. The winch cranked away and Ford rose from the pit. He clenched his shaking fists and wished he'd held onto the weapon. If he had, at least one of those vile, stunted devils would have fallen before him. When he reached the top, he had to be restrained. A dozen valvar had their spears trained on him by the time Roniik arrived and calmed everyone.

"Vrod still has the battle fury within him. He needs time to settle down," he explained. They left Ford chained well after the audience emptied from Mullauk and even then his obvious fury required a large escort to get him back to the slaves' quarters safely.

Ford sank into a pile of unused furs, and drowned in sorrow and regret for the part he had played in these games. He wasn't the only one who had been cruelly used. Jengo didn't deserve his fate. He had been kind and a good worker.

"These are not men. They are monsters," he muttered through a tightening jaw and grinding teeth. His body went rigid with the strain of reining in his emotions, but vengeful thoughts doubled and redoubled upon themselves until he put himself into a trance from which he emerged with a pitiable yowl. The other arena slaves tried to calm him, but the wailing went on. None of them slept that night until the small hours of the following morning. Even then, Ford didn't fall asleep so much as pass out.

Without a respite, it was right back to work the following day. Ford toted the pots and pushed the cart without thinking. He shuffled everywhere he went with his head down and his eyes lowered. The other slaves did what they could for him, taking on extra work and spooning a chunk of fatty meat into his bowl from theirs. If he noticed, he was thankful, but when they tried to speak with him, he wouldn't answer. Days went by in which he did not speak, responding only in grunts. He hardly noticed the passage of time. To him it could only be measured in the length of his thoughts: what he had done, what had been done to him, and revenge. Even if he tried to banish the thoughts, they often snuck up on him like a gang of thieves in the night, overwhelming him before he realized what was happening.

Roniik was not a sensitive man, but he knew better than to mess with Ford around this time. More than a week passed before he attempted to continue Ford's training. No sharpened blades were used. Also, no games were held at Mullauk that week. Rumors spread among the arena slaves that Ford's condition was the reason for the delay. It may have had something to do with it, but the reason was more so because the wild game hunters still hadn't returned to the city. Most assumed tragedy had befallen the hunting party. "Surely something's happened to them," the people would say. "It's foolishly dangerous to go out there in the freezing cold amongst all those blood-mad beasts!"

Whatever the task, whether it be training or picking up trash, Ford's mind was always elsewhere. It was often mired in the past, eating away at the saner side of him like a festering disease consuming healthy flesh. His inevitable return to the arena loomed over him like a taunting specter.

"I can't do it. They can't make me do it," he would mutter aloud to the other arena slaves. Of course, what he did or didn't want to do didn't matter. If he refused, they had means with which to make him fight. The people wanted Ford, the man who had slain the hated Khoratan, one of their symbols of evil. They wanted to see more of their hero. After missing out on a week's entertainment, some were demanding a show at Mullauk. They counted on the Master of Games to provide them with something to talk about, something to buoy their spirits.

Kalev could see no reason not to enter Ford into the arena again. He had few options aside from the big Aelwydian, but he hadn't exhausted them all yet. Late in the second week, he paid a visit to the city's animal wrangler. This earthy man without regular friends, aside from the creatures he cared for, was so delighted to have Kalev pay him the compliment of a personal visit to his home that he readily agreed to the game master's request to use one of his beasts in the arena, for a reasonable fee of course.

"It was worth a try," Kalev muttered to his wife two days later as they watched Joord, the most veteran of arena fighters cowering behind a low wall recently built in the center of the pit, while the yeti-esque Avar sat on the other side sniffing the variety of scents wafting about the arena. Roniik had been instructed to send Joord into the pit with Avar to see how he fared. If Joord could put on a good enough show, perhaps it would satiate Kamen desires and they would forget about Ford. Kalev did not want to lose Ford in a hopelessly deadly performance against Avar, but so far, the attempt was falling flat. The previous entertainments that day hadn't been particularly interesting: two slaves doing halfhearted battle with one another and a few old games rehashed with little success. It was the first time in a long time that the audience had shown their displeasure at Mullauk. "Fah! Fah!" they brayed while repeatedly kissing and splaying the fingers of one hand to mime projectile vomit exploding from their mouths.

Kalev had dug clear to the bottom of his bag of tricks. The wall, built of loose stone from the mines, had been an invention of necessity meant to prolong each fight and flesh out the evening's entertainment. The original intent was a maze that would encompass the entire pit, but what they ended up with due to time constraints was nothing more than a five-foot-tall cross section about ten-by-ten feet in the center of the pit. This was no maze. It was a minor obstacle. Instead of adding intrigue to the battles, it merely got in the way. Avar crouched on one side of the cross, only mildly curious of his surroundings and unaware of the presence of Joord, who was sweating profusely and breathing heavily on the other side. Neither man nor beast had moved in a while and the audience was getting restless.

"Tell Roniik to send in the giant," Kalev commanded his personal attendant. Nodding and bowing, the slave scurried down one of the tunnels to a stairway leading to the arena holding chamber, where Roniik awaited with Ford. A heavy guard escorted Ford toward Mullauk at a brisk trot and without trouble. Sleepless nights and mental exhaustion had rendered him mostly sedate.

However, upon hearing the unsettled masses and sensing the arena was near, his breathing became strained and his chest heaved. His manacled fists clenched, having nothing to wrench and twist as they wished. Sensing the tension, the valvar behind him trained their poisoned spear tips upon the center of his back and Roniik picked up his marching step. Kalev met the group at the entryway and introduced Ford to the audience by throwing up his hands in a theatrical flourish and beaming a winning smile to all. He and Roniik put on a good face upon entering the arena, even though neither was pleased with the situation. This would not be a fair fight. Joord was only alive because Avar hadn't noticed him. As soon as the beast woke to the prey presented to him, he would rip apart Kalev's two most valuable slaves. Roniik rued the loss of the time and effort he put into their training. "Such a waste," Kalev muttered between his smiling lips.

Now that Ford was favored by the audience, he would always be lowered into the pit by the winches. Once he was securely harnessed, and only when he was securely harnessed, did the valvar remove his manacles, force him over the balcony, and hand him his weapon.

The moment they began lowering Ford, Avar lumbered toward the spot where he would land. Avar's jaws ground in anticipation. Spittle dripped from his lips. A meal was on the way. Ford saw what awaited him. As all slaves did, he thrashed about as if he might somehow get away, but his twisting body and churning legs soon came to rest. He had been thrust into this situation before and his natural self-preservation kicked in. Taking his weapon up by the middle of the shaft, he reared back and aimed with the intent of spearing Avar. If he missed, he would be weaponless when he landed. As Avar waddled around the low stone wall, his hungry eyes never leaving Ford, his muscular fingers gripped the stonewall just inches from Joord's head. The arena slave jumped up and scampered away. Avar tore off after him and together they went around and around the wall, stepping wide at one point to avoid the rock urchin.

Ford hit the ground at the same moment Avar discovered he could climb over the walls in the center of the pit and go straight for his prey. At the height of his climb, he spotted Ford and came for him. Joord ducked behind the wall. Ford ran around the cross and made a pass by Joord. Their harness chains tangled and Ford jerked Joord off of his feet, sweeping him along with him. The chains went taut and yanked the two off their feet. They spun away from the ground together in a wide arc that swung them around the pit. Avar bemusedly stopped and watched them fly by in the opposite direction.

When they came to rest, the rock urchin stood between them and Avar. Seeing the strange spikey creature blocking him from going straight at his prey, Avar wailed in frustration. He had encountered its kind before and did not forget the pain it had inflicted when he poked it out of curiosity and felt its sting. With their chains tangled up, Ford and Joord stumbled along together, trying to keep the urchin between them and Avar. For the time being, it worked. Avar would come no closer. But then the urchin lurched toward them, its spikes coming within inches of Joord's leg. Ford held it at bay with the blade end of his weapon. Avar stepped laterally and then lunged for them in one of his frightening bull rushes. The two men shuffled behind the urchin. Avar came on. Purely as a gut reaction, Ford flicked the blade up and catapulted the creature through the air, in the same way he and his brother once used sticks to flick muck at each other at the old swimming hole. The urchin somersaulted into Avar's chest. The beast reared back and howled.

Ford untangled his chain from Joord's and they fled around the stone wall, leaving a frustrated Avar wanting to rid himself of the painful spikes, but not daring to touch the urchin. Wheeling about in agony, he stumbled blind with rage and agony, each step ever closer to the two slaves. Joord ran, but Ford stayed, letting the great brute come on. Avar whirled about and presented his back, Ford jumped forward and made a stab for it, but Avar's body kept contorting. The rock urchin flew from his chest and Ford's blade plunged deep into Avar's abdomen. The beast howled, the audience gasped, and Ford found himself on the ground, struck by a backhanded blow unlike anything he had ever felt before. He stumbled about like a ship tossed in a hurricane. Unable to see straight, he groped for his footing and weapon, and found neither. Avar's pungent musk filled his nostrils. The beast roared in his ears. Huge fingers wrapped around Ford's neck. He couldn't breathe. Blood pounded in his ears. Avar's massive teeth flashed before his face as his vision began fading to black. His grip loosened and the heavy ball end of his unbalanced weapon dropped like a lever, lifting the other end and driving the blade within Avar up into his chest cavity. The beast's limbs convulsed and jerked rigid, as if electrocuted, before he fell dead from as lucky a stab as had ever been seen in Mullauk.

The Kamen were shocked. Avar should have been feasting upon the two slaves. Admittedly, at the start their loyalties had been torn between Ford and their beloved Avar, but even so, they were certain that he was invincible. Some wondered if they weren't hallucinating the scene before their unbelieving eyes. Children asked their parents why Avar wasn't getting up. The uneasy, confused hush of the stunned crowd gave way to dissatisfied rumblings as they filed out of the arena.

"So, my friend, what do we do with our giant now?" Kalev asked Roniik over drinks after the show at The Salt Lick, a clean but crypt-like public house serving a well-off clientele. He had to raise his voice to be heard over the din of the disgruntled grumbling and clinking of ceramic mugs surrounding them. Patrons just arrived from the arena filled the drinking establishment with an agitated buzz.

"You call that a show?" someone angrily shouted from across the room over the heads of dozens of sour-faced Kamen.

"I paid good gold for…for what? What was that, Kalev?" complained the man who owned a monopoly on the town's trade in koer oil. His sour breath could have been smelled halfway across the room. Having it in his face when the man stomped across to speak his mind turned Kalev's stomach. He felt queasy for more than that reason alone. A tide of complaints rolled in with another influx of patrons. The show had been a disgrace, the people said. The animal wrangler was weeping in his chambers, they said. Such an outpouring of sympathy and compassion had never been lavished upon the man before in his life. A few in the crowd called for Ford's execution. The vehement reaction to his slaying of Avar was so unexpectedly furious that the two Mullauk men decided to take their conversation elsewhere.

"A glass of well-deserved wine, while we discuss this problem," Kalev said to Roniik back at the Master's home as he poured out a pair of deep beakers. But when he sat down, Kalev found there was little left to discuss. "It's obvious we can't keep him as is. Something must be done with him."

Roniik sat on the edge of an overstuffed stool with his elbows resting on his knees and his beaker cradled between his hands, while he gazed absently around the Master's spacious and comfortably furnished den, lit and heated by a colorful array of warm rocks. Padded seating, a pair of superfluous servants, and a few wooden implements, such as utensils that were actually used for eating, displayed a wealth well beyond the trainer's means. He stared down into his wine while contemplating the evening's show, hoping to find a wisdom he did not possess somewhere within the murky depths of this expensive beverage. Being a practical and focused man, his mind was rooted to the present. He hadn't given future possibilities much consideration, so when put to it, he had little to say on the matter. Never had he been asked to come up with an answer for such a perplexing quandary as what to do with a perfectly useful slave. After a rare moment's hesitation from him, he said, "I would hate to lose such a valuable fighter. Would it be possible to use him as an evil one?"

"Turn him into a villain, you mean?" Kalev said blandly.

"He is hated now. It would not be difficult," said Roniik, shifting his weight in the chair to hide his embarrassment for suggesting such a wholly unoriginal solution.

"Yes, that would seem to be the only thing we can do with him now. I can think of nothing better. But of course, we will lose him either way. The people won't stand for him winning once more. He must die in the very next games. Either that or it will be my head they will be calling for! They're on the verge of it already, the ungrateful savages." Kalev let slip a mirthless laugh that soon died away, leaving behind a lingering silence during which they both drank and Kalev reflected upon his grim future.

A polite knock at the front door was answered by one of the house servants and a moment later he led into the room a Hikarite dressed in the finest robes worn by any slave within the city. His name was Mukhayato, but the Kamen considered three syllables too lofty for a slave to possess, so they called him Muk. As the personal translator and ledger keeper for the Vanagz family, Muk kept an orderly house and finances. At times he could be a very busy man. Yet, regardless of whether he was run off his feet or left with nothing to do for hours on end, he consistently comported himself with an air of utter boredom. He was not lazy and would never do anything as impertinent as lounging about in front of his master or any Kamen for that matter. It was simply that he had no interest in the world around him. His utter indifference gave him the half-lidded eyes and motionless face of sleepy bullfrog. Whenever he spoke, no matter the language, it all came out in a monotone. Muk would be considered an uninteresting individual in most cultures, however, for a slave of Daragkivi he stood out in more ways than one. Not only did he wear some of the finest clothing permitted a slave, he also had been allowed to grow out his hair, which was mostly hidden by a large skullcap to avoid offending Kamen sensibilities. Also, he stood with an erect posture that even Roniik had to admire. It was as if standing with an impossibly straight back was as relaxing to him as slouching was to others.

While Kalev did not go so far as to offer him a seat, he did treat the Vanagz's slave with more civility than he would most other servants, so their conversation maintained a courteous and respectful tone throughout. After pleasantries and even an offer of wine, Muk got down to business.

"I have been sent by the good wife of my master to transact the purchase of your stock," he said.

"My stock?" wondered Kalev.

"One of your slaves."

"And which one would that be?" asked Kalev with an indulgent smile as he leaned back in his chair, stretched out his legs and crossed them. He always tried to appear aloof in these matters, but the fact was, he had few slaves left and he had a good idea which one Muk was talking about. He fought his eyebrows down, which liked to rise up his forehead and levitate there for the duration of intriguing negotiations. As luck would have it in this case, subterfuge was unnecessary. Muk's mistress was terrible with money and had instructed her servant to give Kalev whatever he wanted. The frugal Muk had a far greater understanding of finances and would have struck a favorable bargain. Since he didn't care how Vanagz's spent their fortune, he handed over a bag filled with his mistress's offer along with his answer. "The large man who fights at Mullauk. The slave known as Vrod."

"Ford? You want Ford," said Kalev, his pulse quickening. He took one look in the bag and his heart outpaced his head. Nothing could hold back his eyes from bulging at the sight of the abundant gold, silver, gems, and more within. He drew out the handle of a hairbrush bereft of its bristles. This simple piece of wood could be sold for more than he had expected to get for Ford at this point. Before he could leap up and kiss this god-sent slave, the tiniest twinge of scruples pricked his conscience. Muk's master provided the ferocious beasts needed for the arena. He and Vanagz had good trade relations, which he didn't want to spoil by taking advantage of his wife's loose purse. If he gave them Ford as a gift, it would be a nice gesture, one that would curry favor. Favor for what, Kalev asked of himself. Who else would buy Vanagz's wild game? He trapped the dangerous beasts alive and was paid more than handsomely specifically because the Mullauk arena existed. The argument for and against was getting muddled by his innate greed. It would have been foolish, even suspicious to turn down such an offer. Instinct even told him to ask for more, but the absurd amount of valuables in the bag was already tantamount to a raider's plunder. In the end he found that weighing the options was as simple as weighing the bag in his hand. "He's yours."

Muk wanted to take Ford immediately, but Kalev convinced him with Roniik's backing to give them time to "properly prepare the slave for Mistress Vanagz." Arrangements for delivery were made for the following day and Muk left without showing a hint of his feelings regarding the transaction.

Kalev turned to Roniik unable to contain his amazement at what had just happened.

"Well, well, well, Vanagz's wife," he said, then threw back his beaker of wine, drained the remainder, and filled it again. "You never know who's going to come raining gold upon you." They laughed together and toasted to the Mistress Vanagz and her extravagant generosity.

"The giant lives after all," said Roniik.

"Yes, yes," said Kalev with the rim of his beaker poised at his lips. After a moment's pause he laughed. "But after she's done with him, he's going to wish he died in the arena!"

Chapter 15
Not Too Blind To See

In the exclusive Ulemine Alu section of town, where rich families lived alongside the chasm across from the Revane Steps, the Vanagz house occupied a fair stretch of the cliffside where the northern most point of Dargkivi touched the icy coast. There were more desirable locations on this strip of rock, but the Vanagz wanted more room. The sprawl of the family's living quarters took up an impressive amount of land.

The front door set the tone for the whole dwelling, for this prized possession was made of wood. "Entire doors all of wood," astounded people from the lower towns would often muse when tales of the Kamen elite trickled down to them. Passing through the door, one entered the central common room, where the family received and entertained guests. This room housed the most impressive collection of furs and hunting trophies in all of Dargkivi. These treasures were illuminated by a dazzling crystal chandelier, a lighting feature which came into vogue in Ulemine Alu soon after the Vanagz had theirs installed.

Doors and hallways branching off of the common room led to the rest of the house. Each member of the family had their own spacious bedroom with a massive wardrobe stuffed with furs and the fashions of the day. Each bedroom included at least one annex, such as the son's playroom. The Vanagz owned one of the city's more impressive kitchens, and it was put to good use morning, noon and night, although there were but three family members. The lady of the house made sure her larder was stocked at all times with the freshest and richest food Rikaswelt could provide, as well as delicacies from around the world. Slabs of white elk and grand mammoth from her husband's most recent hunting expeditions hung in their own personal cold cellar, which also housed exotic spirits from far-flung lands.

The Vanagz house was so excessively spacious that it contained a number of rooms that were never used. And yet, all of the family's servants save one were made to share a single room furnished with cots and little else. A bodyguard, cook, housemaid, and now Ford all had to cram into the spare, stuffy space just off of the kitchen. The sole exception being Muk, the personal translator and ledger keeper, who had been given his own work and living quarters due to his importance.

At one time, the Vanagz house was the most visited in the entire city. People wished to view the trophies, as well as the stylish décor and odd lighting choices. Lanterns with colored glass sides threw a variety of hues about the rooms, which some visitors considered eerie. Others appreciated the fanciful variation, as did Mistress Vanagz, who tended to suffer from mood swings during the winter months. The lady of the house felt that the color lifted her spirits. A variety of methods were employed by the Kamen to stave off depression. For instance, in this house many rooms included windows and balconies. Though they provided views of little more than the frozen sea, the main point was to let in the sunlight. There was even a solarium of sorts.

"Follow. This way," said Muk in an attempt at Aelwydian, which wasn't bad, though Ford thought it sounded a bit funny in a Hikarite accent. Everything sounded funnier than usual to him. Roniik had slipped him a crystal compound with a strong measure of spirits that brewed up a warm, fuzzy complacency within him. He followed dutifully, happy to find the ceilings were high enough that he didn't have to crouch in some of the rooms. "You are to be prepared. You meet Mistress Vanagz."

Ford stood erect, tried to blink away the indistinct blurring of his eyes and appear alert. It was not that he cared about making a good impression upon a Kamen, but he had to admit, he was dumbstruck at not having died in the arena or apparently having to fight there ever again. Now, here he was, once again in a new situation with no clue what was expected of him.

On their way through the kitchen, they stepped over sacks of root vegetables and wire baskets of seafood, while ducking and dodging hanging pots, pans, and bowls of bread and dried fruit. The cook, a queen of her domain, hurried the intruders along with blasted invective and a long metal spoon to the backside. Muk ushered Ford into a small adjacent room cluttered with mops, brooms, brushes, buckets, rags, and a large tin basin placed in the center. The basin had a few inches of water in it already.

"You wait," said Muk and turned back to the kitchen to address the cook. "Alee?"

Without looking up from the beef she was pounding with a tenderizer, the cook repeated "Alee!" but in a hoarse shout lacking Muk's discretion.

"Move off clothes. Go in water," Muk instructed Ford with the same bland enthusiasm as he employed for everything he said.

Since the start of his enslavement, Ford's modesty had been greatly diminished. He needed no prodding to disrobe in front of others. Once naked, he stepped into the basin and danced circles in the frigid water while awaiting the translator's next command. When none came, he looked to where Muk had been standing and found instead a slight woman of perhaps twenty dressed in a smart olive frock. Despite lips which drooped at the corners and perpetually downcast eyes that gave her the appearance of a mourner, high cheekbones and curling lashes went a long way in improving upon such a somber face. To Ford's surprise, she grabbed one of the rags, got down on her knees and began washing him. He had been made to wash that morning before being handed over to his new master, but he wasn't about to stop her. Her tender, almost massage-like circular wiping motions felt too good. She scrubbed him all over, even in places he didn't bother with much.

Suppressing his pleasure as best he could, he allowed his mind to spin with the dozen and more questions he wanted to ask her. It took a good deal of restraint to hold back, but he knew the dangers of talking out of turn in front of a master, and at this point he didn't know if she was his new master or not. After all, Muk had said he was about to meet Mistress Vanagz. This woman kneeling before him was quite short, but then again, her head was smaller than a Kamen's, more in proportion with the rest of her body. Perhaps she was a Manerd. Very little light penetrated from the kitchen into this closet of a room, so he couldn't tell whether her skin was dusky or dusty. Also, she wore a cloth headwrap which hid her hair or lack thereof. She began drying him off with one of the softest pieces of cloth ever to touch his skin. When she did what she could, he stepped out of the basin and she patted down his feet. This couldn't be his new owner, he reasoned. Not only did her features point to a race other than Kamen, no Kamen master would do this sort of work.

"Are you from back home?" The words tumbled from him, albeit in whispers. Still, he could hold back no longer. "I mean, Aelwyd? Can you understand me?" he kneeled in front of her, trying to meet her eye to see if there was any recognition. The young woman averted her gaze and offered no answer. She turned to a lumpy sack by the door and began taking from it pieces of his arena outfit, struggling with the heavy ring armor shirt.

"Hold up now," he said, leaning away and throwing up his hands to ward off the hated apparel. "I'm not fighting no more." He folded his arms. She tilted her head and her brow creased in confusion. She may not have understood him, but his distress was unmistakable. The cook, with her eyes locked upon the meat she was trimming, hollered something over her shoulder at them from the kitchen. All Ford garnered from it was that the young woman's name must be Alee. "Nobody's making me go back in that hole," he continued. Alee shook her head, which he mistook for an answer. "Good. Glad that's settled." She pressed the gear into his arms, all but the hybrid mace and halberd weapon, which had not been included for safety's sake. Donning the short skirt again made him go as red in the cheeks as he did the first time he had put it on, and when he finished dressing he was glad to find Alee gone.

"Follow. Follow," Muk said, reappearing in the doorway wearing the expression of someone who had better things to do.

"What's all this? Why am I made to wear this? They don't mean to make me fight again, do they? The girl said I didn't have to and I tell you I won't!" A headache was forming in the center of his forehead just thinking about it. He wasn't going to kill for the Kamen again. The pleasure they found in pain made him sick. He didn't bother explaining all of this to the translator, because it soon became obvious that he would get no answer. It wasn't Muk's job to answer another slave's questions, especially ones that sounded impertinent, so he made it a point to ignore the other servants as much as he could. It seemed like a good idea to get this new one used to the treatment straight away.

Ford did receive a meaningful glare and frown when they passed through the common room and he tripped over a bearskin rug. From there, they made their way down a hallway and into a cozy, dimly lit lady's salon. The air was choked by perfume. Randomly strewn plush chairs, footstools, Kamen-sized tables covered in tiny bottles, and a miniature daybed cluttered the space so that they had to weave about to get from one side of the room to the other. There wasn't a single mounted trophy here.

In the low lighting, Ford thought he spotted a stuffed boar across the room, but it turned out to be a chunky guard sitting slouched on a stool by the door they were approaching. This former valvar had left city service to take up employment as a hired bodyguard. The pay was higher, the workload less demanding. It only made sense and any valvar who could get the work took it. By the look of him, this drowsy-eyed man with a salt and pepper beard could still do a fair amount of damage with his bare hands alone, but he also wielded a needle spear, as well as a short sword. Muk and the bodyguard exchanged no words, not so much as a grunt, so Ford followed suit when they passed by.

When they stepped into the next room, it was as if someone had clamped hands over their ears. All echoes ceased and the edge came off of every noise. Shuffling feet and the swish of cloth whispered without sibilance. Nothing snapped or crinkled here. The thick carpets and heavy draperies that lined all surfaces in this room absolutely killed sound. Ford's eyes fought to adjust to the strange lighting. A pair of colored warm rock lanterns played tricks on one's vision.

Once his senses rebalanced, he noticed the room's décor. Bowls filled with glinting baubles sat atop pedestals, chests and tiny tables. Countless necklaces hung from the corners of a gigantic mirror with a gilded frame propped against wall. Everything about the room pointed to the designer's attempt to create a veritable shrine to comfort. A brazier off to one side kept the space heated like a furnace, which in this climate was a pleasure. In the center of it all stood a mound of plump mattresses stacked three feet high. Such a tall bed required a set of moveable stairs for it to be mounted by the mistress of the house.

The ruffled bed covers shifted and a groan crawled out of what appeared to Ford to be a fuzzy cushion among the pillows. The cushion rose up slightly and blinked in his direction. With a colossal effort, the covers were peeled back to reveal the ghastly pale, gelatinous form of Wivvek Vanagz, the mistress of the house and the person who had bought Ford from the Master of Games. Seeing her lying there before him was like seeing the shell of a clam pried open to reveal the squidgy muscle within. When she rolled over the mattress toward him for a better look, her belly and breasts sloshed to one side. Her fingers and toes looked like beans growing from the ends of stalks. Everything melded into one.

Her many sickly grunts and groans, coming as if from some dying animal, made Ford wonder if they had brought him in to care for her. If so, he thought, they would have been smarter to bring in the priest Will. The impression of illness wasn't helped by the glass lanterns casting blue and yellow hues from either side of the bed, which combined to turn Wivvek's skin a pallid green. This and the smeared make-up she had worn for three days straight did nothing to improve her looks.

Perhaps *good* looks at one time, thought Ford. He wasn't wrong. Prior to her marriage, at least three of her many suitors pursued her solely for her beauty. However, after wedding Vanagz she dove headlong into the indulgences of wealth and put on the kind of weight that created a brow heavy enough to droop, pressing her eyes down into horizontal slits and giving them the illusion of permanent disapproval. Her tiny cherry nose was buried between enormous peach cheeks that also crushed her lips into a permanent pucker. Under the lips, her walrus's chin was bookended by a massive pair of jowls, like cow udders in need of milking. Everything on her person drooped, save her hair. Her eyebrows had been curled up and encrusted with mica dust and her frizzy hair sat atop her head like a haystack.

"Ze zevalimus horklik," slurred from Wivvek's lips as if the words had been dropped into a vat of butter and had to climb back out to be heard. Not wanting to exhaust herself by speaking too much, she resorted to silently eyeballing Ford. The sight of him in his arena outfit lifted the corners of her lips and aroused other parts of her body as well. He looked just as she had imagined he would from the description her friend had given her. Wivvek never made it to Mullauk these days. In fact, she seldom left the house at all, so she relied upon friends and servants to collect the playthings she desired.

Ford stood awkwardly in the center of the room wondering what was expected of him. He didn't know what to do with his hands, and his feet kept shuffling. Like the previous room, there were no stuffed trophies in this room either, he noticed while staring goggle-eyed about him. The detail seemed remarkable only for the fact that there were trophies everywhere else in the house but these two rooms. Even the kitchen had a massive set of antlers hanging above the hearth. Ford doubted he would have noticed if he didn't feel the need for his fluttering mind to latch onto something.

Wivvek took up a thin stick she used for multiple purposes, such as ringing the servants' bell over her head, and waved Ford toward the bed with it. He took a single step forward. The stick whipped through the air with an irritable jerk. Ford took another step. Wivvek hooked the bottom of his skirt with the end of her stick and lifted the front. Ford fought the urge to knock the stick away. Nothing good would come of resisting, so he stood still while she admired his manhood. The stick tapped the mattress repeatedly in the way one would pat the ground beside them when they wanted a pet dog to sit next them. Ford sat on the edge of the bed.

"Koraltama ma." The words flopped from Wivvek's lips. When Ford didn't react, she raised her voice into a sluggish shout, "Koraltama ma, ze trattal harg-kukk!"

"Mount me, you idiot ox-cock," droned Muk from where he sat on a stool in the most distant corner. Ford jerked upright and twisted around so fast he nearly fell off the bed. He thought the translator had left. The surprise of finding him still in the room quickly turned to embarrassment, because now he knew what Wivvek wanted him to do and he wasn't too pleased about doing it in front of a stranger. The guard sitting on the other side of the door was one thing, but having another man with his eyes on you in the midst of the act was another thing altogether. It didn't matter that Muk stared straight forward at the wall and his bullfrog face looked as if it were bored of catching flies. Wivvek grumbled and muttered a string of Kamen that Ford couldn't make out at all, but which Muk apparently understood as: "Make relations with my parts! Or I cut away your seeds!"

After some initial half-hearted thrusting, in which her pendulous breasts sloshed back and forth between her chin and belly, he tried to think of other things. The bed covers were incredibly soft. They made the towel that Alee had dried him with earlier feel a cat's tongue in comparison. But that was all the distraction he could muster. His mind reluctantly wandered back to the disturbing present. "Like bumping into a bowl of jelly," he said to himself. "She's got the strength of a bucket of slops." The only effort Wivvek made the entire time was to shift on to her side halfway through. One of her breasts rubbed against her own hip. He stared in amazement, not believing it were possible.

Muk kept up with his translations. Lines like "Mine me deep!" and "Spear me with speed. With speed," were repeated without the slightest interest. Finally, "Feed me your jewels. Pop. Pop," finished the session. The repulsive nature of the act and the distracting commentary made Ford's performance a trying labor, but Wivvek didn't need him for long. Her pent-up desires unburdened themselves quite quickly.

Ford was summoned to her bed three times that day and twice each the next two days. He relished a short-lived reprieve on the fourth day before having to go back at it again on the fifth. By the end of the week he was fairly exhausted from having some of the least arousing relations he had ever had with a woman. He was also growing a little tired of her stick. At one point he did something wrong—he had no idea what—and she used it to whack a tall, thin glass vase off of the table next to the bed. It had smashed across the floor and Muk crawled about picking up the scattered gems and colored glass it had contained, all the while repeating, "Idiot. Idiot." On the positive side, it was during this same session when Wivvek began crying out, "Za! Za! Za!" that Ford became very excited, because he understood that *za* meant *yes* before Muk had translated it. That put him in a good enough mood to finish with a vigor that pleased Wivvek.

During his first week at the Vanagz house, Ford recovered in body and soul from his experiences in the mines and arena. In many ways, he was in a better place. The threat of life and limb didn't hover constantly over his head, provided the performance of his current duties met expectations. Other than that deplorable task, life in the Vanagz household was by far the best situation he had been placed in since the outset of his enslavement. The house was a pleasant place to live. Better than the mines by far. The hint of a scent still given off by the wooden shelves and walls of the house's interior reminded him of home more so than the usual rock tunnels and caverns of Dargkivi. The new clothes he was given were the finest he had ever worn. Slaves owned by wealthy Kamen were decently dressed and made presentable, because it reflected well upon the owner. A shabby slave meant the owner had fallen on hard times. In these days of plenty, being poor was tantamount to committing a crime.

Wivvek aside, his household duties were minimal. The worst of them being the disposal of the family's waste, but even that job didn't require him to walk any farther than a chute just off of the kitchen, which dumped everything down a cliff toward the sea. Ford didn't know where the chute ended. All he knew was that the dark hole blew in cold air and it was better to shut and latch the little hatch as quickly as possible. Mostly Ford spent his time wrangling the family's only child, an unruly handful of trouble named

Vaavo. Whether the boy was three-years-old or thirteen, Ford hadn't a clue, because all Kamen were no taller than the prepubescents where he came from. Vaavo didn't come up much above Ford's knee, a fact Ford became painfully aware of when his first encounter with the boy concluded with a headbutt to the kneecap. Like his mother, everything about Vaavo's body tended to be round. The likeness to a ball and the boy's irascible nature soon fostered in Ford a keen desire to boot Vaavo across the room after a few short hours of minding the child.

Vaavo's favorite pastimes of wandering through the halls or playing upon the bridge over the gorge kept Ford busy. Half a day might be lost in tracking down the boy and luring him back home. Tag and other such games could often get the child headed back in the right direction, but sometimes he had to be coaxed with goodies or hauled home kicking, screaming, and clawing the whole way. During one chasing game, Vaavo turned his ankle slightly and demanded to be carried home. After that, being carried back by Ford became a common occurrence. Every day he wandered farther afield and usually he didn't have it in him to repeat the journey all the way back.

In their way, the adults were no different. The rich of Ulemine Alu liked to drink stronger spirits than they could handle. Hauling a passed-out Kamen home became an almost nightly ritual for which Ford could be called out of bed at all hours. Compared to what he had endured in Dargkivi up until now, this was nothing to complain about, and he was disappointed when it all came to an abrupt end. The way it ended made him want to turn into a mouse and disappear into the walls.

During one of his grunting and sweating sessions with Wivvek, Alee sprinted through the bedroom door with the cook and the family's bodyguard at her heels. Muk had a devil of a time translating her frantic words as they tumbled over one another.

"Man come…Your man comes…" Even under duress, Muk maintained his bland cadence and only once became perturbed enough to ask Alee in her own language to speak slower. While this carried on and the issue became clearer, the bodyguard discretely slipped from the room and shut the door behind him. "Master Vanagz is in the house," Muk finally announced.

The two servant women flew into action. Muk was cajoled into stalling the master with excuses that his wife was bathing and readying herself for her husband. Ford's arena outfit had to be hidden. Waved hands and sheets dispersed the air's sweaty musk. The giant Aelwydian had to be yanked on to the floor beside the bed. As the blankets descended upon Ford's body, covering him completely from head to toe, it seemed to him that these two had done this sort of thing before. They had, but usually the master sent a messenger ahead to alert the household of his imminent arrive so that a meal could be ready for him. That had not happened this time.

"Are all dead? Where is everyone? Why are you transla—" came Muk's voice as he translated the gravelly Kamen words shaking the wooden walls of the house. The heavy oak door of the bedroom gave way to the rotund chest and belly of Dagmar Vanagz. He took one look at his wife and did nothing to disguise his disgust. "Why the party? What is the cook doing in here? There is nothing to eat in the kitchen and I'm starving!" The shock of graying black hair atop Master Vanagz' square head wobbled back and forth as he shuffled left and right to scan the room. With such a short neck, mountainous shoulders and prominent, bearded jowls, it was the only way for him to take in a larger panorama. In his youth he cut a powerful figure, but time and a healthy appetite allowed his gut to catch up with his chest.

The room remained silent. The servants stared at their feet and the mistress of the house refused to answer her husband. Handling his moods exhausted her.

"Why is your room always a mess?" He pointed at the pile of blankets. Everything he said, he said in a shout. Even if he wasn't angry, the cutting timbre and volume of his voice, as well as a permanent wrinkle above his long nose, between a pair of shrub-like eyebrows, made it seem as if everything under the sun angered him. He carried on hollering with the occasional curse thrown in for good measure, because it never seemed to hurt and sometimes won his arguments for him. Eventually, when he realized there was nothing to win, he calmed down somewhat. Muk translated to the servants only what was necessary. "I have a side of elasmutterum coming up. We'll have that tomorrow, but right now I need something in my belly."

The cook's head remained bowed as she made for the kitchen. Master Vanagz had a few more things to say. His wife answered a question or two, but asked none of her own and already seemed bored with her husband, whom she hadn't seen in over a month. Having never left the door frame, Master Vanagz took one last look at his wife's bedroom, gave a derisive grunt, and left to light a fire under the cook.

From the moment of Dagmar Vanagz' arrival, the atmosphere of the house changed. The cook showed a more tender side to Alee and only quietly bossed her about. Muk shed his most blatant shows of apathy and spent most of his time at the table in his private room, making sure to have some papers and writing implements in front of him at all times, instead of just a mug of some warm beverage. The bodyguard no longer slouched. Whatever wall he had his back to, his back ran perfectly parallel with it. Alee made herself scarce as much as possible, avoiding Dagmar when a few days passed and he began showing up in the kitchen inquiring into her whereabouts. All of the servants became a good deal quieter and kept to themselves. Ford was fine with that. Since Polecat Island he had become more subdued and introspective. After his experiences in the mines and arena, he wanted to be left alone. For his part, since Dagmar's arrival, he spent less time hovering about the kitchen hoping for a handout or a sniff from one of the expensive spice jars, and more time on his chores. He would empty a waste pot the moment it had been used. His liaisons with Wivvek ended immediately, to his relief.

When the master was gone, no one worried about being caught mucking about, because if Wivvek ever got out of bed, everyone knew about it, and for the short time she was up she never ventured beyond her favorite few rooms. However, the far more restless Dagmar moved about the household, sometimes appearing around a corner when one least expected it. The servants blessed his carrying voice and frequent shouting for giving away his whereabouts. While the other servants were merely annoyed by the master's intrusion into their usual routine, Ford was especially worried. If the master of the house found out that a servant had been sleeping with the lady of the house, whether or not by choice, surely it would mean a swift execution.

Everyone was on their best behavior, except for the boy Vaavo. He didn't misbehave in front of his father, but he did spend even more time sneaking away from home. Master Vanagz chalked it up to a wanderlust in keeping with his own, but the real reason was that the boy feared his father.

"Vaavo?" Ford said to a bent-backed widow late into an afternoon's worth of chasing down the boy, who had long since slipped from sight. It was getting on, his back ached from bending under the low ceilings, and he needed help, so he appreciated seeing her full-moon face of astonishment poke from her doorway. Vaavo's noisy rambles through town happened so often that few residents still paid either of them any mind when they tromped through their neighborhoods, one shrieking and the other calling out for the child.

Ford held back a sigh when the old woman launched into a fully one-sided conversation. From the few words he picked up now and then, she seemed to be speaking of her ailments. She lived in the heart of Rask, a somewhat affluent neighborhood whose old-money was tied to trade with the provinces. Dargkivi's ailing elderly preferred living in Rask to take advantage of the town's attempts at the healing arts. The city's secretive alchemist laboratory was rumored to be located somewhere nearby. In her dotage, the widow had very few friends left, and since her husband died and her salt-addicted daughter had dropped into a coma, she longed for companionship and to unburden her woes upon someone else for a while. Even this frighteningly enormous slave was better than nothing. Ford's scant knowledge of the Kamen language reduced him to nodding and smiling until he could interrupt without offending. Saying the child's name and looking inquisitive did the trick. The moment the widow pointed down the tunnel, he was off.

"Vaavo!" Ford called down a dark tunnel with a barrel vault ceiling. There was no response but his own echoes, so he turned back and made for the fork in the passage he had just passed. Clearly, he had misinterpreted the old woman's directions. Getting back on track, he found the other tunnel proved to be nearly as dark and empty. However, there was a faint light ahead. He picked up his pace and continued calling out. With such a lead, the boy could be in another part of town already. He hurried on. When a faint series of random, warbling hoots came from somewhere not far ahead, he knew he was on the right track. The boy liked to make odd noises during his trips through the tunnels. It helped to release pent-up energy.

Rask's wide striped wall pattern continued on down this tunnel, where the light grew stronger as Ford passed around a sharp corner. The source of the light at the end of this passage was being blocked by a pair of figures a hundred or so feet ahead. A tall robed man down on one knee was speaking with what appeared to be Vaavo from the outline Ford could make out against the backlighting. Beyond them, a mirror propped against the far wall cast daylight down from a vertical shaft in the ceiling and sprayed an iron gray illumination into this lower passage. The first time Ford had seen this sort of device in use elsewhere in Dargkivi he was awed by the simple-but-smart ingenuity.

The robed figure patted Vaavo upon the shoulder. Ford didn't know what to make of the scene at first. Obviously, the man was a non-Kamen and thus a slave, but he took dangerous liberties in handling a Kamen boy so familiarly. The man ran a hand affectionately over Vaavo's head while standing up. The unfurling of his lanky body looked familiar. Vaavo skipped to Ford. Ford slowed down, but he didn't stop. He kept moving toward the man, as if an unseen force propelled him inextricably forward. Perhaps it was nothing more than curiosity. Vaavo came up to him, took a swipe at Ford's shin and then ran down the tunnel and around the corner. Ford hardly noticed. His eyes had adjusted to the light and he could see that the robed man, now waving and smiling at him, was Will. Ford wanted to go to him, to say something, but Kamen voices coming from the doorway next to Will stopped him in his tracks. If Ford didn't go after Vaavo, he would lose the boy again. The chase had taken too long already. Ford couldn't afford to stand around in the tunnels talking to another slave, not with Kamen masters within earshot. Ford held up his hand just as Will slipped through the doorway and disappeared.

Though he walked away disappointed, Ford took heart in finding Will alive and in apparent good health. Now that he knew where to find him, perhaps there would be a chance to speak with him in the future. Vaavo's wanderings would surely take them down to Rask again sometime.

"Vaavo! Damn the boy," Ford shouted as he began the chase all over again.

Ford may have regularly cursed Vaavo, but he didn't think he was such an awful child. Having been a rambunctious boy, who did some wandering of his own in his youth, he could empathize. Besides, when Dagmar was away, the boy would often stick around the house. Occasionally he would venture into his father's rooms to play with the weapons and strange artifacts on display there. Ford learned to check Dagmar's rooms before traipsing about the city and more than once found the boy there reaching for a sabre, trying to lift the bronze maul from its pedestal, or stabbing the air with a dagger in the midst of some fantasy. Even if Vaavo was a bother, chasing down a noisy, troublesome child was better than walking around the house on egg shells and having to listen to his master and mistress screaming at one another.

"Why the giant?" Dagmar asked his wife one evening by the fire when they were well in their cups. The drink had calmed him down enough to have a relatively civil conversation at a normal volume. The question was prompted when Ford carried in a haunch of meat for their evening meal. Since his return, Dagmar and Ford had been in the same room together on more than one occasion, and yet the master of the house hadn't noticed the new servant at first. This was due to his habit of daydreaming himself into oblivion when he was home. He often strode about or rocked back and forth with his hands clasped behind his back, staring into a glowing warm rock, an actual fire, or out a window. His gaze went beyond sight to visions of far more interesting places than this set of rooms, which he hardly thought of as a home.

"A gift. For you," Wivvek replied with a breathy sigh between sentences. She was really beginning to feel the extra weight these days. When she stood, her belly hung down to her tree stump ankles. Her husband's presence within the home got her out of bed and into clothes. Wivvek did not want to give him the satisfaction of knowing what a trial it was for her to leave that bed. So, when he was home, they dined together.

The fluffy white fur cloak she wore this evening transformed her into a fuzzy snowball sitting in a high-backed chair by the hearth. The trip from her bedroom to the dining room reddened her face and stole her breath. "I saw him in Mullauk," she eventually went on. "He would be good...for the hunt."

"So, you bought him for me...for *me*?" Dagmar eyed her over his cup while he drank and pondered her motives, which were suspect whenever it came to generosity toward him. "If he's for me, why isn't he down in the stables? Even you know that slaves for the hunt are stabled." The city stables deep down near the provinces' market included servants' quarters for the workers who looked after the pack animals. Wivvek hadn't thought of this. She didn't give much thought to anything beyond her own desires and, when it came down to it, at this point she didn't much care if her husband knew she had bedded another man.

"He is good..." she began and then stopped. The taunt forming in the darker recesses of her mind seemed like a good idea at first, but she decided to hold back. Infidelity with another Kamen was one thing, but admitting to Dagmar that she had done so with a slave would give her husband the power to smear her name across town, utterly cripple her socially, and cast her aside without a coin to her name. The servants were aware of what was going on, but she needn't fear them the way she did her husband. She took another drink before going on. "For the house."

"He's good for the house," said Dagmar, soaking each word in doubt.

"And the boy."

"He is good for the boy, too?"

"For collecting the boy. They tell me."

"Of course you were told. You wouldn't know for yourself, would you? I'd bet wood you didn't get out of bed while I was gone, not more times than you could count on your little piggy hand." His lip curled and he turned away, unable to look at her any longer. She was supposed to be eating less and dropping the pounds she had packed on since their union. Before he had left on this last hunt, she had promised to lose weight. While most Kamen women were vaguely oval in shape, she had gone to extremes, and if anything, had grown larger since he last saw her. His accusation and the peppering of insults regarding her weight which followed, propelled the conversation into an evening-ending argument. Wivvek stormed off to her rooms and wasn't seen for two days. Dagmar was happy to have the rest of the house to himself. His only regret being that his wife kept Alee cloistered in the bedroom with her the entire time.

After the first frustrating day of sitting alone, fidgeting with his hunting gear and installing a newly stuffed long-clawed tiger in his secondary trophy room, Master Vanagz grew bored and cantankerous. He had nothing left to do, but stroll through the rooms admiring his treasures, and that only entertained him for so long. Too soon for anyone's liking, he began nosing into the servant's affairs, finding fault in Muk's bookkeeping, criticizing every meal his cook placed before him, and complaining that the house was filthy. The rooms rumbled with his petulant grumblings about Alee being taken away from her work. After the second day, he began straying from home, spending his time visiting friends and drinking at The Salt Lick.

In the early hours of a morning midway through his second week back, Vanagz barged through the front door locked arm in arm with a group of up-and-coming merchants he had spent the night with gambling and getting blind drunk. These *New Beards*, as they were nicknamed for their youth, shaved their beards short and wore their mustaches long, setting the newest youth trend in male hairstyles. Though short and stocky like all Kamen, they were also among the slimmest and trimmest men in the city, and far younger and smoother of voice than Dagmar's usual leathery, long-in-the-tooth gang of friends. That night they had drunk just as much if not more than Dagmar, and yet they were still as spry as they had been when the evening had begun.

After his usual cadre of drinking buddies had dropped by the wayside and Dagmar was left standing, the New Beards swooped in to ply him with drink and pry hunting stories from him.

As they fell through the front door of the Vanagz home, one was trying to tell a joke over the wailing song of the others. Dagmar liked the song, but they'd been singing it all the way across town, and the joke teller was sure he would get a big laugh, if he could just get to the punchline. Each of them yearned to impress the man who had awed them all night long with tales of his daring adventures. Not one of them had traveled much beyond their own neighborhoods, let alone into the far reaches of Rikaswelt. The din created by their carousing woke up the entire household, just as Vanagz had intended.

"I've an annou'ment to…to say!" he bellowed before being interrupted by a belch that he laughed off. The entire household, even Wivvek, had gathered in the common room waiting to hear the news. They watched with trepidation as the mass of sweaty, drunk men swayed dangerously about in one another's arms, threatening to collapse a spindly-legged pine table if they leaned any farther to one side. "Me and these…fine men," Dagmar shouted, pausing again in order to squeeze the shoulders and necks within his grasp. "We are off hunting!" He stared down his wife through blurry eyes. "And I'm taking your giant with me!"

Chapter 16
Happy Together

"You are stupid. Most stupid."

It was the following morning after Ford had been assigned to the stables. Dagmar ordered Muk to those cold, dark, stinking stalls at dawn to translate for the Vanagz slave overseer, who stood before Ford like a clenched fist full of strength and fury.

"You not understand…no…Do you not understand?" Nerves and the difficulty of his task had Muk fumbling over his words. He trembled before the overseer, whose rough and rumbling speech was a chore to follow, especially under the stress of fear. "Slop little bucket. Not slop big bucket…Little bucket. Little bucket go slop. In big bucket go dung. Dung for big bucket. Understand, stupid? Stupid, you understand?"

Ford nodded and turned his face away from the musty musk radiating from the overseer's hunched body and from his hot, rancid breath. Spittle shot from cracked lips which barely covered a mouthful of stony teeth. Ford's show of disgust enraged the overseer further. The breath came hotter as the pinched face moved closer, a face hanging upon a knobby head, too small for the wide body beneath it. A face terribly crowded by a flat nose, low forehead, and broad chin as battered as a ram that had busted in a castle gate or two in its day.

Through one of the other stable hands, Ford had pieced together what was known about the overseer. They called him the Walking Rock. Vanagz's slave overseer stamped his unusually wide webbed feet to get Ford's attention, but Ford only stared down at the webbing; not thin and membranous like a duck's foot or a bat's wing, but thick and leathery. Not unlike a snowshoe and no doubt good for running over ice and snow. The skin covering the Walking Rock's entire body was so tough and resilient against the cold that he hardly needed to wear clothes at all. If he would only stop stamping his feet and thrusting his fists, Ford could see how the creature could be mistaken for a dusty rock pile or a moving snow-covered mountain of muscle. Almost hairless, but for near-translucent eyelashes, his albino skin was marbled by faint pink creases, taut sinew, and scars cut upon his chest.

From a stable hand, Ford understood this massive ball of muscle's name to be Kaltzek. It seemed Dagmar had named him. He and his people came from a distant—perhaps the hand had meant *remote*—valley where they chased prey around their home mountain. The details were vague and difficult to follow, but it sounded as if Master Vanagz had captured his Walking Rock during a hunt with the intention of selling him to the Mullauk fighting pit, but Dagmar took a shine to the strange and immensely strong creature. It seemed Kaltzek had a knack for wrangling the pack animals, captured beasts, and even the hunt slaves. Before long, Dagmar made him slave overseer for the stables and hunt. Quick to anger, he would often knock other slaves down in frustration and take over the job when they were not pulling their weight. Not that Kaltzek minded the extra work. Hard work pleased Dagmar, and pleasing Dagmar meant everything to Kaltzek.

At first Ford couldn't fathom why such an impressively powerful being as Kaltzek would remain willingly under the yoke of the man who captured and essentially enslaved him. The answer was in the eye. Kaltzek's most entrancing feature was his false eye. Ford was sure he had misunderstood this part of the stable hand's story, but apparently Kaltzek's own people had plucked the eye from its socket and exiled him for some unknown offense. As a gift for loyalty and good service, Dagmar had a false eye fashioned from gold and enamel with a large ruby as the iris. The false red eye contrasted disconcertingly with the natural black of Kaltzek's good eye, giving him a cock-eyed leer. Regardless of the off-putting irregularity, the gift imbued a potent devotion in Kaltzek. He would go to great lengths for his master.

This was not the case for all of Vanagz's servants, as Muk would attest if such an admission could be pried from him. The translator exuded annoyance at having been called all the way down to the stables to translate nonsense among slaves and having to listen to the overseer's child-like attempts at the Kamen language, which Muk then translated into his limited Aelwydian.

All around them, servants ran to and fro over frigid flagstones from storeroom to stables preparing for a hunt. They gathered cold-weather packs of extra clothing and survival gear for the wilds of icy Rikaswelt: picks, hatchets, rope, cleats, fuel for fires, and armloads more. They loaded sledges with greased runners and harnessed anxious and annoyed animals. The chaotic activity left behind a mess that would be cleaned up by the dusky Amita boy being left behind to watch over those untrained pack animals too immature to be trusted on the trail. Dagmar's stables would be orderly and spotless before they returned, otherwise Kaltzek would take the hide off the boy.

A ripe stream of feces plopped down next to Muk, much to the relief of a nearby ivory ram, one of many from a robust stock of docile and nimble-footed creatures that made good Kamen mounts and adequate sledge teams. Muk danced away from the hot steamy mess quicker than Ford had ever seen him move. The translator grumbled something in his own language. Kaltzek cut off his complaining with a snarl. They began talking at one another in Kamen, but after a few laborious lines, Kaltzek went rigid, standing almost as erect as Muk. His master was striding through the staging area.

"You're coming too," Dagmar shouted at Muk through a passing servant, who cringed and shrunk down next to nothing before slinking away.

"Pardon, master?" The translator couldn't have looked more perplexed if he tried.

"You heard me! Grab a heavier cloak, some proper boots, whatever you need. You're coming on this hunt!"

Muk never attended the hunts, being useless when it came to tracking and slaying beasts. Alarm and protest rose to the tip of his tongue and was swallowed back down. It was no use. Dagmar wouldn't change his mind, and Kaltzek was liable to do anything if he felt another servant had disrespected the master.

While they spoke, Kaltzek stood by rocking from foot to foot, uneasy in his hardened skin and wishing the packing had been completed before Dagmar's arrival, as it had been for every hunt prior to this one. It would soon be finished, but he still resented the difficult translator and this dimwitted new slave for distracting him and causing the delay. Luckily for them, they were not the worst of the problems that morning.

"Where are they," Dagmar muttered with his arms folded and a foot tapping. A few sour oaths rumbled out of him. The young men who were supposed to accompany him on this hunt should've been there by now. Just as he was about to send a runner back up to Dargkivi to rally them, they finally staggered into the stables. The one in the lead struggling to tighten his belt stumbled as his loose shoe slid half off.

"Have you seen my hat?" asked the one behind him after a yawn and a rub of his half-lidded eyes. Neither of his companions responded. The last of them seemed to trip along on clouds as he followed behind with his eyes shut. Dagmar looked them up and down in disgust. They all wore city shoes, not boots. Their shirts and cloaks were too light to keep them warm. Their tall and wide-brimmed hats would blow away as soon as they stepped outside. Even Dagmar's slaves were more appropriately attired in wool and fur-lined coats, hard-soled boots, layered leggings, and gloves.

"Is it always this cold down here?" wondered Elvo, the weakest and most well-read of the three New Beards. His shivering shook the little confidence he had in this venture. The stoutest and most slovenly of them leaned against a pillar and slurred something in agreement. This one they called Gelee after the soft, jiggly dessert made from rendered animal bone. Of the three, he was the most excited and least prepared.

The young, inexperienced hunters would all require refitting out and that would take time. Dagmar relieved the annoyance building within him with a deep sigh through his teeth. Delays irked him. He had grown accustomed to a smooth-running operation. His usual hunting companions knew just what to do, but none of them could make this trip. The turnaround between hunts had been too quick for them. Their trade and families needed looking after.

Master Vanagz set Kaltzek to work repacking and finding proper gear for the New Beards, who dazedly stood back, letting him dictate to their own servants. Dagmar took up a station in the middle of the stables slapping a strap into his palm repeatedly. He had a passionate longing to be away. Once everything was ready, he immediately ordered the sledge train in motion, foregoing the usual pre-hunt aperitif.

The sledge runners scraped over the stone floor through a cavernous tunnel to the provincial market on the outskirts of town. This enormous oblong room—with a ceiling tall enough for Ford to walk under unimpeded—teemed with drovers, butchers, porters, and buyers and sellers, all constantly active and chattering. Around the perimeter, Kamen merchants traded at alcoves cut into the rock. Groups bartered in rapid shouts across stone slabs covered in cuts of red meat and pungent fish. Sacks full of shellfish or red root vegetables packed stalls. A lengthening line of talkative Kamen waited their turn at the market's official weights and measures stand in the center of the room. A clamorous auction was taking place off to one side against a wall, much like the slave auction Ford had been sold at. Here, the stock was large quantities of meat and produce. A few hanging braziers provided light, but much of the room was lit from the daylight coming in through the open gates at the far end.

The sun behind the cloud-choked sky cast a white luminescence against the snow-and-ice-covered ground that half-blinded the hunting party as they slid out through the market doors. The glare set everyone to squinting, pulling down their hats, shading their eyes with hands, or at least keeping them lowered to the dirty gray ground of the road where the reflection was not so bright. Towering banks of ice and rock flanked either side of the road and blocked the view in all directions but straight ahead. But even when the road rose and the banks diminished, one could see very little through the windswept ice particles which created the appearance of a perpetual blizzard over much of Rikaswelt. Judging distances became nearly impossible with a white-on-white landscape and hardly a landmark of note. A gray rock or ice mound thirty yards away looked much the same as a mountain thirty miles away. In the open, the wind cut through fabric and fur alike. One of the New Beards' wide-brimmed hats sailed away, rolling somersaults up the road and out of sight.

At least the wind was at their backs, mused Ford as he pulled his cloak tighter about him. Now that he thought about it, he didn't feel quite as cold as when he first arrived in Dargkivi. He and the other slaves were shackled to the back of the pack sledges, so that they could help push the train into motion. Once it reached traveling speed, they walked behind. If the train slowed, they were to push. If it ever picked up its pace, on a smooth patch or a downward slope, the slaves were expected to run and keep up.

The road became a flat, hard-packed mass reaching straight out into the bleak white beyond. A low range of hills ahead to the east was just coming into view. Out here upon a glacial plain, the Kamen masters trotted at the head of the train in a close pack upon their husky rams. The New Beards felt ill at ease in such wide-open spaces, an environment wholly foreign to the confines of home. Dagmar had grown used to the unsettling feeling. They tried to match his poise and mask their nerves with boisterous banter. Their forced laughter was loud enough to hear over the howl of the wind a few hundred yards back where the servants trudged over the granular snow surface of a frozen lake. They would have redoubled their pace without the help of Kaltzek's whip had they known of the scaly, tentacled leviathans residing under the layer of ice beneath their feet.

The New Beards brought the sledge train to a halt for an elaborate midday meal designed to impress their host. Their slaves pitched and prepared a hot, sumptuous meal in a cauldron that took hours to heat. Dagmar appreciated none of this. He loved his food and drink as much as the next Kamen, but these young ones had none of their elder's urgency. The older he grew, the more Dagmar realized that time was indeed of the essence. Time spent unnecessarily out here in this vast wasteland was time wasted. He had a gnawing impatience to get to the town of Siltsvesi, which normally could be done within a day's brisk travel. This leisurely attitude of the New Beards ensured that they would not make it there in a day. Dagmar sunk into a sullen mood which could not be ignored.

"Have we done something to offend you, Master Vanagz?" asked Adelar, who was by far the soundest of the three New Beards. With better companions, he might have been molded into an industrious trader like his father, but his foppish friends held him back.

"We should be much farther along by now," was all Dagmar would reply.

Packing was done in an embarrassed haste, a sweat-inducing haste for the servants, and no one spoke another word until later in the afternoon. The road had vanished altogether and the sledges crunched over frozen snow.

"Is that Kohle?" Elvo finally summoned the courage to ask.

"No," said Dagmar. Kohle was a deserted mining town some two hundred and more miles to the southeast and they had traveled less than twenty. It was the arrowhead-like peak of the hill directly ahead and its vague resemblance to the mountain in which Kohle was buried that had unearthed the worthless nugget from deep within Elvo's now depleted mine of geographic knowledge.

"Where they coming from?" Gelee asked as a team of drovers led a flatbottomed sled stacked with pelts past them on their way to the city. Dagmar had ridden ahead of the pack and neither of the other two New Beards had an answer. Had Dagmar been with them and in the mood, he would have informed them that they had passed numerous Kamen settlements since leaving Dargkivi. These close-knit family clans were hidden away to either side of the road among ravines or buried within some craggy hill.

"This is Kalnamada," said Dagmar when the day was through and he could no longer will the rest of the hunters on. Unaccustomed to riding, the exhausted New Beards had been drifting off to sleep uncontrollably for the last hour. Gelee had fallen off of his mount twice. The New Beards pried open their eyes and saw nothing but a snow-covered hill. Dagmar led them around to an exposed rock outcropping on the backside. The people of Kalnamada lived within the rock's cracks and crevices, which had been burrowed out to create snug chambers for the few indomitable Kamen who squeezed out a living from the cold, hard rock of this inhospitable land. "It is not ideal, but better than nothing, we'll stay here the night and continue on in the morning. First thing in the morning."

Such prestigious visitors provided a respite as good as a holiday for these miners and small game trappers. The squat figures in black and brown furs said little, but rather preferred to hear news of the larger world beyond their ken. While Dagmar made do with the sparse accommodations, the New Beards took no pains to hide their contempt for the primitive lodgings. The cheerful dignity of the Kalnamadans, who presented their meager but well-intentioned offerings of plain food and watered-down drink at the start of the night, were reduced to shame-facedly leaving a plate of salted meat on the table for their guests in the morning before slipping off to work.

The night before, Ford had been confused while standing outside feeding the animals. Darkness had not descended. A dusky light lit up the sky all night. It was as if the sun had forgotten to set entirely. When Kaltzek kicked him awake and drove him out into the light of day, he panicked at seeing the sun, assuming he had overslept and was about to be punished. But no, the overseer only wanted him to prepare the animals for the day's travel. Everyone else was still asleep. When the rest of the hunting party awoke soon after, they seemed unfazed by the brightness of the day this early in the morning.

"Does the sun never go down?" Ford asked a bleary-eyed Muk upon seeing him shuffle from the cave mouth. His question went unanswered, as usual. The translator had spent the most uncomfortable night since being bought by Vanagz, having been made to bed down with all the other servants like a pack of dogs upon the floor. It was not his idea of the treatment due a dutiful servant, so he was in no mood to speak with anyone, let alone an impenetrably-thick slave, who should have known it was summer and that nightfall never truly enveloped Rikaswelt during the summer. The sun only dipped below the horizon for a few hours before returning. He turned his back on Ford and hurried off in search of a private place to relieve himself.

Dagmar was up and out the door, ready to go before his breakfast had reached his belly. Once mounted, he trotted ahead of everyone else. The New Beards scrambled to keep up.

"Vanagz is in some haste," said Adelar through a raspy throat newly awoken. His friends nodded sleepily. Gelee wiped crust from his eyes and fell farther behind.

The miles they made over the previous day revisited them in aches and pains. Servants unused to long walks looked every bit as miserable as their feet were sore. If Dagmar felt it, he didn't show it. By midday his head could only occasionally be seen bobbing away over a low rise ahead as he put more distance between himself and the rest of the party. Kaltzek whipped the pack animals and slaves to quicken their steps and gain on him. The slave overseer wished fervently to be at his master's side out here in these perilous lands where anything might ambush him and bring an end to the man around whom his life revolved. However, it was Kaltzek's duty to look after the slaves, animals, and gear, and all of these things were being held up by the lagging New Beards. When Dagmar disappeared entirely around a range of foothills, Kaltzek cracked his whip at the slaves' backs and went into a paroxysm of angry growled commands and insults, ostensibly hurled at his charges. The New Beards cast wary glances back at him and doubled their pace.

In the midst of the hills were a few jagged outcroppings that shot up some hundreds of feet above their lesser, smoother brothers. One in particular stood out in height and girth, like a mammoth among mice. A shift in the earth had cleft this mountain in miniature in half. The best stone from the rubble of the crumbled half went into the building of a plain and sturdy barbican set in the middle of the smooth rock of the intact remainder. The twenty-foot-tall gatehouse, with two round flanking towers reaching heights of thirty feet each, contained slender arrow loop apertures and a bank of wider windows above them. Its solid gate had been thrown open for the arrival of the hunting party. A valvar in a lookout window in the rockface some two hundred feet above had spotted them coming from miles away.

The sledges flew up the short ramp and straight into the gatehouse. The rams' eagerness to get at the awaiting leafy greens and salty pap had them salivating since first spotting the barbican. In an adjacent mud room off the main gatehouse room, the New Beards removed their wet and soiled garments, and were presented dry, clean cloaks and soft slippers by their obliging hosts.

"Now this is something more like it!" said Gelee, rubbing his sore backside.

"They ought to know how to treat a person, after all, this must be Siltsvesi," said Adelar. The three New Beards looked about as if expecting wonders to leap from the very walls. Their families ran in elite circles, so they had all heard the rumored secrets and some of the truths about the place.

Founded as an outpost for Kamen refugees fleeing west, Siltsvesi later transformed into a renowned retreat for the rich of Dargkivi, who were willing to travel such a distance to enjoy Siltsvesi's hot springs, a network of consistently warm pools underneath the rocky peak. Over time, Dargkivi developed entertainments and pleasures of its own and Siltsvesi fell by the wayside. Adapting for its own survival, the residents developed farming in the natural caverns that had been created by the waters and also relied on the generosity of men looking for a place to sequester their bastards. Caring for inconvenient offspring maintained the comfortable living standard of the inhabitants of Siltsvesi.

"So, this is Siltsvesi," Elvo mused as he stood in the middle of the gatehouse main room, letting his new, light cloak hang open. The windows of the gatehouse façade created an airy space, but also one that was perceptibly warmer than just the other side of the open gate and the un-shuttered windows. The difference had less to do with the deadening of the wind and much to do with the hot water springs beneath the town, which heated the floors and blew warm and lazy breezes through the tunnels.

Kaltzek vanished into one of the side passages, as his master had done when he arrived, withdrawing into a sanctuary reserved for him when the hunting party was in residence. This left Ford and the rest of the slaves in the hands of Siltsvesi servants, who were made up of an even more motley assortment of colors and sizes than at Dargkivi. They were also decidedly less dour and downtrodden. Ford and the others were fed and then allowed to roam free, save a few areas reserved for Kamen. This left to them a variety of grottos with warm water pools and the open-air fields of cabbage and carrot-like vegetables growing along rocky terraces within steep ravines, land transformed into an almost temperate zone by a microclimate created by the hot springs.

Ford and two stable slaves went straight to the nearest pool. When they stripped down and slid into the water, it felt to Ford as if he was finally thawing out his bones. His fingers and toes caressed the creamy coating layering the rock. It was like having a balm rubbed on his palms and soles. He and his companions enjoyed an hour's respite, even sleeping, while they soaked. Before turning in that night, they played a game of dice among the servants in the large, oval kitchen which served most of Siltsvesi's people. Actually, Ford wasn't sure it was a game of dice, not the sort he was used to. The small square crystals with etchings on the facets appeared to be dice. Whatever the game may have been, he was fairly sure he was losing. It didn't matter. They played for fun and everyone was very pleasant. Afterwards, they were shown to their quarters. Sleep came easy that night.

The following morning, after eating and serving up breakfast for their masters, the two stable slaves who Ford spent the previous day with took him on a tour of the town. The three New Beards had each brought along a slave to take care of them, but these were insubstantial domestic servants accustomed to indoor duties. Ford's two companions were hunt slaves and had no interest in associating with the house servants any more than they had to. Parvan, a lanky and long-necked Gel na Nadi man, couldn't stand their simpering submissiveness. The other was a man from Aral of the Southern Isles with dark skin so taut that it shone with a deep blue tint. Those who captured him mistook his name and called him Dam, which simply meant *man* in his language. Neither man was nearly as imposing as Ford, but both were rugged and knew how to use just about any weapon placed in their hands.

Their walk took them through the ravine fields on a path passing along a steep wall. A tiny irrigation canal flowed on the level just below, passing on to the lower tiers by a series of dams and sluice gates. The steamy water warmed the ground and air, nourishing the soil and making it possible for hardier vegetation to grow. They were helping a stumpy little farmer pile rocks back up along a section of retaining wall that had given way when Ford gasped out, "Look at the size of that rat!" A large furry brown rodent lounged by the canal, listlessly watching whiffs of steam rise and sniffing at a leafy stalk lying by her side.

"Ivet. Ivet," said the farmer. Through repetition and pointing, he finally made them understand that Ivet was the creature's name. She was a three-foot long marmot who lived among the Kamen at Siltsvesi. Many like her could be found in the caverns which had been cut out by hot springs that riddled Rikaswelt's underbelly. Much of the region's flora and fauna survived and sometimes thrived in these underground ecosystems, surfacing occasionally to migrate from one to the other tundra oases. The farmer scratched the whitening fur about Ivet's shiny nose to show how friendly she was. Dam and then Ford tried to pet her, but she shied away. When they brought her leaves and roots and laid them before her, she looked down at the offerings, then back up at them, not terribly interested until they began handfeeding her. Strangers or not, Ivet warmed to anyone who fed her. They knelt down and stroked her back. She nibbled their fingers at first and then gave off pleased snuffling noises.

After spending some time assisting the town valvar in the constant occupation of chipping away built-up ice around the barbican windows and tunnel ceilings, the hunt slaves spent the afternoon back in the hot water springs. This time, instead of returning to the same pool as the day before, Ford exercised his freedom of choice and picked another spot that they had passed that morning. This was a labyrinth of steaming caverns with low archways connecting one pool to another. When they arrived, they found the cheerful, tinkling laughter of children echoing throughout. In the middle of their soak, young boys and girls of all colors and sizes gamboled through the knee-high waters with a lethargic, smiling matron following the pack and holding two of the littlest children by each hand.

These were the Kamen bastard offspring, often of master-slave relations. They were well cared for, regardless of the mixing of race and parentage within them. The children were used to visits from Dagmar's hunting parties. In fact, one of the children belonged to him. They loved his visits and called him Uncle Marmar. They were comfortable enough with Parvan and Dam to start a splash fight with the three slaves. However, when Ford stood to join in, they shrieked and ran from the grotto, laughing and calling out to one another in their pidgin Kamen.

"Ogre! Run!"

"The ogre come get you, Viktor!"

Knowing Ford always wanted to see something new, on the way back Parvan and Dam took him on an alternate route over a tiny arched bridge spanning a canal, down a long passage that deposited them onto a balcony, which opened to a light and airy cavern. The light and air came from grated windows in a half-dome roof, which had been built into the side of the mountain. Below them was a peaceful grotto. Cozy seating for couples carved into the surrounding rock walls ringed the hot spring pool. A short causeway of flat stones led to a small island in the center just large enough to hold a cylindrical hut of fine masonry. An ornamentally-crenelated rooftop made the building look like a crown. The grotto was deserted but for a single couple strolling arm in arm near the edge of the water. Parvan and Dam silently motioned to Ford to come away. Before they could drag him from the balcony, he recognized the male of the couple below as Dagmar. Master Vanagz was speaking softly to the woman who leant on his shoulder. She was of his height and build, though less bulky, and wore her bright red hair in a tall pile upon her head. Her hip playfully bumped his with every other step she took. After the fourth or fifth bump, a joyful laugh rippled out of Dagmar. She giggled at the sound of it, happy to have made him happy. His twinkling blues eyes spoke of an ebullient nature. Years had melted away from his graying head and his creased and sagging face beamed youth once more. The desire to laugh and love was still in him. It just needed a spark. The pair disappeared into the hut.

"So, that's why the old man was in a big hurry to get here," Ford mused as he and his companions made for the slave's quarters. He didn't blame Vanagz for finding love or wanting to spend his days in Siltsvesi. If Ford had to spend the remainder of his days enslaved to the Kamen, he would have preferred to do it in as nice a place as this. The people weren't mean, not that he'd seen so far. The warmth of the hot springs seemed to seep into their hearts. Every aspect of life here was more laid back than in Dargkivi.

Yet, even if it were possible, he knew living here would do him no good. The tiny taste of liberty the place afforded a slave had brought back his hunger for freedom. The word meant more to him than just some satisfying place to live out one's servitude. To live as a free man, that was the goal, a true treasure trove worth making a grab for, regardless of the danger.

***

"Siltsvesi is a wonderful place," said Adelar. He and his two friends were drinking together in one of their rooms later on the third day after arriving. "Master Vanagz was right. And I have enjoyed myself." At Vanagz's suggestion, all three had done an admirable job of enjoying themselves: soaking in the warm waters until their skin pruned and soaking their insides as well on the local zivivesi, the name given to an arak made from a carrot-like root grown here in abundance. "But I understand your complaints," he said, veering the discussion toward a minor quandary they found themselves in. "We did not come to lounge about, wonderful place or not." It had taken them much less than three days to see and do all there was to be seen and done in Siltsvesi, and they had grown restless. Now all they did was sit in their plush rooms drinking to repress the unkind thoughts cropping up whenever they thought of their host and the exciting hunts he had promised.

"He spends every waking hour with that woman," said Elvo staring blankly into his cup through bloodshot eyes. "If I had known this was what he intended all along I would never have come."

"Yes, yes, I agree. But he's our host and leading this expedition. What do you want?" replied Adelar.

"I want to hunt! That's what I want," said Gelee throwing back another drink.

"We all want to go hunting," said Adelar. He'd grown tired of hearing his friends' repeated complaints. "That's why we came. Whining about it won't do any good. The question is, what's to be done?"

"No, whining never does any good," said Dagmar from the doorway, where he leaned against the frame with his arms folded. Their heated conversation had reached his ears as he passed along the hallway. He wasn't surprised to hear their grievances. One of his usual hunting companions voiced something similar during the delays of their last expedition. Dagmar threw Gelee a charitable smile to show the goofy Kamen boy that he meant no disrespect. He was in a good mood, but his three guests were too mortified to see the smile as anything but an angry grimace.

"Master Vanagz—" began Adelar trying to rise up from his chair, but finding the room a bit too wobbly.

"Dagmar! I told you to call me Dagmar."

"Forgive me. It slipped my mind."

"Well, you seem to have other things weighing it down. What can I do to lift that weight?" He wasn't going to give them what they wanted without them working for it. These soft boys needed to sweat a little.

"We wondered…" Adelar stopped to sip from his cup. His throat felt suddenly dry and he was sure it would seize up if he didn't wet it.

"You wondered what?"

"We wondered if, or rather when there might be some hunting?" Adelar despised his own weakly worded question, but now that it had been cast, there was nothing he could do to reel it in. The other two hardly noticed Adelar's embarrassment, for while he spoke Dagmar caught each by the eye and held their gaze for longer than the two young Kamen could stand.

"Growing bored, are we?" he said.

"No! No, of course not! This is a nice place—"

"A marvelous place!" put in Gelee.

"Yes, a marvelous place to visit, but…" Adelar looked to his two companions, seeking support. They were such young, inexperienced men, boys really. Challenging one of their heroes was not what they had signed on for. Adelar summoned the courage and finished his thought, "…but the hunt?"

Dagmar's lips twisted into a smirk that unnerved his companions. Companions who were little more than acquaintances, he reflected. They were not comrades, nor contemporaries, not in the least. He had tried to make Siltsvesi feel like home for them. On the first night he introduced these fancy-boy milk-suckers to sweethearts, whom they might call their own, or at least for brief liaisons. The kept women of Siltsvesi were a secret just as hushed up as the village's horde of illegitimate children. Of course, none of the women were whores, but a few of the unattached young ladies or the older widowed women were not averse to keeping a man's bed warm at night. Yet, these New Beards had barely touched a single one of them. None of them, as far as Dagmar knew, were married or even contracted to a woman back in Dargkivi. For all he knew they might be man-fanciers.

"Soon," he told them. The words slipped from his lips with a ring of insincerity. They tried to seem pleased with a show of chipper nods and declarations of thankfulness, but even Dagmar wasn't buying his own deception. Delaying tactics such as this would not do. As much as it annoyed him to admit it, he needed the New Beards. Managing a hunt alone was difficult. A large party was necessary to handle the creatures they would encounter. Furs and exotic meat made up a fair share of his profit, but taking live beasts of the wild back to the arena in Dargkivi brought in the real money. And with the way his wife spent their coin, he needed this hunt to be a success. Yet, resentment and a selfish will made him want to send these spineless boys back to the city, so he could be left to his pleasures. There was love for him here, far more love than he ever felt in that place called home. But none of that mattered now, practically speaking. Right now, he had to march on and over the obstacles in his path until he could reach his goal and live life on his own terms. "Tomorrow. First thing tomorrow we set out."

In the middle of the night, Kaltzek invaded the slaves' quarters and turned it upside down. All available hands scrambled to tackle an impossibly long list of tasks in an incredibly short amount of time. The cooks were roused from their beds and the kitchen hearth remained stoked all night to prepare sustaining rations, as well as extra delicacies for Uncle Marmar, who spent the time enjoying every last bit of his paramour's warm bed. Before the haggard slaves of the hunt were allowed to crawl to their beds to seek whatever sleep they might scrounge before dawn, they were taken to a storage room and fitted out with heavy coats and boots. Small snow shoes were doled out, too. Ford tried on a pair that barely extended out beyond his long feet.

Everything was ready by morning. Instead of the sledges they had used on the way to Siltsvesi, flat-bottomed sleds were loaded with weaponry, the foodstuffs, bedrolls and other comforts against cold weather for this leg of their excursion. The owners of the sleds proudly slid them into the barbican where they were hitched to splay-hoofed muskox, instead of the rams that had been used for the trip out. The powerful limbs of these shaggy muskox made them ideal for hauling heavy loads over rough terrain.

The half-awake New Beards shuffled into the barbican the following morning and found all of their gear, animals and slaves clustered in the center of the main room with Kaltzek squatting before it all, like a hound keeping watch over the flock. But there was no Dagmar. They wanted to ask why he was late, but Kaltzek's brooding vigil repressed the urge to say anything against his master. They meekly fell in with their servants without a word.

A dreadfully long and increasingly tense half hour passed before Muk appeared and spoke with Kaltzek. By the end of their short conversation the translator was lightly perspiring. He beckoned to Ford. Surprised to be addressed, Ford hesitated. Before he knew what was happening, Kaltzek grabbed him by the arm and led him away. Muk followed behind, but Ford didn't bother asking him where they were going. The translator had ignored him so often that he knew there was no point in asking. Kaltzek jerked him around corners and down tunnels with an iron grip. Ford worried his bones might break, and thought that if Kaltzek wasn't actually made of stone, his hands certainly felt as tough as rock.

They entered warm passages filled with fresh air and ornate carvings framing wooden doors to either side. One of the town's few valvar stood before one of them and pushed it open. Kaltzek shoved Ford through the doorway and into a room containing a bear so large that its back brushed against the ceiling even though it stood on all fours. Its wide-open mouth revealed a dangerous array of ripping and grinding teeth. The unexpected shock rocked Ford back into Kaltzek, who shoved him back. Ford stumbled into the bear and realized it was dead, just another stuffed hunter's trophy.

Kaltzek grabbed Ford by the arm, yanked him upright again and held him so that they stood side by side facing an octagonal room of cottage warmth and abandoned responsibilities, hominess infused by a sensual sense of retreat. The décor, though not Dargkivi-extravagant, nonetheless was lavish. The woman who spent day after day here had created something practical and livable. The man who visited only sporadically showered wealth upon the place in a desire to indulge a secret love. Painted vases crowded about the comfortable furnishings. The white fur of a nine-foot-long saber-toothed cat took up much of the floor. Trinkets in colorful glass bowls cluttered wall nooks originally intended for usable cups and plates. Though braziers, hanging lanterns and oil lamps were strewn about the place, the only light came from a glowing warm rock sitting on top of a tall candleholder. It lit up the room enough to reflect off of the glass eyes of a menagerie of stuffed and mounted animals. Most were quadrupeds common to Rikaswelt, such as a diamond-chested ram, a flat-tailed elk and a woolly boar. Thinking his secret love might find it a cute little oddity, Dagmar had placed what he thought was the stub of a stalactite on the boar's head to make it look like a unicorn. The foot-long, cone-shaped object was encrusted with small, dark crystals and could be quite dazzling in the right light. The remaining space was decorated with hunting paraphernalia both hefty and deadly: wide butcher's blades;

spiny forks; jaw-like traps of iron. The warm rock cast just enough light to illuminate a thinly-veiled archway at the back of the room, beyond which lay a bed. The lumpy form of a body rumpled the woven coverlets over the thick mattress. By the archway, Dagmar sat at a small wooden table eating a plate of sausages.

The valvar came into the room, closed the door and leaned against the bear. The guard was half asleep and a little annoyed at having to leave his cozy bed at such an early hour. He couldn't understand why he needed to keep an eye on Dagmar's big slave, as friendly and docile a creature as Ivet the marmot, as far as he could tell.

Dagmar frowned and glared from under a heavy brow as he chewed. Muk slid in beside him and everyone waited. Once the last sausage was on its way to his stomach, Dagmar gestured Ford forward. Kaltzek pushed Ford in the back and made him kneel so that he was eye to eye with Dagmar. Both of Kaltzek's stony hands clamped down on his shoulders. Ford doubted he could stand if he tried. Dagmar muttered something to Muk and nodded at the chair next to him. The translator reached down to the seat of the chair and picked up a collar and manacles. Without making eye contact with Ford, Muk stood before him and fastened the restraints on his neck and wrists. A sturdy chain connected wrists to neck. The liberating ease and lifted restrictions of the last few days vanished when the studded leather strap tightened around his neck. The fleeting return of freewill, however infinitesimal, called up all of the rebellion left in him. His fists clenched. Kaltzek felt his muscles tense beneath his hands and snarled a warning so sharply that the valvar slid off the bear and grabbed for his spear. Ford fought down his primal urges and remained steady and silent.

The valvar laughed off his own fright and cursed. "The damned rug jumped up and bit me!"

Muk slithered away to his master's side again. Kaltzek dug a knee into Ford's back, making him stumble a few feet forward on his knees, just close enough so that Dagmar could lean in and speak straight into Ford's face.

"I know your dirt cock be in my wife. I know…" Dagmar spoke low, grinding each word.

Muk wedged himself a little farther behind his master's chair. His translation came out in a tremble and he seemed to be skipping some of what was being said, most noticeably when Dagmar jerked a thumb at the translator. "Dump you rocks in my wife whore?...She nothing!...She my wife! Not for you!" Dagmar pounded his chair's armrest and shouted, speaking quicker than Muk could translate. "...I give good life! No thank! No thank slave!"

So, the truth had been discovered. It seemed Muk had given him up. Ford knew he was in for it now. Whatever the punishment, he would take it without complaint. After all, there was no point in complaining. Better to keep one's head down and focus on the future: *Get through this. Your time will come. Get through this. Your time will come.*

Dagmar gripped both armrests and steadied his voice enough to speak in a snake's hiss. "I use you. For hunt, I use you. After hunt, I no use you." He shook his head and stared directly into Ford's eyes. "After hunt, I end you."

Chapter 17
The Hunt

"Ma-haw-hawn! Ma-haw-hawn!" The plaintive cry, like a cross between a wounded animal and the bleating of a calf, filled a steep, ice-sided hollow. One end of the hollow opened to the gaping maw of a cave deep in the desolate northern reaches of Rikaswelt. Ford lay on his side bound hand and foot a few feet away from the mouth of the cave. He kept his forehead pressed against the ice, not daring to look up and into that foreboding orifice, out of which might charge salivating horrors hungry to sink their teeth into his flesh.

"Ma-haw-hawn! Ma-haw-hawn!" Dam called again from under a white fur where he lay hidden up against one wall of the hollow. The depth of the hollow was enough to shield those within from some of the wind above their heads tearing over the barren wastes all around them. Down here in the relative calm, Dam's perfected call carried well enough so that anything within the cave would hear it and perhaps come out to investigate. Any predators would be too curious to pass up what sounded like an easy meal, and any predator spotting the defenseless human bait before the cave could not help themselves.

The hunters were stationed on the surface all around the edge of the hallow, except Kaltzek, who was perched on the rock above the mouth of the cave with a heavy net at the ready. From there he would be able to leap down upon anything that attacked Ford, trapping it alive. The Kamen masters knelt behind sleds, camouflaged in white canvas with crossbows in hand. Dagmar was trying to keep a steady vigil upon the cave, but the New Beards kept popping their heads out from behind their blinds on the far sides of the depression. Their sudden, jerky movements caught his eye every damn time. Likely their prey would see it, too. He wanted to fire a bolt into the next head he saw bob up. Maybe he wouldn't have to. If his eyes didn't deceive him, Elvo was holding his crossbow backwards.

After two days of constant wind whipping past one's ears and ice crystals spearing one's cheeks, the hollow created an eerie calm, as if the world held its breath in anticipation. Kaltzek's ear caught a crunching sound, like a footfall, but whether it was soft and stealthy or simply remote, not even his superior hearing could deduce. A moment later, everyone heard a moan slip through the whistling of the wind. They held their breathes and strained to listen. Ford's entire body contracted. He had tried to remain absolutely still, but he couldn't stop shivering.

Whatever had blown upon the wind to their ears never manifested before their eyes. The New Beards grew restless and began talking among themselves. Their whispers, from sled to sled, irritated Dagmar. He could appreciate their desire to be in on the first kill and the excitement they had shown up to this point, but these boys were as impatient as children. Still, he wanted to show them a good time, impress them even.

"Something should have come up from below by now," he said when he called them all together. This site and others nearby were tried-and-true hunting grounds. To make sure nothing was cowering within, Parvan and Dam were sent into the cave to search its deeper nooks. They stalked through honeycombed passages decorated in places with stalactites, icicles, and layers of water table stratification, making their way to a small pool of lukewarm water, all that the once-powerful geyser could now produce. No longer did the scalding jet shoot up through the rock and fill the hollow above. The decline of the hot spring provided a relatively warm place for repose and a source for fresh water. Dagmar was right, there should have been something here. But it wasn't long before Parvan and Dam returned to report the place empty.

"What is wrong? What has happened?" Dagmar wondered aloud in front of the befuddled New Beards and servants. Past hunts here had taken down great prowling bears and cats, or at least some hooved or horned beast. "There's always something here, even if it's nothing but a mangy marmot." Privately, he considered the possibility that the spot had been hunted dry. After all, he had come back here regularly, because it was convenient to Siltsvesi. His plan had been to pile up a few furs and quickly retire to the arms of his beloved, as he had done in the past. It appeared that the plan needed to be altered. "We'll have better luck elsewhere," Dagmar said with a dismissive wave at the cave.

While the Kamen stood about munching on cold meat and discussing their next move, their servants pulled the bulky canvases off the loaded sleds and shoved them back into the cages where they were normally stored. Ford had not been allowed crampons, so he had to be dragged up the icy slope out of the hollow with a rope. They untied his hands from his feet, though his hands remained bound together, and then they yoked him alongside the muskox. He had been tied up and made to be pull a sled along with the beasts since leaving Siltsvesi. Sometimes, when the ground was particularly icy, he would slip and fall, and be dragged by the muskox until he regained his footing. He'd receive a lashing each time he fell.

"Why the punishment?" Adelar had asked the day before. Dagmar explained how he had eventually wheedled the truth out of his translator back in Siltsvesi and discovered what the big Aelwydian slave had done with his wife.

"Ah, we wondered why you bothered bringing the translator!"

"That and I need someone to fluff my pillows!" Dagmar said it and then tossed off a jesting laugh. However, there was truth in the statement. He did need someone to look after his domestic needs on the hunt. Since the New Beards hadn't thought to bring their own hunt slaves, Parvan and Dam would have to work extra hard and hadn't time to prepare meals. But Dagmar kept all that to himself. These young ones would learn and come better prepared next time.

The New Beards all agreed that Ford deserved what came to him and that he posed a high risk of running away. "Considering the circumstances, depriving a potential runaway slave an easy means of escape is prudent," said Elvo and received blank stares.

"Can't let them get away," clarified Adelar and the others nodded vigorously.

Gelee had taken a particularly sharp set against Ford. "You want me to castrate him for you? Chop off his filthy rocks? It's only what the animal deserves," the stout young Kamen had offered. Ford had realized they were talking about him, but mistook the meaning behind their smiles and laughter until Gelee sneered and spat at him. Gelee took his behavioral cue from the severe way in which his father had dealt with his mother upon learning she had cheated on him. "All such vermin should be flayed and left for the wolves," he liked to say. On the other hand, Dagmar's infidelity did not bother him in the same way.

The expedition moved on from the cave to a pass within a range of low jagged hills, where a game trail regularly used by reindeer herds and the giant wolves that chased them was expected to improve their luck. Huge boulders and high escarpments narrowed a bend in the trail, making for excellent natural cover. This did away with the necessity of setting up the canvas blinds. They hunkered down and spent the remainder of the day in the pass, and saw nothing. In such desolate land, this was not unusual. However, what surprised Dagmar and Kaltzek was a total lack of sign: no tracks, no scat, nothing. It was as if this once-frequented game trail had been abandoned altogether. Dagmar declared it a waste and they returned to low ground to make camp.

The next morning a visit to a crack in a rock, which opened to a cavern susceptible to cave-ins, also proved fruitless. It had been suggested simply because it was close by. By now, failure had become so depressingly predictable that at the last location of the day, a small grotto which never failed to attract game, they didn't even bother setting up the canvas blinds or have Kaltzek bother with his net. Dagmar simply sent Parvan and Dam in to confirm that the place was empty.

"Barren, it's all barren," he said in disgust that evening while they sat about eating and drinking at their encampment, a lean-to built with loose stones against an overhang at the base of a crag. Many such encampments could be found throughout Rikaswelt. They were sometimes leftovers from previous civilizations, as well as the Kamen migration or were more recently constructed for hunting. The structures varied. Those that were Kamen-made often included doors and hearths, and might be stocked with provisions and fuel if they were particularly frequented. Others were simple caves made more comfortable. All of them had stacks of rock piled either atop the structure or upon some nearby height where the landmark could be spotted from afar.

"Something's not right," Dagmar went on. "Who knows, but maybe the whole rotten place is cursed! There's always been something around here that wanders back in after we've come through. Even a mangy shrew would be better than nothing!" Dagmar toyed with a sausage he hadn't so much as nibbled as he spoke from a reclining position on one of the many cushions the New Beards had packed. "Usually, it's just a matter of flushing them out!"

Very little reply came from his guests. They had no suggestions. The New Beards were out of their depth when it came to hunting. That realization coupled with this string of disappointments had turned them somewhat sullen and bored. Gelee let out a long loud yawn and then the camp went uncharacteristically quiet.

Muk was the one person in the confined quarters still in a good mood. The translator-turned-hunt-servant sang in his native tongue, talked at the other servants and even interrupted Dagmar at one point. Once put in his place again, he retired to a corner and resumed singing to himself in a low murmur. Dagmar had given his servant a jug of strong zivivesi for having informed him about the goings on between Wivvek and the giant Aelwydian. Muk had made impressive progress through the bottle all on his own. Ford watched Muk from the corner where he had been bound and mutely vowed revenge.

"I'm sure something will turn up tomorrow," said Adelar after an unbearably long stretch of silence. His friends agreed, dredging up a round of ready nods and overly enthusiastic grunts. Dagmar only grumbled. He could take their brooding, but not this placating nonsense, not from a pack of know-nothing boys.

During the first half of the following day, Kaltzek guided them to a watering hole. This was another geyser, one which was clear of ice this time of year. Unfortunately, it was not a popular spot for wildlife, except for the few animals that could stomach the water's sulfurous flavor.

"Well, I didn't hold out much hope," said Dagmar when they arrived and found nothing - not even a set of tracks in the surrounding snow.

The expedition moved on and spent a few fruitless hours on a former game trail on their way to the next encampment. Setting up camp upon the wind-whipped tundra was a miserable experience, which the New Beards did not enjoy, so they were greatly relieved when just past midday they spotted the stones stacked atop the northern most Kamen hunting lodge in all of Rikaswelt. Made with Kamen proportions and comfort in mind, the resulting squat structure, which was set against a rocky bluff and an abutting scree, resembled a tiny ziggurat of loose stones. The hole of an entryway was small enough that someone of Ford's size would struggle to climb through. Parvan reached it first, knelt upon the steps and stuck his head in. His shriek blended so perfectly with a growl that it seemed the harmonic duet was intended.

Kaltzek and Dam drew their weapons and rushed forward, while the others watched on in confusion and wonder. Parvan stumbled back from the doorway and fell onto his back. Some of the onlookers had to turn away from his mauled face and the open gash spilling blood from his neck. A woolly wolverine, even larger than the one Ford had faced in the Mullauk fighting pit, leapt from the doorway onto Parvan with flailing claws. The violent eruption of the creature's sudden appearance threw Dam back upon his heels, but Kaltzek's powerful mass surged past and stabbed into its flank. The wolverine jumped away snarling as it surveyed all the men surrounding it. The muskox shied away and none of the men were prepared for the attack, but their numbers were intimidation enough. Before the hunters could react, the wolverine retreated behind the piled stones of the lodge, appeared on the other side scurrying up the scree, and disappeared between a gap in the rocks near the top of the bluff.

"There's your reason why we haven't seen anything!" Dagmar shouted as he pointed up at the bluff, dancing from foot to foot as the adrenaline coursed through him. "Those bastards will decimate a herd just for fun! They scare off every damned thing!" One of his slaves lay dead before him, yet his elation was not diminished. Here was a ready excuse for the poor hunting, which also absolved his blame for overhunting the area. And now they had prey to pursue. "It'll be back, just you wait and see!"

There was no burying of bodies out here where the ground was frozen solid. Nor would the hunters inter Parvan's body within the lodge and forever close it up for future use. The slaves could understand and accept this, but they could not accept what became of his remains. The Kamen, in hopes of luring the wolverine back using the scent of fresh blood, left Parvan's body out in the open as bait while they hid quietly behind their white canvas blinds for the rest of the day. This was deemed reprehensible by the slaves. When Ford had been given this treatment, it was understood and accepted as a just punishment for his transgressions. But Parvan did not deserve this, even the house servants he did not get on with agreed. Their simmering anger and the subsequent gloom that overcame them went unnoticed by the Kamen. Even had the Kamen noticed, they would not have cared. This was the way of things and had been since before any of them had been born. Their one concern was their prey, which never showed.

"And there's no point in tracking the damned beast," said Dagmar. "The ground being all rock and ice, we won't find a trail." The spirit of the hunting party dipped lower than ever.

Ford was nodding off in his corner that night when Kaltzek grabbed him and dragged him outside. The others slept through the whole thing while Kaltzek ripped away at his bonds. Ford threw up his arms to protect his head, assuming this was the end. He would put up what fight he had in him, the little good it would do against this iron-fisted foe. But then Kaltzek thrust Parvan's long-handled fork into Ford's hands and began teaching him how to wield it. After that, he showed him how to toss a net and tie up captive prey. They went over the working of the locks on the cages and how to secure a tripwire line. Ford couldn't understand why all of this was happening until it dawned on him that Parvan's death necessitated another pair of hands for the hunt.

After a few hours with Kaltzek, Dam was woken and made to carry on the training. So, while his head lulled and his eyes began closing of their own accord, Ford learned through Dam's unintentionally silly pantomime how they dipped the tips and edges of their weapons in a potent sleeping draught in order to subdue violent beasts, which could then be caged and sold to the Master of Games back at Dargkivi. Ford's new importance to the expedition did not free him from his bonds. At all times, at least one foot remained tethered to a loaded sled. He had little doubt that Dagmar still intended to execute him when he was no longer useful.

The New Beards awoke slowly and only reluctantly started the day. The trip had been a disappointment and they were losing their taste for hunting, if this was what hunting was. They wanted to go home, but were too timid and ashamed to say so. Dagmar was ready to pack it in too, but he wouldn't order the sleds back to Siltsvesi. He wouldn't be the one to give in and quit, so he told himself the night before.

"The wolverine has laid these grounds to waste," he said to them over a morose breakfast. The words from his own mouth surprised him. Why had he repeated something already established? It sounded like an excuse. He realized it was. Without meaning to, he was building a foundation for a way out of this hunt. He wanted to quit as much as these boys. A shudder ran through him and in his head his father's voice shouted "weak!". Every ounce of this unworthy, un-Kamenly act flooded him with embarrassment. To stamp out the shame mounting within and to prove his bravado, he blurted out, "We're going to Veks Miris!"

Elvo stifled a gasp and Adelar carefully laid down his mug while staring with trepidation at his host. Dagmar beamed back at them. If they wanted action and excitement, he thought with devilish delight, he would give it to them.

Chapter 18
Veks Miris

"What's Vek Smeers?" asked Gelee looking from his host to his friends and back again.

"Veks Miris is dangerous, is it not?" said Adelar trying to appear casual, but with his arms folded over his stomach in hopes of calming his fluttering innards as he anticipated Dagmar's answer.

"What is a hunt without danger?" bellowed Dagmar, who had previously lost a friend and two servants in Veks Miris.

"It's supposedly a ruined citadel made by ancients and abandoned long ago, or so I've read," Elvo informed Gelee and then turned a quizzical eye upon Dagmar. "But is it not purely myth? *Maad ohn Rikaswelt* is vague and devotes less than one half page on Veks Miris."

"No, of course it's real!" Dagmar went on to describe in brief the isolated and remote ruins built and abandoned by an unknown people before the arrival of the Kamen. "It's not easy to find, if you don't know it's there. It's tricky to get into and getting back out is no treat. Lots of climbing and slippery as a koer!" Distance, danger, and the arduous, time-consuming task of hauling game out of Veks Miris was the main reason Dagmar avoided the ruins. However, a profitable day or two at Veks Miris might save the whole expedition.

"Is it far?" asked Adelar.

"An easy two days north of here!" said Dagmar, throwing off a careless laugh meant to show that distances and danger meant little to him. "And once we're there, I promise you more game than you've ever seen in your lives!"

"Then what are we waiting for? Lead the way!" Gelee's fearlessness and exuberance warmed Dagmar's heart and won over his friends.

The journey took three days. On the first, they dragged Parvan's body behind the last sled in hopes of luring in predators. By the second day, they cut loose what was left of the stinking corpse. Every mile they made farther north came slower and slower. The increasingly steep and rocky terrain overturned the New Beards' top-heavy sleds more than once. Extra stops to rest slowed their progress. It was quite late on the third day when Dagmar finally called a halt in the midst of a long row of stone and ice foothills which looked like something made by a giant's moulboard plough. Kaltzek and his master climbed atop one of the many boulders jutting out of the earth at odd angles and had a look about the land. He knew of only one way into Veks Miris: a scalable shoulder between two tall spurs where enough space remained for the muskox to drag the sleds over with some help. Finding it was not always easy. One peak looked much like another and vision was cut down to nothing by the wind that picked up grains of ice and blew them into their faces. Dagmar cursed into the shrill gusts and ordered Kaltzek off to find what he could not see.

The others hunkered down to wait between the tall rocks that served, like kite shields, to buffer the wind. Ford took a good look about him for the first time all day, another day spent with his head bowed and his shoulders pressed into the yoke. Only now did he see how high they had climbed. The craggy stretch of sharp peaks jabbed at the sky like rows of sharks' teeth.

"Ha-hah! We've found it!" Dagmar called down to the others when his scout Kaltzek returned with the good news.

The taxing climb up and over the pass exhausted them all, while descending into the valley beyond scared the life out of everyone save Dagmar and Kaltzek, the only two to have been here before. The tired New Beards carried on gamely, not wanting to admit to weakness. Likewise, they kept mum about their fears at the sight of the icy chute that might end with a cracked skull up against one of the boulders awaiting them at the bottom. Had the slaves any say in the matter, they would've balked at the descent.

However, the animals had hoofs made for this terrain, which safely carried them all down to a level plateau large enough for a camp to be set up. All of the sleds and muskox would be left behind at this base camp under the care of the New Beards' most trustworthy house servant, while the rest of the party carried on into Veks Miris. The remaining slaves' backs were loaded with gear and provisions packed well over their heads. They carried on in their descent with knotted ropes tied together to help them reach the bottom.

Veks Miris, a city for giants, was located deep within a valley, tucked away in its own ravine, lined with high, sharp ridges. Whether the founders had been true giants or simply large humans, the Kamen couldn't say. Everything in Veks Miris was on a larger scale than the Kamen were used to. However, it was plain that the people who built the temples and houses were at least Ford's height or taller. Nothing could be seen of the ruins from the heights where the sleds had been left behind, even on a clear day. Not until reaching the bottom of the valley, turning toward the eastern valley wall and passing through a natural arch into a narrow gorge did signs of civilized handiwork meet the eye.

"This isn't big," said Gelee, staring in some dismay at a thick stone wall which barely rose above his head.

"Come here, boy! Have a look," said Dagmar, who led them all up to the wall. At a clear patch where they could see through the ice, the wall reached down another ten feet beneath them, perhaps more, but that was all they could make out. The wall had once sealed a gap in the inner ravine ridge within the larger main valley, completing the natural fortifications that successfully protected the inhabitants of Veks Miris at one time. Without the layers of ice, the wall would have stood twenty-five-feet tall with a stout gate in the middle. The wood of the gate had long since returned to the earth and the top of the arched gateway had broken into ruin.

The Kamen hunters and their burdened servants passed slowly, with as little sound as possible through the gateway. The wind droned high above their heads, whispering past their ears. Their boots crunched over a dusting of ice crystals. Nothing stirred, aside from themselves. The ruins breathed the life of the dead. Those who held weapons clutched them a little tighter. No one commented upon the empty, snow-blanketed courtyard they entered. Nor did they speak when they turned about in the middle of the wide space to study the surrounding walls. They were but plain stone walls, yet the New Beards looked at them in wonder, as one does when arriving at a new and unusual destination.

Dagmar led the way northward down an easy slope of ice that encased a stairway beneath their feet. At the bottom, all four of the Kamen hunters walked abreast through a long avenue with ponderous stone retaining walls to either side. The road extended for hundreds of feet before a bend cut off their view of what lie ahead. In some spots, the ravine had spilled its boulders and toppled ice chunks over the retaining wall into the avenue. After a hundred yards the ravine widened and the walls morphed into blocky living quarters that doubled as bulwarks against failing debris. Windows and doorways of the original ground floor were buried beneath the ice. Only occasionally was the keystone of a tall archway visible at their feet.

"Someone important must have lived here once," said Adelar gesturing to the façade of a lordly hall. The frames of its many wide windows were more intricately carved than neighboring buildings. It had been constructed upon a rise and half of its larger than normal doorway still remained above the ice.

"Looks to me like a holding house for goods," Dagmar said, suggesting only what his practical mind could supply. He waved them toward the doorway. "We'll have a little something to eat and then leave the equipment here and see what's about."

While the servants unburdened themselves and began setting up a temporary encampment within the hall, the Kamen scouted ahead for tracks and any sign that game had passed through the area recently. Though it was getting late, a reinvigorating meal gave the New Beards the desire to hunt the new location immediately. Dagmar took them farther down the avenue to where one of the walls had given out and the resulting collapse partially blocked the road just around the bend. This created a funnel that forced migrating game through the gap.

"A perfect killing field," Dagmar proclaimed. While he installed them in windows and doorways with ideal vantage points, Kaltzek set up Ford as bait once again, dragging a claw across Ford's arm and letting the blood dribble into a small pool. Then he wrapped the wound, bound Ford hand to foot and left him in the middle of the road. Dam started up his enticing call and the waiting game began.

As instructed, the New Beards kept their heads still, but before long one of them started whispering to his neighbor. It was Elvo's girlish voice, thought Dagmar. He jumped to his feet with a burning desire to thrash the boy on the backside like he did with his son when he misbehaved, but instead, he sat right back down. In the same instance, Kaltzek jerked upright. They and everyone else had heard the distant wailing of an animal in the throes of misery and torment. It sounded to the young hunters like condemned souls shrieking for salvation, a screech through the ether aimed precisely at their unwilling ears. This eerie cacophony, seemingly conjured from nothing, quickly returned to nothing, leaving the listeners to wonder if they had actually heard anything at all.

Ford inched his bound body across the open avenue toward the shelter of fallen rocks beside a crumbling wall. He didn't care if the Kamen beat him for it, he didn't want to be in the street if whatever was making that horrendous sound came through the gap at the bend. Dagmar and the others lifted their heads, then came out of hiding and stood side by side to stare wide-eyed down the avenue. They heard only the whipping of the wind over the peaks above. This relative calm was merely the eye of an audible storm. One singular and instinctual cry culled from the very core of being, dredged from the gut and drenched in the essence of despair, screamed out of the depths of Veks Miris to annihilate the hunters' flagging courage.

"What deviltry is this?" begged Adelar.

"We should go!" insisted Elvo.

"It's not but some unfortunate beast meeting its end. Nothing more," said Dagmar softly to help calm the New Beards. Since he normally spoke in shouts, his unnaturally quiet voice only heightened their alarm. The truth was, he didn't know what had cried out, but there was no need for the others to know that. He thumped the heads of his nearest, paling guests in a most avuncular manner. "It is nothing! But come, now we know for certain there is game to be had here! Let us see if there is something to be salvaged!"

When on a hunt, strange noises came with the territory, and Dagmar had heard his share. The wailing of a dying animal wasn't going to send him home with loaded pants and an empty hand. Gelee was game, Adelar cautious, but Elvo was ready to go home. Dagmar guessed the boy's bladder had released already. But as long as he kept his mouth shut and didn't worry the others, there would be no trouble.

With their servants in tow, the Kamen followed the avenue around the bend and down a gradual slope. The sun had long since set, so no light shone upon this continuation of the avenue. In fact, very little direct sunlight ever touched the valley floor. Most of Veks Miris remained in perpetually shaded gloom. Defense and the presence of a natural reservoir was the original attraction to the location, not light and beauty.

"Leave off! Leave off," Dagmar commanded of the New Beards, who had begun tiptoeing along with their weapons drawn as they peered tentatively into open windows and doorways on either side of the road. "Anything here would have been spooked away by now. Come! Follow me!"

He took them through an archway into a tunnel which delved straight into the side of the ravine. Iced-over snowdrifts built up on the floor close to the ceiling, so close that the tunnel appeared as if it were Kamen-made. However, the oversized proportions returned when the short tunnel ended in a massive cavern lit by two other entrances and a few windows quite close to the half-dome ceiling some twenty-five feet above. The round, smoothly hollowed-out space had once served as the premier temple at Veks Miris. The idols or relics which had once filled the few alcoves around the perimeter had been pilfered.

All that was left to inform visitors of the former inhabitants' religious practices was a large altar near the back wall. The five-foot-wide, pentagon-shaped obelisk sat upon a broad dais which stood nearly as tall as Ford. Though its plinth-like base was made up of unadorned granite blocks, the altar was decorated in bas-relief carvings of figures working fields and at war with vaguely beast-like humanoids. Circular designs and syllabic writing wrapped around the altar at various intervals. Most of it, as well as some of the figures, had been defaced with chisels. The whole structure was topped with thick horns that nearly grazed the ceiling. Steps with a two-foot rise led up the front to the altar. These were meant for worshippers and penitents to kneel upon in prayer or a pulpit from which priests might preach.

"There is something behind the altar," said Elvo, overcoming his fears and moving closer to the altar. The room's historical import intrigued him.

"It's a door," said Dagmar, referring to a concealed doorway in the back wall tucked away behind the altar.

"No, on the floor. There, see."

"He's right. It looks like a helm of some sort," said Adelar.

Between the altar and the back wall sat a small helm on its side. Rusted and battered, it was little more than a skull cap with a neck guard and face plate protection attached. Dagmar picked it up and plunked it onto Gelee's head. The young Kamen had been sore about losing his hat early on in the expedition, but now he laughed and yanked the helm down over his thick hair until he could see out of the eyeholes. The face plate did not hide his toothy grin. "Suits me fine!"

"The door appears to permanently be jammed open with this spike," said Elvo pointing to an iron wedge lodged under the door. His finger shot out toward the doorway beyond which a landing before a flight of descending steps was stained with a dark red smear. "What is that?"

"Dried blood," said Dagmar stepping to the top of the stairs. "See, streaks of it go down. This wasn't here last time—" A piercing scream, as if from within a canyon, echoed up the stairs. The New Beards fell back, but Dagmar and his servants remained calm.

"What was that?" asked Adelar.

"It sounded like a woman!" said Elvo.

"Was nothing but one of those marmots," said Dagmar. "They screech like little girls. It is nothing to fear. Rather you should rejoice! Game isn't far off! Follow me and we'll find out where this blood leads!"

For all of Dagmar's bold words, it was Kaltzek who took the lead, with Dam a step behind on the gradually spiraling staircase. Ford had trouble fitting through the cramped stairwell. His bulky pack, sticking out on all sides, kept dragging along the walls and the top of his head clipped the rough stone ceiling. The stairs straightened for a few feet before terminating at a spacious landing. Two open doorways led to a pair of chambers. The dried blood streaks crossed the landing and passed through the closer of the two doorways. Less than a half dozen persons could fit into the windowless and almost dark rooms, so the servants waited while the Kamen crammed in to investigate. In a pool of dried blood, they found the top of a skull, a torn cloak, an overturned oil flask, a punctured wineskin, and a dagger with its tip snapped off. The other room was empty. The Kamen had no idea who the person had been.

"Doubt he was Kamen," said Dagmar. "Few huntsmen other than I ever come out here." They left the remains behind with a shrug and took the last few steps down into a veranda overlooking a high-walled courtyard.

"This was once a hanging garden," Dagmar told them, repeating a guess made by one of his regular hunting companions. The windows of rooms formerly occupied by the temple's priests dotted the walls around them, except to the north, where terraces three and four stories high contained large plots of frozen-over earth from which a variety of ornamental and edible vegetation once grew in abundance. Buried in ice beneath them was a fountain surrounded by flowerbeds and large pots.

"It must have been peaceful and pretty here back then," said Adelar.

Dagmar grunted and crossed over to the center of the courtyard to sit upon the flat stone surface of the top of the fountain where it protruded from the ice. "It's as good as anywhere to ease our feet." From there, he gave a stationary tour of the courtyard and the buildings enclosing it. "The whole place seems to be a sanctuary of sorts."

With a boost from Ford, Elvo was able to see into a few of the windows. "There are pieces of cloth, clothing in here. Shredded mostly. A mangled boot," he reported.

"It must have belonged to the unfortunate fellow who lost his life upstairs," Adelar guessed.

While the harsh Kamen language erupted from his master and rattled back and forth between the other Kamen, Ford sat by his pack and looked up at the square patch of pale sky visible above him. He couldn't have cared much less if it were a midnight sky or one of pure bright blue. At the moment, his mind was busily constructing an escape plan. He thought he might have something cooked up, but there were obstacles. The main one being that he was not trusted to keep watch alone at night, which was his preferred time to slip away. Even through there was no cover of darkness, at least the Kamen would be sleeping. However, there was someone else awake with him at all times, always a servant, since the Kamen never took a turn at keeping watch. They slept as much as they pleased. So, he would have to reason with at least one servant, perhaps incapacitate them if need be, preferably without ending a life. All four of the Kamen could die a horrible death for all he cared, but if he could spare a slave, he would. Kaltzek was a whole other story. The Walking Rock posed the most difficult obstacle. Ford wasn't sure he even slept at night.

As his gaze came back down to earth, his eye caught sight of a head framed in one of the windows. At first, he wasn't sure what he was looking at. It appeared to be a diamond-shaped stone perhaps two feet wide and a yard long perched upon the sill, but he didn't recall seeing it there before. Then it moved with a lightning-fast jerk to one side. The dark oval of an eye on the side of the head became distinctly visible. A lead-gray body about as wide as the head slithered and jittered from the window and down the wall. Five, six, seven feet long and counting.

"Snake!" he shouted and tried to back away, but his legs were bound at the ankles and he couldn't move much faster than a toddler. As the creature gained, Ford toppled onto his backside. Fifteen feet of segmented, plated body swiftly skittered to the bottom of the wall, over the ice and across the courtyard toward one of the house servants. Its upper body reared back, revealing dozens of legs in two rows along its underside. Slim pincers clipped onto the struggling servant and pulled him close. The iron-like plates along its back, which Ford mistook for scales, were exoskeletal segments. Under the diamond head a pair of clicking mandibles opened wide to strike down upon the incapacitated servant, who let loose a high-pitched scream to rival the eerie one heard earlier. Dagmar shouldered Elvo aside and fired a bolt from his crossbow into the creature's head. It released the servant and fell to the ground writhing and twitching. While everyone else scattered, Kaltzek dove in with his wide-bladed sabre and delivered a severing blow that ended the fight.

"Ho, my boys! What a nasty sneak he was to come upon us while were unprepared!" Dagmar shouted and laughed. "This thing here will have been what caused all the fuss!" Dagmar propped a heel upon the creature's head and looked along the length of its body, while everyone else crept back for a better look. The servant who got the worst of it couldn't control his shaking, but the rest of the expedition soon pulled itself together. "Those damn things scare the life out of a critter!"

"I don't doubt it," muttered Elvo as he massaged the elbow that had stopped the fall he took during the melee.

"What's worse is, they're no use to man nor beast! Can't use them in the arena and they're poison to eat. What a waste!"

None of the New Beards had ever seen such a thing in their lives. The encounter left them jittery, so that, although the day was growing late, there would be no sleep anytime soon.

"Let's carry on before another of those things comes creeping out of the windows of this horrible place," said Adelar.

"Those giant bugs only ever travel in ones," said Dagmar. "But yes, let's find a new patch. This one's spoiled."

With the assistance of their servants, the Kamen climbed through one of the bottom windows and passed into a warren of mostly bare rooms neatly carved into the living rock. Kaltzek took the lead and Dam lit the way with an oil lamp for the rest of the expedition until they all emerged into the dull glow of a midsummer's night in Rikaswelt. They rejoined the main avenue at a broad square carved out of the cliff walls where it pushed in, creating a narrow gorge.

"Is that a well?" asked Adelar, pointing to where a foot's worth of circular stone masonry stuck up out of the ice.

"A cistern, I should say," said Elvo, examining the structure without going near it. "At least fifteen steps across, by the eye. It's larger than any well I've seen."

"Neither! It was a tower," said Dagmar stepping up to the edge. "Come and see! The steps along the inner wall are frozen over, but they are there. Ah, and that's not all!" A giant marmot was trapped at the bottom some ten feet down. "Must've panicked and fallen in." The walls were too steep for it to climb out. Kaltzek leapt in and landed on his sturdy legs as if the ten feet had been but two. The animal squealed and Kaltzek silenced it.

Obeying his master's commands, he dragged the marmot's body around and around the square, leaving a thick coat of warm blood encircling the tower ruins. The body was left by the wall. The hunters hid themselves in the adjoining cliffside abodes and waited. Within the hour, a marmot shriek of alarm could be heard close at hand, then others joined in. They never did show themselves and apparently had dispersed, as they were not heard from again.

Soon after, the relative silence and the long, tiring day finally wore out the New Beards. They dropped off to sleep where that sat, concealed within open doorways and windows with their crossbows cradled in their laps. Even Dagmar's eyes were shutting when a karvane slevkavve dropped from an upper window down into the courtyard with a heavy *thump* that woke everyone. It sat back on its haunches snorting in the air and taking in its surroundings. Once satisfied, it leaned forward to rest most of its weight upon its thick forearms with its knuckles pressed firmly flat upon the ground. Its broad, muscular back faced Adelar a mere few feet away. The young Kamen's head popped up in his window to see what the commotion was. He held his breath and slowly slid back down out of sight.

As large as the famed Avar, this creature was even more agile. In a sudden burst, it rushed across the square and loped around the tower ruins with its nose to the ground sniffing and licking the blood. Adelar hadn't even thought about his weapon by the time Dagmar let loose his crossbow. The bolt flew into the karvane slevkavve, but disappeared in the churning arms and legs. Whether it struck home or sailed straight through, no one could tell. The karvane slevkavve never reacted, but rather carried on to the marmot's corpse, scooping up the animal like it was nothing more than a feather pillow. Then it bounded through Elvo's doorway. Elvo squealed as shrill as a dying marmot. The karvane slevkavve leapt back through the doorway and disappeared from the courtyard down the avenue deeper into Veks Miris.

Gelee stumbled from a window. "It'll get away," he cried, desperately upset at seeing their first real trophy slip away. The chase began in earnest for half the party and warily for the other half. Dagmar, Kaltzek and Gelee ran after their quarry, trying to keep it in sight. Adelar, Elvo and the servants followed cautiously behind.

"Hold up! Hold up!" Dagmar called out, red cheeked and heaving in huge breaths. Gelee's ear-to-ear smile faded. The eager New Beard had been about to enter a doorway alone, but Dagmar restrained him. "It's no use, son! No use! It knows we're about! I'm as broken hearted about it as you, but we'll try again tomorrow! It won't go far! We'll have it tomorrow!"

Dagmar was determined to capture the creature. If he could manage to bring it back to the city alive, the price he could get for it would mean he could go for months upon months without hunting again. Of course, he would, or so he told himself, but it would be nice not to feel pressured to do so. The problem was finding the damned thing. He had seen the creature's speed and agility. It would find some hidden place to gorge itself upon the marmot. After such a meal, it would likely sleep away the following day. That would give the hunters plenty of time to track it down. For now, they simply needed to keep it within striking distance and find a safe place to camp for the night.

The New Beards deferred to his superior knowledge, following his lead as the hunting party delved deeper into Veks Miris. Soon after the square, Dagmar anticipated an avalanche obstructing the avenue farther ahead, and so even though fresh blood droplets trailed away in that direction, he took the party on a detour.

They passed through a long, low-ceilinged former armory and smithy. The space was mostly barren, although Dam's lamp did reveal scattered light brown and gray hairs where animals had recently bedded down in the more hidden of recesses. Coming out the other side, they found themselves on a cramped landing facing the sheer cliffside. The only option was a sharp right turn down a long stairway that had transformed into an ice slide. The cliff and the building paralleling this slick chute provided nothing to grip, so a knotted rope was used as a guidewire to assist their descent.

At the bottom of the slide stood a stout cross vault topped with an ornamental hammer. One side was walled off by the abutting cliff. Its opposite side led into a former stonemason's workshop. Straight ahead was a short curving lane that emptied back into the main avenue.

"This is different," Elvo said, running his gloved hand over the inner rim of the arch supports, which were coated in a crystalline substance.

"Ice does strange things," Dagmar said.

"It appears to be more than just ice."

Dagmar still dismissed it. He had little interest in the natural world beyond what it could bring him in glory and gold. "We passed the avalanche. From here on watch yourselves. Watch your footing and keep an eye out. Have your weapons ready." His switch from boisterous shouts to a subdued tone kept the New Beards on their toes.

They passed under the cross vault, along the lane and out onto the main avenue. To their right, along the southern route, they could see the huge chunks of ice and rock in a massive pile that created a barrier blocking their way, Dagmar's avalanche.

The passage north snaked about, twisting and turning through an ever-narrowing gorge. The expedition was crowded into a single file line as they passed between thick buttressing retaining walls that towered overhead. A smattering of the crystals Elvo had discovered before, speckled the walls to either side from the ground up to about as high as a Kamen could reach. Again, he ran his gloved hand over them and tried to imagine how spectacular they might appear in better lighting.

There was little else to see in this short stretch of road before it split into two lanes. Dagmar took them down the wider of the two into what was once a residential area of modest housing built into the cliff walls. Against a wall off to one side sat a mound of Elvo's crystals about the size of a giant marmot.

The shape was odd. The erudite young Kamen was inclined to investigate, but passed them by with only a longing second glance. If Dagmar saw no value in them, then they must be worthless. However, when they entered another town square, they happened upon a second mound of crystals that could not be ignored by even Master Vanagz. If the marmot-sized pile could be called a *mound*, this one could only be referred to as a hill. It took up half the square. The light of Dam's tiny lamp created a dazzling display as it played upon the multifaceted surface. More lamps were lit, so they could have a better look at the strange object.

"It's as tall as two or more of the giant!" Dagmar jerked a thumb at Ford as he said this and then wheeled about to poke a finger into Gelee's side. "And almost as big around as our friend here!"

"It looks like a statue or monument," said Adelar, walking around it to get a better look at a pair of long, sabre-like protrusions coming out of one side.

"I don't recall it being here before," said Dagmar. "I would have remembered this."

"Is it ice," said Gelee as he drew back his iron-shafted glaive and cracked the butt of it into the mass of clear crystals. A chunk of crystals chipped off and rolled a few feet across the square. Elvo retrieved it and held the piece up to a lamp, turning it so that the light reflected the countless irregular facets. While he examined the piece, the others took swings at the giant mass. Chunks and chips sprayed the air. The Kamen wore out their arms, so Kaltzek was given a turn. He smashed open a window-sized hole in the side of the crystal mass.

"What do you know, it's hollow!" bellowed Dagmar in surprise. Lamps were gathered about the newly made hole and the congregated illumination lit up the interior so that it twinkled a thousand times brighter than a starry night sky.

"It's like a giant glass skull," said Adelar over the excited gabble of the others. The more they stared, the more interesting details were revealed to them: space for four stumpy legs; a long trunk-like nose; protruding tusks. The glinting facets created too much confusion to discern much else, but it soon became clear what they were looking at.

"It's some sort of behemoth," said Elvo.

"The grandest of grand mammoths," put in Dagmar.

No signs of physical remains, such as bone or hair, could be seen from Kaltzek's hole, leaving them baffled as to its creation or significance.

"Maybe it *is* a statue," Adelar suggested.

"Yes, maybe," said Dagmar, whose interest was flagging. The crystals were an odd anomaly, but all this messing about was not hunting and he was growing bored. "Whatever it is, it's no use to us." The command was given to gather up the gear. Before everyone was ready, Dagmar had already stalked out of the square.

By the time the rest of the party caught up with him, they found they had passed into a section of Veks Miris quite dreary and full of shadows. The rough gorge walls, some with modest abodes built into them, closed in over their heads, like the garrison structures of Ford's homeland. The road squeezed down to a slender footpath. In the poor lighting, only marginally improved by lamps and lanterns, anyone taller than a Kamen had to be wary of overhangs which dipped down into the passage. Everyone was watchful of holes in the ground. Sudden drop-offs to the left or right would plunge one into a crevasse of indeterminate depth. From time to time, they had to cross chasms upon yard-wide stone bridges.

"I have only ever nosed into these parts but once. Watch your step," said Dagmar as he yanked Gelee back from a nearly fatal misstep.

Their path poured them into a uniformly miserable enclave of puny, maze-like burrows. This depressing, comfortless shamble of rooms molded out of natural caves was on a scale smaller than anywhere else in Veks Miris. Walls and ceilings were often left rough. Rocks too hard to remove still jutted up from uneven floors. Even the Kamen had to duck under the oddly-shaped doorways and the few windows found here were never larger around than one of their heads. A few bones lay scattered about in some of the rooms, dusty litter from predators' meals.

"What a horrible place! Who could live here? They must have been the most desperate of the poor," said Adelar and the others concurred.

"They lived like animals," said Gelee.

To Ford's eye, the confined conditions were as stifling as any Kamen dwelling and reminded him a good deal of Drek. The New Beards were oblivious to the similarity, having never visited the mining town and having no idea that their own people lived in such squalor.

"As poor as it is, one of these caves will make an easily defended encampment," said Dagmar in what for him would be considered a whisper. He was on his guard, walking and talking carefully and quietly. He didn't want to worry them, but karvane slevkavve would attack a Kamen as likely as a marmot. There wasn't much of a chance of that happening since the one they were hunting had recently fed, but there was no sense in tempting fate.

They made camp in one of the more comfortable dwellings. Its three chambers contained only one door and one window, making it fairly easy to defend. The two remaining house servants were installed in the innermost chamber, the smallest of the rooms and the one with the window. They blocked up the tiny window with debris, which would tumble out and clatter upon the floor should someone or something try to enter from that direction. The Kamen took the middle chamber, it being the largest and least drafty. The duty of guarding the entryway chamber went to Ford, Dam and Muk since it was their night to keep watch. The watchman would take his shift sitting outside the doorway, which offered the best vantage point. Kaltzek had been sent back to the valley pass to obtain more supplies for the following day, as well as to check on the servant waiting there.

"If a bear gets you down on the ground, stay there," Dagmar said to the New Beards sitting on cushions gathered about him in a circle around a single oil lamp. After some prodding, he had begun telling hunting stories while they ate. Their questions led to him dolling out tips and tricks he had picked up through experience. "It might leave you alone, especially if there is easier prey about or competition to worry it, but the moment you try to get back up and get away, it will chase you down and it will catch you and you will not get back up. Never again."

This was the third of his anecdotes which had either ended in the death of a hunter or at least alluded to it, and the New Beards were becoming decidedly less eager to hear more. Elvo squirmed in his seat, and when he could take no more, he interrupted his host with, "Do you believe in the old stories of hidden treasure somewhere in Veks Miris?"

"Maybe it's out there. Maybe it isn't." Dagmar waved a non-committal hand and went on. "I've never found any treasure. But then, there must be deeper, darker holes in Veks Miris than even I've ever visited."

"Deeper and darker than this? I would hate to imagine," said Adelar looking into the shadowy crevices of the chamber, where the sloping walls met the floor in an angle of pitchy blackness that their lamp did not illuminate. At least two of the three New Beards were certain they didn't want to dig much deeper into Veks Miris, not after stories like this, nor after their own experiences thus far. Never in their lives had death snuck up on them with such intimacy.

Ford pretended to sleep while he listened to the Kamen talk in the adjacent room. It seemed like their conversation would never end. He wished they would go to sleep. For a while now, Dam had been sleeping like a baby wrapped in a blanket, cradled between two smooth rocks. They'd stopped giving Ford a blanket to cover himself. He lay on the cold ground on his side facing Dam a few feet away. Outside the entrance, Muk sat alone propped against a rock, keeping watch and finishing off his bottle of zivivesi. A sliver of midnight light shown down through the narrow gorge and gave him something to drink by. It lit up his legs enough that Ford could see them from the knees down. He opened his eyelids to slits and watched Muk's heels tap the ground as he beat the time to some unsung song. Eventually, the empty bottle clinked down on a rock and a faint humming could be heard coming from the tipsy translator. Ford would have loved to go out there and give Muk what was coming to him, but now was not the time to muck about.

The Kamen's animated nattering slackened into little more than grunts. Between the final few sluggish words, the house servants collected, cleaned and stowed away tin plates and mugs. Bedrolls were ruffled and soon a solid snoring started up. Ford's heart began to race. He had come up with a plan to escape and tonight he would set it in motion.

Gradually propping himself up with an elbow and cocking an ear, he let slip by what seemed like an eternity before he was satisfied with the repetitious sounds of sleep reverberating throughout the dwelling. His backside scraped across the rough stone as he tried to sit up, making him hesitate, stop, and start again more slowly. Every movement he made sounded incredibly loud to his ears. Surely, he thought, someone would hear him, and yet no one stirred, not even Muk.

Next came the part he feared most. He had to creep inch by inch across the floor with one hand tied to its opposite foot. Hopping across on one foot would have been much quicker, but the chance of falling and waking someone with the noise seemed too risky. So, he began dragging himself across the floor by hand and heel.

Scoot and listen, scoot and listen, one inch at a time.

The snoring rattled on. All seemed well. Ford sped up, otherwise it would take him all night to get to the pile of packs stacked against the far wall. Still, care was needed, because he was attached to Dam's wrist by a length of rope. Dagmar insisted upon it, assuming Ford would try to escape at night. The man was too clever for Ford's liking. He would have to be quick and at least as clever to outwit him.

Once he'd crossed the room, there would be no more stopping and listening. Ford knew exactly which pack contained the sleeping draughts. Once he had them, he would pour them into the remaining water supply. In the morning, everyone's waterskins would be refilled. Before breakfast was over, they should all fall back to sleep. Then he would slip away, during broad daylight. They wouldn't expect it. How could they? And when making camp, Ford had arranged the packs so the one with the draughts was on top. That would make things easier on him. Still though, opening it up and digging through it without making too much noise would require time. If he rushed it and they heard him, there would be trouble. His ready excuse was that he was preparing to refresh the dose on the weapons. All the previous day and right up to this moment, he repeated the words "for hunt" in Kamen to himself. Saying those words correctly might save his skin. True, it was too soon to apply the dose. The weapons weren't supposed to be coated with the stuff until right before a hunt. This had been explained to him, but he could always feign stupidity. The plan was laid out as perfectly as he could imagine. The path to freedom was in a vial a few inches from his fingertips.

As he reached for the canvas, tinkling and crackling noises from outside arrested his hand in midair. It sounded like the grinding of glass or perhaps the crunching of hail underfoot. Perhaps Muk was smashing his bottle or maybe walking about on those little crystals that seemed to be everywhere down here. Ford lay back and pretended to sleep. When the sounds continued with little change in their tempo or volume for a formless length of time, Ford ruled out footsteps. He doubted a perfectly comfortable drunk man would bother getting up and walking around. However, it might have been the grinding of a stationary person digging a toe or heel into the icy ground. Muk gave a stifled groan, as if disturbed in his sleep. Not long after that, the noise subsided and was replaced by a deeper and less frequent snap and crack. Ford had heard iced-over ponds make such a noise during a period of freezing or thawing. The association eased his mind. Perhaps it was nothing more than the shifting ice on the surface of a pool of water somewhere in the plunging crevices of the ravine. He propped himself up again. From this angle, Muk couldn't be seen through the doorway at all, not even his feet. The snaps and cracks subsided.

He began pawing through the pack. The vials were in a padded pouch of their own. A grumble from one of the Kamen and the rustling of a bedroll from the other room sent Ford's head to the ground yet again. One of his balled-up fists pressed into the rock beneath him. He fought down the urge to punch the ground. At this rate he would never finish his task before Dam awoke.

The tinkling and crackling resumed even louder, but he wouldn't let it dissuade him from his task. The moment the man-made noises within the camp calmed again, he went back to work, locating by feel the remaining water supply in a large and thick-skinned sack. Shivers rippled down his spine. He thought it was nerves, but a chilling draft had swept into the room and the temperature dropped.

One by one, he plucked the glass vials containing the sleeping draughts from the pack. Each vial had been wrapped in cloth and stored in the padded pouch to keep them from breaking against one another. There were three vials. One was full, one was empty and the last had about a third of the solution left. In his excitement and haste, he yanked on the rope connecting him to Dam, not once but twice, and twice as hard as ever intended. The man was a sound sleeper, who knew how to get his forty winks whenever he could, but still, Ford was surprised the motion didn't wake him. He took a peek over his shoulder and saw a shambling heap of crystals crawling on top of Dam. The whole mass twisted and writhed, like the embodiment of a water spirit or earth elemental in the form of glass shards or a mound of frozen spikes come to life. Its every movement was accompanied by a cascade tinkling clinks.

Ford stumbled back, rolling over and falling toward the doorway to the Kamens' room. The rope connecting him to Dam pulled taut and jerked Dam's hand into the air. Ford yanked on the rope, but there was no give. Crystals spreading from the creature onto Dam had created a bond between the two and attached them both to the ground. Already Dam's head and shoulders were completely anchored. The pile of crystals rose a yard above him and was at least as wide. The creature shifted constantly, making it nearly impossible to pin down its shape and size. A sluggish swirl of icy wind whirling about the crystalline form drained the warmth from the room. Ford gasped. While the bitter cold of Rikaswelt attacked from the outside, probing one's apparel to prick at the skin, this uncanny tenfold frigidity seemed to suck up and annihilate bodily warmth. Light from the doorway bounced off of the crystals and flashed a dull luminescence about the room. Dam's face in miniature reflected back at Ford in more than a hundred facets. Whether Dam was awake and aware, Ford couldn't tell. He could barely tell whether he himself was awake or dreaming.

The crystal mound slid down Dam's body, continually coating him in multiplying layers of crystals. It inched closer to Ford, who clutched at his neck as the freezing air constricted his throat. He feared he might pass out. Before it was too late, he pulled on the rope, putting everything he had into it. Dam's arm leapt about. The jerking of its victim drew the crystal mound's attention to the rope. It slid with a fluidity belying its mineral composition from Dam toward Ford along the length of the cord. The clinking came faster than ever. Ford fell back into a skirting crab-walk that wrapped the rope around the crystal mound and shortened the distance between them. Pulling harder only lodged the rope deeper in the shards. The invasive, radiating cold aura froze the breath in his lungs and sapped his will to live. He wished nothing more than to curl into a ball upon the floor and sleep forever. He would have called for help, but it felt as if he breathed another breath, he would breathe no more. As his sight dimmed and his head swam, Ford wound the rope around his free hand and leaned back with all his weight. It would be the last time he pulled upon the rope, a rope gone brittle from the cold and worn thin by the jagged edges of the angular shards rubbing against it. Ford's vision darkened just as he fell over backward. The rope had snapped. His tumble to the far side of the room distanced him enough from the crystal mound to clear his head. He got to his hands and knees and scrambled out of the cave dwelling.

Still hobbled hand to foot, he tripped and stumbled over Muk, clutching the zivivesi bottle in his lap where he sat by the entrance, the entirety of the translator's body encased in crystals. Not a moment did Ford spare for the man who had betrayed him and put his life in peril. As he slid across the ground, frantically reaching and pushing with his free hand and foot, each inch, foot and yard came at a great expensive to his remaining strength. He never looked back to see if the strange crystal mound still pursued him or turned its attention to the inner room where the Kamen lie sleeping.

A light crunching, as if the ground were covered in a layer of hail, accompanied his hobbled escape. Tiny crystals coated the walls throughout the cave dwellings where the passages closed in enough to touch his shoulders to either side. He prayed as he crossed each thin bridge on his belly, fearful of losing his balance and falling into the chasm below. His muscles burned and his throat begged for water. His fingertips turned raw and bloody from clawing at the ground, but he kept crawling. Once he tried leaping upon the foot that was bound to his hand and hopping, but the position was too precarious and awkward to be worth the strenuous effort.

Eventually, though he couldn't say how long it took, he came to the main avenue and the avalanche that blocked it. There was no way of climbing over such a massive pile of rock and ice chunks, not tied hand to foot. Instead, he found the side lane and the cross vault topped by the ornamental hammer at the base of the steep slope. The knotted rope they had used in their descent was still in place. Without it, the climb would be impossible. The knots had been made for the Kamen, so they were close together, which would help. Even if they weren't, he would have tried anyway. This was his only hope. He took hold of the rope and jumped, but missed the bottom most knot. It took four tries before the side of his foot caught the knot and held his weight. With his scrunched-up body pressed against the slope, he hoisted himself up with his one free arm. Reaching as high as he could, he tried for the next knot and missing, sliding back to the bottom.

Again, he tried. Again, he failed.

His grip was weakening. Holding on became as difficult as the leap for the knot. Two was the most knots he managed to scale before falling down. The awkward position, his own clumsiness and exhaustion were doing him in. He tried once more before sliding back down and remaining in a heap at the base of the slope, hope diminishing but not lost.

He sat with his back against the cliff wall under the cross vault, resting while trying to think of a solution or another way around. If there was another way around, he didn't know it. The thought of backtracking toward the Kamen, even a few steps, didn't appeal in the least. There was no alternative but that the bonds must come off. Either that or he would never get out of

Veks Miris. The length of remaining rope tied to the studded collar around his neck could wait. He had already tucked it into his tunic to get it out of the way. Now what he needed was something sharp, something with an edge to sever the rope binding his wrist and ankle together. Nothing within sight would do, but before him sat the open doorway to the former stonemason's workshop.

Scooting over the ground and through the doorway of the single, long room of the workshop, he navigated the stout pillars down its center in search of anything of use among the piles of broken stone and the few small stacks of blocks. Kicking at the debris, he unearthed a piece of metal which might have been a trowel blade, but it had rusted away so thin that the brittle piece came apart in his hand when he lifted it. The best he could find for what he needed was a square block. Its corners still had a decent enough edge to sever the bonds, if he had the time to rub the rope against the rock. For all he knew, that crystal thing or his Kamen master might be coming for him. Getting his hand and foot up against the corner was not easy. Rubbing back and forth was tiring work and difficult at such an odd angle. He tried a sitting position first and when that seemed cumbersome and slow, he tried standing. It was no better. There was nothing to do but sit there and work at it. A rumbling sound above the rasping of the rope against the rock caught his ear. He stopped and listened to it grow louder. Something was sliding down the slope outside. He dove behind the block, which only stood a little over a foot high. A lumpy shape flopped down in the doorway at the base of the slope. It was one of the packs the Kamen had brought for the hunt. An even louder rumbling and scraping came down the slope. Kaltzek slid into the pack. Ford ducked behind the block and tried to make himself as small as possible. The encounter with the crystal mound had driven Kaltzek from his thoughts. He caught his breath and tried not to move or make a sound. The blood pounding in his ears blocked the rustling of the pack being lifted from the ground and tossed about, as well as the thump of Kaltzek's heavy footsteps. If the slave overseer found him it would mean pain or a swift end if he were lucky. Ford forced himself to look and saw nothing in the doorway, no sign of Kaltzek.

He went back to rubbing away at his bonds as fast as he could, one eye on the rope and one eye on the doorway. The rope fibers gave way ever so gradually. "By the gods, please," he begged the stubborn threads which would not give in to his fierce, abrasive thrusts and drags. Then, as if it were nothing at it, the cord snapped. Rope ends still dangled from his hand and ankle, but at least now all of his arms and legs were free. He ran to the doorway, peered about. Kaltzek was nowhere in sight. If he was truly gone and for how long were questions with answers that didn't matter, not if Ford couldn't get up the slope. He grabbed hold of the knotted rope and attacked the climb once more. Hand over hand, each foot landing on a knot, made it seem like child's play when he reached the top. From there, the way out of Veks Miris should have been simple, but in his haste, he made wrong turns and had to double back before finally finding the half-buried wall of the gateless entryway.

The dutiful house servant still waited with the rest of their baggage, the empty cages, and the team of restless muskox. The man had not been idle. The canvas had been tented over the encircled sleds to create a semi-enclosed encampment, which cut down a good deal of the wind and provided at least a sense of security for those sitting in the center. When Ford crawled up the slippery pass, he found the man stirring a simmering pot of broth over a flickering flame.

Relieved to see someone aside from the intimidating Kaltzek, the house servant fairly fawned over Ford, fluttering about, feeding Ford, and asking in basic Kamen after his health and that of the others. The man had been riding his heightened nerves to the breaking point ever since they left him behind, so he was happy to do something productive and useful, a bit of work to calm his shaking hands and disperse the fear of the lonely night.

Ford noticed a wide circle of blood soaked into the ice and snow next to the encampment. When he gestured toward it, the house servant tried to tell the story of how one of the muskox had been savaged by a wolverine, probably the one that had killed Parvan, and Master Kaltzek had had to butcher the remains of the beast while he was here, which was why he had been so late in getting back. Did Ford see him? They must have passed each other along the way. What had Ford been sent for? All this was delivered in a mix of languages and very little of it was understood. Ford didn't much care, but he was happy to allow the servant to feed him and assist in finding more clothing to layer over his own.

The near-witless fellow was eager to help until Ford began sorting through the gear and rearranging it onto one of the sleds. While they harnessed the muskox, the servant began questioning Ford's motives and wandered if there was more to the story behind the bits of severed rope wrapped around his neck, wrist and ankle. Ford recognized and ignored the man's questioning tone, but once everything was ready, he faced him and tried to explain, parsing out the few Kamen words he knew which applied.

"Death! Death!" he kept repeating and articulating the word with his huge hands. The servant's eyes bulged. Ford fell back more and more upon his own tongue, until finally he gave in entirely. "Your master and all the others may be dead by now," he said, taking the servant by the arms and looking him in the eye. "If you stay here waiting for them, you might wait forever. Come with me!" The servant looked back blankly. "You come with me! You!" Ford poked the other man in the chest. "Come! With! Me!" It did no good and only served to worry the servant more. However, when Ford pointed to himself, the loaded sled, and to the south, a light dawned in the servant's eyes.

All of the New Beard's house servants empathized with Ford's plight and fully understood why he would risk an escape. It was common knowledge that Dagmar's slave was not long for this world and it made perfect sense that he wished to strike out across this desolate and deadly tundra, but the New Beard's slave wanted no part of such a forlorn hope. He foresaw only hardship and inevitable recapture, if not death between the jaws of some hideous monster somewhere out in this godless, frozen wasteland. The servant backed away shaking his head. Ford let him go. He didn't have time to convince the unwilling and had already wasted too much of the precious little he did have. He jumped on the back of the sled and reached for the reins, but just then, the house servant ran up to him brandishing a knife. Ford reeled back. The servant threw up placating hands in a peaceful gesture.

"I help! I help," he said in Kamen, reaching for Ford's hand. Ford let him slide the sharp, three-inch blade along his wrist under the leather thong between the iron studs and slice up, severing the bond. He did the same with the one around Ford's neck and ankle. No, he would not join Ford, but neither would he try to stop him. Parvan's death and the Kamen's mistreatment of his body still rankled him.

"You go. I say no thing," he said, miming a hand over his mouth to show he would not give him away when the Kamen came around asking questions. Ford embraced him, hopped back on the sled, and flicked the reins. The sled rocked, wobbled, and nearly toppled as it cascaded down the pass. The house servant watched with a touch of longing and regret. When the sled disappeared from sight, his loneliness and fears returned. He went back to the encircled sleds, climbed into one of the cages and awaited his fate.

Ford drove the sled in a frenzy southward. In this ice and rock landscape, the tracks the sleds had made on their northward passage could only rarely be seen in the snowdrifts skirting out from boulders and escarpments. The way back from whence they had come was a mystery. He had to trust his own judgement and read the sun when he could to keep the sled headed in the right direction and get him out of the northern reaches of Rikaswelt. Once down from the foothills, the muskox took over with their sights set on Siltsvesi. Ford loosened his grip on the reins, gave them their head, and collapsed face first onto the packs piled before him.

***

Into the second week since the hunting party set out, a valvar drowsily keeping watch at Siltsvesi caught sight of something interesting while leaning against the lookout window in the rockface some two hundred feet above the barbican. He had been daydreaming of frogs and questioning their existence when his languid, roaming eye spotted a speck of a figure some miles away crossing the broken terrain. He took it for a small herd of the large, four-legged animals common to the area, not an exceptional sight. But then he made out the sled and instantly the muskox sprang to mind. Obviously, it must be Master Vanagz's hunting expedition returning. He picked up his chisel, which had slipped from his hand when he nodded off earlier, and went back to scraping ice from the window frame. The task quickly lost its charm and his listless gaze returned to the barren horizon and featureless lands surrounding the town. When he spotted the sled again, he could have sworn its course had been diverted to one which would take it farther away. He stared awhile. His eyesight was excellent. It was the attribute that got him the job, more so than his physique. From what he could see, there appeared to be one person with the sled, and not driving it, but rather leading the muskox. The figure was too tall to be Kamen. Curious, he thought, that whoever was with the sled would not come to Siltsvesi. Yes, whoever it was, they were most definitely leading the muskox away. The valvar left the window, forgetting his chisel on the sill, and made his way down the stairs to report what he had seen.

Once Siltsvesi was out of sight, Ford stopped the sled in a shallow depression. The land had leveled out and the winds whipped steadily over head. While the muskox rested, he pulled open the packs and took stock of his provisions. What was left might last him two weeks, if he were good about rationing. The feed left for the animals wouldn't cover half as long. He hunkered down beside the muskox, nestling in their thick black and brown wool while he ate and considered his options. The animals would have to be jettisoned soon. If he had been wiser, he would have set them loose already. Their hooves sunk through the crusted snow now and then, providing a trackable trail. But without them, he wouldn't have come so far so fast, nor would he feel half as refreshed. Whatever happened, he would always think fondly of the two charming beasts and what they had done for him.

A stiff wind tugged at the many layers of cloaks and clothing he held tightly wrapped about him. To the south there would be warmer weather. How much farther south he did not know, but what was loaded on the sled would take him a fair distance from the Kamen, far from their lands, perhaps out of their reach. He had food, clothes, a few essentials to make a fire and set up a camp, everything he would need for a long journey. He was as far south as he had ever been in Rikaswelt, as close to an escape as ever. Elation at the very thought of this almost tangible freedom drove the cold from his bones. So, it was a great surprise, even to himself, when he turned the sled westward and made for Dargkivi.

Chapter 19
The Return

At the base camp on the plateau of the Veks Miris pass, the New Beard house servant left behind to watch over the animals and sleds went from grinding his teeth to biting off the ends of his fingernails. The wait for the return of his master or anyone from the hunting party had been interminable, especially since he had assisted in the escape of the slave known as Ford. A lie to cover the truth was needed. He grabbed the bits of rope Ford had left behind, went back to the cage and locked himself, then tried to bind his wrists as best he could. The lock could be undone from within the cage, if one knew how, and the binding job was loose and easily unwound. He doubted any of it would hold up under the scrutiny of the inevitable interrogation that would follow upon the hunting party's return, but it was the best he could come up with on such little sleep.

The house servant had passed the whole night with hardily a wink and as midday approached, he was beginning to succumb to a drowsy fog. The crackling and snapping of granular ice barely registered as he dropped in and out of sleep. He considered himself to have a vivid imagination, as most do, and reckoned the noises to be the waking fancies of a rattled mind. Nothing more than deluded dream fantasy. On the other hand, if it were a dream, it was persistent and repetitive. It even seemed to grow louder. He sat up and saw a white mound laboring up the slope. The shambling form shuffled closer, stopped when it reached the plateau, and turned to face him. Only then did he recognize Kaltzek.

The heads of the other two house servants crested the rise behind Kaltzek, who laid down the cumbersome bundle burdening him and unbent his back. Seeing the servant in the cage, he growled commands to the New Beard house servants with him. They rushed to the cage, undid the simple gate lock, and untied their fellow servant. Kaltzek removed the blankets covering his bundle and made the prostrate form wrapped within more comfortable. Distracted as he was, Kaltzek never noticed how easy it had been to release the supposedly trapped servant. Assumptions had already been made and so the slave was spared the need to fabricate much of a story to cover his actions. His sputtered tale of ambush and the loaded sled being taken by force sufficed. Kaltzek could easily imagine it. After all, the servant had no skill in arms and his negligible strength would have been no match for Ford.

Kaltzek's attention returned to the bundle. He drew back the blanket which exposed Dagmar's pallid face and quivering blue lips. Master Vanagz had survived the encounter with the strange moving mound of crystals. Though paralyzed from the waist down and never to walk again, he had fared better than his companions. All three of the New Beards were still in the Veks Miris cave dwellings, entombed in crystals, their corporeal forms being drained of minerals to provide sustenance for what Elvo had called with his expiring breath, "Lord of the Endless Winter," as if reading the name off of a plaque. Through sheer will and a natural resistance to cold, Kaltzek had withstood its frigid radiating attacks and delivered his master from danger. In the confusion of the melee, the house servants had saved themselves.

Kaltzek called for water. A servant brought a skin. Kaltzek lifted it to his master's lips, but Dagmar drank little. He wanted no more assistance, no more coddling. Rigid but for an occasional shivering tremor, Dagmar's dark and sunken eyes were alive with anger. The hours it had taken to be dragged out of the ravine gave him time to think. After it appeared that he wasn't going to die, he regained some semblance of calm, at least enough to unravel the situation and realize that one person from the hunting expedition was left unaccounted for. Now that he had heard the story of Ford's escape, his suspicions were confirmed and he relaxed in relief at finding someone upon which to lay the blame for the disaster. A target for revenge had presented itself. A hatred brewed for the slave who had cuckolded him and caused the death of his friends, his dear friends as he now remembered them. This fugitive slave deserved a wrathful, merciless end. Dagmar motioned Kaltzek closer and rasped out, "Track him down. Return his body." Kaltzek nodded, but Dagmar was not finished. "Bring him pain."

***

Ford lie prone upon a long knoll paralleling the road to Dargkivi. The city's market gates were just in view but miles away yet, too far to make out the valvar he assumed stood guard there. He slid down the backside of the knoll away from the road and remained hidden there for hours while he worked out his plan to sneak into the city.

When he first located the road, he found himself trailing a small caravan of drovers some miles ahead. He had dropped back and watched them disappear through the gates. This gave him the idea of trying to pass himself off as a drover. He still possessed his muskox and sled. The packs they carried might pass as wares. Then again, maybe not. No slave he knew of was allowed to travel alone outside of the city. He would have to attach himself to a caravan. "But then the drovers would ask questions. Use your head man," he chided himself. Any Kamen with half a brain would wonder where he had come from and what he was doing out here all alone.

He sat huddled with the shaggy beasts that had pulled the sled what felt like halfway across Rikaswelt. They had grown used to him and were willing to let him curl up with them for warmth. One of them gave a plaintive bawl out of frustration. The moment they met up with the road to Dargkivi, the muskox were on familiar ground and expected the next stop to be within the city, where they would be warm and fed well. They stayed put, but only reluctantly, and occasionally gave a dissatisfied bellow.

Ford tucked his hands deeper into his midsection to keep them warm while he ran over the few ideas he had come up with thus far. It didn't take long to settle upon the only option which made any sense. Of course, it could be said that none of this truly made sense, not to the selfish side of him. Why enter the lions' den when you didn't have to? Yet instead of fleeing south like any sensible soul, he had come back to this cesspit of half-sized demons. Why? The only answer he could think of, the one he kept reminding himself of, was that he came back to do what needed doing and to avoid the regret of not having done it. Already in his short life, regrets had piled up for things he had done and things left undone, and the weight of it all was becoming unbearable. If he added to it, he wasn't sure he would be able to stand himself much longer.

The scraping of sledge runners along the road jolted him out of his abstracted thoughts. He crept up the knoll and peered over it as a Kamen drover team passed his hiding spot on their way to the city. He scampered down to his sled. This was the moment of truth. The moment to summon every ounce of courage within him.

Gathering the reins, he led his muskox back onto the road. The Kamen drovers were well ahead of him by now, too far ahead. He wanted to be close enough to be associated with them, but not so close as to draw their attention. If these farmers questioned him, he had no ready answers for why he was alone and where he had come from. Likewise, if the valvar at the market gate didn't think he was a part of the farmer's team, they would want answers to the same questions. Ford spurred the muskox on. They were not animals built for speed, but rather a steady plodding. Even when he got off the sled and helped push, it hardly gained them much momentum. The distance between the two closed to a few hundred feet, but they neared the gate and the guards could be seen clearly. His nerves were high, but he felt his chances were good if he stayed directly behind the drovers and if none of them looked back. The grinding of their runners upon the ground masked the scraping of his sled. He prayed that his muskox would keep quiet and not be tempted to return the calls of the drover's ram teams. If he could play the part of the laggard slave, something the Kamen would recognize and think nothing of, his plan might work. However, if he lagged too far behind and the caravan reached the gates well ahead of him, the valvar would have him.

As much as he urged the muskox on through the reins with a rapid flicking and a tight grip, it did no good. Only his lighter load helped close the gap between them. As the drover's team came to within a couple hundred feet of the gate, a leathery turnip-like vegetable, which the rural Kamen grew in their hot spring caves, toppled from the back of the last sledge. Someone short and springy leapt down and chased after it. At first, Ford thought it was a Kamen, but it turned out to be a spry young Bzinsani girl of ten to twelve years. After snatching up the vegetable, she straightened up, looked directly at him, and gave a little start, confused by his unexpected appearance. Ford caught his breath and felt his stomach lurch. But the girl said nothing, alerted no one, and after hesitating to watch him for a moment, she caught up with her master's sledge as it passed through the gates.

The muskox dragged Ford's sled over the smooth flagstones before the arched entrance. He hunched over, kept his head down close to the packs and pressed on. The valvar at the gate hurling friendly insults back and forth with the newly arrived farmers were too preoccupied to notice Ford. The muskox jerked the sled over the stone floor straight into the bustling crowd of the cavernous marketplace.

The shouts of buyers and sellers as well as the scrape of many flat-bottomed sleds and runner sledges masked noise, but by no means did the flurry of brisk trade make Ford any less conspicuous. He would never move through a crowd without comment about his height, unless he walked among giants. Remarks on his size and the usual old jokes about "the view up there" flew at him in Kamen from all corners. One elderly merchant went further. Having retired on the wealth he had amassed over a successful career, he had plenty of spare time to waste on other people's affairs. Being a stickler for tradition and always mindful of keeping a slave in their place, even when the slave did not belong to him, he pointedly shouted at Ford from across the scales platform, demanding to know why the slave's hair had been allowed to grow so long. Ford's hair had only recently begun settling down upon his scalp again, but that was far longer than the shorn pate allotted slaves. Not understanding much of what was shouted at him, Ford feared the worst, pretended not to have noticed, and pressed on through the crowd. His plan had been to take some of his provisions with him, but the old merchant's persistent shouts made him give up the sled and leave the muskox where they stood in the middle of an aisle. The seller whose stall he blocked shouted at him to "come back and take these stinking beasts away!" Ford doubled his pace, slipped into the stables, and left the hubbub of the market behind.

Within the hour of Ford's return to Dargkivi, a fire broke out in Ulemine Alu. Something in the Vanagz dwelling caught alight and the entire place went up in a destructive conflagration. Fire was not usually something the Kamen worried about since so few of their possessions and structures were made of wood, but at the Vanagz home there were wooden walls, furnishings, and other combustibles, such as rugs and tapestries, all of which rapidly took flame and produced a choking smoke that kept back those few neighbors who rushed to the family's aid. Most fled the area when the alarm went up. Others came to gawk. One of the earliest onlookers to arrive on the scene claimed to have spotted the Vanagz's giant slave standing in the midst of the blaze among toppled oil lamps and lanterns with a sabre in hand and the valvar who acted as the family bodyguard dead at his feet. However, that supposed witness had taken a nasty bump on the head and some doubted his account.

When the place was reduced to smoldering ruins and the choking smoke had been ventilated from the rooms and surrounding tunnels, neighbors gathered to search the wreckage and found that most of the household had made it out safely. All but the family's young son could be accounted for.

"Vaavo! Vaavo!" screamed his mother from where she had collapsed into a neighbor's chair.

The ear-piercing shrieks of Vaavo Vanagz cut through the tunnels and echoed into the far reaches of Rask. The residents had heard it before and ignored it as best they could. Only two slaves new to the town, pushing and pulling their dung cart from door to door, actually saw Vaavo. They couldn't help but notice the boy and the person with him when Vaavo came tearing around a corner toward them with a growling bear in close pursuit. The slaves fell over one another in panicked flight, but when the boy burst out laughing, they turned back to see the bear sprawled upon the ground with a spilled sack and a bundle of fur in front of it. Human hands scrabbled about from under the bear picking up chunks of meat and shiny stones spread about it. The great head of the bear slid askew and the skin slipped away, revealing Ford beneath. Immediately recognizing a fellow slave, they began laughing too as they watched him fumble about in a frantic attempt to shove everything back into the sack.

Tram ma! Tram ma! The boy's shouts rang through the tunnels as he passed the two slaves. Ford wished he had a third arm as he grabbed up a haunch of lamb, tucked a spare bearskin under one arm, and centered the head of his own bearskin on top of his head before resuming the chase.

Steering the boy toward the more remote parts of Rask had not been easy. Vaavo went where he wished. But he was also thoroughly enjoying this game and wanted it to continue on forever, so whenever Ford fell behind, the boy would wait for him to catch up. When Ford took a wrong turn, the boy raced back and passed his pursuer, going down the new passage as if he'd intended it all along. After this happened a second time, Ford caught on and used it to his advantage, finally guiding the boy to the tunnel with the wide stripes carved into its walls, which was followed by a turn into one of the Dargkivi passages illuminated by mirror-reflected light.

Vaavo was fascinated by the unusual lighting, but another temptation had drawn him to these distant depths. The boy knew he could get sweet treats, rare in all of Dargkivi, by pestering the kindly servant at a particular Rask residence toward the end of this tunnel.

Ford felt a tangible relief when Vaavo broke for the door. He dropped the items he had taken from the Vanagz household and pressed his body against the wall beside the entrance. Vaavo beat on the door until it was opened by a bald-headed and robed servant, whose height forced him to stoop deeply in the short doorway.

"Ah, Vaavo!" said Will, the Aelwydian priest, in his soft and genuinely pleased voice. Ford's comrade from their Polecat days touched the boy with the flat of his hand on the top of the head in a respectful version of the Kamen greeting. "I will find you a sweet," he said as he stood and turned back through the doorway.

"Will," Ford whispered.

Will spun about and stared. His indulgent smile for the boy widened to an ear-to-ear pleasure at finding Ford at his master's door. His mouth opened, but whatever was on its way out died before it hit his lips when he saw that Ford had his back pressed against the tunnel wall and wore a deadly serious expression. Ford nodded down at the bundled items at his feet. "Come away," he whispered. Will stared at the lumpy sack, the bearskin Ford wore, the spare skin on the floor, and then searched Ford's eyes. He found the same desperate daring he had seen in them when the two men escaped with a small group from Polecat Island.

Vaavo pulled on Will's robe and loudly demanded the treats he had come for. Ford's head snapped back and forth, up and down the tunnel. Unwanted attention right then could undo his whole plan. There were but few households in the area and no one cared enough to check upon a squawking child. Will muttered something softly and slipped inside. This quieted the impatient boy, but Ford's heart sank at seeing his friend disappear back into the Kamen abode. Vaavo began to dance from foot to foot. The willowy slave who dispensed nuggets of sugar was taking longer than usual. Ford too began rocking back and forth, nearly dancing with impatience.

Ford noticed the door had been left ajar. He thought of rushing in, killing every Kamen within and dragging Will out. If he had to cut his way out of Dargkivi, so be it. His trembling hand sought under the bearskin for the sabre at his waist which he had taken from Dagmar's collection. A muffled exchange of words from within tightened his grip upon the hilt. He drew out the sword and raised it above his head, letting it hover above the lintel of the doorframe. When a figure emerged, he nearly brought the blade down upon Will's head. Will crouched and handed a pouch to Vaavo. The boy dug into it and pulled out a fistful of sugar encrusted gelatin nuggets.

"Ava gar ze," said Will and the boy's eyes shot wide open. He couldn't believe all of it was for him and him alone. Before they could be taken away, he shoved a half dozen into his mouth and chewed in voracious ecstasy. Vaavo's day of fun had just gotten a whole lot better.

Will reached back through the doorway and produced a flask as well as a small, deep red warm rock. The produced such minimal light and heat that it could be held in the hand continually without scorching the palms, but it would keep the frostbite from the tips of fingers in conditions of extreme cold.

Vaavo pirouetted a few times and then ran back up the tunnel from where they had come. A shout from him already sounded far off. "Tram ma!" Will reached to close the door, but Ford grabbed him by the arm and off they went.

"I knew you would come one day," Will said between labored breaths while trying his best not to lag far behind. Even when in prime physical shape, Will was not a swift nor graceful sprinter. When running determinedly and with abandon, he wasted a lot of energy pumping his elbows and knees sporadically and at odd angles, as if his body chose to do away with rhyme and reason. After weeks-worth of work done for his master in the cramped accommodations provided him, his muscles had atrophied. His legs felt wobbly and his lungs burned from the exertion almost as soon as they set off. "Where do we go from here?" he gasped.

In a few words over his shoulder, Ford explained his original plan to recover the sled with its pile of provisions. "But now I don't know." Two slaves going down to the market to steal a sled and drive muskox through a crowd of Kamen didn't seem like such a good idea.

"What then?" asked Will when they caught up with Vaavo and stopped to accommodate the boy's commands to put on the bearskins. Ford handed Will the spare, a fluffy white fur with the head and paws still attached. While helping him put it on, tying the arms around his neck, Ford began explaining another idea that had struck him earlier when passing the two dung collectors. Before he could finish, Vaavo let out a triumphant whoop at having doubled the bears at his beck and call. The boy took to his heels with a peel of laughter.

Now seemed like a good time to leave Vaavo behind. Twice Ford and Will tried to change course and veer off at a fork in the tunnel, but as soon as they deviated their path, Vaavo would catch up with them and take the lead again. The third attempt and failure turned out to be a stroke of good luck. A Kamen couple casually strolling the tunnels seemed to be about to ask what the two slaves were about, both dressed as bears and a variety of random items. Vaavo's shout of "Tram ma!" allowed Ford and Will to spill past the couple without explaining themselves and disappear into the tunnels of the next neighborhood.

In this carnivalesque manner, all three navigated to Dargkivi's south side. Vaavo had never been this far away from home before. He remained ahead of Ford and Will, but not by much. He wanted to touch every door handle and wall sconce, and investigate all of the alcove shrines they passed. When they arrived at the southern waste gate, the chute that slaves used to dump the pots of urine and feces they collected, Vaavo was dying to know what was beyond flapping leather-covered grating. The cold radiating from the circular portal could only mean the frigid outside world, which Vaavo wasn't terribly interested in, but the grate was out of reach behind the iron gate and that made anything instantly intriguing to such an inquisitive child. The boy stood at the gate rattling it something fierce.

"Hush, boy! Stop that," Ford hissed as they caught up. He wanted to keep the boy from making any more noise. His plan was to wait until a slave came along with some pots to empty and then somehow escape through the grate. Admittedly it was a plan lacking forethought. He had no idea if anyone would be coming along for the rest of the day.

"Come away," said Will laying a hand upon Vaavo's shoulder in hopes of guiding the child from the gate.

"This is it. This is how we escape," said Ford over Vaavo's incessant rattling. He nudged the boy aside, laid a hand upon the iron bars and gave the gate a tug of his own. "One of my jobs was dumping muck through that grate there. You open it up and on the other side is a chute, the outside."

"Our doorway to freedom is a shit chute?" Will asked. Ford shrugged his shoulders. "Oh, don't get me wrong," Will said, "I'm not complaining. It just seemed too appropriate."

"Nakke! Nakke!" The chastising bark of an old man from somewhere down a darkened tunnel stood all three of them at attention, at least briefly. Vaavo's hesitation was short-lived before he threw himself at the bars with renewed determination. He sensed the approach of someone who might alleviate his distress. Here and there during the boy's Dargkivi wanderings he had come across objects such as this which obstructed his desires. He found that if he persisted with enough volume, someone would eventually come along and alleviate the problem for him. As if in answer to his wishes, an aging Kamen tottered out of the darkness toward them with a ring of keys jingling in one hand and an oil lamp in the other. This was the semi-retired valvar who acted as gatekeeper here in order to continually afford indulging himself in the koer crackling he dearly loved. The stooped man didn't waddle because his age was so very great. The crimp in his back and his creaky knees mostly came from having done as little as possible over the past few years.

"Hide! Make haste!" Ford commanded at first hearing someone coming. He gave Vaavo a shove into Will's arms. Will tucked away the warm rock he had been using to illuminate this lightless section of tunnel. Ford pushed them all toward the nearest corner, but it was too late. The gatekeeper had seen them. Ford's tongue tripped over itself as he dithered in his search for a plausible explanation for having bothered the old man. Even if he had an excuse and knew enough Kamen to deliver it, the ruse of acting the part of a sanitation slave would not work without a cartload of pots as props. The gatekeeper grumbled a couple questions at them. For starters, he wanted to know why a pair of slaves were wearing bearskins tied about their necks. Ford had no idea what was being asked and it made him nervous. His hand moved to the sabre tucked away under his bearskin.

The delay and the jingling of the old man's keys proved too much for Vaavo. In a series of high-pitched squeaks, he demanded the gate be opened immediately. The old man was taken aback. Now he truly did not understand what was going on. He stopped and clutched his keyring to his chest. A call for the ulemvalvar was forming upon his lips.

"This gold-born boy," said Will, stepping forward and delivering the words in near-perfect Kamen. He gestured to the overly excited boy, Vaavo, whose sugar-induced mania had him climbing the bars of the gate. "He wish...wishes to see the..." Will had to stop a moment to conjure the right words or at least something that would do. "The window to the world."

The old man's frown and creased brow softened. He knew about the spoiled children of rich families and didn't care much for the brats. On the other hand, he also knew that by denying their wishes one risked reprisal. Even children of Vaavo's age could make life uncomfortable for a lowly retired valvar if the boy went whining to his parents. The gatekeeper found the key, grumbled to himself, and opened the gate. Ford could have kissed the old man, Will, and even the boy. Dizzy with excitement and forgetting himself, the sabre slipped from where he had it concealed between his arm and the side of his body as he ushered Will and Vaavo through the gate. The blade came within an inch of hitting the floor before he trapped it against his leg under the bearskin.

The gatekeeper eyed the sack Ford carried, looked the bearskins up and down, thought what a strange situation this was, and muttered a few words about irregularities. All would have been routine and he would not have been troubled in the least if only they had been sanitation slaves with a dung cart. The presence of a nobleman's son muddled his mind all the more. One thing he did know for certain, it would not take them long. They would have a look, see that there was nothing to see, smell the stench of the spilled slop, and feel the chill wind, and that would be the end of it. He tapped away at one of the bars with the key, as if counting down time until this was all over and he could go back home, settle into his chair, and see if he couldn't get in a nap before it was time to sleep.

Vaavo dashed through the gate and danced about before the grate waiting for it to be opened. Ford's hands being full, he nudged Will forward. "You'll have to open it, brother." After a glance back at the gatekeeper, he lowered his voice and went on, "And when you do, jump straight through headfirst. Fast as you can. I'll be on your heels."

The bar across the grate was heavy enough that Will had to tuck the flask under his arm to use both hands. The leather over the grate acted as a sail so that the wind blowing outside whipped it open upon its hinges with a tremendous squeal. Vaavo leapt in front of Will and stuck half his body out of the opening. The wind whipped his hair about and carried away his hoots and yelps. The temperature of the room plummeted and the old gatekeeper barked out a complaint which was buried by the whistle of the wind passing across the opening. A sinking feeling came over Ford and Will as they watched their plan being dashed at this crucial stage by the child blocking their escape route.

"No!" Ford bellowed as he lunged forward, seized the boy by the shoulders, and pulled him back. A clang of metal made them all look down to where the sabre had clattered upon the floor. The old man held up his oil lamp stared at the sword shining in the light. Disbelief crossed his face and then he let out a long, loud creaking cry for the ulemvalvar.

"Go!" Ford shouted. Will's thin frame dove through the narrow hole and his long gangly legs kicked like flippers until every last bit of him disappeared. Ford shoved the squirming boy into the old man and the two fell over one another. Grabbing up his sabre and the sack, he pushed them through the hole and shoved his head through. His broad shoulders and the fur covering them lodged in the opening. He backed out, tucked the bearskin about him tighter and made a run at it headfirst. Though it was a tight squeeze, this time he popped halfway through the hole and wriggled the rest of his body out. Something fell upon the back of his legs, like a sack of potatoes dropped from a height. He guessed it was the old valvar making a grab for him, but then Vaavo sang out a joyous cheer as they both began sliding down the slope at an alarming speed.

This was not the gradual slope that had been here when Ford last dumped waste down the chute. The gradient was much steeper now. Ford hadn't considered the effects of summer temperatures and was unaware of the procedure the Kamen used of occasionally pouring hot water down the chute to reduce buildup. The gradual slope was now a near vertical drop.

"This is the best day of my life!" Vaavo shouted as they shot down the hill. Ford felt sure this would be the last day of his life. If he wasn't pummeled to death by all of the bumps of lumpy solid waste frozen to the chute, then crashing into a stone building sitting directly in their path at the bottom of the hill would surely kill him.

The definitive u-shape of the chute at the top turned into a shallow depression of yellow ice the farther it went on, and it was funneling them straight at an archway in the side of the conical, domed building. The arch had no more than two feet of head room and looked too small for the both of them to fit through from what Ford could tell as he flew headfirst toward it. There was no way to stop or avoid the building. A moment before impact, he rolled over and pulled the flailing boy down. They slid through the archway into the building and crashed into Will.

"Are you hurt?" Ford asked, rolling over and releasing an agonized wheeze to ease the sharp sting in his tailbone and the revibrating twinge in his elbow. His fingers tenderly squeezed and prodded the sorest parts of himself searching for broken bones. The boy, whose landing had been softened by Ford's body, jumped up and began investigating the new location as if he were an explorer whose ship just landed at an exotic island.

"Nothing broken. I don't think at any rate," said Will, though his grimace and the way he rubbed one of his shoulders said different. "This poor fellow provided a buffer." He leaned back so Ford could see a shaggy-headed Kamen man in filthy clothes crumpled against the wall just behind him. The unconscious ruddy-cheeked man had a trickle of blood running from a cut along the crown of his head. As the lone attendant at this station, his job was to keep the sewerage channel clear. Much of his day was spent chipping away at urine-soaked ice and shoveling the chips from a trough at the end of the chute to a channel set at a right angle to the trough. This channel drained the refuse all the way down to the sea.

Ford shook clear his dazed head, took in hand a lit oil lamp tucked away in a wall nook, and crawled about the dank, stinking interior. On the shelf where the lamp had been there were spare wicks, flint and iron pyrites, wool, and a bottle of oil. "These will be useful," he said setting them aside to store in his sack, if he could find it again. Most of their possessions had scattered during the wild descent.

"Very much so, as I seem to have misplaced that handy, little warming rock," said Will patting the spot where he had stowed it upon his person. "I must have lost it on that unexpectedly exhilarating trip. You didn't warn me it would be so...so thrilling."

"Didn't expect it to be," said Ford as his search moved to a stone block being used as a small table. "It was never that steep before." He found a waterskin and an oily rag wrapped around bits of fatty meat. A pile of scrap metal, mostly bits and bobs discarded along with the waste water, had built up beside the trough. The rich often threw away broken items which the poor could find use for.

"What about him?" Will asked while kneeling beside the Kamen man and placing fingers upon his neck. "He lives yet."

Ford tore himself away from a stunted, grime-covered door he had discovered positioned along the wall between the chute and channel. Being as blackened as the walls, it blended in to the point of disappearing. Everything within the waste station was dark with filth. The two archways for the chute and channel let in a white light, but otherwise it was as dreary a place as any of them had ever been in. Ford sat by Will and searched the Kamen, finding nothing of value on him aside from his sealskin cloak. Will had his bearskin, but otherwise was not well-attired for the outdoors, so Ford gave him the short cloak to wear as a mantle under the fur. He then took the Kamen by the back of the neck and britches, carried him across the room, and sent him sliding out of the building through the channel archway.

Vaavo laughed at seeing the inert body slipping away. It was the only thing he enjoyed about his new surroundings. Having thoroughly nosed about the squalid station and discovered it did not please his nose, which wrinkled back into his curdling face, he was quite ready to leave.

"And the boy," said Will waving down Vaavo's initial squawks. "What do we do with him? We can't leave him."

Leaving the boy here sounded like a perfectly fine idea to Ford. Someone would come along and collect him soon enough. Then again, if they didn't, the boy would likely freeze to death. Vaavo hadn't done anything to deserve that. The little boy's lips were already blue. "Where does this lead?" he wondered in a flash of inspiration at seeing the small door in the wall between archways. If it led to somewhere safe and warm, or at least safer and warmer, they might trick Vaavo into it and shut the door behind him. It would be better than nothing. But getting the boy to do what you wanted was never easy.

Ford lifted the heavy bar keeping the door shut and pulled it open, revealing a cramped tunnel. It led down to the distant mining town of Drek. The people of Drek provided the small workforce needed for this station. Ford saw that the door could be barred from within as well as without. When a worker was on duty, they barred it on the outside. This helped keep slaves in and the more sinister of brute beasts out. When Ford swung the door open wide, Vaavo leapt in front of him to stare down the long dark tunnel on the other side. Before Ford laid a hand on the boy, Will lurched forward and shoved Vaavo through the opening. Instinctively, Ford slammed the door behind the child. He shot Will a look of surprise and then dropped the bar back in place.

"If an unpleasant thing has to be done, best to do it swiftly," Will said with a shrug of his shoulders.

Weak pounding and cries of complaint carried on from the other side of the door as they gathered up everything they could use and pushed it all through the archway before sliding out through the opening themselves. Outside they searched the ground for their lost possessions. The sack was located nearby, but neither the sabre nor the warm rock could be found. The gray stone, white ice and sullied snow to either side of the chute made up a mottled patchwork where small objects might disappear, and the pitted and veiny ground of the slope could hide such items in a crevice quite well. Ford darted this way and that in search of the blade.

"We shouldn't linger!" Will called over the wind. He didn't want to give up on finding the warm rock, but it wasn't much larger than a pebble and it could be anywhere.

"Help me find it!" shouted Ford. They would need to protect themselves. To his mind, the sword seemed vital to the success of their escape.

"We can't dally here! They could be upon us at any moment!" Already, high upon the side of the rock Dargkivi was built into, Kamen faces had poked from the hatchway at the top of the chute and were shouting down at them, their warnings lost to the wind. Will caught sight of them and pointed. "Look!" Ford saw the Kamen, saw reason, and the two fled southward away from the city.

Their feet slid over slick ground that dipped into a wide depression leading down to precipitous bluffs, which would flush them into the frozen sea if they lost their footing. Already Ford was ruing the loss of the sabre, which could have been used to stab into the ice to maintain traction. They climbed to a gentle knob of wind-blasted stone and ice in order to skirt the slippery depression. The hike took them a quarter of a mile out of their way inland before they were on level land. On the other side of the long, exposed rock, Will suddenly stopped for no reason that Ford could see. "What is it?" he bellowed through a spray of ice particles darting between them.

"I don't want to leave them behind!" Will shouted back.

"Leave who?"

"The others!" Will pointed toward Dargkivi. His words came out a tremor caused as much by his own misgivings as the wind penetrating his bearskin. If he had his way, they would save every enslaved soul trapped within that cold, hard rock.

"We can't go back!" Ford shouted as he took Will by the arm and pulled him closer, hoping his words might better sink in if there was no space between them. "They'd catch us and we wouldn't save anyone!" Queasiness overtook him at the very thought of being forced back into slavery. Images of the mines, the fighting pit, Dagmar, and Kaltzek shot through him like bolts of lightning. When the shudders passed, he added, "Not even ourselves!"

"I know, I know," said Will. Ford's distress could not have been more apparent to one as empathetic as he. And he knew his wish to save everyone was an impossibility, but it was something that had to come out of him. He returned Ford's grasp. "You're in the right. We're lucky to have got this far. And I thank you." Ford said nothing of his own desire to free every slave and burn Dargkivi to the ground. There was nothing more to be said.

Ford led the way over flat ice and rock. A mile's worth of dips and even deeper gullies hindered them from keeping up a steady pace. To stay on a southerly heading, they aimed for a trio of peaks looming in the distance. The air being so clear and the land colored in various shades of white, they didn't know whether they were looking at hills or mountains. The vaguely outlined points ahead might have been rock mounds a few hundred yards away for all they could tell.

"The important thing is, we're headed in the right direction!" Ford shouted through the wind back to Will. After a few more steps, he concluded, "I think."

An hour after the sun sank below the horizon, they toed up to a deep fissure in the ice too wide to leap. Cutting inland, they eventually found a passable spot where the fissure wasn't so deep and the escarpments to either side were scalable. Rocks had been piled waist high at the edge of the fissure and at the bottom they discovered a three-sided stone lean-to.

"It's Kamen built," said Ford.

"Must be," said Will of the squat structure. The doorway was so small they had to crawl through it on their hands and knees. Even less comfortable than the waste station, it was at least a shelter against storms, and more than one Kamen traveler had huddled here for warmth when caught by an unexpected squall. Ford and Will sat curled up in a corner each, quite cramped and still cold, but glad to be out of the cutting wind coming off the sea, at least for the time being.

While Ford had layers of clothing and good boots, Will was not nearly as prepared for their journey. He hadn't complained, but he was beginning to lose feeling in his toes. Ford guessed as much. No one could stand such unforgiving conditions for very long dressed in a bearskin loosely wrapped over a flimsy robe. Using this blessed reprieve from the battering elements, Ford distributed the clothes they had equally between them.

"I insist," he said when Will tried to decline out of some deep-seeded sense of politeness. However, once attired in Ford's extra clothing, Will was able to use the short Kamen cloak to wrap his feet and that relieved much of his discomfort.

"I feel like I could withstand whatever the winds wish to hurl at me," he said as heartily as Ford had ever heard him speak. "It's amazing what a little warmth will do for a body." They both felt a good deal better after resting a while and chewing on some of the fatty koer meat which had been meant to be the sanitation worker's mid-shift meal. "I confess, I didn't hold out much hope for our chances, but now I feel the spirit of possibility flowing through me."

"If luck's with us, we'll make good on this."

"I believe we shall. I believe we shall."

Their spirits were up and they would need to keep them up. After leaving the lean-to, the ascending land ahead grew rougher by the step. The broken terrain forced them either inland or toward the sea. They chose the sea in hopes that the smooth-looking frozen surface of the water might support their weight and make walking all the easier. They might also find seals, birds or some other form of sustenance. The chance seemed far likelier than in the barren wastelands inland.

A crack opening to a larger gorge allowed them to leap and crawl from rock to rock down to the seaside, where they found incredibly slow rolling waves dropping huge chunks of semi-frozen seafoam onto the beach. The sluggish undulations made it clear that the water's surface was far from solid and not safe to walk upon. As if to nail home this northern sea's inhospitality and the utter futility of relying upon it for any sort of relief, they saw not a single animal, not so much as a bird soaring in the distance. But something they did see spooked them.

"What kind of magic is this?" Ford pointed to the northeastern sky at a band of shimmering streaks of pale green light snaking above the clouds of a dimming night sky.

"I've no earthly idea," said Will. As they gazed upon it in wonder, the light seemed to writhe almost as if in concert with the sea.

"Do you think it's dangerous?"

"It could be some benevolent magic to light the evening. Or reflecting light, perhaps? Such as with the mirror in the tunnel in Rask."

"But is it a danger to us?" Ford asked again without taking his eyes off of the wondrous vision in the sky. A wave of eerily invisible-but-audible magic had been the undoing of a friend of his back home, and ever since then he had been more reticent of any kind of wizardry he did not understand. He was about to ask the question a third time when Will clutched at his elbow and drew his attention up the coast. There sat the Bay of Riches, the harbor at Dargkivi, looking not much farther away than when they first escaped down the chute. Ford breathed in deep to steady himself from the shock, and then exhaled forcefully, as if he might expel the wretched feelings welling up within him at the sight of the despised place.

"I thought we were farther away than that," he said.

Without another word between them, they left the sea for an inland route and hastened southward. After a mile, their hectic pace slowed to a plodding walk. They felt spent. Every direction but backwards was now leading them uphill. They knew it, but didn't realize how steadily steep the increase in the incline was. Anyone could have been deceived by the gradual rise of this ill-defined landscape. Not until they found themselves in the midst of rugged foothills and blundered to the edge of a cliff overlooking the sea far below them did they get the sense of having climbed hundreds of feet higher. They pressed on, loath to take even a single step back toward Dargkivi,.

"My legs, they feel as if they may give out," Will admitted sometime in the middle of the night. The admission slipped from him in warning that he might drop at any given moment, rather than any desire to stop. If Ford wanted to press on, he was right there with him, for as far as his legs would take him.

"Mine burn as well," said Ford.

With the Kamen still so close and a search party no doubt trailing them, neither wished to stop. However, they could not go on forever. Sleep must come soon. By morning's approach, their eyes often closed of their own accord and they were all but crawling on their knees. When either spoke, it was to mutter supplication from any being within earshot. It seemed Gwency, the Goddess of Luck, heard their prayers and put them in the path of what meager shelter could be conjured in such inhospitable lands: the convergence of two massive boulders, beneath which a cavity provided enough room for two to curl up in and comfortably tuck themselves away from the elements and searching eyes.

"Getting out of the wind feels like climbing into mothers' arms," said Will while they fought with stiff fingers to light their oil lamp. Ford couldn't recall such a feeling, but he understood what Will meant. Relief from the relentless beating wind gave their bodies a chance to warm themselves.

"Everything will go well with us, as long as we stay warm," said Ford, his eyes glazing over as he stared into the lamp's tiny flame.

"And dry," said Will. "You remember escaping the island, when crossing the water and the poor soul who fell from the boat and succumbed? Being cold is bad. Cold *and* wet is dangerous."

"That's why I went and got you, to keep us warm!" Ford said it with a smile, but immediately realized how unkind it sounded. Also, it wasn't the entire truth. "One of the reasons," he amended.

"The other?"

"I owe you."

Will often took time to consider questions and answer, but it didn't take him long to ponder over this. "Owing one weighs heavily upon you, doesn't it?"

"Never owe a man when you don't have to."

"Some say giving is better than the receiving, but you don't always have to feel obliged to give in return for something you receive, especially in acts of kindness."

"Saving my life was more than an act of kindness."

"Well then, you are generous in your thanks," said Will, cracking a smile and rubbing his hands over the lamp flame.

Ford began heating strips of meat taken from the Vanagz larder. After a mouthful each, they laid on their sides, wrapped their arms around their knees and fell asleep almost instantly.

"I'm awake! I'm awake!" Ford remonstrated at the hand shaking his shoulder. It was only Will. He had woken in a panic, not knowing how long they had slept and fearing it had been too long. Fear of being recaptured roused Ford from slumber faster than ever before. They broke camp in a mad bustle and scurried out of their hole.

Both of them ached from head to toe, but of the two, Will felt worse. His muscles had seized up from so much walking the previous day. Being in far better condition, Ford made a point of scouting ahead and being the one who took those few extra steps necessary to insure they were on as direct and smooth a path as possible. For his part, Will forced one foot in front of the other again and again, refusing to be a burden. Loose stones and slick ground conspired against him, but he kept pace as best he could, falling no farther behind than shouting distance.

They fared better the following day. Will's aching muscles became more accustomed to the strain. Also, they happened upon a long and winding snow-covered lake, which Ford was determined to cross lengthwise. The lure of a flat, unimpeded surface for as far as the eye could see was too great to pass up. "It will take us farther faster."

"If you think it's safe," Will said while taking his first tentative steps away from shore.

"There'll be ice under there thicker than my skull. Sure it's safe!" Ford gave his forehead a rap as assurance. The granular snow crunched and compacted under their feet. The ice held. The ice would have held the entire population of Rikaswelt, but the two travelers couldn't know its thickness under the layer of snow which would retain their tracks for weeks to come as a memory of their passing.

After the lake, they found other waterways, but the foothills threw up impenetrable crags and precipitous embankments which rendered most of these captive tarns inaccessible. Peaks became impassable, climbing in and out of canyons impossible. Great rifts of ice and rock forced them farther inland. A day passed in which they barely made a mile of southing. Worse yet, their supplies were running low.

"At least water's easier to come by," said Will. A lift in temperature created enough thawing at midday so that they were able to pack their skins with snow. The shelter of increasingly common rocky nooks and crevices was another consolation.

"But we're being driven up and up the mountains," said Ford when they halted upon an outcropping to get their bearings. "Didn't mean for it to happen, but we can't seem to avoid 'em."

"They spring up around us like blades of grass in summer," said Will. No matter which way they turned, the prongs of the peaks stood in their way. The mountains grew in breadth as the miles passed and their shoulders spread about them from the east to the west. The two travelers still caught glimpses of the sea now and then between the crags and boulders, though it was distant.

Both men were loath to leave it, for the sea was a link to the world beyond, to home.

On a night when the strange lights in the sky disappeared behind the suffocating gray Rikaswelt clouds, Ford and Will stumbled upon a loose-stone structure akin in style to the Kamen lodges near Siltsvesi, only taller. The doorway was covered in a tanned hide held in place by stones. Ford broke up the ice binding the stones together, yanked back the makeshift door, and ducked into a rectangular room, narrowly confining and reminiscent of a tomb. Neither complained. There was adequate headroom and plenty of floor space to sleep stretched out. Small gaps between the stones let in a hiss of wind, but it didn't blow hard enough to stop Will from lighting a fire in the lodge's small but serviceable hearth. A sack tucked in a nook containing balls of hairy dry lichen provided the tinder and two bricks of peat stacked by the door made up all the fuel they had to burn. No trees grew in these parts, so it was more than they could have hoped for. The lodge alone was more than they could have hoped for.

"I don't suppose we should stay here long," said Will. Each word dropped from his lips in a descending tone mirroring his flagging strength. He would have been happy to stay here for a good long while.

Ford shook his head. "The longer we stay, the greater the chance they track us down."

"True." Will sighed. It seemed to him that he was dredging his last reserves of strength. He would go on summoning what will was left within him for as long as he could, but it couldn't last. His body was still in recovery, for his time in Dargkivi had been the stuff of nightmare. While Ford had been ill-used by the Kamen, Will had been intentionally brought to the brink of death time and again during their tests of his divine gifts.

Ford was not unaware. At various times since setting off, the wind billowed the layers draped over Will's shoulders to reveal the cut marks and scorched skin of his arms. He never said anything, never asked for the precise details behind the wounds, because he had taken plenty of his own and he did not wish to relive the memories, nor inflict the burden upon another. Likewise, Will didn't ask where Ford had gotten the raw marks around his neck and wrists. They had both been through a lot and nothing need be said.

"Looks like nobody's been here for a good long while," said Ford. He would have gladly stayed in the lodge to rest and recover if they were a thousand miles farther away without a chance of recapture by the Kamen, but that was wishful thinking. "We'll warm ourselves and go."

However, knowing a truth and acting upon it when mind and body want to shut down is an entirely different matter. The crackles of the lichen taking light evoked warmth. When the smoking peat gave off something like the real thing, however trifling, they huddled close to the smoldering brick, encircling it with their palms and pressing the tips of their cold noses close for as long as they could before turning away to breathe. Even if it didn't truly warm them through and through, the smell of smoke and its association to a roaring fire, helped subdue their shivering.

Ford's eyes drooped and his head nodded forward while they burned through the brick. He was nearly out when Will broke the silence and dragged him from the brink of a welcome slumber. "How can one man sell another?" It was a question posed as much to the air as to Ford.

"Huh?"

"I don't understand why man cannot live peaceably together. Why do they treat each other's lives with such contempt?"

Ford glanced from the peat brick to Will and caught a glassy glimmer in his companion's eyes. The watery glaze might have been caused by the smoke, but Ford doubted it. "I don't know. I don't know," was the best reply he could come up with in the moment. Will's ideas encompassed a larger concept than he could comprehend. The injustice of it all had pricked the simple Aelwydian warrior's ire the moment they had been sold into slavery, but he lacked Will's erudition and eloquence. His mode of expression, had he the chance, would have been to bash a few Kamen heads and be done with them. He lacked art, not the heart.

While smoke filled the lodge, dense reverie fogged their minds. Neither sensed the approaching footsteps until the flap over the door pulled back. Into the rectangular daylight of the doorway stepped a figure so thoroughly clad in fur from head to foot that they couldn't tell for certain it was human. A furry hood pulled tight hid the face. Whatever the race, a hideous sculpin, all spines and mouth, strung from a belt, indicated a fisherman. Then again, the belt also held the curved blade of a scimitar. The figure staggered back a step. The scimitar flashed out and was leveled at them.

Chapter 20
Under and Over

The wielder of the leveled scimitar jerked its hooded head left to right, looking for others and gauging the danger. The sword did not have a large blade, nor did it gleam with a razor-sharp edge, yet it was nonetheless a deadlier weapon than anything Ford and Will possessed. They remained crouched by the fire holding out their empty hands to show they meant no harm. There was nothing else they could do. The ragged figure framed in the doorway, clad in furs worn thin over time and matted with fish gore, could have been human, or some form of humanoid, but whether brutish and savage or kindly and benevolent remained to be seen.

"We apologize for trespassing. We meant no offense," said Will as steadily and agreeably as he could muster in the face of the blade's looming threat. When he received no response, he tried again, but in Kamen. The mute figure swayed, whether from the words or wind they couldn't tell. The scimitar rose, described an arc in the air, and was stowed back in its belt. And just like that, empty and uplifted palms were displayed all around. The new arrival's gloved hands went through a series of dumbshow gestures from mouth to stomach. They had to assume a mouth, because a kind of scarf covered the lower half of a face otherwise shrouded in a furry hood.

"Is this a promise of food?" wondered Ford, much relieved at the prospect. The subject was never far from his mind, especially now with their limited provisions and untold miles of snow and ice-covered land to cross ahead of them.

"I believe so, unless we're wildly mistaken," said Will. The sudden appearance in these desolate lands of someone who wanted to feed them seemed like astonishingly good luck. He looked at the figure as an answer to his prayers and nodded while patting his belly to show he understood. Ford clung to his suspicions, having developed a mistrust of anyone since his enslavement. Even so, they couldn't pass up a free meal and any other aid this person might be able to lend them in their escape, so he nodded and patted his belly, too.

They were motioned to follow and so they did, from the shelter down into a valley, then higher to a thin ridge on the far side. Nothing was said between them and both parties kept their distance. At one point, Ford nudged Will and pointed out the unusually wide feet of their host, but otherwise they followed behind quietly and respectfully. Upon cresting the ridge, they found a glacier valley on the other side. This half-mile wide river of ice stretched beyond sight in either direction. Its pitted and jagged surface looked a misery to cross.

"We'll have to travel well inland to pass this," said Ford.

"I don't think we intend to. See," said Will with a nod ahead to where their host had picked up a footpath passing parallel alongside the sheer wall of the glacier rising above.

On this side of the valley, the glacier and the land it rode upon separated from one another for the span of a few hundred feet. Ford and Will watched their footing on the broken slate detritus of the path. A slip or a rock slide might send them all on a rough trip right under the glacier shelf. Neither of them wanted to find out how that would end. The path terminated at a stairway which cut into the earth and plunged beneath the glacier through a crack in the ice. The crack had been chiseled into a larger, serviceable tunnel.

"I've never seen the like," said Will in a childlike voice floating away in amazement. Their host encouraged them with a wave and led the way to show it was safe. They delved into the glacier itself. Sunlight shone through the walls of the tunnel, illuminating the bubbly, gel-like texture of the sparkling ice, which ran from white to a richer blue hue, the color growing darker as the stairs went deeper.

"This is a sight for the gods!" Ford exclaimed as he took in the underside of the ice flow.

"I've never seen…" said Will quite lost in awe.

"A sight for the gods," Ford echoed. As his words trailed away, a boom followed by a sharper snap made them both jump.

"The ice cracking perhaps?" wondered Will as they looked to one another for answer. Their host had taken no notice of it, so they did the same.

The tunnel began as an arch, but the farther they went the more shapes it took on, shapes as much dependent upon handcrafted measures as glacial stratification. At one point they found themselves squeezing through a crack so steeply angled that they had to lay on one side and slide against the wall to get through. After that, the steps were no longer made of rock, but rather cut out of the ice itself. Ford and Will lost their footing repeatedly, but not their host, whose rudimentary crampons clung to each step.

The stairway of ice ended when the tunnel leveled out and funneled them into an oval-shaped cavern with a domed ceiling, like an enormous air pocket. To enter the cavern, one had to duck beneath a large shelf-like sheet of slate which must have weighed tons. It had been carried by the glacier and now sat above their heads like a doorway lintel. Half of the slate was still encased in the ice, the other half jutted out into the cavern. If much more melting took place the rock would come crashing down. Ford and Will rushed past it and into the cavern. Once in the cavern, they noticed that along the walls and up through the ceiling they could see numerous rocks similar to the piece of slate trapped in the ice as if suspended in midair, like surreal planets or gray clouds.

The floor looked far less celestial, but enough sunlight filtered down through the ice to make out a bed of smooth rock and rounded stone. Water spouted from between two boulders against the base of one wall into a pot with a protruding lip, which caught the water, filled, and spilled over. The spillage trickled across the floor, disappearing among the rocks and reemerging thirty feet away at a small pool. A rivulet slowly drained from the pool into the vanishing darkness of another tunnel on the far side of the cavern. From the ceiling of this farther tunnel, a few long and thin crystal stalks with branch blooms hung down like small inverted leafless trees. Next to the pool, an oval piece of slate had been propped upon stones to make a table that appeared to be used for filleting. Strips of drying fish flesh had been stacked to one side of the table. Under it were a dozen or so clay pots. Behind the table, a midden of bones was piling up against the wall.

Their host threw down his fish and initially made for the farther tunnel, but then stopped. Though they hadn't seen his face and no words were exchanged between them, they had decided he must be male after a loose stone turned his ankle and he let loose a deep and gruff grunt.

"I don't think he entertains many guests," Will whispered to Ford.

"But somebody else lives here with him," said Ford, whose eyes had adjusted to the low light and had caught sight of five greasy waterskins laid flat on their sides near the water spout. There were also a few long, stuffed sacks laid out like bedrolls wherever the ground appeared least lumpy.

With a perfunctory sweep of a gloved hand, their host bid them sit down where they wished. He then picked up a clay pot, propped it atop the table, and removed its lid. Since there were no chairs, Will moved to take a seat upon one of the sacks, but Ford arrested him by the arm. The rotten egg stench of fermented fish coming from the clay pot had filled the cavern and turned Ford's stomach. Will caught the repulsive sulfur smell a moment later.

Just then, footsteps approached from somewhere deeper within the glacier. Their fur-clad host barked out a string of harsh exclamations in a guttural language as, from the ice tunnel on the other side of the cavern, another figure garbed in matted furs emerged. The newcomer's hood was thrown back. The lower half of its face was wrapped in a filthy rag. The top of its bare head was covered in stringy hair and strikingly rough, gray skin dotted with moles. It strutted into the cavern raising a four-fingered salutation as it swung its sharp shoulders with each confident stride. The newcomer's jovial welcome vanished at the sight of unexpected guests.

Ford leapt forward, reached down, and drew forth the scimitar from their host's belt, then whipped it back in a high arcing swing that tore through the fur and opened a gushing gash along the side of his neck. Blood spurted across the cavern and splattered against the ice wall. The victim of the murderous blow spun around and reached for the blade. He wavered after one faltering step, his eyes rolled back, and he collapsed upon the rocks. It occurred so quickly that to Will it seemed like a single fluid motion.

The newcomer, an insubstantial youth, let loose a howling war cry and yanked the rag from his face to reveal a jawless maw. Only a flap of skin hung over a small plate-shaped bone where a jaw should be. The telltale Skala mouth flashed a ghastly half grin even as his cry carried on. Unphased by a sight and scare tactic known to him, Ford howled back, slashed the curving blade of the scimitar through the air between them and charged. The Skala pulled out a small gutting knife, the only weapon he had equipped just then, and pointed it at Ford for a moment before fleeing back down the dark tunnel from which he came.

Ford chased the Skala into the tunnel, smashing the inverted ceiling crystals with the top of his head and casting a shower of shards across the floor. The darkness descended upon him with the shocking suddenness of a strangler's grasping hand stealing breath. He might run straight into anything down here and not realize it until too late. He couldn't even be sure of his own footing. "Ford! Ford!" Will's calls returned him to reason. Ford halted. With one hand on a wall to catch himself from falling in the dark upon the slippery ground, he listened to the cries of the young Skala disappearing into the distance, then turned, and headed back.

"Gather what you can!" he shouted at Will as he loped into the cavern. The instructions had to be driven home with a second shout before they shattered his companion's state of shock and initial abhorrence of the sudden carnage. Will was not a man born to violence, although, the more time he spent with Ford, the more he learned the necessity of force in a world that could be dishearteningly cruel.

While Ford kept watch on the dark tunnel for fear more Skala were on the way, Will darted about the cavern frantically filling their sack with dried fish, the waterskins, a spare spool of fishing line, and whatever else he thought might be useful. He even ripped open a bedroll and used it as a sack of his own.

"Take the shoe spikes off his feet too," Ford instructed.

Will pulled the crampons from the bottom of the Skala's boots and called back, "I think that's everything!"

Ford stalked back through the cavern and kicked over the pots of fermented fish. A fetid cloud erupted into the already putrid air. It made them gag, but he had no regrets. The blood-letting and this little act of retaliation relieved some of his pent-up hatred of the Skala for having sold them into slavery.

"Back up the passage!" he shouted as he led them out of the Skala lair with his sack slung over his shoulder. Will followed on his heels, grabbing up the bearskin that had slipped unnoticed from Ford's shoulder and casting glances back to make sure they weren't being pursued.

The light of day temporarily blinded them when they reached the top of the stairs and began climbing the path along the side of the valley parallel to the flow of the glacier. There was only one way out: back the way they had come. The steep-sided ridge hemmed them in. Ford forged on with his head bowed to keep an eye on his footing where the loose rock was most treacherous.

"Ford!" Will cried out. Where the path led over the hill crest some two hundred yards ahead, three Skala were coming straight for them. There was no way around, no alternative path. Ford dropped everything but the scimitar. He thought he could take them. Only one appeared as large as the Skala warriors who had attacked their ship so many months ago. The other two were no bigger than the Skala he had scared off. The narrow path by the lair's entrance, where the edge of the glacier and valley wall nearly kissed, left little room to maneuver. Wedged in here he might swing his blade and take them on one at a time. It could work, as long as they bore no bows or others weapons which might strike from afar. The sight of a spearhead silhouetted against the sky sank his spirits. The Skala slowed and then stopped. The largest, a warrior clad in gray skins and a horn-topped helm, pointed down at them and raised the Skala war cry.

"Down!" Will shouted as he headed back into the glacier. Ford was loath to retreat into the lair of the enemy, but that spear would skewer him before he could get in a single swing of his short blade. Seeing no better option, he followed Will.

The three Skala sprinted down the footpath into the valley and alongside the glacier. The largest of them led the way, as was fitting for the clan's Tarken Hoof, a title bestowed to Skala chiefs. His leathery fists had fought for everything he had ever gained. Spilled blood built his ancestry. The spear Ford thought the chief carried was actually a solid iron spike with a long shaft used as a chisel to break ice. It worked as well for bludgeoning. The other two less-substantial Skala chasing after the Tarken Hoof were scouts and fishermen. One of them hefted a heavy hammer, used for beating the spike through frozen lake surfaces. He took a practice swing on the go. One could easily imagine the hammer making a head-crushing blow that would impress the chief and garner the warrior esteem among the clan. The smallest of the three dropped their catch and fishing gear to draw her knife.

The Skalas' howls echoed through the tunnel as they tromped down the steps toward the cavern. Their calls reached their clanmates in the deeper recesses of the lair to alert them of the prey in their midst. It wasn't often these landbound Skala had the opportunity to capture potential slaves. Gifts had fallen in their laps and they did not want them to slip away.

The Tarken Hoof skidded to a halt in the tunnel under the hanging slate shelf before entering the cavern and the other two fell in behind him. At the back of the cavern, a bear rising up on its hind legs and clawing at the air stole away their courage with a menacing, but oddly high-pitched growl. Something was off with the bear's underside. It looked more like the cloth of robes and cloaks rather than fur. The chief bellowed a command and all three Skala dove into the cavern to attack the phony bear. Ford leapt down upon them from the slate shelf over the doorway, but his ill-timed ambush missed and the swipe of his scimitar hardly grazed the chief's back. Instead, he landed upon the hammer-wielding Skala, driving the warrior's body into the ground and his head onto a rock. Skala eyes blazed with surprise and indignation that slaves-to-be would have the audacity to attack them, the master race of these lands. Even lesser landbound Skala as these felt the predators' pride of their piratical seafaring bothers. The cavern rang with war cries and hisses through flapping lower lips.

Ford struggled to one knee and swung at the chief. His clumsy two-handed swing, like a man chopping down a tree, was easily dodged. A sting to his back jerked him upright. He spun about, whipping the blade around with a backhand swipe that overshot the female, the shortest of the Skala. She ducked and shoved her stubby blade into Ford's layered fur and cloth. Ford picked her up by the neck and drove his enemy backwards into the ice wall.

Above the tumult rattling about the cavern and distorting Ford's senses, a screaming tiger's roar from behind jolted him to his core and left him paralyzed. The primal fear he could fight back, but when he tried to face the danger, he couldn't turn around. His feet would not budge, nor any other part of him. The hold on him was complete. The Skala female remained within his grasp, but loosely. A child could have broken free, but she stayed put, gripped by the same bewitching paralysis that held Ford. He feared the chief's inevitable attack from behind, from where the ceaseless roar drilled into the back of his skull, but he could do nothing to prevent it. He couldn't even let his body collapse upon the ground.

The unearthly dissonance blared away from a gnarled and flared seashell that the Skala chief had pressed to his lips. His strangely elastic lower lip reached up like a finger from his chinless bottom jaw to clamp about the shell. He blew through a hole at one end and the blast came out of a trumpet-like aperture pointed directly at Ford's back. To everyone else within earshot, to the sides or behind, the roar was nothing more than the distant snarl of a housecat. Only those in the path of the blast felt its true power.

By order of a Tarken Hoof of ages past, the shell had been imbued with a shaman's magic to entrance and arrest bodies in motion. That one of the current chief's fellow clansmen had been caught in the shell's cone of effect was an unfortunate but frequent side effect in the fury of battle. The Tarken Hoof deemed it a fair price for subduing such a dangerous foe as this pale barbarian from over the seas, who had already killed one of his warriors and now wielded his scimitar.

When the Skala burst into the cavern, Will stood at the back doing his best bear impression. It wasn't convincing. To the Skala, he appeared weaponless and inconsequential. They had ignored him to focus on Ford. Now, one Skala lay lifeless on the ground and another was entranced, and yet the chief still had command of the situation. He gripped the seashell at his lips in one hand, hefted his iron spike high above his head in the other, and aimed for the back of Ford's skull. The clink of loose, trodden rocks recalled to mind the shrinking dog in the back of the cavern. The Tarken Hoof twisted about, ready to deliver another war cry that would cower the craven, weaponless one or perhaps end the annoyance entirely with a thrust of his weapon. His head came around and Will plowed into his ribs, knocking the shell from the chief's lips and the wind from his lungs. They pitched forward together onto the rocks. The sharp shock of knees and elbows smacking stone shot through Will's limbs. He rolled and tried to rise, but his fingers were pinched between stone and bone. Something prodded his back. The three fingers and thumb of a Skala hand mined for his throat. Will rammed his one free knee up into something solid, but to no effect. A gurgle escaped him and then nothing more. The scant air left him would be all he ever breathed again, of this he felt sure. His arms and legs thrashed at random, trying to break the pincher grip upon his throat or beat back his attacker. The top of his head knocked against the stones. The cold abrasion of wet rock against cheek accompanied the darkening of the cavern. The friction dulled, the darkness deepened, and all went black.

Womb warmth. A coddling comfort. The stunning cold trauma of birth. Will reawakened to the harsh world in a fit of jerky seizures that soon subsided and found himself within Ford's arms. His immense companion had him half off the ground, as if he planned on carrying him out of the cavern if need be.

The Skala bodies lay strewn across the ground. Ford caught his flickering eye and shouted, or rather had been shouting, Will realized.

"More are on the way!"

"How do you know," Will slurred. He didn't really doubt it and hadn't even meant to ask. In his groggy state, it simply tumbled out of him.

"I can hear them!" Ford hoisted Will onto his feet and left him wobbling there while he picked through the bodies with one hand and held the scimitar at the ready with the other. "Take what you can with all haste! We can't stay here!"

Will steadied himself, he wasn't in a condition to do much else. His fingers wrapped around the hammer pressed into his hands. The ice chisel was too cumbersome to bother with and the magic seashell was forgotten where it lay obscured among the stones. Ford had never seen the shell, so he didn't know what to look for and Will was too dazed to think straight and search for the valuable item. Ford shoved the Skala chief's helm onto his head and made for the exit.

"This way!"

Will followed on stiff, tottering pegs for legs. They snatched up their sacks from the steps on the fly and stuffed the fish into them which the Skala had dropped, then fled the Skala lair, scattering loose pebbles and causing mini landslides that disappeared under the glacial shelf. Angry shrieks speared their ears from the mouth of the tunnel behind them. Ford stopped at the top of the hill and looked back. Will was catching up. A pair of Skala faces peered out from the mouth of the tunnel. Another two joined them. Knives were brandished and the tip of a spindly javelin caught the light.

"Come no closer!" Ford growled and barked at the Skala, as if they were wild animals badgering his flock and he meant to scare them off. It seemed to be working. The Skala hovered no more than a step or two away from the tunnel. After Will overtook him, Ford swiped at the air a few times with his scimitar. "Be gone! Be gone or be cut down!"

Ford and Will ran eastward along the ridge. They passed a conical boulder which stood out from the rest. It bore a line of runes and an etching of a war hammer with a head resembling a seashell. Farther on, in a rocky dell below them, the remains of an abandoned encampment poked out of a slate scree. They hadn't noticed any of this on the way in, but now signs of the Skala appeared everywhere.

From what Ford and Will had known of them, the Skala were a seafaring race, so they turned away from the coast and headed inland. The idea was sound, but upon mounting the next ridge after a slight dip, they found themselves staring down at a broad lake several hundred yards away covered in ice-fishing Skala. The distant figures stood or crouched over their holes in ones and twos spread out across the entire lake. The closest of them unbent his crooked back and waved an arm over his head. Others noticed and joined in. Soon the entire lake's worth of Skala had acknowledged them.

"Oh dear," said Will. His knee buckled and he had to catch himself from falling.

"There must be close on a hundred of them," said Ford.

"If they come for us…"

Ford measured the distance from where he stood down to the lake and then looked around him at the miles of barren landscape. There were hills and valleys, but no tree cover, nothing to disappear into. Their options were few. They might outrun some of the Skala, they might even fight a few of them off, but they would never survive a full-on attack by the whole clan.

"Walk on," he murmured. With their heads down, they kept up a steady pace along the wind-blasted, slate-strewn ridge paralleling the lake, ignoring the salutes all the while.

"They're not coming for us. They're only waving. Should we acknowledge them?" Will whispered.

"Walk on."

Ford might have been only half as wise as Will, but something in his gut told him this was the right course of action. Will didn't disagree. After all, it was working. As soon as they were able to pass over the glacier, they left the ridge and the lake behind, ducking out of sight of the Skala and making a dash for it in a southerly direction.

"The helm," Will said when they finally slowed their pace, more out of necessity than desire. He had stopped for a breather on an incline between what appeared to be a pair of steps. The squared off rock might have been natural. Its uneven surfaces seemed too rough to be manmade. Either way, smooth edges indicated where feet might fall and told them that the Skala came this way frequently.

"What about it?" Ford wondered, pulling off the fur-wrapped and horn-topped helm to give it a closer look.

"I think it saved us. They must have thought you were him, the one who wore it before."

"I don't look as ugly as all that, I do?" Ford asked with a shadow of a smile.

"From a distance, anything is possible."

Running into the horde of Skala at the lake left them wondering whether to keep to the heights or stay down in the valleys. To see or not be seen. They couldn't hike through the length of this land along its ridges, where they stood out like a pair of twinkling stars in an otherwise empty night sky. Yet, the need to know what lie ahead was of the utmost importance. If they didn't, they risked walking straight into a valley full of Skala. Who knew how many more there were out there and where their lairs might lie? While they thought it over, the aches and pains of battle began to sink in. Will's head throbbed and Ford still felt a phantom hold over his body. In the end they opted to do both, occasionally cresting a hill to spy ahead and then slinking back down to less conspicuous paths at lower elevations.

After traversing more hills and valleys, passing a pair of frozen tarns devoid of fishermen, and seeing no sign of Skala at all, their confidence rose enough to walk across a five-mile-long lake upon its smooth black ice. The opportunity to devour so many miles over a flat surface was too good to pass up. They strapped on the crampons taken from the Skala and dug the metal cleats into the ice to keep from slipping. A gathering wind that had helped push them over the tops of the last two hills now came screaming down the valley, ripping through them and plowing directly toward a massive blue-tinted wall of ice at the far end of the lake, where streaming clouds coalesced from thin air into vertical white ribbons flinging themselves over the cliffside and reaching into the sky, adorning it with swiftly swirling braids. The gale shoved at their backs with such force that they had to lean into it and dig their spiked shoes into the ice just to stay upright. Even so, Ford ended up using the point of his sword as a pike to stick into the ice. His new helm blew off more than once. The first time he retrieved it. The second time he let it go. No great loss, he mused. The thing didn't fit well and its horn kept him from using his bear head as a hood. Besides, it stank and reminded him of the Skala, which he didn't want. Will fell down repeatedly, sometimes violently. Both legs would slip out from under him and he would land on his back. After his fifth collapse he stayed down.

"What is it? What's wrong?" Ford worried Will had broken something, but his shouts could not compete with the wailing wind.

"Sit down! Sit down and let go," Will shouted back. He tried to explain the idea that had come to him, but Ford didn't catch all of what was said and didn't understand what he did hear. Will demonstrated. Sitting on his backside, he spread his arms wide and lifted his feet from the ice. The bearskin draping from his arms and tucked under his legs caught the wind and soon he was creeping away. Then he began sliding quite quickly, faster than they could walk. Ford got down and, after struggling against the wind and having his bearskin nearly ripped from his grasp, he joined Will in a ride across the lake that matched the terrifying slide down the waste chute for speed and exhilaration. They left behind long gouges in the ice from where they dug in with their crampons to brake and steer. The wind whipping over their eyes drew tears, but they cried for joy and laughed aloud, too, as the miles flew by. Traceable marks were being left behind, but they didn't care. With the traces, they were leaving behind the horrors of the north.

The sun hit the sheer, towering wall of ice and cast off dazzling shimmers of white and blue bright beyond the mortal eye's endurance. As they approached, they pulled in their arms, shielded their eyes, and dug in their spikes, hoping to slow down and avoid dashing their brains against the wall, but the wind thrust them on. Ford flipped onto his belly and dragged the tip of his scimitar along the surface. Will did the same, but with his hammer and with less success. The wind blew his lighter body like an autumn leaf, tumbling over and over. He flipped onto his back to see how close the wall was. The sun no longer reflected off of the cliff into their faces at this closer angle, so he could make out dark forms in the ice, like vague splotches of paint upon a white wall. Bodies, dozens of them, hovered above with outstretched arms like a welcoming party of ominous specters. A few feet before the wall, built-up snowdrift corralled them both. It deadened the impact for Ford, but Will was swept up the drift and the wall a few feet before somersaulting back down onto the crusted snow, luckily none the worse for wear.

"Do you see this?" Ford shouted, while they fought to their feet and stared up into the ice.

"Yes!"

"What are they?" As near as the closest body was to the cliff face, they could not definitively determine if it was human through the distorting lens of the encasing ice.

"Not one of *them*," said Will referring to the Skala. Race and gender could only be guessed at, but the closest appeared to be a woman in a drab frock. Her long dark hair was caught forever in flowing waves. Her arms were not stretched toward them as they originally imagined, but rather uplifted in the attitude of one reaching for the sky in supplication to gods beyond the clouds. A few others had been locked in this posture, but many were suspended in frozen space curled in a ball or on all fours. Most were buried too deep within the ice to be anything more than vague shapes. They could do nothing and nothing could be done for them.

"There's something unnatural about all this," said Ford, pushing himself back from the ice.

"They are quite inanimate," Will assured him before giving one last look and turning away from the perfectly-preserved remains of a small unfortunate band caught in the wrong place at the wrong time. Trapped by a landslide or flood, he guessed.

The unrelenting wind kept them pressed against the base of the ice wall until they reached the edge of the lake, where a scalable incline ascended into the hills once more. After the first ridge, they passed along a ravine and saw at the bottom a crumbling pile of stones containing what looked like a doorway. It may have been another lodge, but they never bothered to investigate. A comfortable harbor from the wind and cold beside a nice fire would have been pleasant for a spell, but they didn't dare stop, not after their previous encounter at a similar lodge. And of course, building a fire was out of the question, what with the inherent risk of rising smoke giving them away. Besides, they had no fuel to burn.

"Oil's running low, as well," said Will trying to see into the flask during a quick stop to rest their weary legs and make an inventory of supplies.

"We're running low on everything," said Ford with his head buried in a sack. "Everything but rocks, ice, hills and mountains."

Not long after, those troublesome hills quite abruptly died away and turned into what appeared to be an utterly flat plain for as far as could be seen on that overcast day. Behind them and to their left and right, the long march of coastal mountains continued unimpeded, but ahead the panorama offered nothing more than an unfathomable white void topped with a dull gray sky.

"Such limitless ambiguity," said Will in an awed voice. "It's as if we stand upon the precipice of a plane of nonexistence. Limbo." Only the stratified furrows of a cloud mass retreating to the southeast broke up the monotony. "It must be the Jatti Valley."

His memory of a map glimpsed along with Cadogan during their brief respite between imprisonment and slavery was sound. This was that broad basin between the Zoudenz Mountains paralleling the coast and a massif known as Heikki Linna to the east. Heikki Linna was nowhere near as imposing as the Zoudenz, but the massif's oblong whirlpool-like swirl of rock, as a soaring bird might see it, lent a more than adequate helping hand in cupping the land's water and channeling it into the Aarne River. Near where Ford and Will stood, the basin collected mere trickles into an innocuous, whispering stream. It slipped through the middle of the valley under thawing ice and snow, rarely bubbling to the surface. The two travelers saw no river or stream. All that caught their eye was the blissful lack of hills and mountains.

"No rocks for those rotten fish-eaters to hide behind," said Ford. He and Will stood on the side of a barren slope a thousand feet above the valley floor. Anger welled within him just thinking about the Skala, but he said no more. If he were alone, he would have screamed to the heavens for release. Instead, he held back such unbridled emotion and stole a glance at Will, wondering if any of his inner turmoil had been detected. His anger melted away at the sight of his companion. Will's flushed cheeks and raised eyebrows made him appear almost whimsically pleased. All the corners of his face were upturned.

"No rocks," Will murmured barely loud enough to be heard. He laughed a soft amused titter at the thought that this vast open stretch of white nothingness ahead of them was clear of Skala and perhaps did not belong to anyone but themselves for the time it took them to cross it.

"What do you find funny?"

"All this open land, all to ourselves."

Ford allowed this to sink in and carry him with a lighter heart and step alongside his cheerful companion the rest of the way down the hill. Both men looked forward to stretching their long legs over open country. And they did, covering far greater distances over a fraction of the time spent in the mountains. The going was easy and the weather fine. If anything, they found it too warm when the sun was at its peak. The worst of it was the blinding brightness of the sun shining off of the snow. There was a very real danger of going snow-blind out here in this unending field of whiteness. With no shade and nothing to break up the reflected sun glaring back up into their eyes, they soon longed for the dreary, often sunless Rikaswelt skies.

"Everything's gone pink and red," said Ford in some alarm as he pressed his fingers into his eyes in hopes of rubbing away what felt like grit. Will suffered the same. No amount of massaging the eyes or flooding them with water helped. After a day of stumbling along with their eyes closed or at least heavily lidded and shaded by hands and hoods, they took to resting when the sun was at its fiercest and traveling when it dipped below the horizon each night, or when there was cloud cover during the day.

Late into the third day, they spotted the outline of the Heikki Linna massif. It was also on this day when their food ran out.

"Fish never lasts," said Ford, who hadn't wanted to eat the stuff to begin with, because it reminded him of the Skala. Now that they had run out, he wished for more. What was worse, they realized they had no hook for the fishing line they'd taken from the Skala. Water they could come by, but the snow they packed into their waterskins never melted fast enough to quench their incessant thirst.

"What I would give for a fire," said Will as they walked through a night of plunging temperatures. "To warm these bones for even a short while."

"If we came across the only tree in his whole damn land, I would light it afire and curl up in its branches." Even as Ford said this, they were walking past ankle-high bushes. The hardy flora didn't grow in profusion, nothing did here, but there were plenty of bushes lying around the valley floor which could be gathered up and used as tinder. Since they were leafless and covered in snow, their presence had gone unnoticed.

On the morning of their fourth day in the valley, they found the Aarne. Though iced over and no more than a few feet wide at this point, the discovery nonetheless excited them.

"See if you can't break the ice with your hammer. Here. Let me," said Ford. His first swing glanced away, but the second put a sizable crack in the ice. The third broke through. Beneath the ice ran a slow current of fresh water over streaming strands of clean golden grass a foot down. Ford stuck his face in the hole and slurped up the frigid water.

"Not too much! Not too much or you'll chill your innards," Will warned. But when it was his turn, he did the same. Neither suffered from the chills. In fact, the day was already warming enough to leave their bearskins and cloaks flapping open.

"Now if only a meal on four legs would offer itself up, the day would be complete!" Ford immediately wished he hadn't thumbed his nose at the capricious gods so flippantly. "Not to tempt fate, that is, but a full belly would be a blessing." After a moment's more consideration, he added with all solemnity, "I am grateful for the water. The water is enough."

Feeling refreshed and having filled their waterskins to the brim, they followed the river with a livelier step. Their tired feet no longer bothered them and hopeful notes lightened their conversation. Both had begun to feel more and more certain that they had truly escaped the Kamen and eluded the Skala. When the sun lit up the snow, they didn't mind stopping to cover their eyes. The wind died to nothing and an almost absolute silence enveloped them. All they could hear was each other's rumbling stomachs.

The draining of the mountains had swelled the little river to twice its size within a few miles of where Ford and Will first happened upon it. Again, Ford used the hammer to break the ice. They had no desperate need for water, but the gathering of it became habitual. "Makes sense to top off the skins while there's a chance." The first hole he smashed open filled with mud. They kicked away at the snow until the center of the river could be established and another hole was attempted. Cracks in the ice spiderwebbed out from the splintering impact, spreading under their feet, and a wider hole than intended broke open to reveal crystal clear water to a depth of nearly four feet.

They sat in the snow beside the river with their eyes shaded, drinking already warmed water from their skins. Neither spoke for the longest time. The only thing either could think of was food, and that was a topic best left unbroached. To stave off the boredom and keep his legs from cramping up while they rested, Ford kicked at the snow, plowing it away from himself with the soles of his feet.

"If you build that any higher, you'll have yourself a castle wall," said Will squinting at Ford's yard long, foot-high bank of snow.

"Maybe I'll make myself a cozy little home."

The notion brought smiles to their faces. But after some reflection, Will said, "Why not?" Ford's jest and the sight of the growing pile of snow had given him the idea to build a shelter in the style of the Haunan domed temples back home. "It wouldn't take long and it would provide relief from the sun and wind. We might even steal a few hours of sleep in relative warmth and peace! Well, not true warmth, but something close to it."

Ford needed very little convincing. A lengthy rest would be welcome. So, they kicked, pushed, and rolled snow into a circle, continuing to build it up and then inward, until they had their very own temple dome. An archway large enough to crawl through faced the river.

"Amazing," said Will.

"It is rather good. Never would've thought of building a home out of snow," replied Ford.

"Yes, but I refer to the grass and dirt. See?" Will knelt by a patch of earth where Ford had stripped the snow completely clear, revealing brown dirt and matted grass instead of bedrock. "The earth is still solid with cold and the grass may be quite dead, but still, it's not rock!"

Ford seemed perplexed. "You should meet my cousin. You'd get on. He gets excited over nothing as well."

"Don't you see? The grass, the dirt? You'd never find that anywhere on the Kamen's cold, hard rock."

"Oh. Oh!"

"Yes, precisely! And look at this!" Will nearly fell over himself scrambling across the ground to one of the tiny, leafless bushes scattered about the valley floor. Ford had knocked the snow off of it while building the dome and yet its existence hadn't made an impression until now. "There's more over here! And there! Help me gather them and we can make a fire! I wonder what else we might find."

Will and Ford ranged about the valley, all but skipping at times as they passed over the river and back, while picking armloads of the dry vegetation. Once a little wavering fire had been started, their hunger rushed back upon them to starve out all other thoughts, such was the evocative scent of smoke.

"Maybe there are fish in the river?" Ford wondered. Will held his tongue rather than remind him they had no hooks for their line. It wasn't long before Ford's head drooped between his shoulders and a groan sighed out of him.

"Something will come along," said Will.

"I wouldn't hold out much hope of something delicious hopping along and serving itself up to us," said Ford looking about at the bare lands around them.

The open fire incinerated the bushes in no time and gave off little appreciable heat. All the same, they gathered more fuel and tossed the spindly plants onto the meager embers. "Perhaps if we build up a hearth around it," said Will, but neither had the energy to get off their backsides more than they had to.

The wind picked up and the sun brightened enough to trouble their eyes once more. They climbed inside their dome, laid down shoulder to shoulder in the cramped confines, and tried to think of pleasant things, such as home, what they would do when first they arrived there, and what they missed most about it. Against the will of their best intentions, the conversation inevitably reverted to food and drink.

"Did you know, I know how to brew ale now," said Ford, momentarily forgetting that Will was with him on Polecat Island. Those days seemed so distant, almost another lifetime ago. "I think I might go in for a brewer. Set up my own brewery. Maybe a tavern of my own one day." How he would afford such an undertaking hardly crossed their minds. Reality was not the point of their musings. They were speaking their dreams. "How 'bout you?"

"Me? I'd have a long lie down beneath my favorite tree. I'd probably sleep for days. A nice, long, peaceful sleep."

"The old tree at the grove in the city?" asked Ford. The fires which swept through the city during the recent rebellion or the needs of the impoverished people had probably done that tree in by now, but Ford thought better of mentioning either. Will simply nodded.

They both wished only to think the most pleasant of thoughts about home, such as family, favorite haunts, and the like. The past bubbled out of them and within an hour they knew one another as well as old friends. Ford loved a good story and listened attentively to Will as if he were a bard. However, toward the end he grew distracted, and when Will went quiet, he asked, "But how do we get back?"

"What do you mean?"

"I mean, I don't know where we're going. South seemed to make sense, but after that it's all beyond me."

"South does make sense. I believe the south to be warmer in whatever lands you may find yourself in. But also, and more importantly, to the south lies Valtavastad."

"Valtavidstad?"

"It's a city. At the southern end of these mountains, I believe." Will pointed in the direction of the Zoudenz, those impassable peaks which kept them from the ocean. "The city does not allow the purchase and selling of slaves. Although, if I understand correctly, they do allow the recovery of escaped slaves within the city bounds. All the same, if we make it there, we shall be as nearly free as ever, for within Valtavastad there is a goodly order of generous women who practice charitable acts. Mostly they care for the Haunan faithful, offering sanctuary and protection from being retaken. They might even help us return home."

"That's good enough for me!" Ford let fly a triumphant fist, tattooing his own thigh and then Will's. "That's where our journey leads!"

The path had been decided, their moods were buoyed with hope and purpose, and yet the core of Will's nature rebelled against a celebration that not all could join in. "I wish we could have found a way to bring out the others."

"So do I," said Ford.

"I don't mean to cast a gloom over our joy," Will said quickly with an apologetic smile. "And don't think for a moment that I'm not eternally grateful for what you did."

"No, no."

A silence followed that made Will feel as if he hadn't said enough. "To be honest, I think Aeddamon…that's the priest Aeddamon Born…I think he's found a suitable calling. I saw him once and he had taken entirely to his new position as clerk and translator to a wealthy household. The way he carried on, lording over the other servants, you would think he was the master of the house." The memory made him grin. "He'll be fine. I'm sure they will all be fine."

Ford said nothing to that initially, although there was plenty within him that wanted out. He held on to it for as long as he could, but hunger and fatigue had eaten away at his reserve. "I dare say some of those sailors got what was coming to them," he said with a snort. "Let them rot!" Will didn't know how to respond and decided that saying nothing was better anything that came to mind. Ford's breathing came in measured huffs and his fingers clenched into fists. "I don't mean that, but—"

"I know."

"If I could have saved…" The cloak and bearskin wrappings slipped from his arms as his fists rose into the air.

"I know."

"I would have gotten them all out, every last one of them!"

"I know."

"But I couldn't," Ford said, his arms dropping to his sides. "I didn't know where they were or if they weren't already dead. So many were, you know? I saw our people, and not only ours, all kinds, dropping left and right." Ford wiped an arm across his eyes.

"You did all you could."

"They…" Ford turned his head to spit, then thinking better of it, swallowed hard to clear his throat and control the tremble in his voice. "Those Kamen, they didn't care about nothing. Nothing! Nothing but themselves! Any price for a good time!" Visions of death scenes within the fighting pit tormented him. Such visions, he was certain, would haunt his sleep for years to come. Ford held his head in his hands for a long while before looking up again. He turned, caught Will's eye, and wished he hadn't. "I should never have told them about you."

"About me?"

"About your faith. That you can heal. Back at that trading block." Ford whipped out a dismissive hand toward Dargkivi. His bare arm fell to rest upon his stomach and he reflexively unfurled his bearskin and cloaks, from which wisps of steam rose. "I should've kept my mouth shut. I'm sorry. Maybe they would've put you back on the boat and none of this would've happened to you. I'm sorry."

"No," said Will shaking his head. A pink flush highlighted his concerned pallor. "No, if you hadn't said anything, they would have killed me right then and there. I was near to death anyhow. You saved my life."

"Only to go through what you did."

"But I'm here now. And I wouldn't be if not for you." As Will said this, his hand alighted upon Ford's forearm. Ford winced from the unexpected intimacy. In almost the same breath, his flesh prickled from the sensation of being touched by another. After months of brutality, he couldn't recall being touched with kind intent. The sympathetic gesture felt like soothing words in the ear, perhaps even as powerful as the cure to a long illness. Will didn't have particularly robust circulation and knew his boney hand could be painfully cold at times. He pulled away.

Though the hand withdrew, its ghost remained. The physical contact meant little compared with its true, intended significance. Will's forgiveness and understanding unlocked something within Ford, something he wasn't prepared to face. It went deeper than the easy release of rage. That one simple gesture had broken down his defenses. The stock of his father's stoicism within him was not as impervious to finer feeling and tenderness as he believed. The dam to Ford Barlow's deep reservoir of ungovernable emotions overflowed. He sat up, gathered himself in and held on. His shaky hand clasped onto his forehead to massage away a building headache, but slid down his face like a mask. His other hand had a solid grip on his churning stomach. When he finally broke, it was like dropping a barrel and watching beer spread at random. He rocked back and forth, eyes closed and hyperventilating, while the pain and anguish of the last few months spilled out of him with spittle flying. "Why'd they do those things? Why would they do it? Why?" He held back an anguished roar only for it to bubble out in sobs, accidental drool, and a runny nose that couldn't be wiped away. He lost focus and went on repeating "why?" while shaking his bowed head. Finally, he went limp.

Will knelt before him with his hands on his friend's shoulders, the shoulders of someone he could now call a very real and true friend. His empathy knew no bounds when it came to those he cared for. It was nothing for him to imagine in full, vivid detail what Ford had gone through over the past months. The truth of Will's own nightmarish enslavement by the Kamen shuddered through him.

"There is so much love for gold, wealth, possession, one's own people. If only there could be such love for all of mankind. It doesn't seem too much to ask. It cannot be too much to ask. It can not!" He wished to embrace Ford, to absorb his pain. But he didn't possess the power to take it all away. And worse, he was ashamed at allowing himself to be overcome, his own breathing ragged, and his hands shaking. Whenever this happened, he knew it was best to distance himself from others.

Snatching up his hammer, he crawled out of their shelter, not caring that he stuck his hands in and dragged his legs over the ashes of their dead fire.

Once on his feet, he stomped over to the river and smashed away at the ice closing up the hole they had made. Bear fur flew about him with each flailing swing of the hammer. Every crack in the surface and splintering shard released a piece of his fury. Ford watched Will beating away at the surface of the frozen river, stunned to see this side of him. The crack and splash after the hammer came down happened so fast and unexpectedly that for a moment, he couldn't understand why he only saw Will from the waist up, as if, within the blink of an eye, Will had lost both legs. The impact of what had happened struck him only after he was scrambling out of the snow house.

"That wasn't very clever of me, was it?" Will said as Ford rushed to where he stood in a gaping hole in the ice. Ford latched on to one of his drenched arms and hauled him out of the water. Will stood beside the river holding his arms out from his sides while he looked down, amazed at the intensely cold wet cloth and fur clinging to his body from the waist down. "I'll need to dry these," he said through clenching teeth.

Ford looked to the ashes of their fire. Gathering up bushes would take time and armloads would be needed to create a fire that would warm Will and dry out fur. A cursory scan of the valley showed what he already knew, that the tiny bushes were few and far between. Many long trips far afield would be needed. When he turned back, Will was trying to pluck the wet clothes away from his body. Where Ford's forearms had been dampened from handling Will, he could feel the cold breeze being conducted straight through to his skin. It took no whip-smart wizard to imagine how Will felt.

"We got to get you out of those and out of the wind," Ford said as he began peeling off Will's bearskin. The cloak and robe had to go, too. Even Will's shoes would need to come off, he thought while rubbing him down with one of the sacks. By now Will was so stiff with cold that Ford had to drag him through the opening into their shelter. When the last of Will's clothes came off and he crouched naked in the little snow house, Ford pulled off his own bearskin and wrapped it around his friend. Will curled up in a ball on one side.

"Can't you warm yourself?" Ford asked. If ever there was a time to replicate the miracle Will had performed during the Polecat Island escape, now was that time. A wisp of words escaped Will's lips as he laboriously turned his head from side to side. Ford refrained from shaking him and demanding why he wouldn't do this thing. The question was futile and the situation frustrating. His impotent hands hung in the air a moment before he began vigorously rubbing Will's shoulders and back until he thought of something more useful to do. "I'll be back!"

Ford crawled out of their shelter and set himself to finding fuel for a fire. The cold hit him hard without his bearskin to ward it off. The cloak over his tunic and trousers was but flimsy protection in this region. Only his constant running about the snowy landscape kept him warm. The little bushes were not as near or numerous as he wished. Their snow house had to be left farther and farther behind to find the ones they hadn't already plucked up. Every few steps he threw a cautious glance back, partly to keep the little white-on-white dome in sight, and partly to watch out for Will. Having a better understanding of the man's nature, Ford worried Will would try to help gather wood. But even more so, Ford feared Will would die before he could get a fire going for him. Ripping one more bush up from the ground, he rushed back, dumped his load and stuck his head through the snow house doorway.

Will remained curled in a ball on his side, pale, blue lipped, and fighting spasms that racked his body and kept him from speaking or answering questions. Seeing his friend freezing to death before his eyes and not knowing what else to do, Ford climbed in and wrapped himself around Will. It was like hugging icicles. The radiating cold brought the shivers out in Ford, but he clamped Will's naked body to his breast, like mother and child, and hoped not to succumb to the shakes as well. It would be the end of them both.

Ford tried to distract his mind from this awkward but necessary embrace. Out of a random tumble of wandering ideas, the thought occurred to him that while Will was not the strongest or toughest person he had ever met, if it ever came to a fight, you could count on him to be there for you like a brother. After the word *brother* had been evoked, he realized he had been thinking of Will as a friend. Only the honest truth would do for a friend at a time like this.

"The truth is…" he began, as if he'd been speaking all along. The next words addressed to the back of Will's head dug their hooks in deep, initially refusing to be spoken. Ford swallowed his pride and forced them out. "The truth is I never was important for no reason. You said once that you thought I had something to do with your, I don't know what you call it, your miracles or magic or I don't know, and well, that's pretty important. Nothing else I ever did in my life's been as important as that. It means something to me. It means a lot. Maybe more than to you, I don't know, but it's special and I can't…I can't let that die."

He felt guilty for having made it all about him, all about his own concerns. His attention turned back to Will. Will's shaking had abated a great deal. Little more than sporadic shivers quivered through his body now. Ford wanted to leap for joy and then fall to his knees in thankfulness. Instead, he just kept talking.

"And besides, I didn't want to do this alone," he went on with a catch in his joy-lightened voice. "Figured I'd take a friend with me on this miserable trip!" His eyes and nose ran freely and the laughter poured from him.

Within moments, Will stopped shivering altogether. He remained peacefully tucked within Ford's embrace with his eyes closed, seemingly asleep. A deluge of relief washed away the annoyance flickering through Ford at the thought that Will had missed the confession which he had had to drag out of himself like a breech birth. But he supposed it didn't matter. Will would be all right and that was the important thing.

His relief was palpable enough to send him into a deep slumber immediately. By the time he reawakened, the sun had long since gone down. There was light enough to find fuel for the fire which would be needed to dry out Will's clothes, but when Ford shifted his weight and pulled his arm free so he could get up, Will didn't react in the least. His body felt cold. Any warmth Ford sensed, he attributed to himself.

"Will!" he shouted. Nothing. Ford shook him by the shoulder and called his name repeatedly. Will's eyes fluttered open.

"I am here," he said. The glow of blissful serenity transfixed his features into a picture of perfect peace. "And I thank you for that."

***

The sanitation worker from Drek, who was on duty at the waste station when the slaves escaped, felt sure his wobbly legs would give out. His long exposure to the biting Dargkivi winds was nothing compared to the chills assailing him now that he stood in a circle of unwanted attention. Several days prior, he had awoken to find himself sliding down the waste channel toward the sea. After his frigid scramble back up to his station, he found the son of one of the town's wealthy citizens banging away at the access tunnel door. What a strange day that had been. Since then, he had survived an inquiry without losing his job and recovered his health without permanent harm. His ordeal appeared to be over until now, when he had been called up once more to give another account of himself.

"On the day you let two slaves slip past you," said the Head of Sanitation, repeating a line of questioning he had made before in front of the same officials gathered around the gateway to the grated waste chute, the closest scene to the slaves' escape without actually having to brave the cold weather. As before, he let the statement linger before going on. Among officials of his caliber, the art of deflection seemed to be taught hand in hand with delegation. "You did nothing to stop them?"

Alongside the department head was the Commander of the City Guard, an array of local community leaders, Roniik the trainer for the Mullauk arena, as well as the neighborhood's busybodies, who gathered together again to listen to the sanitation worker tell his story. The first time around they had listened without judgement, only wrapped interest. This time, though, his every word was met with disapproving frowns meant to mirror that of the new addition to the interrogations, the Walking Rock known as Kaltzek.

Kaltzek's return to Dargkivi had caused an uproar. News of the Veks Miris tragedy spread like noxious gases through a mine. Wivvek Vanagz received more condolences from nosy well-wishers than when her home was gutted by fire. Some Kamen reacted with fear and demands for heightened security, thinking their lives might be in peril from some new, rising danger. The Master of Mullauk suffered "a collapse" and sent Roniik to shadow Kaltzek in hopes of discovering what he might of Dagmar, and to learn whether or not the hunter would be providing fighting pit fodder anytime in the future. For many, Kaltzek's presence among them was worse than the news he brought with him. "We should be watching monsters like that in the fighting pit for pleasure, not allowing it to roam around the city free," they said.

Kaltzek didn't care what they thought of him. He had a job to do, one of the most important of his life, second only to dragging Dagmar out of Veks Miris, so he would do whatever he needed to do to get it done, which included enduring the sanitation worker's stammering, nonsensical account. He stood impatiently among the Kamen, who gave him as much space as they could in such cramped confines. Only Roniik, having slipped into the role of escort, remained at his side.

The sanitation worker wrapped up his disjointed side of the story and answered all of their remaining questions in rapid mumbles backed by silent prayers that this would all be over soon. When the inquisition did mercifully end, the gathered officials turned their expectant and nervous gazes from one another to Kaltzek. This officious show had been performed once again for his benefit and they wanted to know if he was satisfied, though none wanted to ask outright. No one dared disturb the creature with the perpetually seething scowl and a body that emanated strength and ferocity like white hot coals.

Kaltzek had heard all that could be of use to him. He grunted and left them. The officials heaved a sigh of relief and broke up gratefully. Now he knew. The slave Ford had escaped south, so Kaltzek would go south. Undoubtedly the fool had fled straight into the arms of the Skala. Because of Dagmar's hunts, Kaltzek knew that the closest clan of Skala wasn't far away. However, the slave traders were nomadic, so their latest camp would have to be tracked down. He doubted it would be difficult. They stank of fish and liked to leave markers that were impossible to miss, even if you only owned one good eye. Kaltzek thought of the bejeweled false eye bauble fashioned for him at Dagmar's command and expense to replace the eye taken from him at the hand of his own people. The memory stoked his already enflamed desire to track down the escaped, troublesome slave on behalf of such a benevolent master.

He was ready to get on with the manhunt which had taken him over much of Rikaswelt and would likely take him over much more. However, that intrusive trainer from the fighting pit still trailed behind him through the tunnels. Kaltzek wished the bushy-headed show fighter would leave him be. He wanted no one getting in the way of completing his task. Then again, this Kamen might be useful in talks with the Skala. Communication was not Kaltzek's strong suit and he knew it. So, he said nothing when Roniik, looking like one of Dagmar's overstuffed trophies in his blue-lined, thick fur cloak and loaded down with a provisions pack, caught up with him at the waste station, where they briefly searched for any clues.

Roniik didn't want to be here, just as much as he wasn't wanted. His master had commanded him to shadow Kaltzek, hoping for a chance to snag free or cheap slaves for the arena. Perhaps Roniik might even entice Kaltzek into becoming one of the heroic warriors of Mullauk, that is, if Dagmar no longer needed his services and Kaltzek found himself at a loose end. And if Dagmar never returned, well then, the Walking Rock would make a fine pit fiend, willing or not. The Master had never seen such a perfectly monstrous villain for his shows.

As suspected, the Skala encampment proved easy to find. Its utter disarray was surprising. Apparently, fights had broken out within the clan to decide a new chief after the previous one had been killed. The Kamen trainer was marginally useful in talks with the Skala. All that could be gotten out of them regarding Ford was that two slaves had last been seen heading south, deeper into the mountains. Finding someone in a mountain range, when they didn't want to be found, was not easy. Then again, thought Kaltzek, it might not be so difficult. After all, the ocean was impassable and, at some point for a pair of weak humans, so too would be the mountains. The slaves would have to veer inland.

A few days later, Kaltzek was perched upon a rock on a slope along the eastern edge of the foothills of the Zoudenz Mountains. He had been gorging himself on a hunk of raw meat while surveying the vast, white expanse of the Jatti Valley before him. Tracking the slave Ford had taken longer than he had hoped. The Kamen trainer's need for warmth, shelter, and far too much sleep slowed down their progress considerably. But now, all was well. The wind carried away the blue-lined fur cloak Kaltzek had discarded beside a pool of blood. When he stood and hopped down from the rock, he kicked at the bushy-haired head at his feet and watched it roll down the hill. There would be no more trouble, no more delays.

Chapter 21
The House at Heikki Linna

A towering smoke plume rose over the Jatti Valley. Ford was on his hands and knees beneath it, hovering over a hole in the Aarne River ice with his scimitar poised to strike. He could have sworn a fish had swum by, but now a fruitless hour had passed with no results and he was beginning to wonder if what he had seen was nothing more than a leaf tumbling by in the current.

Looking on the bright side, he no longer felt famished and had more patience for a long wait. After spending a day at their domed shelter drying Will's clothes, they had recommenced their southward journey down the river and happened upon the hindquarters of an elk sticking out of the ice. Apparently, it had broken through, gone headfirst into the river, and drowned on the spot. The exposed parts of the animal, above and below the surface of the water, had been gnawed away by a variety of creatures, but a decent sized chunk remained lodged in the ice, which they had chipped out and thawed over a fire. The last of it was cooking now.

Ford jabbed his scimitar through the hole in the ice at a darting shadow. He missed, but smiled. The flick of a tail before the shadow disappeared was unmistakable. At least now his actions had purpose and possibility, however remote. He was glad Will had declined his offer to use the sword to cut down bushes.

The dried, thin trunks were easy enough to snap by hand. Will knelt by a pile of them which he had collected at some distance from the river. Though bushes were becoming larger and more frequent—some dwarf conifers had even been spotted—they had gone through a good many in thawing out the meat. Out here he found open patches of ground clear of snow and covered in dead grasses, recovering mosses and dormant lichens. In any other setting, their drab blues and pale greens would have seemed dreary, but in this world of ice and stone, the subtle colors and variety of textures created a botanical flourish which leant a velvety softness to the inhospitable landscape. Life was returning to the valley. It may not have been readily apparently, but Ford and Will witnessed signs in the form of deer and bear tracks, the small markings of shrews, as well as some mysterious tracks neither of them could make out.

Will's knees pressed into mounded earth among a lumpy field of palsas and their larger pingo cousins, hummocks thrust up from the ground by the seasonal expansion of boggy water in the dips and troughs between the low hills of the moorlands stretching down from the Heikki Linna range to the east. Beyond feeling obliged to run about the valley gathering fuel for a fire, Will also knelt to give thanks for what Ford had done for him. Will knew just how close to death he had come. Without Ford, he would still be back in Dargkivi. Thanks were also given for having fallen through the ice on a milder day than today, when a cold, moaning wind blew in from the west.

Will liked to wander into the wild to pray in solitude. Out here one didn't have to go far to give the impression of being completely alone. Turning and walking a hundred paces away from his companion eradicated all human intrusion, including sound if the wind picked up. Will was more than a hundred paces out of earshot. Ford was not overly fond of these little excursions. They always seemed to come whenever he thought they should be moving on. On the other hand, Will worshipped for them both, and that couldn't hurt.

Presently, Will wasn't praying, but rather meditating on why he had been unable to save himself from freezing to death. The answer came before the damp ground soaked through to his knees. Concentration had been the missing element. The shock to his body was too great. "Simple as that," he said and smiled at how quickly he'd come to the conclusion. Contemplations such as this could take him all day. His eyes popped open and he hopped to his feet with a lightness of heart. Regardless of the length of time spent, he always felt fuller in mind and body when he came to a better understanding of himself and the nature of the divine energy that sometimes flowed through him.

Shouldering his pile of bushes, he turned back to the river and saw a white wall rising up from behind the mountains to the west. It stampeded toward the valley like a massive, ivory-hued herd of wild stallions and mares. The mass expanded and soon blocked the mountains from view. Before long it would engulf the valley. As it gathered speed and raced ever closer, Will recognized it as a cloud of wind-driven snow. He looked to Ford, still bent over the ice and oblivious to the oncoming danger. Will shouted and ran for the river.

Ignoring the wind as it picked up momentum, Ford stared intently into the ice hole. When that fish came back, it was his. But then driving snow persistently pecked at his cheeks until he gave in and looked up. For several heartbeats, he stared befuddled by the sudden and strange appearance of the oncoming snow squall which had already blotted out the mountains and much of the sky. Just before it hit, he stood and turned away, taking its full force in the back. The howling gale knocked him, slipping and stumbling, off of the ice. The sky darkened. The bare patches of grass were instantly coated white again. Darts of ice stung Ford's exposed flesh. He shaded his eyes and looked for Will, who bobbed over the lumpy land, arms and legs flailing, before the squall swept him up in its battering embrace. The bear fur flew about him. His silhouette lightened into a grayish outline.

"Will! Will!" The roar of the tearing wind obliterated all other sound. Ford stepped toward his friend. The wind at his back shoved him on at the instant Will vanished in a haze of swirling snow. Ford staggered forward and shouted again, but the wind whisked the words away. He started running and caught a foot on a tussock. While stumbling, a blast of air caught the back of him and drove him the rest of the way down. He managed to get to one knee, but toppled over immediately. Facing the wind and leaning into it was the only way to stand. Through the slits of his eyelids, he could see no sign of the river, which should have been at his feet. The packs and provisions, the meat on the fire, not even the fire, he could make out none of it. Walking into the wind was futile. He turned to where he thought he had last seen Will. The wind veered wildly and whirled the snow dizzily about him, confounding any sense of direction. One moment he was trying to find Will or the river and the next he was desperately peering through slivers of flying ice just to see where his feet would land. Wandering blindly into the squall, he found a hummock and fell into it, clinging on and resting until the wind eventually abated enough that he was able to climb atop the knoll to call into the buffeting gusts. Optical illusions, more hope-filled than corporeal, appeared in vague shapes in the shadowy landscape.

The snow squall gave way to a blizzard that surged over the valley like an indomitable horde charging into battle and sweeping the field in a resounding victory. Ford had no choice but to keep moving or freeze to death. Shelter was needed, anything to keep at bay some of the biting cold. He hoped Will would do the same wherever he was. After the storm cleared, they would find the river and reunite, so Ford told himself. A fir tree a few inches taller than himself stood in his path, its slender boughs reaching out invitingly. A fairly snow-free hollow remained at its base. Ford crawled within and hunkered down. Wrapped in layers and shielded from the buffeting winds, he kept warm enough to pass the hours until the chill winds subsided.

Heavy flakes had piled all around him and above his head. He dug out of the accumulated drifts and dragged his weary feet through the deep snow as he walked into a world transformed. The landscape's edges had been smoothed out. Stunted domes stood where once were bushes. Nothing looked familiar.

He kept to the high ground when he could. The soft and squishy depressions, where the snowpack beneath the new powder dissolved into slush, brought to mind the bog which had once nearly consumed him. It wasn't long before he had to stop to catch his breath. Another hundred paces on and his stride shortened, then ground down to a plodding gait. From then on, he had to rest frequently. Whenever he stopped, he built piles of snow, stones, bushes or whatever was at hand in hopes that Will might see them and follow. These stops became so frequent that upon collapsing on his backside after what felt like an arduous trek across great lengths, he looked back to find his last tiny plinth but a mere ten feet behind. Disbelief swept over him. His head lolled, he fell back into the snow, and allowed his most negative thoughts to cascade over his remaining resolve. Not only had he lost Will, but he'd lost an entire river. Of late, he hadn't even glimpsed the mountains. He couldn't tell which direction he was facing. Rather than accidentally walking back to Rikaswelt, he would stay put until the skies cleared and he could see farther than where his next footfalls would land.

Half a day passed before the skies did clear enough to see the sun. The hazy orb showed the way east to west. His southerly course lay between them. Simple enough, as long as the sun was in view. White cones in the gloom ahead transformed into the full-grown firs of a copse on the backside of a long, low hill. This took him into a mildly undulating landscape of scattered trees that reminded one of a sea crowded with shipping. He rejoiced at the sight of them, for there were no trees like this anywhere in Rikaswelt. Surrounding himself with them felt like being wrapped in a bit of home, his true home where he was born and raised in a forested backcountry.

Soon after the sun disappeared below the horizon, Ford built another of his snow plinths and crawled into a hole he dug out from under a tree. Plans of finding the river and reuniting with Will in the morning were coalescing into vows while he curled up, closed his eyes and dropped off to sleep. By the time he had reawakened, the storm had completely moved on, though the sky remained overcast.

Snow fell from his head and shoulders when he stood. The sudden movement sent a hummock bolting with a rumble and flurry of white powder. The snow blew away and the shambling mound transformed into a lone muskox that disappeared over a rise. The temptation of fresh meat set Ford on the animal's trail. Its tracks led through a thicket to where a whole herd of muskox had plowed a broad, compacted path over the snow which was as easy to walk along as any road Ford had traveled. For miles he tracked the herd, followed it up land he didn't realize was ascending. His ever-slowing pace he blamed on sheer exhaustion. The sky cleared enough to see one set of mountains, but not enough to tell whether he was facing Heikki Linna in the afternoon or the Zoudenz in the morning.

The gloom of evening set in once more and matched his mood. There had been no sign of Will, the river was nowhere to be found, and a sudden whirlwind whipped up the snow like a blinding blizzard within a tornado. Caught in the open without cover, Ford tucked his head into his bear fur and pulled it tight around his shoulders. The cold crept over his skin and into his bones. Hunger gnawed away at his innards. Each step of his damp boots dragged through the snow slower than the last. He tottered forward on numb toes.

Among the pointed tops of silhouetted evergreens ahead, one stood out as having particularly broad boughs. He made for it with plans of burying himself beneath. Trudging up to it, he found drifts piled high against its sides. He drove into the piled snow, expecting to push through the heavily-laden boughs to a clearer inner core. Instead, his fists knocked into something solid. A timbered wall rose before him, two in fact, the corner of a tall house concealed by snow. Judging by the section he could make out, it appeared to be as large as one of the great halls of his homeland.

He hailed the house, but the wind carried his shouts away. No one would hear him out here. Perhaps no one was home. The place might be abandoned and he would have to break in through the door or a window, if he could find either. Next to the wall, the snow came up to his chest and the drifts reached right up to the roof. He tried the other side of the corner, where there looked to be a better chance of wading through the snow. There was no walking through the stuff, but rather he fell forward and crawled over it. A whiff of smoke made his heart leap and his stomach rumble. No entry revealed itself, but a new wing of the house jutted out at a right angle. This recent addition was hastily made with green timbers that leaned haphazardly left and right, leaving large gaps between. Frozen hides had been jammed into the gaps to cut down drafts. Worrying he would freeze before he found the door, Ford dug the snow away from the widest of these gaps, cleared it of stiff hides, and then drove his shoulder into the space. With a heave on the logs, he was able to shove in.

What he shoved himself into was a mystery. Instead of the open interior of a home, he found himself in what appeared to be a cluttered mudroom or oversized cupboard or pantry. The air smelt like a smokehouse. The space was jammed with something like irregular posts or tree trunks stacked at odd angles and draped with furs and skins. Weaving between them, his scimitar often got hung up on something or other as he made for a weak glow penetrating through the jumbled mass.

After muscling through the final few feet, he found himself staring into a pair of googly eyes set in a lumpy and ruddy face. A fat tongue poked from chubby cheeks to lick slobbery lips. The head was topped with masses of kinky russet hair and bookended with saggy, uneven earlobes. The face seemed human, though distorted. Malformed, but not entirely grotesque. This strange visage, a few short feet away, morphed through a variety of unusual expressions, none appropriate for the situation. A lack of control over facial muscles seemed evident. Ford slowly reached for his sword where it was still tangled and hidden among the furs and pole-like objects. The eyebrows shot up and the mouth made an enormous oval. With a twitch, the egg yolk eyes disappeared into a squint and a smile broke out which bared rows of corn kernel-sized teeth haphazardly planted. This head hovered on a level with

Ford's own and he could see no body. The room was dim, the light flickered irregularly, and the angle of the figure seemed odd at first, until Ford realized he was looking at someone kneeling on a table. The body was stout for its four-foot length, as stout as the ponderously thick table it perched upon.

Whatever it was, it let out a shriek like a whistle that had Ford falling backward through the clutter. The cry dissolved into a giggle and the eyes flared with a child-like glee, bright with life and alive with fun. There seemed to be no outward menace in the strange thing, none that Ford could make out at any rate. In fact, if he wasn't mistaken, this was indeed a child, the largest he had ever seen. The head was bulbous, outsized for its own body like a toddler's, and the mannerisms were akin to a human child of perhaps two or three. Suddenly, the oversized child erupted into rippling laughter, put its hand to its mouth as if surprised by the noises it made, and then pointed at Ford with fingers dripping in drool. A cackle of garbled words spilled forth. Ford receded deeper into the furs. The noises unsettled him. Something was very odd about all this. At Ford's disappearance, the child struck up a piteous howl. Through the clutter, Ford saw the enormous face approaching his hiding place just before the howl cut off abruptly and the face vanished. There was the thud of a body hitting a floor. After an expectant pause, it let rip the kind of heart-rending wail only a child makes after hurting itself. The crying continued and seemed like it might go on forever, but it quieted when sonorous grunts rumbled out of some other part of the house. Earth-trembling footsteps approached. Ford tried to back deeper into the tangle of furs and skins, but one of the solid post-like objects stuck in his back and barred his way. He caught his breath and hoped for the best. Through his concealment, he could make out unrecognizable body parts, wiry hair, very rough homespun cloth, and a glimpse of one side of the child's face pressed into the flesh of another. The cries were muffled and then died off altogether. The interior of the house went quiet, or at least quieter. A fire crackled and the heavy feet shuffled away.

Ford tried backing out of the house. He did not like what he had seen so far and didn't want to meet that child's parents. Tales of giants and their brutal ways speckled the old tales of distant lands. Like a slap to the face, it dawned on him that he was now in one of those *distant lands*, and unless grossly mistaken, he had happened upon a house of giants. Lingering here was not a good idea. He might possess a sword, but little good it would do him if the blade couldn't pierce a giant's thick hide. And should one of them get their hands on him, his life was forfeit and his body would make tender meat for their next meal.

Tender meat. A savory scent caught his nose and drew from him a subconsciously deep, longing breath. Meat was cooking on that crackling fire. His mouth watered. The hand he was using to extricate his sword from a fur hesitated as he cocked an ear. The sounds of danger had passed. His stomach told him it had been too long since he'd last eaten. The least he could do was to have a look about. This might be his best chance to snatch a little something to eat until only the gods knew when.

Taking a step forward and peering through the cover of fur, he caught the tips of flames rising out of an immense stone hearth beyond the table. The yard-long logs burning away within had room to spare. The source of the delectable smell, a huge side of meat raw on one side and charred black on the other with reddened ribs protruding, sizzled and smoked upon a long iron cooking sheet perched upon the hearthstones directly over the fire. Ford swallowed and licked his lips. If he could just get his hands on even a small portion of what lay so tantalizingly available before him, it would feed him for days. If he could pack away a fair bit, it might see him through the rest of his journey. More dripping fat sizzled upon the iron. The tempting sound convinced him that, while the essence of self-preservation was in keeping one's skin intact, it was also necessary to keep flesh on one's bones. Here was an opportunity to satisfy a need, one he could not pass up.

Though rash at times, Ford wasn't fool enough to saunter out into the middle of a giant's lair. He leaned forward, stretched his neck out, and pushed his face through the furs to take in his surroundings. His view was mostly limited to the kitchen before him, where long utensils hung from a beam, a wide pot with enormous bowls stacked in it sat on the stones by the hearth, and sagging sacks had been piled on the table. One of the sacks looked as if salt had spilled out. He could see little else. Obviously, the house continued on in other directions, especially where it stretched away to the right around one of the stone support walls, but for how far and what was there, there was no telling from where he stood. And he had stood there long enough for at least one of the local inhabitants to mistake him for a fixture. Tiny feet crept up his leg. It might have been a small insect up against his skin or something larger clinging to his pants. Compared to the outside, the relative warmth of this dark and cramped cubbyhole provided an ideal ecosystem for any number of vermin. A twitch of the leg shook it off.

The house's design was an architect's nightmare of lopsided smoke-blackened timbers and crude masonry. Two outer walls were of stone, as were two of the inner load-bearing walls. An attempted arch at the center of the structure had been aborted, and instead, the roof was held up at its peak by a cluster of crisscrossed beams bound together with rope. The beams closest to the broad, circular central hearth were scorched precisely where an overzealous fire had reached up and licked them. The ceiling, ten feet high at its lowest point, was pitch black. Tree trunks and branches, some dead and dry, while others were still green, had been snapped in half and piled haphazardly by the door to be used for burning. The door, too, had been constructed in the same ramshackle manner. Thawing snow and ice against the outside kitchen walls formed a puddle in one corner. A few flagstones remained visible by the hearth, but the rest of the floor was hardpacked dirt or mud.

Ford poked his head farther out. From what he could see and hear, no one was about, and yet he couldn't seem to make either of his feet take that first step out into the open. "Coward," he chided himself inwardly. This was no time to hesitate. The tapered ends of the slab of meat on the hearth were already burnt. It would not be left to cook forever. He urged himself to go and go now, shouting the words in his mind so loudly they seemed to bounced off the inside of his skull. One foot slid forward into the kitchen. For all his determination, it was a tentative step. And for all his hesitant caution, the step was ill-advised. Everything may have been on a larger scale here, but Ford was no mouse, able to slip in and out unnoticed. "Be like the mouse," he told himself. "Make yourself smaller." Getting down on his knees, he crept out of his hiding spot on all fours, looked all around to make sure he was still alone, and then crawled under the tall wooden table which took up much of the kitchen area. His heart tried to pound out of his chest, his breathing sounded like the snorts of a bull to his ears, and as wide as he opened his eyes, he could not take in enough of the darkened house to feel safe.

No one or nothing had seen him, as far as he could tell. Likewise, he had seen no one and little more than table legs, hearthstones, and dividing walls. He blinked away the smoky air from his drying eyes. The hesitant urge to listen for danger nearly stalled him again, but he dredged up the courage to make for the hearth and scurried across the floor. Reaching up, he took hold of a rib and pulled. The hot rib didn't give way like he had hoped. The fibrous meat held firm and yanking upon it to wrench it free resulted in him roasting his palm and singing his wrist on the iron sheet. He jerked back and cradled his hand against his stomach. It was painful, but nothing serious. He blew on his wrist and shook his hand, while desperately trying to come up with a way around the problem. A rusting and chipped blade with a greasy handle had been laid on the stones to one side of the hearth. It was long enough to act as a large dagger or even a short sword for anyone smaller than Ford. He took it and cut off one of the seared tips.

An inquisitive sniff behind Ford spun him around and brought him face to face with the largest cat he had ever laid eyes upon. Its thick fur made it appear more burly than slinky for a feline. Even so, the underlying muscles flexing with each movement spoke to its agility. It slipped around from the backside of the hearth, where it had been sleeping the whole time. Its yellow-brown coat covered in splotches and indistinct stripes stood on end along its arching back. Rounded bear-like ears over fluffy cheeks might have made the cat look friendly, except that the ears were laid back and on the alert. After sizing Ford up as a surmountable threat, it lowered its head close to the ground and cocked its legs to pounce. All through the fluid movement, it maintained eye contact, all but for a single glance at the meat in Ford's hand. Ford knew next to nothing about cats, other than that they liked to eat. He flung the chunk of meat onto the floor between them. The cat inched its nose forward and sniffed. Mistrusting the man, it backed away, but only for a moment. Another deeper sniff and it snatched up the chunk and suddenly everything about the cat's demeanor relaxed and softened. It chewed contentedly, swallowed, and licked its lips. The cat's body relaxed and hope filled its eyes. The morsel was gone and it wanted more. It looked from Ford to the hearth. After burning its paws once before, it knew better than to approach any closer to the flames. Ford reached up and sliced off another piece. His hunger attacked his insides, but the cat had to come first. The slice disappeared in one gulp. The third and fourth pieces it took directly from Ford's hand. It purred while it ate.

Ford was nearly done cutting his own piece when the floor quaked with the heavy tramp of plodding footsteps. He tore at the meat. The knife clattered against the stones and fell to the floor. A tree-sized shadow loomed in his periphery as he dove for his hiding spot. Behind him a mountain's growl and a thunderous stamped foot rattled the bowls. A wooden spoon cracked against the table top, followed by a feline snarl and whine. Scampering paws fled away, leaving behind deep grumblings and the shuffling of leathery feet over dirt and flagstones.

Tucked away between what felt like a pair of cold tree trunks in the fur and skins nook, Ford looked out through the gaps in the wall at the snow and felt the cold on his face. It almost seemed more pleasant and inviting outside than in this madhouse of intimidating inmates. Bolting then and there would have been wise.

A lot of grunting and scrapping was carrying on behind him. A loud sizzling and the slam of a heavy, awkward weight onto the iron sheet told him that the meat, a side of muskox, had been flipped or replaced with another. The cat poked its nose into the furs and nuzzled into the back of his leg. The cool damp nose found his hand and immediately an abrasive tongue went to work on his palm. He brushed it away, but to no avail. Ford took a bite out of the chunk of meat he had ripped off at the last second and handed the rest to the cat. It was a tough piece and when it finally went down it did nothing more than tantalize his wizened stomach. When the cat finished its portion, it plopped down quite close to Ford's hiding spot and proceeded to lick itself thoroughly. For the first time that he could remember, Ford was happier to be in the company of a cat rather than a dog. Any dog would have likely barked its head off and given him away.

Ford twisted around slowly, turning away from the opening to the outside world. He had to make another try for the cooking muskox. With everything covered in snow, this was perhaps the only place for a hundred miles where he might find something to eat. He carefully inched back toward the kitchen until his view was of one of the sacks on the table. A gnarled and hairy hand dug into the sack and took away a clump of coarse-grained salt, close to a half pint's worth. The sheer girth of each finger made him catch his breath. Heavy footsteps retreated from the room. He slid into a more comfortable position. An hour wore on where nothing more could be seen or heard moving about within the kitchen. The fire crackled and some of its warmth reached into his cozy den. A new, wet log had been thrown into the hearth. Keeping a steady rhythm behind its popping and fizzing could be heard a sonorous snoring reverberating from the far side of the hearth. It wasn't long before the drowsy atmosphere wore Ford out.

His eyes popped open. How he had fallen asleep in such circumstances baffled even himself. Perhaps, he guessed, the warmth and exhaustion had conspired against him. But he was awake now, wide awake to the thumping and banging ruckus going on in the kitchen. A peek through the furs brought him a clear and close view of immense watery and drooping eyes, a hooked and wart-tipped nose, a broad jaw full of signpost teeth mashing muskox flesh, and a knotty crown with patchy hair that brushed the ceiling. Two or three guttural words punched the air, bags made of hide rustled, footsteps thumped. Cold gusted into the kitchen after a great creaking of wood. The whole house reverberated as a heavy door slammed shut. A brief silence passed and then Ford spotted bare hands heft a slab of thoroughly cooked meat off the hot iron sheet and toss it onto the table. Stooping over to hack away at the cooked carcass showed a side view of a slouched body through a threadbare and sleeveless patchwork tunic. The tunic fell open, revealing a pendulous breast which could have passed for the udder of an aged cow. Painfully swollen joints forced a limping gait when the giantess took even the one or two steps around the crowded kitchen.

The cat sprang upon the table, keeping low and sniffing as close to the cooked muskox as it dared. A massive hand swatted the cat, which let out a plaintive cry as it flew from the table. The knife sawed back and forth. Some cuts sliced through like butter. A steamy, meaty pungency filled the air. The cat circled the kitchen sniffing. Steaks and chops were laid to one side of the table, so close that Ford could have reached out and snatched one. The cat's head popped above the tabletop and went for one of the steaks. A bellow and a kick sent it skittering from the room. A bowl as big as an ancient tortoise shell was thumped down onto the table. The pieces of meat were dumped into it and a piece of slate the size of a shield was placed over the bowl as a lid. A hairy and rough branch-like arm plunged through the furs and groped around. Ford caught his breath, leaned away, and was shoved aside. A cold slab of beef propped against others like a tilted post was chosen and dragged out. It was then that Ford realized what he took for furs and frozen logs in a disused wing of the house, were actually halves and quarters of muskox in a larder. The side of stiff meat was heaved onto the hot iron sheet. The smell of burning hair and skin choked the air. Eventually it died away and was replaced by the smell of cooking fat and muscle. Upon seeing another slab of meat being cooked, Ford realized she was preparing more food than she and the child needed. This was enough for a large family, maybe a whole clan even.

The giantess' footsteps faded away from the kitchen, but not far. When Ford peered out, he saw those long, leathery feet sticking out from the other side of the stone and timber walls built around and over the hearth. The only pleasing thing about the yellow soles and corn-covered toes with rotten nails curling inward was that they lay absolutely still upon their bed of flattened straw.

Ford pushed his nose through the cover of the larder to see if he could work out how to gather up the most provisions in the least amount of time. He wanted to get out of the house as fast as possible and in one piece. A hungry lemming, spying on him from the rafters, also wanted this new interloper to leave with all speed. Rodents like the lemming had eaten away the bottom corners of two of the sacks sitting on top of the table next to the one holding the salt. Dried herb debris dusted the tabletop near the sacks. Not knowing the contents, Ford had taken his cue from the cat and ignored them, too. Until now, that is. One of those sacks, if filled with meat, could keep him fed for weeks. The logical idea had occurred to him to grab the cold slabs of muskox and whatever else was stacked about him, but much of it was frozen solid and all of it was too heavy to carry very far. The bowl holding the pieces already conveniently cut was a tempting target. The rock slab covering it could be lifted off, but at what price? There was a very good chance such a heavy and awkward weight would slip and fall, either to crash upon the floor or drop with a loud thud upon the table. The noise would likely wake the giantess.

Ford picked another option. He stopped thinking and worrying, and snuck out of hiding, lifted the closest sack from the table, and slipped back into hiding. It was surprisingly light. He upended it and poured out dried sage and other leaves which smelt much like hay. It all fell almost soundlessly onto the larder floor. The lemming's heart fluttered. Slowly and with absolute care, he began tearing strips of the sacking as quietly as he could, the plan was to wrap the strips around his hands in preparation of grabbing the hot meat right off the burner, if needs be. He would use his own sword to cut off the pieces. That would save time.

While he worked, out in the kitchen the cat jumped onto the table and hovered around the meat bowl, sniffing eagerly, annoyed with the piece of slate frustrating its plans. It resigned itself to licking the tabletop where the cutting had taken place. Beyond the hearth, the regular rhythm of snoring continued uninterrupted and the feet never moved. Ford went on tearing and wrapping even after the large headed child toddled into view once more and immediately started pestering the cat. When that carried on for too long, the two set to wrestling around the kitchen, knocking into table legs and bumping into walls. Eventually the roughhousing broke up when they rolled into the puddle in the corner. The cat slipped away to find some private spot to clean itself and the child whimpered as it disappeared behind the central hearth. After a deep groan, the giantess' feet flipped to one side, and a sloppy suckling sound started up.

Ford finished wrapping his hands and waited impatiently while the child's feeding continued. Eventually, when the slurping noises were replaced by synchronized snoring, he slipped from the larder, drew his scimitar, and dropped to his hands and knees. Once under the table, he stopped to listen for signs of disturbance. A *thump* and *crack* from behind him nearly stopped his heart once and for all. The snap might have been nothing more than wood splitting. Houses often made such settling noises. The heat of the hearth working against the cold pressing in from outside wreaked havoc on timbers. The thump might have been one of the sides of meat shifting and falling over in the larder. At least, this was what he told himself in order to summon the courage to get on with the task at hand. He heard nothing more and there had been no suggestion of a stir within the house, so he reached up and knocked the salt sack over. Crystals softly showered the floor. He whipped the much lighter sack off the table. The residual salt would act as a meat preserver and the sack could be tied to the makeshift belt which he had made out of the remaining sacking he didn't need for his hands.

With sword and sack in hand, he crawled out from under the table and stole up against the hearth. The heat coming from the stones made him shy away. Crouching over and leaning back made it difficult to reach up with his blade to saw at the slab of meat. The awkward cutting angle and inability to see what he was doing meant that his blade kept missing the groove or hitting bone. A couple dozen hard strokes with the scimitar, as well as the conspicuous feeling of being exposed out in the open, made him break into a muck sweat. Another *thud* back in the larder didn't help his nerves any.

As beads of perspiration trickled down his back, the blade scraped against bone one last time before an irresistible force plowed into him from behind. Like a boulder rolling over his back, it sandwiched him against the hot hearthstones, shoulder and cheek first. The sensation was like being punched from both sides at once. After the shock of impact, his head swam against a tide of confusion and pain. The side of his face and his arm went fleetingly numb. Stoney fingers and iron limbs wrapped around him: legs around his legs, arms around his arms, in an ever-tightening constriction. Hard white skin, like snow-coated rock, pulled him back from the hearth. For a blinking instant, Ford saw his own blood from his cheek smeared across one of the stones. His eyes cleared and instantly he knew that the rippling forearm beneath his nose belonged to Kaltzek.

As Dagmar's Walking Rock yanked and tugged them both away from the hearth and across the room, a truly absurd thought flashed through Ford's mind: what if the giantess should hear them? As immensely strong as Kaltzek was, Ford didn't doubt the strength of a ten-foot-tall woman with hands that could palm either of their skulls. In the very least, they would be a match for one another.

With a twist and a heave, Kaltzek somersaulted them into one of the table legs. The table shuddered across the floor and crashed into the wall. The bowl of meat tipped over and the slate lid slid off. Meat chunks spilled across the tabletop. Kaltzek scrambled on top of Ford and jabbed his stony fingers into his vitals. The thorny digits found a purchase under his ribs and lifted. Ford's entire chest felt like it was on the verge of exploding open. He pried at his tormenter's wrists, but they held fast to him like iron shackles. Kaltzek tried to stand, but the underside of the table stopped him from lifting Ford any farther. He gave up and slammed Ford to the ground. Ford reached out for anything to strike Kaltzek with. His hands ran over the pile of salt. He threw a handful into Kaltzek's face. Kaltzek reeled back enough for Ford to squirm out from under him and scramble away.

Falling with his back against the hearth, Ford clung to the stones and panted for breath. While Kaltzek remained crouched under the table, blinking and rubbing his one good eye, Ford sought his scimitar all about the kitchen floor. The weapon had flown from his hand when Kaltzek tackled him from behind. After a second glance over his shoulder, he spotted the tip sticking up from the hearth fire, its handle buried somewhere within the embers and its blade rapidly heating. It was lost to him.

Kaltzek lumbered out from under the table and gathered his bulk into a ball of strength and fury ready to be unleashed upon his quarry. Without thought, Ford's hand shot into the fire and pulled out an arm's length of burnt log, charred black at one end and orange with embers on the other. He wheeled around and caught Kaltzek's head with a blow that lost all of its power when Ford's hand was forced open by the burning wood's searing heat. The log glanced off Kaltzek's crown in a burst of embers that flew across the room. Kaltzek threw his hands up to frantically brush away the cinders dancing over his bald pate. The reprieve was brief, but enough for Ford to reach back, grab the large knife off the hearthstone and lunge. The blade plunged into Kaltzek's shoulder. He barely winced. Ford's heart sank as he let go and stumbled back. Kaltzek sneered down at the knife, drew it out, tossed it into the fire, and came on like a battering ram.

The pummeling Ford took was reminiscent of the time a gang of thugs jumped him. Their fists, knees, and feet struck him from every angle in a constant barrage that seemed to last ages. Now, as then, he fought back until his strength failed him. He had gotten in all the licks he would against this foe, whose ambition to do his master's bidding fueled his desire to tear apart such a vile and contemptible slave. Ford's layered clothing padded the blows somewhat, but he still felt like dough kneaded by hammers. The powerful hands and arms, his core of strength, was beyond anything Ford had known, and it soon became obvious that he couldn't win this fight.

Kaltzek had purposefully tossed away the knife. He wanted to *feel* every bit of this death. Cupping Ford's head in his hands, he dug his fingers into his eye sockets, trying to burst the eyes like grapes. Ford pulled at Kaltzek's wrists, ripping at them with his fingernails and trying to bite his hands, but it was all useless. Only Kaltzek's stubby thumbs prevented him from blinding Ford. He shifted his grip down to the throat and squeezed. Ford's red and raw eyes bulged as his air was cut off. The trapped blood throbbed in his head. His killer hovered above him framed in a blue-green haze. Beyond the demonic face and the staring bejeweled eye, smoke and flame rose up from the tabletop where a flying ember had landed on one of the sacks. Ford kicked and squirmed, trying to roll toward the hearth. The heat seemed repellent to

Kaltzek's cold-seasoned skin. It was his last hope. The weight on his chest, compressing his lungs, kept him pinned to the ground. The firelight dimmed. All light dimmed. Ford's vision swam. Nothing made sense. Kaltzek's head was elongating and his menacing scowl switched to surprise, fear, and pain. A crack and a pop cut the air louder than the burning logs as the great cat's fangs clamped around Kaltzek's head and squeezed it like a vice until it split. Broken bone, torn skin, and blood splattered.

Ford threw up arms to cover his head, expecting to feel the cat's teeth upon him. When nothing happened, he wiped the blood and gore from his face, heaved off the inert body pressing him down and crawled to his knees. The cat feasted upon its fresh kill in the middle of the floor, tearing and lapping voraciously. The fire on the table had spread to the other sacks and lit up the kitchen as bright as it had ever been. The snoring beyond the hearth had been replaced by deep, annoyed grunts and groans. Ford scurried about the kitchen, avoiding the cat as best he could, except where he had to reach into the gore to collect all that was worth taking. A giant squawk ended his spree in a panic. Stomping feet and the enormous form of the giantess emerged from behind the hearth. Ford dove for the larder, pushed his way through the butchered and frozen sides of meat until he thrust his aching body through the timbers. The cold wind scoured his warm cheeks, but he sensed only fear and exhilaration as he plowed through the snow on his flight from the giant house at the foot of Heikki Linna.

Chapter 22
The Last Step

Ford lay face down and motionless with his cheek pressed into a log. Knobby and mismatched, the wood rubbed on his bones and chaffed his skin. Ugly welts crowded his naked back like stars on a cloudless night and sweat ran over his ribs. He pried his eyes open and they rested upon thousands of thin horizontal bars. A shock whipped his head up and around to take in the panorama of his surroundings. He had spent time behind bars before and wasn't about to let it happen again, not if he had any say in it. These days, fear of his freedom being taken away was always at the forefront of his thoughts.

He had been through so much. After fleeing from the house of giants at Heikki Linna, his troubles hadn't ended. On a ridge not far from the house, he stumbled upon woolly beasts being herded by a shepherd two heads taller than the giantess back at the house. A frantic chase drove Ford into an evergreen copse. The giant's long strides bound through the snow with ease and gained with every step. Ford dodged between trees and dove into the cover of a thicket, evading the nearsighted shepherd and avoiding having his head caved in with a log-sized club.

Another time, while hunting an aged and limping elk, Ford became the hunted. A gray dire wolf with winter-starved eyes had been stalking him and the elk for miles. The shaggy canine's wide paws sank deep under its immense weight with each step in the snow. When they finally came face to face, Ford held his ground. Though tempted, the wolf veered away in a wide arc and rejoined the elk's trail. Ford followed behind and they both watched their quarry trot ahead, hoping to do as Ford had done with the shepherd and lose itself among trees. As it approached a stocky fir with a few ragged branches, the elk's head jerked to attention and its hindquarters tensed for a leap. Before it could spring away, one of the fir's branches swept down and clubbed the back of its neck. The tree shed the rest of its branches, transforming it into the giant that it was. Both canine and man fled with all haste.

Getting clear of giant country unscathed was more important than catching the elk. However, as the days passed and his provisions were depleted, he became less sanguine about his prospects of finding food when other opportunities also failed. Large, lumbering beaver-like creatures which he mistook for lumpish mounds slipped into nearby ponds at his approach. Grouse hens lured him away from egg-laden nests by faking wounded wings and madly flopping and scrambling over the tundra grasses, as if fleeing for their lives. Whenever Ford closed the gap enough for a leaping grab, they revealed the ruse and fluttered off without the least hindrance.

Descending once more into the Aarne River Valley, he found that the snow had disappeared entirely. As if the summer gods had snapped their fingers to bring on the welcome warmth, fields of blossoms bloomed and light green grasses waved a welcome at Ford's arrival. Buds once blanketed from the harsh elements by cobweb-like encasements shed these coats to bloom in gorgeous violet profusion. Moths gamboled about wildflowers, twitchy wrens on the lookout poked their heads from their subterranean dwellings, while spiders apparated from the earth and disappeared just as mysteriously at Ford's approach. The innate silence of this secluded land was broken by teeming mosquitoes, swarming flies and bees that zoomed from white bell heather to mountain sorrel.

Unprepared for the sudden warmth, Ford had passed out from the heat after a long march through boggy lands where tannins colored the innumerable surrounding shallow pools brown and green, creating suspicious waters he would not drink from. The sweat-soaked and almost useless bearskin he dragged behind him. Every day he vowed to toss it aside, but was glad he didn't. On a slog between and around sluggish water, which made a marvelous breeding ground for a variety of hardened specimens, the clouds of insects seized their brief opportunity at life with a passion and enveloped him. Wearing the fur over his head nearly boiled his brains, but at least it kept most of the biting insects at bay.

At the base of the valley, Ford found the Aarne swollen and flooding over the roots of hemlock stands on either side, toppling some into the river. For days he had traveled along the river's eastern bank and never saw a sign of his lost friend. Once he spotted a tall stack of rocks on the far shore, but they were moss covered and looked to have stood there for ages. The chance of ever finding Will seemed remote, almost impossible. The thought that he more than likely perished in the snowy north sent Ford into a downward spiral of mourning.

A bit of good luck crossed his path late one muggy morning, when he came across the first full-grown deciduous trees he had seen since Polecat Island: spindly white birch fighting for life along the Aarne. Soon after, a tiny settlement appeared through the tender new leaves of elms growing out of a wide bend in the river. Happening upon this cluster of huts could not have come at a better time. He'd been tightening his belt by the day. His sudden appearance out of the wilds, as well as his size, startled the people at first, but the abject humility with which he approached their riverside hamlet won them over. The sandy-blond and stunted inhabitants spoke a tongue full of lilting vowels and slapping consonants, sighing and spitting out words Ford couldn't comprehend. It didn't matter. They fed him generously on fish and fresh berries, provided him with a small pack of the same to bring with him, then escorted him in a canoe for miles downriver. After passing through the labyrinthine waterways of a vast swamp, they deposited him on a weedy shore beside a beaver dam, which they hoped was far enough away to keep this huge and hungry stranger from wandering back to their village. Their relief upon waving him out of sight was palpable, but in no way did this diminish Ford's appreciation of what they had done for him.

From the beaver dam, he had dragged mismatched logs and strapped them together with grass rope to make one of the loosest and most lopsided rafts that ever floated. Poling downriver with the current gave his feet much-needed rest and sped his journey along at a pace unimaginable in the weeks prior. Despite the speed, a constant swarm of black flies and ever-present mosquitos tormented his days and made him glad for his bearskin once more. It could be turned into an adequate, though steamy, tent over his head. But the suffocating heat made him drowsy and often brought on sleep, which made up for the hours lost at night when eerie sounds in the bushes along the banks kept him awake.

Entire days had passed with his head under cover. Aside from the wall of trees encroaching on either side of the river, he didn't think he was missing much. However, while he had rested he passed unique sites of significance and beauty: the majestic waterfalls at Iverad's Gorge; the accursed rock garden known as Spogeest, where a steady stream of determined but misguided priests continually fell to the undead and swelled their ranks; and the impressively tall arched bridge of natural stone leading to the ruins of Laksonnen, where could be found Halkloft's Reliable Scalding Spout. Occasionally, Ford and his little craft had been spotted by riverside folk and pilgrims on their way to take the waters at a mountain refuge or to pay homage at the hermitage of some long-suffering monk. Some came to bask in the ancient wisdom of an oracle presiding at standing stones renowned for the peace of mind and good fortune they bestowed. But he floated by them all unbeknownst to him and mostly unnoticed by them.

The ever-widening and straightening river made drifting easy. Seldom did his raft approach the riverbanks. For many a mile he rode the middle current in peaceful bliss. Then there came a time when a cool, steady breeze carried upon it a peculiar scent. Water lapped along the logs of his raft much as it had for those many miles, but the chirps and twitters coming from the water's edge had changed to deeper warbles, clucks and hoots. He lifted his head from the knobby logs, rose upon an elbow, and blinked his gummy eyes clear. What he'd mistaken for horizontal bars were large swaths of reeds, sedges, cattails, and tall grasses on all sides.

A cough rattled his parched throat and thrust aside all thoughts but his raging thirst. He stooped to drink. The first gulp didn't pass his tongue before he spit it out. "Salt? What…? And no mountains," he muttered. Talking to himself was becoming habitual, almost natural. He squinted at the skyline. It was clear in all directions, from cloud to horizon, for the first time since he could remember. No gray peaks rose above the abundant flora that spiked the blue-sky background like pincushions full of needles. A strong breeze pushed aside some flimsy grasses and opened gaps through which Ford could see the winding waterways that made up the lazy delta he had floated into. His eyes fell upon one such gap and beyond to an apparent grove of straight trees bare of limb and leaf. The tallest of these rod-straight spires, no thicker than a darning needle at this distance, slid in an unmistakably steady drift across the horizon. "A ship!" he rasped out as the vague triangular shape of a sail came into view.

After a frenzy of paddling spun his raft in frustratingly fruitless circles, he leapt in and swam for the nearest tussock. The dense tuft of weed collapsed under his weight and shrugged him off. Such was his eagerness, that from then on the whole of this marshland seemed determined to hinder his every step. Gray-tipped herons and snowy egrets took to the wing, spooked by his flopping and sloshing approach over and around grassy mounds and patches of reed and sedge, where he plunged waist deep into the stinking brackish mud. His wet clothes, matted and filthy hair, and the weeds hanging from his insect-bit body, ensured that he would attain his freedom in the guise of some sinister monster emerging from the saltmarsh.

On a long patch of dry ground closer to the top of the bay, he dodged between salt hay stacks and leapt like a frog desperate to catch a fly out of its reach. Ahead were more sails belonging to fishing vessels plying the coastal trade. None could see him, the closest being two miles away. The bay curved around to his right, where smaller fishing boats congregated like ducks in a pond, bobbing about in front of the many wooden piers lining the long, thin beach. Up the beach, little fishing shanties perched atop a high sandy dune. A clanging toll rang out over the water with all the melody of a calving cow. It recalled to him the clanking charm of harbor bells in Aelwydian port towns. Discordant and flat though it may have been, to Ford it was a siren's call.

His heart hammered away as he stumbled from sandbar to sandbar across the Aarne estuary, each sinking step into the gluttonous mud sapping another ounce of his remaining strength. A parching thirst from his lips down to his knotted belly impelled his feet forward, even when he thought his legs could stand no more. This desert-mouth impetus propelled him to the beginning of the sandy beach, where a maritime graveyard of worm-eaten dories and wrecked remains rotted among beds of seaweed. His hand fell upon the upturned keel of the first boat he came to and he leaned into its hull to rest while observing the fishermen the better part of a mile away at the other end of the beach.

The waves curling in at his feet seemed to carry with them waves of doubt. This might not be the place he thought it was, the town Will had suggested they make for. It looked like nothing more than a hamlet of maybe a hundred fisherfolk. For all he knew, these people traded in slaves and he would be recaptured. At this distance, they appeared to be squat folk with cheeks, nose, and chin scuffed red and orange by sun and wind. They hauled baskets of fish along the crooked piers to the filleting tables and drying racks on the shore.

Baskets of prepared fish disappeared up the dunes into the houses lining the bay or were carried over the sands to locations beyond and out of sight. Now and then chatter drifted Ford's way, but he could make nothing of the stray wisps of words. Someone lifted a jug to their lips and the motion reminded him of his thirst. Temptation thrust him into a few staggering steps toward them, but he caught himself and dropped down in a heap behind one of the overturned boats. There was no sense in revealing himself until he knew the nature of these people. He would wait here, he convinced himself, until the beach cleared. Under the cover of dark he would see what he could find to eat and drink.

Hours of suffering an aching head and fighting off dizziness ended with the sound of shouts and laughter. A golden-headed gang of children in sun-bleached and shredded clothes waded through the foam of the breaking waves toward him. The taller, older of them worked rakes through the sand of the surf, seeking edible clams, especially the quahogs which could be found on these shores in vast quantities. In their rags, the children might have been one with the clumps of thread-like seaweed that the youngest of them hurled at one another. An adolescent toting a basket with their catch also watched over the youngsters and made sure that the least helpful of them at least didn't drown themselves.

Ford's heart lifted. Children he could trust. And if he couldn't, well, he thought to himself, they weren't going to carry him off. With nothing to fear, he stood up from behind the rotting boat. A single pair of seafoam-pale eyes latched onto him at first. The little boy they belonged to cried out and the others froze at the sight of him. Ford lumbered down the beach toward them. A gust off the sea blew his hood, the bear's head, out from behind his back. The sight of the ferocious beast, looking even more monstrous covered in mud, throttled gasps and cries out of the youngest children. Some ran a few yards away.

"Water?" Ford asked before they all took to their heels. He stooped to look less imposing. They stopped, but stayed huddled together, the youngest and smallest behind their elders. "Water? Do you have any water?" His voice cracked and croaked. They looked at him in perplexed trepidation. He repeated himself, trying simply "water" over and over again. When that got him nowhere, he tilted his head back and mimed pouring a flask down his throat. This they understood.

The tallest of them, a willowy androgenous youth with hair of straw scythed at random, was the only one to step forward. Her name was Aallo and she came from immigrant fishermen. Like her hard-working family who overcame odds for a better life, she too could move mountains if it got her what she wanted. The other older children went back to raking, wanting nothing to do with this odd man straying out here in the mudflats where no respectable adult lingered. As far as they were concerned, this was just another strange foreign beggar. Aallo alone stood before him with hands on hips and her head cocked. Some thought her arrogant, but she was simply self-assured and curious. She hefted her rake and pointed it at him until he picked up on her interest in his bearskin.

"You want the bear? You'll give water for bear?" Ford asked, miming all the while. "Water for bear?"

None of the children carried water on them. Apparently, this child proposed to go get some, and all Ford had for assurances were her eager nods. He was hesitant to give up the bearskin. It was all he had left. On the other hand, the matted mess of a thing was hardly worth carrying around. His need was worth the risk. He handed it over. She tucked it under one arm, and when the others grabbed and tugged at it, she shouldered and shoved each aside without taking her eyes from Ford. After reeling off a determined string of words, she nodded. He nodded back, hoping this was her way of sealing the bargain with a promise. She released the bearskin to the children, who passed it around, everyone having a look. Soon a game broke out. They capered about with the skin over their heads, roaring and chasing after one other like a rampaging monster after prey. The pitch of their giddy laughter soared to the height of hawks and eagles and could be heard long after they left him behind. When they vanished over the dunes, he realized he'd forgotten to ask the name of the town.

By the time evening set in and the fisherfolk abandoned their work on the beach, Ford had given up on ever seeing the children again. His thirst had grown beyond bearable. When hearth and candlelight appeared in the closest houses, he decided the time for waiting was over.

He stole along the beach and snuck up to the rickety piers, ducking down between the boats which had been hauled ashore. A few seagulls and other shore birds pecked at the sand and hopped about the breakwater rocks in search of fish offal and any scraps left behind. The choicest remains had already been snatched up by the early birds. Crabs crawled under the gutting and filleting tables, delicately picking up minute pieces of flesh and scale with their pincers. The only thing large enough for a human to bother with was a bizarre-looking, barbed red fish with coral-like fins. The fisherman who caught it had dashed it against a rock and left it in the sand to rot. The absurdly colorful and intensely spiny fish had been wisely disdained by all the scavenging creatures, save one. Ford was so ravenous that he fell upon it up without a second thought and feasted greedily upon its boney flesh, picking those bones clean and lapping up with gusto all the juices he could squeeze from the fish.

Flinging the carcass aside, he stood to return to the search and had to catch himself from falling when a dizzy spell swept over him. "I need something to drink, is what it is," he said while waiting on one knee for it to pass. Although he felt better for the nourishment, his hunger urged him on to look for more.

If there was anything left, the dying light disguised it among the seaweed and pools of water trapped in pockets of sand. He looked longingly up at the houses on the dunes. All was quiet. No sign of the children or anyone. For a moment, he thought he might chance it and hail one of the cottages, but then something, like an uneasiness palpable in the gut, told him it would be best if he made his way back to the rotting boats, to hold out there until dawn. Even if they didn't trade in slaves, he didn't want to be taken for a thief skulking about in the dark.

The trip back took longer in his mind the second time. Halfway there he broke out in a sweat that seemed to defy the mild evening and cool breeze coming off the water. At the same time, a shiver rippled over his skin and his appetite inexplicably died away. A few steps on and a stab, like a needle to the gut, doubled him over. "Must've swallowed a bone," he said as the pain subsided. A few stumbling steps on and another stab dropped him to his knees. He crouched and held his stomach. Beads of sweat dappled his forehead and then ran down his face. When the pain passed, he wiped at his forehead and felt its burning heat. The final few yards back to the rotting boats had to be done on his hands and knees. Collapsing against the hull of the nearest, he clutched at his contracting innards. His backside had barely touched the sand before he was crawling away to retch on the beach where the surf lapped at the dry sand.

The purge did him a world of good, like exorcising a belly full of demons. His appetite returned immediately. He stood, albeit on shaky legs, but still, he stood and shuffled toward beds of exposed seaweed in hopes of finding something edible beneath them. The distance wasn't much, but he veered away before reaching the nearest beds and returned to the rotting boats. A short rest would do, he thought. Perhaps he might even close his eyes and see if sleep would come. It had been a long day. He curled up in the sand with his arms wrapped around his knees, and his knees pulled up to his chest with a boat at his back. Before long, the nausea, sweats, and the chills returned. Hardly had he lifted his head when he vomited where he lay. An itchy electricity vibrated throughout his skin and every joint in his body ached. A numbing tingle rooted itself in his mouth, a feverish languor flooded over him, and paralysis took his hands and feet.

While the spiney fish's toxins attacked Ford's body through the seemingly endless night, he endured a desert-and-tundra seesaw ride within his weakening physical frame. Nightmarish delusion engorged itself upon his most morbid fears, sending him back to the dark, claustrophobic depths of Dargkivi, where he fought a losing battle against faceless horrors and fanged beasts salivating over his naked corpse. "I'm not dying, I'm not dying..." he chanted with hot, swampy breath. Eventually his mantra devolved into, "I don't want to die." In the early hours, his eyes closed on the night and he joined the darkness.

Tenacious flies woke with the sun and found irresistible delight in the skin of his face. Their twitchy feet skittered over his eyelids, nose, and lips, especially the lips. A splash of water dribbled down upon his face and scattered the flies. Like a tiny cloud dispensing relief, Aallo hovered above Ford emptying her flask over his lips. Much of it flowed down his chin and onto his chest.

The tiny cloud left, left his body to the mercies of an early but eager sun and a returning blanket of flies; all alone with just the sun and flies for company, but not for long. Soon a torment of pelts and pokes beat upon him to the madcap accompaniment of a cacophonous choir of scorn. Not recognizing this much-reduced man from the evening before, the gang of children took him for a yellow ghoul and prodded him with sticks or threw stones at him from afar, not wishing to catch the pestilential disease guaranteed by the bite of the undead. Aallo beat them back and hollered down those who protested. This was not the dead risen, she insisted. She called them names and bent them to her will with unassailable argument. Silver could be made from a body. Dead or alive. The temptation won them over.

Like an army of ants carrying a dead grasshopper, the children dragged and rolled Ford down the beach and into the surf. The cold water washed over his inert body, a body too large and cumbersome for even twice their number to move by brute strength. Planks from the gunwale of a rotting boat were slid under him until he floated enough that they could ferry him along the shore to the town, a technique used before to transport found objects too heavy or awkward to carry. The youngest waifs viewed life as one big game, singing songs and splashing circles around the limp body upon the makeshift bier, while the rest carried their prize over the dunes, through the back bay village, and under the old gate into the city.

Lighthouses, watchtowers, and temples rose above sun-faded shops, taverns, trade houses, inns, and the bewildering sprawl of neighborhood districts which filled the flats of the Aarne delta, reaching back into the hinterlands. Every inch of the seaside bays and coves were taken up with the fishing trade. Inland, the old city center was packed cheek by jowl with housing built over the shops. Awnings and garrisons blotted out sunlight and shaded the random warren of streets, lanes, and alleys that spread like worm holes; a haven for thieves, confusing to newcomers. These streets were a battlefield of the senses, as well. Aromatic spices and the pervading smell of fish seeped from windows still shuttered against the morning damps–the marine layer that gagged the city in a daily fog seldom lifted before noon.

Sand crunched under the bier as it was laid down on the cobblestones of a street just waking to the day's trade. Sailors fell out of a tavern doorway and shuffled past Ford's head. A porter cursed the congested street. Most everyone hurried by. One or two stopped and voiced mild interest, even concern. The children told them off and huddled with their heads together to discuss their course of action. Some uttered *vampeer* repeatedly in fear and reverence while peering cautiously over their shoulders down an alley. A red lantern far within the depths of the alley illuminated a miasmic fog choking the narrow passage in a ghastly pink pallor. Aallo alone wished to take the body into this foreboding den. The rest wanted nothing to do with it. They wished to sell their prize to the corpse-takers, who paid good coin for fresh specimens. It was a better deal for them than what they'd get out of the *vampeer*. One boy pointed to the markings of a slave on the man's wrist, which created more contention among them. In the end, the girl's stubborn insistence won out. Most of the gang abandoned her and the whole endeavor in disgust and fear. Those that remained lifted one end of the bier and dragged it into that ominous alley of sickly rouged walls.

***

White. Penetratingly white. A flaring light much too much for the eyes.

Downy caresses and cloud delicacy.

A halo's glow, all-pervasive.

Two crescent gateways to the world opened to golden light. They expanded, coalescing into a single ray shining down from above. From a hole in the sky? No, not the sky. A ceiling painted white. Perhaps yellow. Whatever the shade, the skylight cast its own color down from a pitched ceiling upon an airy, sparsely-furnished room scoured clean. Sage burned in a dish on a bedside table. His eyes drooped again.

A bed. His name was Ford Barlow and he was lying in a bed. Hovering above and off to one side, a pink orb spoke in dove-soft speech and with a voice almost recognizable. The words danced together into familiar phrases. Ford turned his head and there sat Will in a chair beside the bed.

"I found you," Ford rasped through a tender throat as his focusing gaze roamed over Will's new flaxen tunic up to his face: more worn than he remembered; hair growing back; placid.

"Yes," Will said through one of his quiet, inward laughs. "Yes, you found me." Leaning forward, he gripped Ford by a shoulder. Tears welled in his smiling eyes. With an effort, Ford grasped his friend's forearm. It was the most he could do. When they broke the embrace, Will offered up a cup from the bedside table. Ford drained the contents, the liquid running over his parched tongue and down into belly like a spring flood spreading over a dry riverbed. He dropped back on a thick pillow and sighed contentedly.

"I looked and looked," he said upon feeling his wits returning and his strength rebounding. "I looked everywhere, but couldn't find you."

"And I you," said Will, refilling the cup from a pitcher.

"The storm..."

"Yes, the storm." Will's eyes drifted away, as if they might pierce through the walls to view the far distant snowy mountains to the north. "It was impossible, overwhelming. I'd never seen the like." Will's attention faded toward meditations on the recent past. Ford was too entrenched in the present to sit idly by.

"What is this place?" he asked, looking around the room and down at the clean sheets neatly covering him from chest to toes.

"This is the House of the Many Charitable Daughters of Caru, an Aelwydian infirmary in Valtavastad's temple district." Will carried on, rambling into the city's history, but Ford cut in.

"Are there vampires here?" The alarm with which Ford asked the question surprised Will out of his musing.

"Vampires?"

"The children, I heard them say *vampire, vampire.*"

"Ah! Yes, yes!" Will just about bounced in his chair when he understood. Seeing fear rising in his friend, he hurriedly amended, "No. I'm sorry, no. The people here use the word *vampeer* when referring to healing practitioners who apply leeches to draw out blood when it runs too thick or vile with necrotic humors. It's a common practice here. The people may *believe* them to be vampires, but no one here is a vampire, not to my knowledge."

Ford's ribs let go of his lungs and he slid back into bed. Will offered up the cup again and while his friend drank, he contemplated the pleasures of being able to speak in his native tongue once more. Not having to leap back and forth, untangling words and their meanings or their proper order in a sentence, created an ease of mind not unlike relaxing the muscles of a tensed body. This and the ability to finally speak in confidence about the people of Valtavastad with a friend. Though many of the inmates of the infirmary were Aelwydian, most of them had been in the city so long as to be considered natives. He liked them as a people, but everyone has their idiosyncrasies and it was nice to speak of them without the fear of offending.

"I've noted a, oh, I suppose you might call it a *culture of the dead,*" he went on. "It's a curious duality. Though, not entirely dissimilar to the precepts of Hau. Still, the people here seem to revel in the power, good as well as evil, of the eternally living dead. On the one hand, you have those who preach the necessity of destruction and eradication, while there are those who fervently believe more study is required to obtain the source of a soul's, oh how shall I put it, a soul's reluctance to throw off its earthly form, the body, or however one prefers to..." Seeing his friend's eyelids droop, he reeled himself in. "How do you feel?"

"Wonderful." Ford did feel surprisingly well. His joints and muscles still ached, but he imagined it was nothing a good stretch of the legs wouldn't iron out.

"The Daughters work wondrous miracles. A poison had taken hold of you. You looked more than a little dead when the children dropped you at the door. But the Daughters brought you back. Truly wondrous!"

"A miracle indeed," Ford said, recalling the spells of dizziness and vomiting, and realizing both had left him. "How long have I been laid up?"

"The better part of the day."

"Only a day?"

"Most of it. They're attention to your condition has been indefatigable. All that could be done for you had to be done immediately and without hesitation. There hasn't even been an opportunity to bathe you yet, I'm afraid. Antidotes and rest were what you needed most." Ford lifted an arm and saw that he still wore his old clothes. The sleeve was so filthy and the sheet so white that he didn't want to lay his arm down again for fear of sullying such nice cloth. Will gently lowered his arm for him. "Be easy."

While Ford did feel better, there was no denying that his body had been through an ordeal. The simple act of sitting up in bed and enjoying the company of a friend was enough for now. They listened to the occasional street noises traveling down the alley and up through the windows. After a time, Ford thought to ask, "How long have you been here?"

"A week and more. After we were separated, I followed the river and happened upon an old hermit. He claimed to be a holy man, though I have my doubts. I found him to be slightly touched. Quite mad, if I'm honest. An air of danger about him. Wild as the wilderness itself. He kept a mountain lion as a pet. Strange man."

"Popular pet for those parts."

"Pardon?" asked Will, but Ford waved it off and urged him on. "Poor man, he has the ironic distinction of being a frequently visited recluse. Southern Isle monks on a pilgrimage to garner wisdom from him took me back with them by horse and cart. I had a brisk and untroubled journey straight to the city by the overland route."

"Looks like you ran into some sort of trouble along the way," said Ford, gesturing to one of Will's ears, which now missed a small chunk out of its slightly blackened outer lobe.

"Ah, yes." Will brushed a finger past the missing flesh taken by frostbite. "I didn't quite make it back all in one piece." After a brief explanation, he concluded, "No, I suppose it wasn't entirely trouble-free, nor altogether pleasant. More than once I had to make a meal of unappetizing things I found under logs and stones and the like. But it got me through and on the whole, I consider myself quite fortunate." He shrugged it off and smiled down at his friend. Ford's eyes were closed. A wave of exhaustion had taken hold of him. Will rose, thinking it best to let his friend rest, but felt impelled to add a final thought before going. "I would not have had the chance to test my fortunes without you. I thank you for that."

Ford kept his eyes closed and waved the kind words away. Will was being too grateful for his tastes. "Like I said, I owed you," he murmured.

"Yes well, we made it out alive and that's more than some can say." Will hovered by the door. "But not more than can be said by all. Do you remember our friend Cadogan?" Ford's eyes popped open and he sat up.

"Cadogan? He lives? Is he here?"

"He lives, and stays quite close by. He was kind enough to check in on me daily during my convalescence. He's already paid you a visit, almost the moment you arrived. I dare say, you'll see him soon and hear his extraordinary tale."

The pounding of a fist on a door sailed up from the street below. Ford noticed the window in the wall behind him for the first time. An officious exchange passed between two or three parties in tones of inquiry and demand that quickly burst into anger. Will's long, swift strides took him across the room to the window in an instant. Slowly and carefully, he leaned through the frame just enough to see the street well below, where two well-armed and brutish men argued with someone at the front door. An expectant child waited behind them. He looked to be one of the many waifs of the streets, who did odd-jobs for a coin or two. The men Will recognized as *orjaeger*, the regional name for slave hunters. Those in polite society preferred to call them "agents for foreign interests." Morally bankrupt and naturally greedy, they lined their pockets with gold by capturing and returning escaped slaves to their masters. A bitter bile rose to Will's mouth at the thought of Valtavastad's duality on the subject. On the one hand, Valtavastad was not a slave city, and yet it did allow for the recapture of "property," as some termed their human chattel.

Like most of their kind, these orjaeger wore light armor, in this case dusty leather jerkins and breeches. Anything heavier would be too cumbersome in a chase. To make up for the deficiency, they armed themselves well, carrying enough arms for four of the city's guard. When not plying their loathsome trade, most orjaeger drowned their days in alehouses. The bulbous noses and blotchy skin of these two attested to their indulgence in drink and so much more. So, it was no surprise that they were a bit tipsy when they banged on the door to the House of the Many Charitable Daughters of Caru.

The usual sentry, a well-intentioned and repentant graverobber lacking assertiveness or a particularly robust constitution, opened the door upon their arrival. Using sheer truculence and audacity, the orjaeger attempted to coerce him into giving up the slave suspected of being harbored within the infirmary that very morning. However, bad luck and worse timing were their closest companions that day. The infirmary's slight but tireless head physician, who happened by the door when the knock sounded and who had a good idea whom it might be on the other side, dismissed the cowering sentry and dealt with the two burly men herself.

Though she wielded no arms or armor, she did have the law on her side. Slave hunters were not permitted on private premises without proof that, "lawful property was being concealed therein." These two orjaeger were working on the hearsay of a child. They had hoped to trick a naïve doorman or bully a weak priestess with their demands. The head physician was knowledgeable in her rights and far too worldly to fall prey to their ploys. When they cast the law aside, spitting on the ground to show their contempt, the head physician threw the door open wide and launched herself into the street.

"What's wrong?" Ford asked, wanting to know if the commotion coming in through the window was worth getting out of bed for.

"It is…" began Will, watching and waiting to see the outcome. If need be, there was a staircase leading to a back door. With luck and speed, they might slip away to Cadogan's inn. The following few seconds would decide all.

At times like these when agility was paramount, the head physician was grateful to her order's First Mother for agreeing to her request to forego the usual House attire of voluminous robes in favor of trousers and a smock frock. Her custom-made belt was specially designed to hold an assortment of instruments and various pouches containing bandages, medicinal herbs and salves. She always wanted to have her useful scalpel and lancet at the ready, for she was in great demand by the poor of the adjacent neighborhood and never knew when she might be called to an emergency. As an afterthought to the escaped slave's arrival that morning, she had also tucked into her belt the infirmary's wickedest looking amputation knife, which lent her a reckless and bloody-minded swashbuckler appearance as she set upon the slave hunters with flying punches, kicks, and a hail of slaps. Roughly translated into Aelwydian, her motto was, "When vitriol won't do the trick, give the bastards a right good kick." To the flummoxed orjaeger, she was as quick as a hummingbird in a field of wildflowers, buzzing and sticking, sticking and buzzing.

From the upper window, Will couldn't help but admire the way her flailing arms bewildered the two men and rocked them back on their heels. She astounded them by dashing their manacles to the ground, ripping their daggers from their sheaths, and hurling them down the alley. She then whipped out her trepanning tool and jabbed it at the head of nearest slave hunter, who declined her offer to examine his brain with her skull-piercing instrument. One of the children from the gang who had hauled Ford in from the beach waited behind the orjaeger with his hand out expecting a reward for his tip-off. The hunter who ducked away from the lobotomy trampled the boy and fell over backwards. The boy squirmed out from under the writhing man and fled down the alley, snatching up one of the hunters' knives on the run and making off with it as recompence. When the physician reached for the amputation knife at her belt, the two orjaeger called it a day. No good could come from knife fight with a priestess in the streets, even in self-defense. Better to flee the scene, endure a volley of mockery from the few members of the House gathering in the doorway, and regroup back at the tavern. So, they yielded the field to the whirlwind of a woman with a more fiery spirit in her than they had on that day.

"What is it?" Ford had only caught the most incendiary threats and sharpest slaps, but he was sure he was missing something good.

"It's nothing. Nothing," said Will as he left the window and sat back down in the chair by Ford. Realizing he was beaming with pleasure, he went on by way of explanation, "The Daughters are good people, fine people. I've learned a great deal from them in the short time I've been here." He breathed deeply and let out a long, satisfied sigh. "And I believe my service has pleased them. Excuse my immodestly, but you see, they have kindly offered me a position here."

"They offered you work? Here?"

"A permanent position, yes."

The news came as a surprise, quite a welcome surprise actually, as it crushed Ford's assumption that he and Will would set sail together upon the first ship for home. He wasn't ready to part with his friend so soon after their reunion. Flinging forth the grasping tendrils of a desperate mind, he blurted out the first objection that came to him. "But the *Daughters*? How could *you* join them? You're a man."

"Oh, that's just a name. At one time, yes, they were a solely matriarchal order, but that's in the past. Men work alongside the women now."

"Oh."

"I mean to accept their offer. Everyone here at the House has done..." Will was about to say that they had done so much for he and Ford, more than either could afford to repay, but not wanting to point out his friend's obligation to the House, he caught himself and rephrased. "They've done so much good. I admire them tremendously. Their work, all they do for our people as well as the city's citizenry, it's challenging and comes at a great expense. Giving of my time, helping in any little way I might, I should think it would be quite rewarding in its own way."

There was no disputing Will's sincerity, and Ford was not about to disregard his friend's desires and ambitions, however, he couldn't overlook his own wishes. He hemmed and hawed over minor objections, started and restarted, and stumbled over his words until the solution came to him. "Would a donation to the Daughters be in order?"

"Most definitely, if only we had something to give."

"And would it be possible to find a berth upon a ship bound for home from this port?"

"Certainly. For a price."

"And if the price could be met, as well as the donation, would you go?"

"Oh, without question!"

Ford threw back the sheet and struggled with the sacking tied around his waist like a belt. He worked furiously, causing Will to fear for his state of mind. Miracle cures sometimes came with delayed negative side effects which could be deadly. In the very least, such frenzy pointed to a fevered mind.

"If you wish to bathe, I'll bring warmed water to your room, but rest easy and stay covered. For your own good, you must keep warm and stay calm," said Will while trying to pull the sheet back over his friend. Ford pushed it away again. Finally working the knot free, he unwound the sacking and upended it. Out dropped a perfectly round, stone-like object. Ford held up the bauble to let the light played up its gold and enamel. It looked very much like an eyeball. A large, smoothly-polished ruby embedded in the center peeked out like an iris.

"Do you think this would do?"

"I believe it would and then some," said Will, his initial surprise giving way to the dawning of a golden sunrise of a smile.

"Then we're going home!"

"We're going home."

Some Known Words of Kamen as Gathered and Transcribed by

the Adventurer and Chronicler Frans Eino Melnseppa

Alu ~ cave

Attakal ~ back, backwards

Ava ~ all

Dorv ~ town or district

Drek ~ dirt

Ei hakk ~ a phrase akin to refusal, perhaps will not

Elasmutterum ~ a kind of single-horned mammoth creature

Gar ~ for

Groz ~ big, giant

Harg ~ ox

Hohle ~ another word for cave it would seem, perhaps cavern

Horklik ~ delicious, tasty

Kalna ~ hill

Kalt or Kaltz ~ white

Kiiresti ~ quickly, swiftly

Kirivirz ~ warriors

Kohle ~ coal

Komersantz ~ merchants

Koraltama ~ mount, the act of mounting a steed

Kukk ~ fowl

Kungs ~ comparable to sir

Ma ~ me, I

Maad ~ land

Mada ~ house

Met ~ girl

Miris ~ dead, perhaps specific to the ancient dead

Mullauk ~ a pit of refuse

Nak ~ come

Nave ~ one of their numerous words for death

Ohn ~ of, in regards to

Rask ~ hard or a solid substance

Revane ~ fox or some such canine

Rienegen ~ to clean, wash

Selvst ~ self or specifically themselves, themself

Sie ~ this, these or those

Silts ~ warm

Soolz ~ salt

Tagad ~ now, presently

Tarl ~ pearl

Tat ~ the

Toole ~ work, labor, duty

Tram ~ follow or chase

Trattal ~ idiot

Ulemine ~ upper

Uuz ~ new

Uz ~ to, towards

Vana ~ of the past or old

Vanag ~ a predatory bird such as the hawk

Vaslavak ~ best, elite

Veks ~ old or perhaps ancient

Ver ~ birch

Vesi ~ water

Votid ~ containers such as jugs, jars, pots

Za ~ yes

Zan ~ boy

Ze ~ you

Zek ~ muscle, strength and the like

Zevalimus ~ look, appear

Zielkikraksket ~ an arena game using a swing harness

Zivi ~ life, the living

Zivivesi ~ life water, the name given to an arak or brandy-like elixir, Kamen-made by fermenting and distilling a root vegetable grown in many hot water spring caverns throughout Rikaswelt

Zmaragt ~ a precious stone, perhaps an emerald

Many thanks to my wife. She was a beacon of light in my life while I navigated the darker passages of this book. As always, I appreciate all the support of my friends and family. Those readers and editors who took a look at the manuscript deserve more than I could give them. And a couple thank yous also go to Elsie's and Bird Street Brewing, where I threw back more than a few good pints while working on this book during the "*Before Times.*"

About the Author

Tolkien gatewayed Jason R. Koivu into fantasy. *Dungeons & Dragons* made him an addict. A 4th grade poetry prize convinced him this writing thing wasn't so difficult. A degree in writing showed him how little he knew. New England born and raised, he now resides in California with his wife and their cat Sir Ian.

Note from the Author

Word-of-mouth is crucial for any author to succeed. If you enjoyed *A Winter of Chains*, please leave a review online—anywhere you are able. Even if it's just a sentence or two. It would make all the difference and would be very much appreciated.

Thanks!

Jason R. Koivu

We hope you enjoyed reading this title from:

BLACK ROSE
writing™

www.blackrosewriting.com

Subscribe to our mailing list – *The Rosevine* – and receive **FREE** books, daily deals, and stay current with news about upcoming releases and our hottest authors.
Scan the QR code below to sign up.

Already a subscriber? Please accept a sincere thank you for being a fan of Black Rose Writing authors.

View other Black Rose Writing titles at www.blackrosewriting.com/books and use promo code **PRINT** to receive a **20% discount** when purchasing.

www.ingramcontent.com/pod-product-compliance
Lightning Source LLC
Chambersburg PA
CBHW010726100726
47899CB00009B/2940